A Brave Start

By Andrea J. Severson

To London, the city that taught me how to
dream and how to be brave.

Author's Note

This book has been a long-term, labor of love. I started writing it after my first visit to London as an adult in late 2010. Like Eleanor, the main character in this book, I had visited London before, as a 9-year-old girl, and I had very fond memories of that trip. As teen and adult, I developed a love for all things British, including but not limited to Jane Austen, BBC television (especially *Doctor Who* and *Sherlock*!), and British chick lit novels. When I returned from that trip, I couldn't stop thinking about London, so I channeled that obsession into something a little more productive, and that's how this book was born.

Over the course of several years, and numerous visits back to London, I would work on this book in bits. A few chapters here and there at a time. More than half of it was written on my old 1st generation iPad, using a little Bluetooth keyboard (much like Eleanor uses in the book!). I would write in short sessions before going to teach or on a break between classes while working on my Masters and PhD. I would also work on it during my various trips to the UK. A good portion of this was written while staying for extended trips in London and Oxford in the summers of 2014 and 2015. Every visit provided another layer of detail to add to the locations and new places and elements that I wanted to include. Many of Eleanor's favorite places to wander, shops, restaurants, and things to do are my own favorites.

This book is my love letter to London, a city that has come to mean so much to me and a city that has taught me so many lessons about life, love, and being brave. For those of you who have been to London, I hope this book transports you back to London's bustling streets and lets you relive the magic of the city. For those of you who have never been, I hope this book gives you a small taste of the magic of London and that you fall in love with it, at least a little bit.

Prologue

It was an exceptionally beautiful sunny day, especially for spring in London. And on this lovely day, an American family was enjoying an afternoon in Hyde Park. A mother, a father, and their little girl with long brown hair with strands of red that lit up like fire in the sunlight. They were in London for a series of conferences where the father was presenting his research results. But today, there was no conference, just a family, enjoying time as a family in the park.

As she walked through the park with her parents the little girl was blissfully happy. They walked by the Peter Pan statue and her father started to chase her around it in an impromptu game of tag. She shrieked with laughter as she tried to avoid being tagged, but was eventually caught by her mother who swept her off her feet as she giggled. Her father pulled both of them, mother and daughter, into a giant hug.

"My two favorite ladies. What would I do without you two?" He asked.

The little girl watched as her father kissed her mother, and wrapped in her parents embrace she felt so loved and so safe. They continued walking, making their way to the giant pond in Kensington Gardens, which was surrounded by ducks and geese and swans. Her father began making up silly stories about the birds and gave them funny names as they passed each one, causing the little girl to giggle hysterically as the sun sparkled on the water.

They got ice cream from a stand near the pond and sat down in the grass in the shade of a large oak tree. As they sat there eating their ice cream, with the sun filtering down through the leaves of the tree, with her parents sitting on either side of her, the little girl thought to herself, *what a perfect day…*

Chapter 1

The blinding and hot Arizona sun streamed through her window as Eleanor snapped wide awake from her dream as the alarm on her phone went off beside her on the nightstand. She reached out and swiped it off the table, silencing it in the process, and then smothered it beneath her pillow.

"Cursed thing," she grumbled.

6 a.m. is early by most standards, but for Eleanor it was pure torture. She'd never been a morning person. But these days she didn't really have a choice. In her job as an adjunct instructor at her local community college, Eleanor took any classes they would throw her way, no matter how far from her main field . . . or the time of day the class met. Which is how she found herself dashing back and forth between her bedroom and bathroom trying to make herself look presentable and gather all her materials for the day.

"Good morning sweetheart," she heard her mother call up the stairs.

"'Morning!" she shouted back.

In her room, she quickly put on a dark blue pencil skirt and a lightweight white cotton shirt. She pulled a bright pink cardigan from her closet and tossed it in her tote bag. She would need it later in the classroom. Even though it was still early morning, it was also late April in Arizona, which meant that it was already a very warm 80-something degrees outside. Eleanor hopped into the bathroom, slipping a pair of navy blue ballet flats on along the way. Staring at her reflection in the mirror, she finished putting on what little makeup she wore, just a bit of blush, some eyeliner and mascara, and a swipe of lip gloss. She then wound her long, dark brown hair up into a bun near the top of her head. Stepping away from the mirror she gave herself a glance over and frowned slightly, dissatisfied as usual with what she saw in the reflection.

Individually, she liked each of her features, large blue eyes, a perfectly average nose that wasn't too big or too small, full lips that had no need of fillers, but for some reason all combined, her face seemed boringly normal. Her body was the same, normal but maybe a larger than most. Comparison to others can be brutally easy for many women like her, but it was especially so living in Phoenix, the land of "bikini bodies" all year long. She went back and forth on a daily basis between feeling like her body was fine and she needed to accept herself or feeling like she was too fat. Every day was a struggle to feel "good enough," if it wasn't her body she was dissatisfied with it was her career and if not that, then something else. She was getting exhausted from the constant existential crisis. Sighing, she left the bathroom, turning out the light as she went, and rushed back into her room to grab her things.

Racing downstairs with her purse and tote bag she quickly gathered some food for lunch from the fridge and started the kettle on the stove. Once her tea was ready and in her travel cup, Eleanor gathered up her things and walked out to her car. She winced slightly, squinting in the brightness of the early morning sun and shoving her sunglasses over her eyes. The forecast for the day called for sun, sun, and more sun, with a high of around 99 degrees.

6

Summer was roaring in, and Eleanor knew it would be triple digit temperatures any day. She fought off the envy when she thought about the current weather in her favorite city. London's forecast was in the low 60's with mostly cloudy skies. Eleanor laughed at the thought that most Londoners would think her crazy for wanting to swap climates, but after years of living in the desert, cold and rain and clouds seemed like such a novelty and one she'd trade for in a heartbeat.

Driving to campus, Eleanor went over her lesson plans in her head. On Mondays and Wednesdays, she taught two classes, English 101 and Modern Drama, a theatre class she felt she was barely qualified to teach considering she had no theatre experience, but was allowed because she had taken a few courses in Shakespeare and Early American Drama between undergrad and graduate school. She had a three-hour break in between. Since it took her thirty minutes to get to campus and the price of gas was so high, she just stayed on campus, usually going to the library for the duration. The rest of the drive went by in a blur and before she knew it she had arrived at Glendale Community College.

She drove past the student parking and pulled into one of the staff parking spots, collected her things, and locked her car. She had ten minutes to spare before her first class started and was glad she didn't have to sprint across campus in the morning heat. First class of the day was English 101, and being near the end of the semester today was basically just an in-class workshop day for their final papers. Walking into the classroom five minutes before the start of class, she noticed that about half her students were already in their seats. They were all laughing and chatting, showing each other things on their phones and talking about their summer plans. Summer vacation was only a couple weeks away and they were all ready to begin the time off, Eleanor included. She was a little worried about summer though. She hadn't been approved to teach any summer classes, and she wasn't sure yet if she'd be able to get more shifts at the bookstore she worked at. She loved teaching but hated being an adjunct instructor, just a fancy title that translated to part-time with no benefits and no job security. At 27 years old she was living with her mother, and while her mom was ok with Eleanor not paying rent, Eleanor did contribute to the groceries and paid for her own car maintenance and student loan bills. She also tried to split the bill whenever she and her boyfriend Michael went out on a date. So the summer was going to be tight.

"Hi Eleanor! How's it going?" She heard one of her students call out.

"Hi Max, it's going well, how are you doing? Almost done with your paper?" Eleanor replied with a smile.

"Sure thing, you're going to love it!" Max said laughing.

Max was one of her more outgoing students. He was the life of the party in the classroom, always chatting with the students around him and asking Eleanor lots of questions throughout class, some more relevant to the subject of the day than others. But Eleanor was always so grateful for students willing to participate. Especially at 7:30 in the morning.

Over the next five minutes Eleanor got her things set up at the front desk and wrote instructions for the day on the board as the rest of the class came rushing in. At 7:30 Eleanor turned around and began to start the class, just as one last student came rushing in.

"Glad you could join us Shannon," Eleanor said smiling.

"Sorry Eleanor, bad accident on Bell Road, I had to detour around and it took a while."

"No worries Shannon, I'm glad you made it on time," Eleanor replied kindly. She was always concerned about her students. This morning's group were some of the most dedicated students she taught. The demographic of the students she taught was pretty diverse. But in this class, most of them were from less advantaged backgrounds, worked at least two jobs while going to school full time, taking classes in the early morning, late evening, or online to fit it around their schedules. Many of them also were either young parents, or helped to take care of siblings at home. Shannon was one of those students who shared responsibilities for her siblings. Her mom worked three jobs and was hardly home. So Shannon was the one who got her two little brothers and little sister up and ready for school and dropped them off at school just before rushing to class. She had been reluctant to tell Eleanor why she was always rushing in at the last minute, but after a few weeks she finally confided. Other than her tardiness, Shannon was a perfect student. Her work was always submitted on time, if not early, and it always exceeded the requirements of the assignment. With students like Shannon, Eleanor was always willing to bend some of the rules of the attendance policy.

Shannon took her usual seat next to Max. The two hadn't known each other before that semester, but quickly became friends. Eleanor thought Shannon was good for Max. Max was representative of the other half of her students. He came from a solid upper middle-class background, both of his parents worked good jobs and made good money. He always talked about his pride and joy, a customized Honda Civic hatchback that his parents gave him as a high school graduation gift. His parents paid for all of his school expenses and his part time job at Target just paid for his gas and any personal items he wanted to buy or going out with friends. He was taking classes at the community college to get some of his general education credits taken care of and then he would transfer to Arizona State University.

Some of Eleanor's students were at the college because it was all they could afford, others were there to knock out basic credits or just take a bunch of classes until they figured out what they really wanted to do, using the college as a way station between high school and the university. At the beginning of the semester Max had seemed carefree to the point of being shallow and superficial, but by the end of the semester he had mellowed a bit. Less bragging and boastful and more serious about his studies. And Max had been good for Shannon. She had started the semester timid and hesitant, like she was afraid Eleanor was going to kick her out of the course. Now she had an easy laugh and chatted with the rest of the class and participated openly in class discussions. Eleanor loved seeing how her students grew and developed throughout the semester. She also loved seeing friendships and relationships flourish. She hoped that Shannon and Max would stay friends after the semester was over, and the romantic in her hoped they might become more than friends.

The rest of the class passed by and her students' papers were coming along nicely, they were all on track to be done on time, and so far, it seemed like grading them wouldn't take too long. Or at least that's what Eleanor hoped. After the English class was done she headed to the library and did her class prep for the Modern Drama class that started at noon. She had a stack of papers to grade from last week so that took up the rest of the break time between classes. She then had about 30 minutes to herself to read a bit of the novel she was currently reading on her Kindle and eat the lunch she brought with her and then headed across campus to her classroom for Modern Drama at 11:50 am. By that point the sun was directly overhead and it was well nearing 99 degrees. In the direct sunlight, it felt miserable. She had needed her cardigan in the classroom and library that morning but by now it was back stuffed into her tote bag.

She knew it would be back on within ten minutes of entering her classroom, the AC was on full blast in all the buildings around campus today.

The rest of the day passed uneventfully, and she was done with the school day by 1:15pm. Knowing that she would only waste the rest of her day if she went straight home, Eleanor preferred to go to a coffee shop near her home. It was an independent place and Eleanor had become friends with the owner and all of the employees. Walking in she felt some of the tension from the day melt away. Her students had been unusually distracted and unruly in the second class and had kept taking the class down multiple tangents. But looking around the coffee shop with its framed posters of European locations lining the walls made her feel relaxed. She quickly ordered her standard latte, iced, obviously, and a packet of shortbread cookies and headed to her usual table, under a large poster of Hyde Park in London. She often fantasized about moving to London one day, and being able to go for walks in Hyde Park, wishing she could just step through that poster and be there instead of in hot, miserable Phoenix. She spent the next few hours grading papers and then doing some writing.

Eleanor had always loved writing. Ever since she was a little girl. She was always writing something; short stories, poetry, outlines for novels, many of which would be later discarded when a new idea would come up. She loved this time of day. These afternoons were her favorite time each week. She loved teaching and her other work as a writing tutor at a local educational center on Fridays for high school students. Teaching and helping young students become better writers was exciting for her, she loved watching those moments where an idea finally clicked in a student's mind and for a moment they are truly excited about learning. But she knew it was a temporary fix. Neither of her jobs as an adjunct instructor or writing tutor were paying all of the bills, and her Tuesday, Thursday, Saturday job working at the second-hand bookstore was a fun change of pace but that job wasn't taking her places either.

Some weeks she just felt so stuck. She had jobs, but no career. She'd love to teach full time, but finding a full-time teaching position in her current community college system had nearly the same odds as winning the lottery. She'd been applying to every full-time teaching job, at all of the local colleges in town, since she graduated with her Masters, but she'd only made it to the interview stage twice and still never managed to land the job. Thankfully her mother understood, since she worked in the college system herself, so she knew how tough it was and how infrequently jobs were posted. But it was still hard for Eleanor. She was stuck and she knew it, but she didn't know what to do about it. So she just kept writing, losing herself in fictional worlds where problems like that belonged to someone else.

She got home around 5 o'clock and remembered that her mother was going to be late coming home because of a department meeting. Eleanor took her things up to her office. She and her mom shared a three bedroom, two story condo style house. It had a den/office on the first floor that her mom used and Eleanor took over two of the upstairs bedrooms as a bedroom and office with a sitting area by the window, they were separated by a "Jack and Jill" bathroom, so it made it feel like a little apartment. She loved living with her mom, but it was still nice to have her own space to work and relax. After setting things down at her desk and double checking her schedule for tomorrow in her planner, she went through the bathroom to her bedroom and changed into sweatpants and a t-shirt.

Going back down the stairs she went to the kitchen to empty the dishwasher and put a frozen pizza in the oven for herself and her mother. Cassie arrived home from work just as the pizza came out of the oven and the two of them chatted about their days before Eleanor went up to her room and Cassie went into the living room to watch some TV. Normally Eleanor would be happy to sit and watch with her mom but tonight she felt unusually tired and decided to go to bed early. She had to go to the bookstore early the next morning to open and it had been a long enough day already.

As she climbed into bed she checked her phone one more time and noticed there still weren't any texts or calls from Michael. She'd texted him earlier to say hello but knew better than to text again. Michael worked for one of the financial companies in town and was always busy. He didn't like getting several texts throughout the day. She knew she'd see him on Friday for dinner and was already counting down the days.

* * * * *

The rest of the week went by quickly, though Eleanor was still feeling tired. She was beginning to suspect it was more boredom that she was feeling than actual fatigue. Her mother had begun asking her again if she would think about going back to school and earning a PhD or an MFA. Cassie thought Eleanor would have a better chance of finding a full-time job with a terminal degree and was worried that Eleanor was wasting crucial years of her life.

Eleanor was nervous about going back to school. There was always Arizona State University, which was local but she wasn't sure she wanted to go to such a large school or if she wanted to go to back to school at all. It wasn't an easy choice. There had always been a lot of expectations. Both her parents were academics. Her mother was director of the English Department at a different community college in the Maricopa County Community College District, and also did some consulting work on the side. Her father was a prominent Literature scholar and professor at an Ivy League University on the east coast. Her parents had always expected her to pursue an advanced degree so getting her MA had been an easy decision. But she had hoped she'd be able to find a full-time job at the community college level and focus on teaching and maybe do some writing on the side. But the recent economy downturn had hit higher education hard and Plan A wasn't working out so well. She knew that her mom was probably right. Anytime she tried to discuss with Michael, he would convince her it was a ridiculous idea and complained about how busy she'd be and how they'd never get to see each other. Eleanor thought he was being a little dramatic, but after their breakup and reconciliation a year ago she didn't want to do anything to risk their relationship. Right now, Michael wasn't perfect but he was the best thing in her life.

Turning her car into the parking lot of the restaurant she was determined to put thoughts of school aside and just focus on her time with Michael tonight. She had been excited when he'd suggested the little Italian place between their two neighborhoods as the place to meet. They'd had their first date there, more than two years ago. Eleanor had just graduated with her Masters and moved back to Phoenix. All of her high school friends had moved out of town or just out of her life and she was starting over in the social scene. She hadn't wanted to try online dating so she joined an online social group instead and met Michael through a local literature group created on the site. Though Eleanor had focused on Rhetoric and Composition in school she knew she couldn't date a guy who didn't love to read and couldn't share a love of literature.

She had noticed Michael the moment she walked into the first group meeting she attended. He'd been standing to the side, talking to some other group members, everyone seemed drawn to him and he was smiling and chatting

14

enthusiastically with the members. He wasn't very tall, but was taller than Eleanor and a lot of the other women in the group. Eleanor remembered how his sandy blond hair caught the light from the setting sun streaming through the coffee shop window, and how she admired his easygoing nature and friendly smile. There was just a quality about him that made everyone seem to like him. All the guys in the group wanted to be friends with him and all the women in the group wanted to sit next to him. They seemed opposites in some ways, he was outgoing and loved the attention from the rest of the group, easily dominating the conversations at times, whereas Eleanor was shy and reserved, quietly observing the conversations and only speaking when she felt strongly about the opinions being shared. Michael got on easily with the guys and flirted with all the women, while Eleanor made friends with a couple of the women and never really got to know any of the guys.

She'd given up on finding a romantic relationship within the group but was happy with the social interaction and friendships that were developing. But after several meetings, and after watching him chat up most of the other women, Michael approached her after the group discussion had ended. They'd been reading *Anna Karenina* in the group and the discussion had gotten heated. Eleanor found herself speaking up more than usual, and there had been a bit of back and forth between her and Michael during the discussion. At the end of the meeting, and after a continued debate over whether Anna had deserved her fate — Eleanor said Anna didn't, Michael disagreed — Michael had asked her out. The family-owned Italian restaurant was equal driving distance for both of them and a time was arranged.

Now, a little over two years later, they still came here fairly often, though as Eleanor thought about it, the last time they came was three months ago for their anniversary. Eleanor had thought then that he might propose, it had been several months since they'd gotten back together, the timing seemed right. Instead she got a new case for her iPad. Frowning at the memory and then feeling guilty about her lack of gratitude, Eleanor quickly parked her car and headed inside. Michael was already there, waiting at their usual table. He was preoccupied with his beat-up Galaxy Note. Eleanor hated that thing, he was always on it. She leaned down to give him a kiss before taking her seat and he distractedly tilted his cheek up to meet her lips. Disappointed and a little hurt Eleanor put on a brave smile and sat down.

"Still busy with work?" she asked curiously.

"It never ends," Michael replied, finally putting the device back in his pocket. Seeming to see her for the first time he turned and smiled. Eleanor felt a warm happiness spread throughout her body. It had been a long week and that smile was exactly what she needed.

They proceeded to order their meals and then ordered tiramisu and cappuccinos for dessert. Throughout the meal Eleanor felt increasingly uneasy, there something hesitant and unnatural about how Michael was reacting to her. The conversation seemed a little forced and he was becoming increasingly distant and sparse in his answers. If she asked him something personal, like how he was doing, his answers were short. If she asked him about work, he'd go on and on about his latest project. He didn't ask about Eleanor's week, and when she tried to fill the conversation by offering up details and stories of her week, she could see his attention wander. They often had conversations like this, communication had never been a strong point for Michael. She normally basked in his stories and brushed off her feeling that she didn't get a chance to talk much about her day or activities. She accepted their differences in communication styles, that was all it really was, she had convinced herself. It wasn't that he didn't want to hear what or how she was doing. Tonight though, she could tell something was bothering him. At first she assumed it was something to do with work, the difficulties with the project he mentioned earlier. But as the conversation awkwardly halted, Eleanor finally couldn't help herself.

"Is everything alright? You seem really distracted tonight Michael."

He took a deep breath, staring blankly at his hands wrapped around the cup in front of him. As soon as he looked up and into her eyes Eleanor knew exactly what was bothering him.

Her.

She felt her heart pounding, her mind raced, time slowed down.

She could hear him speaking, and see his lips moving. She could see the attempt at sympathy and remorse in his eyes. She'd seen it all before. On a night like this, about a year ago. Finally, she saw him take another deep breath and feeling like the world was rushing at her at a million miles per minute she was able to process the last few words of his little speech. Four words to be exact.

"This isn't working out," he said firmly.

Each one was a dagger to her heart that twisted and drove its way deeper and deeper. When they'd separated a year ago it had devastated her, but he'd seemed so much more confused about it then. Looking at him now she knew this was real. This was final. This is what the end really looked like. Tears sprang to her eyes and before she could stop them one rolled quickly down her cheek and fell into her drink.

Suddenly time sped up and she felt her heart pounding in her chest. Nothing made sense. All the "I love you's" on the phone recently, the cute text messages, silly pictures posted to her Facebook wall, none of it made sense. He'd clearly been thinking about this for a while, the parts of his breakup speech that her brain was slowly beginning to process made that clear.

"I'm not happy."

"We're going in different directions."

"We want different things."

"I feel like something is missing from my life."

"I'm sorry."

His words were hitting her like bullets. Those last two especially, hitting her over and over again.

"I'm sorry."

"I'm sorry."

"I'm sorry."

Suddenly Eleanor wanted to scream. She knew Michael hated scenes, he disliked any sign of emotion or frustration. She wanted to start throwing things, screaming at him, she wanted to tell the whole restaurant what a pathetic, little man he was and how he had wasted more than two years of her life! How she should have never believed him and taken him back after he broke her heart the first time! Her breath came in jagged bursts and the tears were rolling freely down her cheeks, dropping onto the pristine white tablecloth.

Michael reached over to take her hand, which was still clenched around her cappuccino cup. At the feel of his touch she felt like she was being burned and she snatched her hand away, finally looking up at his face, searching his eyes, her own full of questions. But his eyes were clear and final. She knew he meant every word he was saying. He'd already made his mind up, without bothering to share his doubts with her. He'd just been going through motions while he decided. Everything leading up to this evening had been a lie.

"I think you know I'm right," he said softly.

Eleanor paused, trying to find words. She wanted to devastate him as much as he was devastating her.

Nothing came.

She slowly reached up to wipe the tears and smooth her hair. She reached for her handbag and rose quietly from her seat.

"Don't you want to talk about this?" Michael asked curiously.

Finally, with a steadying breath, Eleanor spoke, "I think you've said enough for the both of us Michael. We've spent enough time on this relationship, it hasn't worked out, you want it to be over. I'm not going to sit here and beg you to change your mind. I did that last year. All it did was get me here, one year later, feeling pathetic and hurt. This time I'm going to listen to you. You want it to be over, so fine, we're done. Have a nice life."

Turning on her heel, she slowly but confidently strode out of the restaurant all the way out to her car before the tears started to fall again.

By the time she pulled her car into the driveway ten minutes later she was a wreck. Sobbing hysterically, she sat in her car for another thirty minutes before she shakily walked across the drive and in the front door only to be met by a dark house. She started crying even harder. At that moment, all she wanted was to talk to her mother, who she now remembered was still at school in a late night meeting with her department's adjunct instructors.

Eleanor made her way to the couch, kicking her heels off along the way and threw herself down, clinging to one of the throw pillows, her body wracked with sobs. She cried for at least an hour, until she couldn't cry any more.

Eyes swollen, body aching, heart breaking, Eleanor did the only thing she could think of to make herself feel even remotely better.

She went over to the DVD shelf, took out her favorite movie, put it in the player, and pressed play. The credits came up on screen, quickly followed by the face of her favorite actor, Patrick Reynolds, a face so gorgeous her heart broke a little more. As the familiar film began to play, a story of love and two headstrong people in 19th century England, Eleanor allowed herself to fall into the storyline and away from her own heartbreak.

Two hours later, just as Eleanor sat back on the couch after getting up to switch discs and put Part 2 in the Blu-Ray player, she heard her mother coming in through the door.

"Sweetie? Are you awake?" Eleanor heard Cassie call down the hall.

At the sound of her mother's voice Eleanor felt the tears spring to her eyes again and as Cassie came around the corner into the family room the first thing she noticed was Eleanor on the couch, sitting in the dark, illuminated by the TV, tears streaming down her face and shoulders shaking as she began to sob.

Cassie rushed to the couch and put her hands on both sides of Eleanor 's face, searching her eyes for answers.

"Ellie? Eleanor, what's wrong? Are you hurt, are you sick?" Cassie asked anxiously, quickly determining that Eleanor didn't look injured in any way, a quick feel of her forehead revealed she didn't have a fever.

Struggling to speak between bursts of sobs, Eleanor finally managed to squeak out the horrible truth.

"Michael broke up with me . . . again. This time he means it, it's for real Mom, it's really over this time!"

Eleanor saw her mother's face rapidly move through her emotions, concern, worry, hurt, as her mother wrapped her arms around her. They stayed there like that, curled up on the couch, for two more hours, as the rest of the movie played. As it finished Eleanor's eyes grew heavy and fluttered closed. There was nothing more she could do but sleep. At some point she vaguely remembered her mother placing a blanket over and turning out the lights.

Chapter 2

The weekend passed in a blur for Eleanor. She called out sick to her job at the bookstore and sequestered herself in her room, lying on her bed. Cassie would bring her water and cups of tea, along with various foods and sweet treats, trying to tempt Eleanor to eat something but it would lie half eaten. The only thing that changed each time Cassie entered Eleanor's room was the movie playing on her TV. All weekend Eleanor alternated between films and TV shows featuring her favorite actor and celebrity crush, Patrick Reynolds along with BBC adaptations of 19th century period romantic dramas. *Persuasion, Jane Eyre, North & South*, and more, Eleanor was escaping into them all.

Cassie was worried about her daughter and not more than blazingly angry with Michael. She had suspected that he was using Eleanor, and secretly hoped her daughter would figure it out. After going through her own divorce, she knew that no one could convince her that she had been wrong about the person she loved.

Cassie sighed as she hoped that the new week would see Eleanor rally a bit. Monday morning came and just as Cassie was gathering her things to drive to work Eleanor came stumbling down the stairs, still buttoning her blouse and fighting to keep her bag on her shoulder.

"Darling, are you sure you want to teach this morning? You could always call out for your first class."

"I can't afford for them to dock my pay, not after just having to pay for new tires for my car," Eleanor grumbled. "I can get through my morning class, they can just keep working on their papers. But I don't have anything planned for the afternoon, I didn't do any of the lesson plans that I was going to prepare over the weekend. And I haven't graded their papers from Friday!"

Seeing Eleanor becoming distraught, Cassie walked over and placed one hand on her shoulder and the other under her chin.

"So, your afternoon class isn't one of your writing classes, right?" she asked purposefully.

Eleanor nodded tiredly. "It's Modern Drama."

"What are you going over right now?"

"We finished our class plays, I was supposed to put together a lesson on contemporary theatre," she explained, looking woeful at the thought of the abandoned lesson plan sitting on her computer.

Walking over to the DVD shelf, Cassie quickly plucked a case from the shelf and walked back to Eleanor and handed her their copy the 25th anniversary performance of *Phantom of the Opera* at the Royal Albert Hall.

"Here, show them this. Sit in the back and grade their papers while they watch."

Grabbing her things, Cassie cast one more look at Eleanor.

"Make some coffee for yourself before you leave. We'll talk tonight and I'll help you with your lesson plans for the next week. Consider it a perk of having a Mom in the same profession!" Smiling, Cassie gave Eleanor a hug and said, "Call me if you need me sweetie," then headed out the door.

When Cassie returned home that evening she found

Eleanor once again hunkered down in her room watching another romantic movie. Cassie knocked on the open door to get her attention.

Eleanor glanced up briefly giving a weak "Hi Mom."

"Did everything work out at school? Cassie asked, worried that maybe Eleanor hadn't left the house after all.

"Yes, the film worked and I got the papers graded. Thanks for the suggestion." She replied as she continued watching her TV screen.

"Ellie, sweetheart, this can't be helping you," Cassie said with a worried look.

Not looking away from the screen, "My love life might be in shambles, but at least these movies don't disappoint. Colonel Brandon will always end up with Marianne, Elizabeth will always have Darcy, Jane will always find her way back to Rochester, and Wentworth will always forgive Anne. Trust me Mom. They help. They may be fiction but they give me hope."

Smiling thoughtfully, she grudgingly remarked, "Alright. If you say so. But how about you shut that off for now and come downstairs. I'll help you put together your lesson plans for the last few classes of the semester so you won't have to think about them later."

Sighing, Eleanor turned off the film and did as her mother suggested. They spent the rest of the evening putting together the lesson plans for her classes. With her mom's help, Eleanor felt like she'd at least get through the teaching and grading left for the rest of the semester. She couldn't wait for summer break to start even more now. She'd still have to work, but a break in the routine sounded good right now as she fought, for the millionth time since Friday, to push thoughts of Michael aside. It was just her luck that all of this was happening while both her best girlfriends Grace and Carly were both out of town. She needed all the friends and support she could get right now.

Being able to vent and let out her thoughts with her friends would have helped, she thought. Although she knew her mom understood and supported her, friends were just easier to vent to.

* * * * *

The rest of the week went by in a haze. Eleanor only went to school and when she wasn't there she would be home, lying in bed, watching movies and trying to avoid thinking about anything. Some days she missed Michael so much she thought her heart would burst, others she just felt completely numb. Saturday came and she had to go to work at the bookstore.

While shelving some new books she couldn't help thinking about the current state of her life. Just as she was placing new books on the shelf, she paused, realizing she also needed something new. She knew something needed to change. She couldn't keep going on like this. She'd avoided making decisions for so long because of the life she thought she'd have with Michael. The tears burned as sadness and anger collided as she thought about how foolish she'd been, putting her own career on the side while just waiting for Michael to decide he wanted her. But she didn't know what to do. The thought of doing a PhD just felt too daunting. She wanted to write, but even a three year MFA Creative Writing program felt like too much to attempt and what if she still couldn't find a job? But something had to change. What?

Returning home that evening, feeling exhausted both physically and mentally, she sat down at the kitchen breakfast bar and watched her mother finish cooking dinner. They shared the space for a while, in a comfortable silence. Eleanor could tell that Cassie was giving her some space to think, sensing that Cassie was waiting for Eleanor to begin.

Finally, Eleanor spoke. "I need a change. I can't keep living my life as it is right now."

"What do you mean darling?" Cassie asked with concern. She'd known this was coming, she'd hoped that the breakup might finally prompt Eleanor to finally take some control over her life. Cassie loved and supported her daughter, who'd been through so much over the years, but she agreed that Eleanor needed a change. She sipped her coffee, bit her tongue, and held her breath, waiting for Eleanor to continue.

"I mean, I'm not happy. I haven't been for a while. What happened with Michael is disappointing but I've realized it's not the only thing making me feel so miserable. I don't know what I'm doing with my life. I love teaching but I wanted to be more than just an adjunct instructor, working for low pay and no benefits who has to work retail part time to earn extra money and still doesn't earn enough to support herself!" Her voice rose with her frustration.

Cassie cheered inwardly at her daughter's words. She knew this had been bothering Eleanor for a while but every time Cassie tried to make a suggestion for a change Eleanor shot it down, partially due to her relationship with Michael.

Slowly and cautiously Cassie spoke, "Eleanor I think you need to be honest with yourself and figure out what it is that you really want to do with your life. If it's teaching, you need to go back to school. If it's writing, you need to focus on that and look into creative writing programs or workshops if you don't want to go back for another degree. What do you *want* to do Ellie?"

Hesitating, afraid to voice her wants and desires out loud, Eleanor finally said, in a small voice, "I want to write. I mean, I could also teach writing one day, but yeah . . . I want to write."

"Eleanor, do you really want to teach writing one day?"

Cassie said, raising an eyebrow.

"Oh mom," Eleanor said quietly but with an exhausted frustration in her voice. "I honestly don't know what I want to do. I know what I *should* do. I *should* get a job that pays a living wage. I *should* probably go back to grad school in order to get that job. I *should* spend less time with my head in the clouds writing stories that only I will read—"

Cassie cut off her daughter's melodramatic tirade, "Eleanor, stop. You shouldn't do any of those things unless you really want to. You don't have to get a PhD and become a professor just because that's what your dad and I did. And you absolutely don't have to give up writing. But if you want to be a writer you need to share the material you are writing. Stop thinking about what you should do. What do you *want* to do?"

Eleanor rolled her eyes, "It's not that simple mom."

"Yes, it is Eleanor. It really is that simple. When I was your age I knew I wanted to work in higher education, as a professor and also as an administrator one day. I knew I wanted to marry your father and have you. And while things with your dad didn't work out, I have you and you are everything I have ever wanted. Now I just want you to be happy Eleanor. So stop trying to please everybody but yourself. What do you *want* to do?"

Eleanor paused and thought about it. Her mother rarely asked her such direct questions. But the more she thought about it, the more impossible her answer seemed.

"I…I want to write mom. I want to be a writer. And if that means I keep teaching as an adjunct instructor and working in the bookshop until something happens, then I guess that's what I'll do." Saying it out loud still didn't make Eleanor feel like it was the right answer. She still didn't feel like a big decision had been made.

"Then write Eleanor. You're good at it. But you're not going to get anywhere if all you do is write in coffee shops and don't let anyone see it or try to get it in front of an agent or go the self-publishing route. Teaching and working part time in the bookshop are not your only choices for work while you write. You have options, you can make it work if you want it bad enough."

"I guess," Eleanor said with a frown.

Cassie took a deep breath about to speak and then stopped. Eleanor looked up at her mother curiously.

"What?" She prompted her mom.

"I spoke with your Aunt Victoria today."

"You talked to Aunt Vickie? When?" Eleanor asked, trying to follow this sudden change of direction in the conversation. She thought her mom was going to continue with advice not talk about her favorite, okay, only Aunt, she smiled thinking of her Aunt Vickie.

"While you were at the bookshop," Cassie said, trying to sound casual.

"Oh really? What did she have to say?"

Cassie paused.

"Mom? What did Aunt Vickie say? Is she alright?"

"Oh yes, darling, she's fine. But she told me something interesting and I think I should share it with you. She told me partly so I could pass the information along to my students because there's an undergraduate level opportunity, but I also told her about—"

Eleanor interrupted, "Mom, what are you talking about?"

Cassie walked to the den to the side of the kitchen and brought back a stack of computer printouts and handed them to Eleanor. Eleanor stared at them trying to process what she was looking at.

London
Creative Writing Intensive MFA
One Year Program

"Get your work seen by top UK literary agents!"

The words stared back at her from the various pages. Looking back up at her mom Eleanor asked quietly, "What is all this?"

"Your aunt was telling me about it today. We both agreed it might be good for you." Seeing her daughter still looked confused Cassie took another deep breath and explained, "It's a one year, intensive MFA program in creative writing. It would be a terminal degree that could help you get a full-time teaching position somewhere. But its publishing rates of former students is impressive, as are its placement rates in publishing and related industry jobs. The program is renowned and your aunt and I think it might be a good fit for you. It wouldn't be like going back to grad school at a U.S. university, but it would still help you professionally both as a teacher and as a writer.

"They offer it every year as a twelve-month program. They don't follow the usual academic calendar in the UK, so you'd start this August and be done by the end of next July. They have short workshops that focus on creative writing, editing, getting an agent, working in publishing, and so on, and Aunt Victoria knows some people on the admissions panel and is willing to put in a good word for you. There's no guarantee that you'll get in, but with your CV, your teaching background, your portfolio, and your connections we think you stand a really good chance."

Still staring at the computer printouts Eleanor suddenly noticed the price tag of this intriguing program, "How on earth would I afford it? I mean, not just the program, which is expensive enough but to move there for the year, to live, where would I stay, how would I afford rent?!"

Taking a deep breath, Cassie replied, "Your aunt already owns a flat in central London for your cousin Jonathan, while he's studying at London School of

Economics. It's a two bedroom but his current flatmate is about to graduate and move out. Victoria says you can stay there for free as her contribution to our plan. As for the rest, I have some money saved up, I can cover the tuition and you can pay me back as and when you're able. Victoria said with a student visa you'd be able to get a part time job, which should help you cover your food, transit, and other daily expenses."

"Mom, I can't take your savings! Not to go live in London for a year! This is my mess. You and Aunt Vickie shouldn't be paying to get me out of it."

Putting her hand over her daughters, and looking in her eyes, "Honey, you've been miserable for ages. Your aunt, cousin Jonathan, we've all noticed. Part of the money I've saved up was specifically for something like this. I'd hoped you'd eventually find something you'd want to do and I didn't want you held back because of money. I can afford this sweetie, and I want to do it, for you. And don't worry, it's not my retirement savings or investments, it's totally separate from that," Cassie said with a smile before continuing with a wink, "But when you're a famous writer living in London, you can buy a place for both of us when I retire."

Eleanor paused for a moment. The fact that her mom and her aunt had been talking about this, had been worried about her meant a lot. Other thoughts flooded the heartache from her brain and as she thought about the possibilities a new excitement filled her. This program; what it could mean for her future. The idea of moving to London. Finally, she began to speak slowly, "I hardly know what to think. It's all so sudden. London? My London? And creative writing? As much as I want to be a writer is that really the responsible thing to do?"

"Eleanor, I'm sorry, but screw being responsible. You've been doing the responsible thing for your whole life, and

I'm very proud of you. I'm tired of seeing you so miserable. You used to like teaching but now it seems like it's just something you do. You can't be an adjunct for the rest of your life. Number one it doesn't work financially. Number two, it will slowly kill your soul to not be treated with the academic respect you deserve. You've worked too hard up to now to settle for being part-time and not earn the salary you deserve. A program like this will at least help give you the extra bonus to your CV to make you stand out when applying for teaching positions. And if you do well, you probably won't even need to return to teaching! You could go into publishing, be an editor. Or you could be a writer full time, and finally get paid to do it!"

"You really think I should do this?"

"Ellie, you have been wanting to write and desperate to live in London. This is your chance to do that, even if only for a year. Things have ended with Michael, the semester is almost over, and you have nothing really to tie you down in Phoenix." She held up her hand as Eleanor started to object. "OK, other than me."

She laughed knowing her daughter was going to miss being with her and she would miss her. "But we can keep in touch through our messaging apps. So, yes, I think you should do this. You need a new start. London would be perfect."

Eleanor slowly began to smile and when she finally looked up and into her mother's eyes Eleanor's whole face had lit up. Cassie immediately said a silent prayer of thanks, it was the happiest she'd seen Eleanor in months, if not more than a year.

They spent the rest of the evening excitedly working out the details and filling out the online application, with Eleanor carefully choosing the few short pieces to submit as her writing samples. The more she thought about it the more desperately she began to hope that she would be accepted.

The next few weeks seemed to drag on. Eleanor went to work at the school and the bookshop and checked her email and mailbox incessantly, waiting for confirmation that she'd been either rejected or accepted. It seemed like she would have to wait forever.

The semester came to an end and summer began. Eleanor began to lose hope and Cassie watched as Eleanor grew despondent at the thought of beginning another year of teaching as an adjunct.

Finally, while sitting in her favorite spot at the coffee shop after a day of working at the bookstore, Eleanor's iPhone alerted her that a new email had arrived. Opening up the email Eleanor could only stare in dumbfounded silence as her brain slowly processed the words that seemed to jump off the small screen.

"We are very pleased to extend an offer of acceptance to this year's 12-month intensive Creative Writing program..."

Eleanor didn't even realize she had begun to cry until a tear fell from her cheek and splashed off the screen of her phone. The tears began to fall more freely as Eleanor felt relief and excitement spread throughout her entire body.

* * * * *

Eleanor came down the stairs to the kitchen, wearing a simple sundress and flats, and looked around at all the people currently filling her house. Her mother had invited just about everyone they knew, friends, neighbors, colleagues at work. Everyone had arrived to say goodbye to Eleanor before she left the next day. The last several weeks had been a blur of activity as she gave her notice at the bookstore and the community college and began sorting out what she would take with her to London and getting her student visa in order, thankfully the school helped handle a lot of that. Back upstairs her room was packed with two suitcases, two carry-on bags, and two boxes that she and her mom would drop off at the post office the next day on their way to the airport. They had already shipped two boxes of stuff Eleanor would need when she arrived.

Eleanor made her way around the kitchen and family room, saying hello to friends, accepting their good wishes and listening to their recommendations of places to visit and things to do. Eleanor had agreed to the farewell party and she knew her mother just wanted to make a big fuss and share her excitement with their friends and family, but with Eleanor's departure now less than 24 hours way all Eleanor wanted to do was spend one last quiet evening at home. Still, Eleanor headed out to the back patio and spent the next few hours chatting excitedly with Grace and Carly, and enjoyed the time she had left with them.

The next morning came early. Though Eleanor's flight wasn't until later that evening she couldn't sleep, she was so excited. Jumping out of bed she quickly changed into some sweatpants and a t-shirt and grabbed her hydration pack, heading out for a short hike. If she was going to spend all night on an airplane she thought stretching her legs this morning would be a good idea. It was only 8 o'clock in the morning but it was already over 100°.

When she got home she quickly got ready and spent the rest of the afternoon sitting on the couch and chatting with her mom. When the time came they loaded everything into Cassie's car and swung by the post office to mail the two boxes of items Eleanor would need over the next year. They continued the drive to the airport chatting casually and talking about London. When they arrived, Cassie parked in the garage and walked Eleanor all the way to the security check point. At last they couldn't delay the goodbye any longer.

"You take care of yourself. Watch out for strangers and don't forget to look right instead of left first when you cross the street."

"Yes, Mom" Eleanor replied giggling. "Didn't you tell me they have which way to look printed on the pavement?"

"Yes, they do, and don't laugh," Cassie said with a slight frown. "Now that it's time to let you go I can't help but worry. London's a long way away."

"Yes, but I won't be alone, Jonathan will meet me at the airport and will make sure I learn my way around. And Aunt Victoria will check on me as well. I know she's going to be giving you regular reports."

They hugged one last time and Cassie stepped back and watched as Eleanor rolled her carryon through the line at security and kept watching until Eleanor was out of sight.

Eleanor made it through security quick enough, noticing there weren't too many people flying out of Phoenix that night. Once on the other side of security she located her gate and stopped at the Starbucks that was along the way to the B gates. She still had more than an hour before her flight would board, so she settled into one of the chairs with her latte and flipped through one of the magazines she had brought with her, not that she paid any attention to the images or text on the page.

She felt anxious; an odd combination of terror and excitement. This was the biggest thing she'd ever done on her own. She still couldn't believe she was uprooting her entire life, even if only for the year. She'd dreamed of living in London for so long, even though she'd only ever been to the city once as a little girl. It had always been a bright, happy memory among a bunch of not so happy memories, and Eleanor had built it up to be a magical place where all her dreams would come true. But now reality was starting to hit. Would London live up to all of her dreams and fantasies? Eleanor couldn't shake the feeling that whatever happened over the course of the next twelve months, her life would not be the same. Underneath the nerves was another emotion, something much subtler that Eleanor couldn't quite describe. All she knew was that she wasn't going to miss being an adjunct and she hadn't thought about Michael in days.

Finally, her flight was called and within thirty minutes Eleanor was on board the plane.

Chapter 3

The flight lasted about ten hours and Eleanor managed to sleep for about half that time, spending the rest of the time staring out into the empty sky. During the last couple hours Eleanor noticed that she didn't feel that nervous anymore, instead she felt peaceful. When the plane finally touched down, Eleanor felt the strangest feeling of being home.

She made it through border control and baggage claim quick enough, a strange mixture of excitement and exhaustion colliding through her body, and when she came through to the other side she struggled to scan the crowd of people waiting in the arrivals area trying spot Jonathan. Thankfully, at nearly 6-foot-tall, with dark brown curly hair and black framed glasses, he stood out. Eleanor had always marveled at how he managed to pull off a combination of sophisticated "cool guy" and "academic nerd."

Grinning, she felt a surge in energy and began walking a little faster and waved. Smiling widely, Jonathan waved back, rushing forward to meet her.

Grabbing her around the waist, he lifted her off the ground and spun her in a circle, hugging her tightly, before finally setting her back down.

"Hiya cousin!" he said excitedly.

"Hi!" She was excited to see him. Though they didn't get to see each other very often, they were both only children and had always treated each other as the sibling they wanted but never got. They kept up through quick messages and occasional video chat, but that wasn't always as frequent as they'd wanted to in recent years as they both worked on their education.

Jonathan reached down to take her large suitcases, leaving her with her two carry-ons.

"How was the flight?" he asked.

"Long," Eleanor replied with an exhausted sigh. "But relatively smooth, and I ended up with the whole row to myself so that was great."

"Oh yeah, that makes a big difference. Lucky you! Well, welcome to London," he said with a grin. "You've seen the airport, now it's time to experience the Tube. There's also the Heathrow Express, but it's more expensive and I thought I should introduce you the public transportation you'll use most often."

"I'm looking forward to it," Eleanor said with a laugh.

As they walked along, following the signs for the Underground, Jonathan slipped a piece of folded plastic from his pocket and handed it to Eleanor. She flipped it open, seeing it was like a little wallet with two slots inside and a small card slipped into one of the slots.

"It's an Oyster card. Mum had me load it with £25 for you, you can top it up yourself once that is used up. It will let you ride the Tube and the buses. But your school isn't that far from the flat, so most of the time you should be able to walk. What's been loaded on the card should last you a bit." Jonathan explained.

"That's great!" Eleanor said gratefully. "I'll have to thank Aunt Vickie. And thanks for coming to get me, you didn't have to, you know."

"I know, and you would have been fine getting to the

flat on your own, you'll see it's pretty easy. But I knew you'd have your luggage and be tired from the flight. Plus I've been so looking forward to seeing you, I didn't want to wait."

Jonathan's smile was infectious, and as tired as she was, Eleanor felt herself begin to grin like an idiot. She was so happy and excited! She was in London, her favorite city, with one of her favorite people.

They soon arrived at the Underground entrance and following Jonathan's example Eleanor tapped her new Oyster card to the card reader and walked through the gate. They soon made it to the platform and boarded a train. Jonathan stacked her bags to the side of the door and then sat next to her. The train started moving and soon they were outside, views of houses and parks, even a golf course, flew past the window.

"We ride above ground for a little bit, until we get to the edge of town and then we go underground."

"Cool," Eleanor said, somewhat absentmindedly, she was so busy processing everything. It was all so different from Phoenix! She felt like she'd landed on another planet. After dreaming about it for years and playing her childhood memories of her family trip over and over in her mind, seeing it all in person was a bit overwhelming.

Just as Jonathan said they would, the train soon went into a tunnel as they headed underground. Eleanor felt like they were flying through the tunnel. As they went along Jonathan quietly explained how to read the signs and know what the next stop was and what other lines that stop might service. Every now and then the train would pull into a new station and people would get on or off. She listened to the intercom voice politely announce each stop as they approached, occasionally mentioning what attractions were nearby. The closer they got to the center of town, the more people began to fill the carriage.

As they pulled into Leicester Square station Jonathan said, "Next is Covent Garden and after that is ours, Holborn. At Holborn you can also get the Central line, which is the red line," pointing at the map. "You'll find that you'll probably use the Piccadilly and Central lines the most. A lot of the popular stuff for tourists are along one of those lines."

Eleanor was too busy trying to process everything to respond with more than just a nod of her head. Soon they pulled into Holborn station and Jonathan jumped up and grabbed her rolling suitcases while Eleanor quickly followed with her satchel and carry-on. There were a good amount of people on the platform but Jonathan stepped to the side and Eleanor followed suit. Within a matter of seconds the platform had emptied.

"I figured we'd let them all go first," Jonathan said with a grin. "You'll learn that Londoners move fast. It's best to keep up or get out of the way."

Eleanor smiled weakly and nodded, then followed as Jonathan began rolling her bags along the platform. She noticed that instead of arrows pointing to the "Exit" they pointed to the "Way Out" and filed that bit of information away. They went up a short flight of stairs and then a couple long escalators. She noticed the signs pointing to the Central line and made a mental note of that as well.

When they reached the top of the escalator Eleanor could feel the warm humid air blowing in from outside and, following behind Jonathan, she tapped her Oyster card at the exit of the station.

As Jonathan turned to the right he looked back over his shoulder at Eleanor and said, "We'll walk from here, the flat isn't very far. This is High Holborn, we'll walk up just a short way to Proctor Street, and Red Lion Square is just a short bit past that."

"Ok," Eleanor replied, a little weakly. She was fading

fast. The overnight flight was definitely catching up to her. Looking around she tried to take in all the surroundings. It was busier than she had expected for a Saturday afternoon. She shuddered a bit at what a week day rush hour would look like around here. They passed what looked like a drug store, and then a clothing store called Next, across the street were some more shops and restaurants including a McDonalds and a Krispy Kreme. Eleanor cringed slightly, *some things you just can't leave behind*, she thought. They came to a cross walk and Jonathan stopped to wait for the light. He was talking again, passing along more information but Eleanor struggled to keep up.

"...once you've been around longer, but for now wait until the green man lights up on the sign. Behind us is the little Waitrose, if we run out of milk or you want to pick up dinner, that's the one I usually stop at or at the Sainsbury's across the street from the Tube. There's a bigger Waitrose a few minutes more in the other direction from the flat."

Eleanor quickly looked over her shoulder to see what he was pointing to but the light changed and she jumped to keep up with him. She assumed Waitrose was a grocery store of some kind, but she was so tired she couldn't remember if she'd heard of it before. Across the street they passed a gym of some kind and then came to a lovely green square. She saw the sign indicating it was Red Lion Square and excitedly looked around at the place that would be her home for the next year.

The square was lovely. It was a good size, not too small, but not too large either. It had nice, tall trees and overall a very pleasant atmosphere. There was a coffee stand in the middle of the square, and Eleanor noticed a few people sitting at the tables around it, drinking coffee and eating pastries while working on their laptops or reading the newspaper. There were a couple people sitting on the grass, soaking up the sun that was shining through the trees.

Jonathan was explaining that the square used to be much longer, and extended down to something he called Southampton Row, but bombing by the Luftwaffe in World War II had damaged many of the buildings beyond repair and in the redevelopment the square was shrunk down to its present size. They walked further into the square and Eleanor noticed that it was lined with a mix of buildings from before and after World War II. Some were more recent from the 1960s and 1970s but some were gorgeous old historic buildings from the Edwardian and Victorian eras, by the looks of it to Eleanor's untrained eye.

Jonathan caught her looking up in admiration at a red brick fronted pre-war building.

"Welcome home," he said with a small laugh.

Eleanor looked between him and the beautiful old Victorian townhouse. Mostly red brick, with some white brick accents around the column of bay windows down the right-hand side of the building. It was like something out of one of her favorite historic films.

"Wait, what?" She stammered in confusion, trying to look around the corner of the building, thinking maybe Jonathan was referring to another building as their home. When she looked back, she saw Jonathan was already walking up the front steps of the building. She read "Halsey House" printed in little black and white tiles at the top of the front steps. She couldn't believe this was where he lived. Where *she* would live!

She followed him in silence, into the main entrance of the building, which despite being newly refinished, still had some of its original features like the tiled floor and the wood banisters. But the decor around the lobby was very modern and *very* luxe. She felt like she was in a boutique hotel. They walked down a hall to an elevator, Eleanor had just caught up with Jonathan as he was pressing the button to bring it to the ground floor.

"The lift in this building is pretty good, they put it in when they redid all the flats a few years ago," Jonathan explained.

He pressed the button for their floor, and the doors closed with a whisper.

"We're only one level up. I don't usually take the lift if I just have a couple things, the stairs aren't bad. But if I'm carrying a lot of bags from the food shop or have luggage like this, the lift is great."

As tired as she was, Eleanor was grateful for the elevator, or "lift" as she quickly corrected herself mentally. Eleanor's tired brain was trying to file away information as quickly as Jonathan was sharing it but the long flight was definitely beginning to get to her. They arrived at the next floor and Eleanor followed Jonathan across the landing to the front door. The door opened onto a long halfway with a few doors leading off it. She could immediately see her Aunt Vickie's design influence in the gallery wall of pictures along the left side of the hallway. On the right side were two sets of doors that Jonathan said were storage closets. Near the end of the hall, was a door to the left and then a continuation of the hall to the right.

Jonathan nodded his head towards the door to the left, "that's the living room and kitchen, go in there for a bit and check it out, I'll take your bags to your room and then come back and give you the tour."

In a bit of a daze, Eleanor set her bags on the floor in the hall and wandered into the living room. It was a large room that ran the whole length of the left side of the flat, and was painted a cool toned light grey, that looked almost white, and served to enhance the natural sunlight coming in through the two windows along the side of the room. As she walked in she saw the kitchen area was at the back end of the room, closest to the door where she was standing. But she was immediately drawn to the far end of the room and the gorgeous, large bay window that took up most of the width of the room at the front of the flat. There were two large, plush arm chairs in the window, with a small table in between and a large, tufted ottoman that served as both a foot rest and a coffee table for the space. There was a wood tray sitting on it with some coasters, books, and decorative items. Long white curtains hung from the top of the windows, and fell into a pool of fabric on the floor.

Out the window, Eleanor could see the square through the lush green trees, and saw people still wandering around the square or sitting by the coffee stand. She couldn't believe this was her new view.

Jonathan came into the room and broke her out of her thoughts. "What do you think cousin?"

"You can't live here!" She replied with excitement, "I don't believe it. This is some kind of a joke. I'd have found a way to move here ages ago if I knew this was where you were living! This is way too nice for you! You have knickknacks and coffee table books!"

Jonathan laughed. "Not always. You know mum. This is just one of her investment properties. If she was going to spring for a flat for me during uni, did you think she was going to get some closet in Zone 6? This all ends when I graduate, why do you think I stayed on for grad school?"

He laughed again as she raised her eyebrows at him. "OK, that sounds a little privileged, like I'm going to be a perpetual student because my parents are wealthy."

"Jonathon, really, that's not what I was thinking. I know that you need the graduate degree for your career path. I was thinking that luckily for me, you were still in grad school. So I guess that makes me the privileged one."

"OK, let's agree that we both enjoy our parent's success, but never take it for granted."

"And hope one day to give back, unlike my...well, you know." Eleanor's voice dropped.

"Hey, none of that." He said gently, before resuming the explanation of the decor. "It only looks this clean because mum did a photoshoot here last week and she made me promise I'd keep it 'show home' ready for your arrival. Anything you don't like, or don't want to keep, we'll just pack away and mum's assistant will pick it up next week."

"I don't suppose we can keep it all?" Eleanor asked sheepishly.

"If you want, but mum also said not to feel like you had to, she wants you to feel like you could add your own touches. But to be honest, mum comes through pretty much every season to give it a refresh style wise and has it photographed for her business or any magazines she has a feature arrangement with. Wait until you see what she does to this place at Christmas!"

Eleanor's heart leapt with excitement at the thought. Eleanor knew she'd never do a better job at decorating than her fabulous, and increasingly famous, interior designer and property developer Aunt Vickie. She knew how amazing her aunt was, but she had no idea she'd be living in what was basically one of her show homes. She'd had that experience before when she and her mom first moved to Arizona, but the London version of the experience was even more perfect.

She walked back down the room to where Jonathan was standing in the kitchen. The kitchen took up all of the back wall with the stove and oven, a wine fridge, cabinets, a microwave, and a hidden fridge, that was very nearly American sized. The sink was in an island that ran half the width of the kitchen from the wall and divided the kitchen from the rest of the living room. It was all gleaming white cabinets with stone countertops and luxe finishings. It was nicer than her mom's kitchen back in Phoenix. Between the kitchen and lounge, there was a dining table with six chairs around it.

"Let me show you the rest of the flat," Jonathan said with a smile.

They headed down the hall, passing a small powder room, then came to two doors on either side of the hallway. Jonathan pointed to the right and said, "this one is mine," then pointing to left and gesturing for Eleanor to go ahead of him, "and this one is yours," he finished with a smile.

Eleanor walked in to her new room and gasped. Her aunt had definitely been at work in here. Jonathan had been living with another student at LSE, but this room seemed almost perfectly decorated for Eleanor.

As if reading her mind, "Mom changed things up after Fredrick moved out. I'm storing some extra boxes of stuff under the bed, I hope that's alright. This is the bigger bedroom of the two, but we each have our own en suite bathroom and I prefer a window out the back, it's a little quieter. But I thought you'd like having views out the front, so hopefully that, and the extra space, makes up for any extra noise. The windows are pretty good though, so when they're closed the noise isn't too bad."

"Jonathan, this is incredible, I'm sure I won't even notice the noise!"

Eleanor couldn't take her eyes off the room, she started wandering around it, looking at everything in more detail as Jonathan leaned against the door frame smiling at her. To the right of the door when she walked in was a large closet, just as big as the one she'd left behind, and she hadn't brought even half of her clothes from home so there'd be plenty of storage. In the middle of the room was a queen-sized bed, with a gorgeous tufted headboard in the most beautiful shade of blush. Not quite cream, or peach, or pink, but somewhere in between. There was a floral patterned rug on top of the wood flooring that Eleanor had been falling in love with throughout the flat. Against the wall opposite the bed was a tall bureau, flanked by two tall slim

45

bookshelves, that had been thoughtfully styled with some of Eleanor's favorite books or books on her favorite topics, as well as a few decorative items. Aunt Vickie had also left plenty of gaps for Eleanor to fill in.

In the corner opposite the bed from the wardrobes was a large, tufted arm chair in the same fabric and color of the bed with a foot stool in front and a plush throw blanket artfully draped over the back. But as much as she was dying of happiness over the chair and the bed, it was the desk placed in front of the large window that Eleanor had to keep herself from squealing out loud with delight. It looked like an antique, made of a beautiful wood, stained a deep chocolate brown, and had drawers down the sides as well as drawers and cabinets across the top, but not so high that Eleanor couldn't see clearly out the window from the desk. She couldn't believe that this is where she would be living and sleeping and that this desk is where she'd do her work and writing. She felt like she was in a dream.

Looking at Jonathan in a daze, "You live here?" Eleanor asked incredulously.

"Yep. And now you do too. I'm so happy you're here cousin, I can't think of a better flatmate to have. And honestly, mum is so happy you've come to live here too. She wouldn't stop giving me instructions about preparing your room or making me promise to tell you that we can change any of the decor. She really wants you to feel at home here. I think she popped some toiletries in the bathroom for you as well."

Noticing Eleanor's tired face as she tried to stifle a yawn, he asked, "Hey cousin? You feeling alright?"

Trying to shake off the fatigue Eleanor forced a smile, "Fine. Just tired. I'm fine. This is all so far beyond what I thought I'd be walking into. I feel like I fell asleep on the plane and this is all a dream. Thank you Jonathan."

"Listen, why don't you set your stuff down and rest for

a bit. I'll call Aunt Cassie and my mum to let them know you made it and I'll let your mum know you'll call her later after you've rested a bit. I'm glad you're here," he repeated with a smile as he hugged her.

Hugging him back, "I am too," Eleanor said warmly.

Jonathan left Eleanor alone in her new room and she looked around. The furnishings were so lovely, and the decor was beautiful but still neutral enough that Eleanor could add it it with almost anything she wanted. The bed was high off the floor and bending over to look underneath Eleanor noticed it was on taller legs that gave her an extra six inches or so, making for enough clearance to get her suitcase underneath as well as some storage containers if she needed. She saw the couple boxes that Jonathan had mentioned, but there was still plenty room left for her. Standing back up, she took in the bookcases and the bureau, the two small tables on either side of the bed, and the closet. She hadn't brought that much with her so it seemed to be more than enough storage for her.

Overall, the room was lavish but still comfortable and cozy, and knowing her aunt, that was probably exactly what she'd intended.

With a sigh Eleanor sank onto the bed, which turned out to be even more comfortable than it looked and seemed to envelop her completely. Smiling contentedly, she quickly fell fast asleep.

* * * * *

A little while later she woke to a knock at the door, as she struggled to make sense of her surroundings she heard Jonathan let himself in.

"Fancy a cuppa?"

Blinking at him rapidly, as if trying to bring him into focus, she asked anxiously, "A what-a? What time is it?

How long was I out?"

"A cuppa? Or a 'cup of tea' to you crazy Americans. And relax, it's only 5 o'clock. I only let you sleep for an hour. We'll go get dinner soon and then go for a walk. We'll keep you up until at least ten and you'll fall right to sleep tonight and hopefully be up and feeling rested by morning."

"Oh, ok," Eleanor said groggily, pushing her hair away from her face with one hand while accepting the tea cup with the other.

Jonathan left her to freshen up and Eleanor changed out of her traveling outfit of jeans, t-shirt, and cardigan for simple black trousers, a fresh t-shirt, and grabbed her light coat from the suitcase. She thought to herself that she was going to need to buy a heavier coat, probably sooner rather than later, her "winter" coat for Arizona would keep her warm on a cool summer evening or a warm fall day here in London but the first big chill and she'd be freezing.

She heard Jonathan's voice from down the hall, "Elle? Are you ready or do you need more time?"

Walking out to meet him, "No, I'm ready. Where are we going?"

"I thought I'd take you over to the Brunswick Centre, maybe Giraffe? Or Carluccio's? There's a few places over there, and then we can stop in at the Waitrose and pick up some groceries for you, I wasn't sure what kind of food you would want for here at the flat."

"That sounds great. Thanks," she said with a smile.

Jonathan grabbed his coat and they headed out of the flat and back downstairs. Back outside, they cut across the square and Jonathan took her through a series of left and right turns. The roads here were much different than back home. Some of them only lasted for a few hundred yards, or crossed across each other, or ended abruptly in a square like Red Lion. It definitely wasn't the grid system Eleanor was used to back home and she could tell it was going to take some getting used to.

"There's a shorter way to get to the Brunswick," Jonathan was saying, "but I thought you would like to walk along Southampton Row and by Russell Square, and I could point out some things to you."

As they walked Eleanor took in all the cute souvenir shops selling mini Big Ben's and red buses and postcards with London icons and images from Will and Kate's wedding, and Harry and Meghan's, pictured on the fronts. She made a note to come back and get some for her friends back home. They stopped in at a phone shop and picked up a new SIM card for Eleanor's iPhone. They got a "pay-as-you-go" plan, Jonathan explained that it was typically a better value and very common in the UK, especially for expats, since it's difficult to get a regular plan without a credit history in the UK. *Just one more difference between the two countries*, Eleanor thought, the US cell phone companies will lock anyone into a ridiculous contract just to take your money. Eleanor was glad to have a working cell phone, with data usage, she didn't want to be without an app to help her navigate. Leaving the shop, they passed by Russell Square and the gorgeous old Russell Square Hotel, now the Kimpton Fitzroy Hotel, and Jonathan pointed out the way to the British Museum before they turned right, away from the square and come up to the Russell Square Tube station and then to the Brunswick Centre.

Eleanor liked it at once. It was bright and open and had lots of interesting shops with names she recognized from her UK fashion magazines. There was also another Starbucks (she'd counted at least three on their short walk, as well as other coffee businesses) and a movie theatre, or cinema as Jonathan referred to it. At the other end from where they walked up she could see a bright storefront with "Waitrose" lit up above the doors. It was all so different from Phoenix yet still also slightly familiar. Eleanor kept expecting to start feeling overwhelmed again, but it never happened. It was as if her mind was already accepting that this was home now.

She and Jonathan decided to eat at a cute restaurant called Giraffe that had a world culture theme and a diverse menu. She hadn't realized until she sat down just how hungry she was. She ordered an amazing parmesan chicken schnitzel "Kiev" that filled her up. She and Jonathan fell into easy conversation over dinner, she hadn't realized how much she'd missed him. They hadn't been able to spend too much time together over the years, but they'd always felt a sibling connection and whenever they got together it was as if no time had passed. Communication had definitely gotten easier over the years as email came around, then social media, and more recently Skype and FaceTime. So they didn't really have to catch up much. She already knew about his studies at LSE and he had heard all the stories about her students, good and bad. He also knew about her relationship with Michael and had tried giving her advice after her first breakup, being the one male she felt she could truly trust. But she'd gone against his advice and gotten back with Michael when he begged her to a year ago. It had been hard to tell Jonathan that he'd been right about Michael and she'd only given him a brief rundown of her breakup but when Jonathan brought it up at dinner she knew she couldn't avoid it.

"So what happened, do you know?" he asked with concern.

"Exactly what you said would happen," she replied bitterly. "At some point after we got back together last year he realized that he didn't really want to be with me. I think when we broke up the first time he just missed the relationship, not me. He missed having someone come over and cook dinner or do his laundry–"

"You did his laundry?!" Jonathan interjected, eyes wide.

"Not all the time!" Eleanor said indignantly. "Look, I know it's pathetic. Believe me, I *know* that, especially now. But yeah, every now and then when he'd be caught up with a big project I'd help him out. I'd go to his place before he got home and cook or do some cleaning. And before you think that makes me totally horrendous you should know that he did the same for me a few times. If mom was out of town for a conference and I had to work a closing shift at the store he'd let himself into the house and cook or do the dishes, run a load of laundry for me. He's a jerk, who doesn't know how to be honest with himself but he's not a total Neanderthal."

"Well, that's good to know," Jonathan said, but still looked a bit horrified at the idea of Eleanor playing "housewife" for a guy who clearly didn't deserve it.

"I really think he just liked the idea of a relationship but just didn't want one with me. And rather than be honest about it he let it drag on and on. . . I can't believe I wasted so much time. I should have listened to you."

"You did what you thought was best at the time. He said all the right things and you thought it was the right thing. But believe me when I say, you should never go back to someone who's dumped you once. Generally speaking they'll dump you again. You deserve a guy who knows what he wants and that what he wants is *you*. You're too good for anyone else, definitely too good for that arse Michael."

Eleanor smiled at Jonathan's tirade, "Well, I doubt I'll be dating much for the foreseeable future. I just want to focus on school and writing and figuring out my life. But I'm glad I've got you now to look out for me," she finished with a smile.

"You got it cousin," Jonathan said, smiling back. "Come on, let's go get some food and such for the flat."

Jonathan paid for dinner, despite Eleanor's

protestations, and she thought it was interesting that the server came around with a card reader and took the payment right at the table. She knew that may be more common in New York City or Los Angeles, but in Phoenix she had never seen a server use one.

They left the restaurant and headed to the Waitrose. It was nice and big and bright, and Eleanor felt more at home, it reminded her of the ones back home. *I guess a grocery store is a grocery store*, Eleanor thought to herself with a smile. They walked up and down the aisles, Jonathan carrying a hand basket for her. He'd told her it was better not to use a cart or they might get more than they could carry. Eleanor hadn't thought of that but now realized that the grocery store was about to become a much more common chore in her weekly routine than it had been back in Phoenix. As they went through the store Jonathan pointed out things they already had and Eleanor added to the basket things she wanted. By the end, they'd filled up the basket and Eleanor was carrying a couple things in her arms. Jonathan pulled a few bunches of fabric out of his pocket and Eleanor watched as he undid the drawstrings on each and unfolded four reusable tote bags. It was not common to have free plastics bags in Europe and in most stores you had to pay for them. Eleanor made a mental note to pick up a couple to stash in her own handbag for future trips. After checking out they were each carrying a couple bags.

Jonathan led her home via the shortcut he mentioned earlier, taking them through an area called Queen Square that looked very nice. Eleanor was still feeling a bit turned around and she figured it was going to take her a few days to get orientated but she was really enjoying the fact that she could walk everywhere. That couldn't happen in her neighborhood in Phoenix. The grocery store was at least an hour walk away!

Back at the flat, Eleanor and Jonathan sat in the lounge

and chatted for a little bit more until Eleanor's eyelids started to flutter, struggling to stay open. They both headed to bed and Eleanor barely managed to change into her pajamas before collapsing into her new bed.

Chapter 4

The next morning Eleanor woke with a start, the room was dark so she thought for a moment it was still early morning but a check of the clock showed that it was actually late morning. The night before, she had pulled the curtains closed leaving a small opening, thinking the light would wake her up. There didn't appear to be that sunny out so there wasn't that much light coming through the opening in the curtains. Eleanor thought to herself that she'd have to get used to waking up without blinding sunlight streaming through her window. She got out of bed and stepped over to the side of the desk and looked out the window.

She really was in London, it wasn't all a dream, she hugged herself excitedly. She dressed quickly in a pair of skinny jeans, a plain t-shirt, and her white Converse. She tossed a loose cardigan and scarf onto the bed along with her handbag and then went out to see where Jonathan was. After walking around the flat and checking his room, she realized he wasn't in the flat anymore. Walking back to her room she noticed a note taped to her door:

Sorry to leave you alone this morning. I realized I forgot I have a section of my thesis I need to send to my advisor tomorrow, so I ran to the library to get it finished. Forgive me? There's a map on the table; I've circled some things of interest. If you get lost just text me. I also left a couple tenners so if you need to catch a taxi to get home you can. See you back at the flat about 6 for dinner? If I think I'll finish in time for tea I'll call you, so keep your mobile on.

   Best,

   J

Eleanor shook her head smiling, both at the thought of Jonathan being so last minute with his work and at his thinking she couldn't cope without him for a day. She put the note back down and picked up the two £10 notes that he had left for her along with the map. Walking back to her room she put the money in her wallet, in a separate section from her own cash. Sitting on the edge of the bed she looked at the map. Jonathan had marked the flat and Red Lion Square with a big star and then had drawn lines from the flat to various destinations, drawing along the roads she would need to take to get there. He'd also connected some of the places to each other along the roads to get between them in case she decided to visit more than one place. It seemed to make sense but her experience last night showed her that the streets of London are a bit more complicated than she'd anticipated.

Eleanor stood up and wrapped her scarf loosely around her neck and then draped her cardigan through the handles of her handbag. After locking up the flat she tucked the keys into her bag and made her way down the stairs and out onto the street. Looking at the map again she decided to start at the British Museum since it looked like it was the nearest to the flat. Folding the map into a small square so it would fit into her palm and show just the route to the museum she headed off through the square and out onto Proctor Street and then quickly turned onto Theobalds Road and then turned again onto Southampton Row. It was the same route they'd taken to get to the Brunswick Centre the night before but it all looked different during the day.

Looking up she noticed the sun was trying to make an appearance but overall it was a mostly cloudy day. She was moving at a good pace so she wasn't feeling cold but she was glad she brought a light sweater with her. It definitely wasn't hot like Phoenix in August and she was loving it! As she walked in the general direction of the British Museum, she marveled at the different styles of architecture she saw. Most of the area around the flat was pre-war, she recognized the Victorian facades and the Georgian, some styles she didn't quite recognize but the mix was all very interesting. Every now and then there would be a newer looking building mixed in. Eleanor thought again how London had been hit hard by the Blitz in the war, so the newer buildings were usually built on spaces that had been destroyed by the bombings, creating a layered mix of architectural history. She loved it. Phoenix didn't have very many old buildings, and the few that did exist had been turned into museums or heritage sites. They didn't have fast food restaurants in them.

She soon enough arrived at the British Museum and walked through the front gates. As the crowds of people entering and leaving swarmed around her she stared up at the front of the building with its elaborate facade and giant columns. Inside she was mesmerized by the enormous central room with its high glass ceiling and the stairs that wound upwards around a large cylindrical structure in the middle. She spotted an information desk and handed over a couple pounds for a map. Deciding to move away from the crowds, Eleanor headed up one of the large staircases and entered one of the upper floor galleries. The museum was divided up into dozens of smaller rooms, each one leading into the next. She found herself immediately transported back in time and got lost among all the ancient artifacts housed in the museum. The Egyptian sarcophagi and the mummies were amazing. Eventually she wound her way back downstairs and noticed a large crowd gathered around one particular artifact. Out of curiosity she joined the crowd and was soon standing in front of the Rosetta Stone. She could hardly believe it! She'd read about it in school but to be standing in front of it and seeing it with her own eyes was something entirely different.

After grabbing a small bite to eat in the museum cafe, Eleanor headed back out of the museum. The sun was trying to come out and the temperature had risen slightly. Looking at the map from Jonathan, Eleanor decided to head to Covent Garden next. Jonathan had drawn a little shopping bag over it on the map and Eleanor thought it might be good to do a little bit of shopping to get some items that she'd intended to buy in London. She hadn't bothered to bring anything that needed to be plugged in because she knew none of it would fit the outlets, so she needed to pick up a curling iron and blow dryer today, as well as a new charger for her MacBook Pro and a couple spare USB outlet plugs. She also didn't waste space in her suitcase with anything that could be cheaply repurchased, so she had a long list of general clothing and household items that she wanted to buy in the next week or so.

She walked for a bit, crossing several streets and making many left and right turns and soon noticed that she definitely appeared to be in a major shopping area. People passed by her carrying bags filled with their purchases and displays in windows offered an array of products. She let herself be pulled along by the crowd until she spotted a Boots. She knew from her British chick lit novels that this was similar to Walgreens or CVS back home so she ducked inside and began looking around. In the beauty section, she found a nice looking dryer and curling iron for a reasonable price. She also picked up some shampoo, conditioner, and a few other similar items. After checking out at the register, or till as Jonathan had taught her the night before at Waitrose, she walked out of Boots and continued in the direction she had originally been going, quickly arriving in the central piazza of Covent Garden. She stood off to the side to take it in. The crowds of tourists, the street performers, all the shops. Off in the far corner she noticed an entrance to the Royal Opera House.

She continued walking, weaving her way through the shops in the piazza and stopping to watch a couple of the performers. She was drawn to the stalls set up in the Apple Market, which today advertised that it was the "Antiques & Collectibles" day. She wandered around but didn't purchase anything. At the end of the market she found a vendor selling photographic prints and was drawn to one of Big Ben and another of St. Paul's Cathedral. She purchased both, thinking they'd look nice in her room at the flat.

After walking around the rest of the shops in the surrounding area, and staring at the gorgeous clothing in the windows of Hobbs, Whistles, Jigsaw, Zara, Ted Baker, and her other favorite British high street shops, she found herself wandering away from the main shopping area and into a quieter part of Covent Garden. She was trying to follow Jonathan's map, and was walking towards Kingsway Road where he'd marked a couple coffee shops and directions back to the flat. She'd just glanced down at the map in her hand again to double check that she was going the right way when she suddenly collided with something very tall and very heavy.

She felt herself starting to fall backwards and flailed her arms in a vain attempt to correct her balance. Just as she thought she had lost her balance completely and was bracing herself for a hard landing she felt two strong arms reach around and catch her. With her head still spinning she tried to focus her eyes on the face that was looking down at her. At first, she thought she must be hallucinating. Blinking her eyes rapidly, she tried to clear her mind and focus, but the more she did the more she began to believe that the concerned eyes staring into hers were indeed the eyes of Patrick Reynolds...*the* Patrick Reynolds. Was staring at her. Was holding her, tightly, in his strong arms...*very strong arms* she thought.

"Are you alright miss? I'm so terribly sorry, I was walking far too quickly and not paying the slightest attention to where I was going," he said in his famously deep, rich voice and classic English accent. The same voice that Eleanor and her friends sighed over and longed for every time they watched one of his movies. A voice that would melt even the hardest of hearts.

She closed her eyes, thinking for sure this had to be a dream, but when she opened them again he was still there, and looking more concerned than before.

Get a grip, she thought. *He's going to think you're a crazy person.*

Scrambling to get her legs back underneath her, she felt him lift her back up into a standing position. Brushing herself off a bit, and straightening her hair, tucking one strand behind her ear self-consciously, she looked up to meet his eyes.

He's taller in person, she thought immediately, *much taller*, and bit her tongue before she could say that out loud. But he really was taller than she'd expected, she had known he was tall, but standing so close to him, he towered over her. His hair wasn't long, but was long enough to tell it was naturally curly. He was wearing jeans with a loose fitting, vintage style t-shirt in a faded blue that matched his eyes.

He had a distressed brown leather satchel slung across his body, with a small reusable coffee cup clipped to the side. Finally, she was able to respond.

"No, um, I'm the one who's sorry. I'm, um, I'm sure that was my fault. I wasn't looking where I was going, I, uh, was checking my map—" she broke off realizing she was no longer holding Jonathan's map, she began to look around, a bit frantically, as she realized she didn't know if she'd be able to find her way back to the flat without it.

Patrick followed her gaze and began looking around as well.

Bending down and reaching behind Eleanor, he stood back up and held the map out to her, "Is this what you're looking for?"

Taking the map gratefully, "Yes! Thank you. I'd be lost without that. I only just arrived yesterday, and my cousin left me directions for getting around, I was so busy looking at this I wasn't paying attention to where I was walking, so I'm sure I was the one at fault, I'm so sorry…" she trailed off weakly, realizing she'd been rambling, and sure that she was coming across as an absolute fool.

Smiling the smile that caused Eleanor and her friends to go weak in the knees Patrick replied, placing his hand across his chest, "No, I'm sure it was my fault. Serves me right for rushing everywhere. Please accept my heartfelt apologies."

Seeing that smile, and feeling the full force of it in person, Eleanor nearly lost her balance again. *Seriously, get yourself together!* she thought ferociously. Steadying herself she looked up at him and said, with a calmness that betrayed the jumbled mix she was feeling inside, "Apology accepted, though not necessary."

She didn't think it was possible but he began to smile even more brightly. Glancing down to check she still had all her bags and clutching her map, she looked back up and said quickly, "Well, I won't keep you any longer. Thanks for, um, catching me. Have a, um, good day." And before she could make a bigger fool of herself she ducked around him and rushed down the road, not even sure if she was going in the right direction. She thought she heard him say something but she just put her head down and hurried ahead. She got to the end of the road she was on and looked up at the sign on the corner of the building and realized she was at Kingsway. She didn't feel like stopping for coffee anymore, so with a quick check of the map, she hurriedly walked back home. She didn't slow her pace or stop until she reached the flat. As soon as she let herself in she closed the door and pressed her back against it.

She closed her eyes tightly, and let out a long, slow breath. Then she smiled. When she opened her eyes, she saw her reflection in the mirror at the end of the hall. Her eyes were bright, her cheeks were flushed. Her hair was in a bit of disarray but actually looked decent and prettily windswept. She replayed the events that had just occurred back in her mind, and could feel Patrick's arms wrapped tightly around her again. He hadn't just caught her, he'd *held* her.

Giggling, Eleanor pushed herself away from the door and down the hall to her room. Feeling kind of dazed and a bit silly, she dropped backwards on her bed and just stared up at the ceiling, replaying that moment over and over again in her head.

Sometime later she woke up, surprised that she had fallen asleep. She heard Jonathan coming in the front door and walked out to meet him.

Seeing Eleanor, Jonathan asked with a smile, "Did you have a fun day?"

Grinning, "It was pretty fantastic. You'll never guess who I bumped into. Like, literally *bumped* into!"

"Who?"

"Patrick Reynolds. Can you believe it?!"

"Who?" Jonathan replied confoundedly.

"Patrick Reynolds? The actor? British heartthrob, loved and adored by women on both sides of the Atlantic?"

Jonathan looked at her blankly.

Eleanor's face dropped, "You seriously don't know who Patrick Reynolds is? He's more famous here than he is in the States! I mean, he's not George Clooney or Brad Pitt famous, he's still getting started, but he's done a lot of work over here. Don't you watch any TV or go to the movies?"

"I rarely have time to go to the cinema. And if I watch the telly it's usually football. Sorry cousin," he said with an apologetic smile as he walked into the living room and set his bag down on the dining table. "Unless he's a footballer I probably wouldn't know who you're talking about."

"Ooh, he played a soccer player in a movie once, I think it was a few years ago. I watched it on YouTube."

Looking at her quizzically, "You watched it on YouTube?"

"I don't think it got a U.S. release. And it's only available on Region 2 DVD, so YouTube is the only way I could watch it," Eleanor replied, shrugging her shoulders.

Noticing the crazy look Jonathan was giving her, Eleanor sighed, "What?! He's a good actor. I wanted to see more of his work."

"Riiiight," Jonathan replied suggestively.

Eleanor snatched up a throw pillow from the sofa and threw it at him, which he caught neatly. "He's a good actor," she repeated defensively.

"Ok, ok. Actually, I think I remember him, and that movie. He was pretty good. Sorry cousin. I'm rubbish with actors, just not my thing. But still. You're obviously a fan and I can appreciate how cool that must have been to run into him."

Somewhat placated, "It was, but mostly it was a shock

and also a bit embarrassing."

Walking to the kitchen Jonathan asked over his shoulder, "Why embarrassing?"

"Because I was completely blocking the sidewalk! He was a total gentleman, tried to take the blame and was so apologetic. He said he had been walking too fast and not paying attention to where he was walking. But I was the one standing in the middle of the sidewalk, fixated on that map you drew me–which was fantastic by the way, thanks–"

" –You're very welcome.

" –so there I was just standing there when he knocked into me."

"Sounds like you were both at fault to me," Jonathan said with a laugh.

Giggling a little, "Yeah, I guess we were. But he wouldn't let me apologize."

"So then what happened," Jonathan inquired, raising an eyebrow.

Looking confused for a moment, before realizing she was being teased again, Eleanor replied indignantly, "Nothing! I said I was sorry one more time and ran off before I could act like a bigger idiot than I already felt like I was being."

"You should have chatted him up!" Jonathan declared.

"You're crazy. That's the last thing I should have done."

"You're the one who's crazy. If he's as popular as you say he is, wouldn't most women give their right arm for a shot with him? He was standing right in front of you!"

"You don't know what you're talking about. The last thing I need right now is a relationship, particularly with some actor I don't even know, who was just being polite, and who would normally never give me a second glance."

Joining her on the sofa, Jonathan said, "But I thought you loved the guy?"

Eleanor turned to look at Jonathan just in time to catch

him fluttering his eyelashes and simpering like a silly school girl.

Throwing a second pillow from the sofa at his face, "You really are an idiot, you know that? I love his *work*, I know nothing about the guy in real life, other than a few random bits from his IMDb profile."

"What, like he likes long walks on the beach and named his childhood dog Biscuit?"

Eleanor was so stunned by this ridiculous answer she couldn't say anything for a moment. Shaking her head, "Um, no. I was thinking more along the lines that he's from Oxford, did a degree in English Literature there before getting into the Royal Academy of Dramatic Arts."

"Ooh, he went to RADA," Jonathan said in an exaggerated accent.

"Oh, just stop it. I bumped into the guy, I thought it was cool. End of story."

"Ok, seriously then. That's cool, and I'm glad you got to meet him."

"Thank you," Eleanor said as she headed towards her room. But before she could close the door Jonathan called from the lounge.

"I still think you should have chatted him up. A little flirting never killed anyone and you need to move on from your loser ex."

Eleanor had no comeback to that, so she just shut her door. Glancing at the time and doing some quick math she knew that it was late morning back in Phoenix. Fortunately, Grace was a grad student with a flexible schedule and Carly worked for a PR firm with her own office and free rein over her time. So Eleanor quickly logged on to her computer and opened up her Skype app. Grace and Carly were both logged in to Skype as well and in short order Eleanor had both of them connected to the call.

"You will never guess who I ran into today…"

Chapter 5

Still riding high on the excitement of being in London, and bumping into her favorite celebrity, Eleanor spent the next few days preparing for school to start the following week. She did some more shopping and managed to find a gorgeous knee length, belted wool coat. It cost her more than a few pounds at Marks & Spencer, and she didn't dare convert it into US dollars, but knowing that she would wear it so often here made it seem worth the price and her mom and given her a generous "gift" of $500 to buy herself some winter clothing, a gift that was matched by her Aunt Vickie. So with $1000, or roughly £600 in her account, to be spent solely on clothing, Eleanor knew she'd have fun doing a bit of "retail therapy" over the next few months and was determined not to spend it all at once.

On another trip to Covent Garden she also stopped in at Paperchase, and stocked up on some whimsical pens, notebooks, and folders, feeling much like a student again and getting excited for the first day of classes. She knew it would be different. This wasn't a university program and she was beginning to feel a little nervous about just how "intense" this intensive writing program would be. Pushing the nerves away for the millionth time, she put another set of folders into her basket and walked up to the till.

On Monday, she headed out from Red Lion Square apprehensively. The school was in the City of London, so it wasn't a long walk. Jonathan had told her it would probably take her about thirty minutes, depending on how fast she went. She'd thought about taking the Tube but Jonathan told her that it was only a few stops away and the walk would be easier. Jonathan had given her detailed instructions on how to find the school, and Eleanor had reviewed them several times.

She turned on her music and listened to it as she walked towards the City. Jonathan had explained that within Greater London there was the City of London, also known as the Old Square Mile and was the part of London that had been around since the Roman times and that had been burned to the ground in the Great Fire of 1666. There had also been more damage done by the Blitz in this part of London and further East. She marveled to herself about what an incredible history London had as she came up to St. Paul's Cathedral. Eleanor was instantly captivated by the Cathedral and wished she had more time to linger, but she didn't want to be late.

Making a mental note to come back later and explore, she turned and started walking towards the river, she could see the Millennium Bridge stretching out before her in the distance. She turned again and headed down a road parallel to the river before coming up to a nondescript building among all the other office buildings in the area. Around here was a swarm of City workers in suits rushing into the neighboring buildings. It seemed a strange place to put a school but Jonathan had told her that the City was home to a number of more creative and artistic places, including the Guildhall School of Music and Drama, and the London College of Fashion wasn't far either, so it wasn't all banks and financial businesses.

She entered the building and went up to the third floor.

By the look of the directory the Harrison Centre for Writing took up the top two floors of the building. She followed the signs for new students and collected her student ID card and other materials with information for the incoming group. Looking beyond the registration table she could see a large common area with a back wall consisting of large windows that looked out on the river. She couldn't wait to explore the school more. She was given her schedule and headed up to the top floor, using an interior staircase.

Walking into the classroom Eleanor saw that a few other students had arrived and that all the desks were facing the center of the room, forming a giant circle. As more students came trickling in Eleanor became increasingly nervous. They all looked so much younger than she was, and she was the only American as far as she could tell.

"Hiya!" said a voice beside her. Glancing over quickly Eleanor realized that a young, male student had sat down beside her.

"Hi," she replied tentatively.

"You're the American, aren't you?"

Eleanor's heart sunk. "*The* American? Does that mean I'm the only one?"

"Don't worry, it's cool. I heard there was an American in the program this year. I studied in the States for a year when I was at Uni, so I kind of understand being out of your element. I just wanted to introduce myself. I'm Jack Taylor."

He seemed like a nice guy, about 5 years younger than Eleanor by her estimation. He had a kind smile and she was grateful.

"I'm Eleanor Gordon," she replied with a shy smile. "But how did you know I was American, is it that obvious?" she asked, glancing down at her outfit, she'd so carefully planned out her 'first day of school' outfit, choosing slim fit black trousers, that just grazed her ankles, fuchsia flats with bows at the back of the heel, and a matching fuchsia top that was fitted through the body, but had loose sleeves that were three-quarter length and billowed around her arms, showing off the stack of bangle bracelets on her right hand.

As if reading her mind Jack laughed, "No, it's not obvious, I was behind you downstairs when you gave your name at reception. Your outfit's reyt good, you definitely look the part."

Confused, "what good?"

"Ah, soz, even Londoners have trouble with my accent. Reyt. Like, if something is reyt good, it's really good."

"Gotcha," Eleanor said smiling. "And soz?

Jack laughed, "Luv, I'm going to have to teach you so much. Soz means sorry. You'll hear a lot of people use that one. But reyt is more of a northern thing. I'm from Sheffield originally." Looking back at her outfit, "Isn't that top from Zara?"

Now it was Eleanor's turn to give a small laugh. "Yes, it is. But I got this a few months ago at the one back home."

"Nice! Where do you live? New York? LA?" Jack asked.

"No, Phoenix. They're finally getting civilized as far as shopping options go. And for what they still don't have what ASOS usually provides," she said with a smile.

"ASOS has the best stuff! Oh, it's so nice to meet someone who understands!"

"I know! Jonathan thinks I'm crazy for all the shopping I do."

"That your boyfriend?"

"Oh, um...no, Jon's my cousin. Though, my ex never understood my shopping habits either," Eleanor replied with a grimace.

"Soz, I can tell that's a bit of a sore subject. Was it recent then?"

"Recent enough," she said with a frown. "But it's fine now. You have to move on right?"

"Aye!" Jack replied enthusiastically. "So, how long have

you been in London?"

"About a week. It's all gone by in a blur."

"Are you staying nearby?"

"I'm staying with my cousin, he has a flat in Holborn."

"Holborn, eh? Nice area."

"Seems pretty nice, this is the first time I'm visiting him here. His parents lived near Cambridge, and his mom lives in Bath now, so I've visited them there before. I haven't really spent time in London, other than once when I was little."

"What does he do? Is he a barrister?"

"No, he's a student at LSE. But don't ask me for more information than that, because I really don't understand his major. Something to do with politics and the economy."

"I have a cousin like that. He's at Cambridge. He's studying astrophysics. Family gatherings are so boring, he doesn't know how to talk about anything else."

"And what about you?" Eleanor asked curiously.

"I read English Literature at uni up in Manchester," Jack replied. "It was fun, and I ended up with a job at a publishing company here in London. Nothing grand, just proofreading, but it's a job, and it provides enough free time for me to write. This program seemed like a good way to force me to write more. I can get a little lazy about it sometimes. What about you? Where did you go to uni?"

"Oh, um, I went to uni back in the states. My home state, Arizona. I did my undergrad at Arizona State, that's in Phoenix. Well, technically Tempe, but most people outside of Arizona don't know Tempe."

"Nope, can't say I've heard of it."

"It doesn't matter. Anyway, I then did a Masters at University of Arizona, which is in Tucson. Both were English degrees."

"Oh, Literature?"

"No, in undergrad I didn't really specialize. I took some

Lit, as well as Rhetoric, Advanced Composition, Creative Writing, basically as many English classes as I could, including some Shakespeare and Early American Drama classes in the School of Theatre. For my Masters, I was a Rhetoric and Composition focus."

"Rhetoric? So that's like speeches and persuasion and the like, yeah?" Jack pondered curiously.

"Basically, it's a little more specific than that, but I won't bore you with the details," Eleanor replied dismissively.

"Oh no, I don't think it's boring! Believe me," Jack said, dropping his voice and leaning closer to Eleanor, "You would not believe how boring some of these lads and lasses here are. I've been talking with some of them this morning, a lot of rich kids with mummy and daddy paying the bills, finished uni, but want to keep avoiding getting a real job and starting their lives. I envy that you've been to graduate school before! I didn't have the energy. I'm just hoping I'll get through this program!"

"I know, me too," Eleanor admitted nervously.

"Oh, with your experience I'm sure you'll be fine."

"But you've worked in publishing, you've seen the type of work we're supposed to be preparing for."

"I like you," Jack exclaimed suddenly. Eleanor started a little bit, taken aback by his abruptness. "No, don't get me wrong, not in an 'awkwardly-forward-run-and-hide-from-the-creeper' kind of way, just, you seem a really cool person. And I'm glad to meet you. I feel like this year will be easier with friends here who know what this is like. So, if you ever want to meet up to work on our writing or just chat about the program or ideas, that would be cool."

Jack suddenly looked so nervous and vulnerable, and Eleanor immediately warmed to him. She could tell that he was truly offering friendship. He had an energetic personality, one that made her smile and feel at ease. There was a quirkiness to him that she instantly related to. And he had a point. Right now, her only "friend" was Jonathan and though he's a student too, LSE and the work he is doing is completely different. Eleanor suddenly realized how nice it would be to have a friend here at school, someone who would understand what she'd be going through over the next twelve months.

Smiling, "I think that would be really nice."

Jack beamed, "Brilliant!"

At that moment, the instructor walked into the classroom and the rest of the day got swept away in a blur of introductions to the program, what the students could expect from the next twelve months, what would be expected from them, going to the Monday seminars and workshops, and Eleanor ending up feeling completely overwhelmed.

She'd read all the information about the program but being there was completely different. There would be different seminars and workshops every day, Monday through Thursday, with Friday designated as a "writing day." There would be classes on everything from grammar and format to genre workshops. Eleanor thought she was good at grammar and formatting and hoped she'd have an edge there, until she realized that the British have different ways of doing things and a lot of what she knew and did were considered incorrect here. And she'd never really thought about genre, she just liked writing stories. She was interested in the business side of things they were going to be covering but by the end of that seminar session her head was swimming at the thought of writing the perfect query and submission letters. Eleanor and Jack had stuck together through most of the day, but got separated before the last couple of workshops. By the end of the day Eleanor felt like her brain was going to explode and she fled from the building.

She got out onto the street and nearly collided with a

man in a very nice suit, yelling into his cell phone. He gave her a dirty look and continued on his way in a rush. She felt herself getting swept up in the crowd of City workers rushing off to dinner meetings or the pub after a long day of work. She knew she was going in the wrong direction but she didn't care. All she wanted to do was get as far away from the school as possible. Eventually she calmed down enough to stop and get her bearings and soon made her way home to the flat. On the way home, she passed by pub after pub with laughing and smiling people outside, enjoying pints and cocktails and chatting about their days. Eleanor felt tears prick her eyes. All she wanted was to fit in and to have a life in London. But now that school had started she felt like more of an outsider than ever. Her optimism from the first week was starting to fade.

By the time Jonathan got home about an hour later he found her sitting on the sofa, crying into one of the throw pillows.

"Ellie! What's the matter? Are you sick? Hurt?!" Jonathan asked, concern etched on his face. Taking her gently by the shoulders and looking into her eyes, which were red and filled with tears, "Elle, talk to me, what's wrong?"

Eleanor just sniffled in response, and pulled the sleeve of her sweatshirt down over her hand and used the hem to wipe her nose. Jonathan reached up and wiped her tears away and then sat down on the couch next to her, wrapping his arms around her. A fresh wave of sobs came out and Eleanor just held on to her cousin.

After a time, she was able to calm herself down a bit and she finally was able to say, in a voice so quiet Jonathan had to strain to hear it, "I don't think I can do this."

Pulling Eleanor closer and wrapping his arms more tightly around her, Jonathan gave a small but kind laugh, "Oh poppet, you *can* do this. You're already doing it.

You've moved yourself halfway around the world to pursue something you love and something you're already good at. I've heard the stories about that program of yours so I can imagine what today must have felt like, but you can do it. I'll bet you a tenner that a year from now you'll look back on today and laugh at yourself right now."

"No I won't," Eleanor croaked out petulantly.

"Is that a bet then?" Jonathan asked, smiling.

"Jon, this isn't funny. You don't know what it's like!"

"Well, it can't be harder than grad school at LSE! I wanted to run out and quit the program halfway through my first class I was so terrified! I assume you made it through the whole day before you fell apart?"

"Barely," she said quietly.

"Well there you go, you survived day one. Only eleven months and 29 days to go. Look, it's true, I don't know what your program is like, but I know a couple people who've done it. They said it was the hardest thing they've done and the first day was one of the worst days. But they also said it was one of the best things that they've experienced. Ellie, the first day, hell, the first week or even *month* is the hardest! You're just starting and you haven't made any friends yet. But you can get through this, and you'll be so happy and proud of yourself once you do."

"Actually, I think I did make a friend," Eleanor said, brightening a little. "That helped for most of the day but then we have different schedules for the afternoon and we got split up in the shuffle and I didn't get his number," she told him, frowning again.

Laughing, Jonathan replied, "It's ok! You'll see him tomorrow. And you'll get his number then, if he doesn't ask for it first. Was he cute?"

Looking sideways at her cousin, "What? Er...yeah, I guess. He's young, way too young for me if that's why you're asking. He's got to be 23, tops."

"So? What do you have against younger men?"

"Nothing, as friends. But if I can't even get a 36-year-old to commit to me, how am I going to get someone only five years out of high school." Eleanor thought for a moment and then added, "Plus, I think he might be gay. He seemed to know an awful lot about fashion."

"Well, don't make any assumptions, we London men actually care about what we wear, unlike your Arizona men in their shorts and trainers."

Eleanor looked at Jonathan suspiciously, "He knew my shirt was from Zara even though it's a few months old."

"Hmmm, ok, he might be gay, but I still say don't assume too much until you get to know him better. I'm rubbish with fashion but I have a few very straight friends who care more about their wardrobes than some of my gay friends. So don't rely on stereotypes missy."

Eleanor smiled.

Jonathan smiled back and continued, "But I suppose you really shouldn't be thinking of starting a new relationship right now anyway. You need to be single for a bit. But I'm glad you made a friend. And you should make some more. Come out with me tonight."

"What? Where?" Eleanor asked, feeling drained from her emotions, she tried to keep up with the sudden change in the conversation.

"I'm meeting some friends at a pub near school. We all had deadlines today for end of summer projects to our advisors and wanted to celebrate and relax a bit."

"I don't know, I have to be back at school early tomorrow and have a writing piece I'm supposed to start working on."

"You need to eat, don't you? Look, I promise we won't be out long, two hours tops, my mates and I have work of our own to do. But you need to get out of here. You look like you've been sitting here crying for hours."

"I've only been home for an hour!" she cried defensively.

"Well, that's long enough. Come on now. Go pull yourself together, I can't be seen with you looking like that. You look a fright."

Punching his arm, "Thanks. Jerk."

"Ow!"

"You deserved that. No wonder you're still single."

Getting up from the couch, Jonathan ordered, "Seriously, go get your bag or whatever and let's go eat."

Eleanor grabbed her handbag and cardigan and they left the flat. Jon led her to a pub near Holborn station. Once inside, Jon found his friends and made all the introductions and then left Eleanor at the table while he went to get their drinks and order their food.

While she waited for him to come back she began chatting with Jon's friends, who were all graduate students at LSE with Jon. There was Zaf, a French Algerian who'd done his undergrad in Paris and was now at LSE studying Economics. He had a warm smile that made Eleanor feel instantly at ease. Then there was the very serious looking Malcolm, from Scotland, studying International Health Policy. Henry, was in the middle of telling a story about a girl he had met on the Tube that morning, and based on the way he was gesturing and playing with the inflections in his voice and switching between his light Nigerian accent and the Welsh accent of the girl on the Tube, Eleanor was not surprised to learn later that Henry had started in drama school before switching to Data Science at LSE. Ioan (spelled I-o-a-n but pronounced Ian, Jonathan explained), was a kind and studious looking guy from Wales, studying Philosophy and Public Policy, and had kindly moved his coat to the ledge behind them to let Eleanor sit next to him. After a few minutes Jon came back to the table, holding a Guinness for himself and a cider for Eleanor. Beside Jon was a tall and very handsome young man.

"Ellie, this is my mate Mark Butler, he studies International Relations. Mark, this is my cousin Eleanor, she just moved here from America to study creative writing," Jon explained.

Mark slid into the open space next to Eleanor, "Hi Eleanor, it's a pleasure to meet you," he said pleasantly and offered his hand. Eleanor noted he had a nice handshake, firm and strong. His eyes sparkled a bit in the low lighting of the pub and Eleanor noticed they were a light green color. He also had a kind smile and Eleanor instantly liked him.

"Hello, pleased to meet you as well Mark," she responded politely, and somewhat shyly. Looking around the table at all of Jon's friends she realized she couldn't remember the last time she'd hung out socially with such a large group of men, or even a group of strangers. The past several months she'd only spent time with Michael, her mother, or her best girlfriends, but overall had had a relatively quiet social life. Now here she was sitting in the middle of a busy pub in central London, surrounded by a group of guys, roughly her age, who were all laughing and making jokes at each other's expense. As much as they were joking, they clearly cared about each other.

They spent the next hour talking about their work at LSE and Eleanor did her best to follow along. She and Jonathan had talked about school before so she understood some of it, but graduate programs were different in the UK compared to the US. Between her exhaustion and still feeling slightly out of place, she kept quiet and just listened as the jokes and stories flew back and forth around the table, trying to feel like part of the group instead of like an outsider like she'd felt passing by the pubs on her way back to the flat. She finished her first cider, enjoying it more than she thought she would, she thought it was much better than beer, which made her think about all the times Michael had teased her for never being able to take her out drinking. He'd always complained that it was a shame she didn't have a taste for beer because cocktails were so much more expensive.

She didn't realize she had been frowning until Mark touched her gently on the arm and said to the table, "I think we're boring our gorgeous new friend, gents." Turning, to look in her eyes, he apologized, "I'm so sorry that we've been talking only about ourselves, so rude of us. You've come all the way from America and we're just ignoring you."

His concerned look and warm smile were so genuine and sincere, it warmed Eleanor's heart and made her feel a little less jittery. She shook her head quickly and protested, "Oh no! You're not boring me, I promise. I'm sorry if I seem like I'm not paying attention. I am enjoying listening, it's just, well, I'm a little tired today."

"It's true," Jonathan said in her defense, "poor thing is knackered. She's had a long day and I had to force her to come out tonight."

"Jon said you were doing a course in creative writing, how's that going?" Mark asked interestedly.

Eleanor tried to keep her face from clouding over, but felt tears beginning to prick her eyes. She blinked rapidly, trying to stop them before they started and forced a small smile. "It's fine. Today was the first day, so it's still too early to tell."

"What school are you at?" Malcolm asked politely.

"It's the Harrison Centre for Writing in the City," Eleanor responded.

"Oh, that's a good school," Henry said, sounding impressed. "They don't accept just anybody, I hear competition to get in is quite intense."

Wryly Eleanor responded, "I don't know about that,

they let me in somehow."

"Ellie, stop," Jonathan said sharply. "Your writing is brilliant, at least the rare bits you've ever let me read. You're a good writer, and you've earned your way into that program. They're lucky to have you."

"But you don't completely believe that, do you?" Mark asked her kindly.

"I guess I do," Eleanor replied. "It's just hard. I've always loved to write, but studying it is different. And I've always done well in school but this is unlike any of the coursework I've done in the past. Today was just overwhelming." She sighed, and suddenly felt even more exhausted than before. She knew it was only a little after 7 o'clock, and still too early for bed, but she just wanted to crawl away and hide somewhere.

The table was quiet for a few moments when suddenly, out of the silence, Malcolm, who had been the next quietest of the group besides Eleanor, said simply, "I nearly dropped out after my first day at LSE."

"What?!" Jonathan asked, shocked by this revelation. "You're the smartest of all of us! You always make it look so easy!"

"Aye, well, looks can be deceiving, can't they?" Malcolm responded wryly. He looked across the table and into Eleanor's eyes, "First days are always terrifying. It's new and unfamiliar, and everyone is trying to make themselves seem impressive to the others to prove that they belong there, when inside everyone feels like a fraud about to be found out. Your first couple weeks will feel scary and a wee bit shaky, but you'll get the hang of it, I promise. If you got accepted to that program, your writing is good, they wouldn't have let you in if it wasn't. So trust in their decision, even if you don't trust in your abilities."

"Thanks," Eleanor said softly. "I'll try to remember that."

Malcolm and Eleanor exchanged small smiles across the table.

"I need another drink," Jonathan said, breaking the hush that had fallen over the table.

After hanging out in the pub for a little bit longer Eleanor and Jonathan headed back to the flat and Eleanor went straight to bed. She wanted to believe Jonathan and his friends, but she still couldn't help feeling anxious about school the next day.

* * * * *

The next day dawned and found Eleanor awake after a somewhat fitful sleep. She was dreading school but forced herself to get up and get ready and head out to school. She stopped at a Caffè Nero on the way for a latte and a croissant and then headed the rest of the way to school. As she approached the building she was still feeling nervous but managed to keep herself from turning on her heels and running away. She hesitantly entered her first classroom, looking around for Jack.

"You came back," said a voice behind her.

Eleanor jumped slightly and spun around. Suddenly feeling very relieved to see Jack standing behind her.

"Hello again," he said grinning.

"Hi!" she responded, a little too eagerly, causing Jack to smile even more.

"I was worried about you yesterday, we got split up and I realized I didn't get to say goodbye. How did the rest of your day go?"

As they moved to take their seats, "Well, it finished alright. I must admit I was a bit overwhelmed...I still am."

"But you're here."

"But I'm here," she agreed with a small smile. "My cousin took me out to meet his friends at the pub, they're all

LSE grad students and they managed to give me a bit of a pep talk. I'm not entirely sure I understand why I came back today, part of me really didn't want to."

"But the other part?" Jack questioned gently.

"I don't know. I guess the other part knows that a lot of people went to a lot of trouble to help me get here. I'm scared to try to actually do this but I think I'm just a little more scared to have to explain to people why I quit. So, here I am," Eleanor explained, suddenly feeling even more anxious, her heart starting to race again.

"For what it's worth, I'm glad you're back. And I think you're going to be brilliant here. The first day is always designed to scare off the weak ones. Look around, there's at least a few lads and lasses missing, they're either not coming at all or they're stuck on the front steps hyperventilating. So, good on you for coming all the way inside," Jack said with a smile.

"Aren't you nervous?" Eleanor asked curiously.

"Sure, but I'm here. What's the worst that can happen?"

"They find out I'm a total fraud and can't write at all and I'm sent home in disgrace?"

Jack's eyes grew wide, "Flippin' eck," he exclaimed. "You don't over think things at all, do you?" He said, his face not quite hiding the urge to laugh.

"I've been a grad student, and raised by two academics. I was trained to over think things. It's what academics do. You should meet my parents, especially my dad."

"What does your dad do?"

"He's a professor at Columbia, he teaches English Literature. 19th century British Lit. All my life he taught me to question everything, to always search for the deeper meaning in things, to find the subtext."

"Wow, um, that's a bit intense don't you think? Can't you just take things at face value or enjoy something as it happens?"

Frowning slightly as she thought about it, Eleanor finally replied, "Rarely, and not without great effort." Offering Jack a wry smile, "It's a problem."

Jack laughed, "We'll have to work on that. And for the record, from what I know about this program they rarely kick anyone out, people usually just drop out on their own. As long as you show up and do the work you'll get through it. And so what if they don't like what you write? That's not the point. You'll still have a lot to gain from understanding how the business side of this works. You'll also pick up better editing skills. Trust me, you want to stick this out, even if they hate everything you write, which they won't. If they hated your writing you wouldn't be here."

"That's what my cousin's friends said," Eleanor responded.

"Listen to them. And stick with me. Together we'll get us through this," Jack encouraged with a smile. And for the first time since leaving yesterday in despair, Eleanor actually started to have hope.

The morning class started and went well, Eleanor still felt a bit shaky but she stuck with Jack for most of the day and she started to feel a little better. They had lunch together, chatting about the morning's lessons, and made a plan to meet up outside the school after their separate afternoon classes. They had a cup of coffee at a Pret a Manger across the street from the school and compared notes on the day.

* * * * *

Over the next several weeks Eleanor quickly fell into a routine. School during the week, with two hour writing sessions with Jack right after, in the Starbucks in Paternoster Square, where she could hear the bells of St. Paul's Cathedral. If the sun was out they'd sit outside, enjoying the last bit of summer weather that was trying to hold on. Then home to have dinner with Jonathan, sometimes staying home, sometimes going out with his friends. Friday's were spent writing in the morning on her own, either at her desk in her room or sitting in one of the chairs in the bay window, and then meeting up with Jack in the afternoons to workshop their writing and review each other's work. In between all that she fit in her part time job in the writing center at the Harrison as a writing tutor in a program they ran for local secondary students preparing for GCSEs. It didn't pay much but it kept her fed and clothed.

On the weekends Eleanor would do more writing and homework. The rest of the weekend Eleanor would spend window shopping, going to museums, or simply sitting in coffee shops watching London go by outside. Jack teased her about her coffee shop addiction, joking that instead of going on a pub crawl she went on coffee shop crawls. Eleanor laughed when she agreed he was right. She particularly liked the Caffè Nero on Kingsway where she would sit in one of the large chairs by the front window and watch people walking by outside, around her she'd watch locals come in for a lunch or coffee break and tourists come in for a rest between seeing all the sights. Sometimes she wrote, sometimes she just observed her surroundings.

She had picked up a few more pieces for her "London" wardrobe, and Jack loved to joke with her that she was looking more and more like a London girl. She was constantly making notes of how the women around her dressed. As the weather had shifted, cute sundresses with sandals or airy silk blouses with slim pencil skits, had been replaced with sweater dresses or wool trousers that swished around the legs with gorgeous knitwear tops. And my goodness, thought Eleanor, but London women love their boots! Tall boots, short boots, ankle boots, boots out of every fabric and color, though black was definitely the strong preference. When the temperatures started to drop, Eleanor caved and purchased a pair of boots she'd been lusting after in Office, they came up to her knees and had a slight heel, enough to give her a bit of a lift and shift her posture but low enough that she could still dash around the streets of London. She wore those boots nearly every day, with either a dress and tights or with jeans or black skinny trousers tucked in. With her hair loosely pulled up into a top knot and her trench coat she was indeed looking more and more like a Londoner, though she still felt like plain old Eleanor from Arizona.

She didn't notice but others were looking at her quite differently, Jack and Jonathan both noticed how much more confident and comfortable she seemed with both school and London. And after dinner with Jonathan and his friends at the pub one night, Eleanor was more than surprised when Jonathan told her that Mark was becoming very interested in her.

"What do you mean?" she asked, brow furrowed, after Jonathan dropped that bomb while she was washing dishes one night.

"He likes you," Jonathan replied simply, walking out of the kitchen and over to the sofa.

"But what do you mean he 'likes' me? What does that *mean* Jonathan?" she demanded, following him, hurriedly drying her hands on a dish towel.

Jonathan looked at Eleanor curiously, "I *mean* that Mark said he likes you. He's attracted to you and thinks you're very interesting. I told him I didn't know how you were feeling and that you've just gotten out of a bad relationship and that his best bet was to take things slowly and not spook you. Why? Was that the wrong thing to say? You should get back out there eventually, but I certainly don't want you to rush it. I care about you both so I wouldn't want either of you to rush into something. But I did want to give you a head's up so you didn't get surprised. I don't think you realize how different you are now."

Brow furrowing even more, "What do you mean, *different*?" Eleanor demanded again, voice rising a bit.

Jonathan sighed. "Eleanor, when you first arrived you were excited, giddy even. You were a tourist more than anything else before school started. Then school started and you were scared and timid but over the last several weeks you've become so much more confident. You disappear for hours on end on the weekends, goodness knows where you go or what you do, but you come home and you're so happy! You've bought new clothes, you wear your hair a little different, you've got color in your cheeks, and I may be your cousin but I'm not blind. I can see what Mark sees. You were beautiful when you got here but with the confidence you've gained since school started and you've settled in to London more you're absolutely gorgeous!" Noticing Eleanor blush Jonathan hurriedly added, "And I'm not just saying that. You may not notice it but everyone else has."

Looking down and playing with the towel in her hands Eleanor said quietly, "Thanks. It's nice to hear that." Smiling slightly, "I'm not sure I completely believe it, but it's nice to hear."

Walking over to give her a big hug, Jonathan said, "Well, I'm just going to have to keep telling you until you do believe it. Because Mark's interest aside, you *are* gorgeous and even more, you're very special. And you deserve a guy who can see that in you."

Eleanor suddenly felt a rush of emotions and confusion, thinking about Mark and Michael and everything that had been going on over the last several weeks. She knew London could potentially change her life, but she still felt unprepared for what might lie ahead.

Chapter 6

October arrived and the first term of the program ended on the 7th. When classes got out Eleanor went to the usual spot to meet Jack. When he walked up he smiled widely and announced, "Change of plans!"

"What?" Eleanor responded in confusion.

"I said, change of plans. A little bird, possibly named Jonathan, told me that today is your birthday. I can't believe you didn't say anything, naughty girl," he finished with an accusing tone.

"I didn't want anyone to make a big deal! I'm just 28, it's hardly a milestone birthday." she replied defensively.

"Well too bad luv, because I am so making a big deal! Today is your birthday and we're going to celebrate. Come along," he ordered, linking his arm through hers and dragging her towards the Tube.

"Where are we going?" she asked, trying to keep up with Jack's excited pace.

"You'll see," was all he would say.

They rode the Tube for a bit, changing at Tottenham Court Road for the Northern Line and then got off at Charing Cross. Soon Eleanor found herself in Trafalgar Square with Jack directing them straight for the National Portrait Gallery. "I know how much you like it here, I do too. It's fun to make up stories about the people in all the portraits," Jack said with a grin.

Eleanor smiled crookedly, "So I'm not the only one who does that huh?"

"Not by a long shot luv," Jack answered with amusement, linking his arm through hers.

They spent the next couple of hours wandering the gallery and sharing the stories they made up about the people in the portraits they viewed. Then at 3 o'clock Jack surprised Eleanor with afternoon tea on the top floor at the Portrait Restaurant. They sat at their table by the window, one of the best tables in the place, with views across Trafalgar Square and straight down Whitehall with Big Ben and Parliament in the distance. Eleanor had a fantastic time, they ordered champagne with the tea, and the three-tiered tray the server brought out was full of the most delicious sandwiches, sweet treats, and amazing scones with cream and jam. Eleanor was in heaven. It all felt so quintessentially British, between the tea and the food and the epic view from their table. The days were starting to get slightly shorter, so throughout their tea the sun was getting a bit lower in the sky, casting incredible light and shadow through the clouds over the streets of London below them.

After tea Jack announced, "Nah then, Phase One of Birthday Fun Times is over. Time for Phase Two."

"Phase Two?" Eleanor said with confusion written all over her face.

Taking a small envelope out of his messenger bag, Jack held it in front of Eleanor, "Phase Two: your mission, should you choose to accept it, it to take the contents in this envelop and follow the directions to the letter."

Eleanor looked more confused than ever and Jack handed it over with a grin. When Eleanor opened it she found a card inside with a Visa Gift card included. She gasped when she saw the amount, £400 pounds, signed from both her Aunt Victoria, her friends Carly and Grace, and her mother. She started to cry at the sight of it but soon started laughing when she read the instructions from her aunt who had written that Jack's part of this mission was to take Eleanor to Covent Garden and help her spend the money on a birthday outfit for that evening. But when she started thinking about all the planning that had clearly gone into all of these surprises today she started to cry again, putting her hands up to cover her face.

"What's the matter?!" Jack questioned anxiously.

"Nothing," she said, wiping her eyes dry. "It's just that this has all been so thoughtful of all of you. How did you get this?"

"Jonathan gave it to me. We've been planning this for a while," he said with a proud grin. "Now come on, are you ready to spend that? We have about three hours before Phase Three starts."

"Dare I ask what Phase Three is?"

"Party time! And that's all I'm going to say about that. Now come on!"

They paid the bill and then hurried out of the museum and headed in the direction of Covent Garden. Eleanor felt like the whole experience was a blur as Jack dragged her in and out of a number of shops but eventually they had found a dress at Oasis and some jewelry at Zara, shoes at Kurt Geiger, and a cute sparkly clutch at Accessorize, and miraculously had some of the gift card left over for Eleanor to spend on more clothes later. Together they dashed back to the flat and got ready for their night out. When Jack had picked up the instructions and card from Jon he'd dropped off a bag with a suit and dress shoes to change into, they'd clearly gone through a lot of trouble to set up the surprise. Eleanor fixed her hair and reapplied her makeup. She then slipped into some sheer tights and her new outfit and switched some items from her handbag to her new clutch.

When she stepped out of her room both Jack and Jonathan were waiting in the lounge for her, dressed sharply in suits. She noticed both of their eyes go wide as they looked at her new look. She stopped immediately and looked at them in concern.

"Is something wrong?! Is this all too much? I didn't know where we were going but I figured with this dress I should do hair and makeup to match—"

Jonathan interrupted, "Ellie, you look amazing, absolutely stunning."

Jack nodded in agreement, "Luv, even as a gay man I can say you look incredible. Jonathan and I are a couple of jammy blokes getting to escort you tonight."

"Jammy?" Eleanor asked with a laugh.

Jonathan replied before Jack, "He means we're lucky, and he's right."

Eleanor looked at him, "I didn't know you spoke northern. This one—" she said, pointing to Jack, "—is constantly coming up with words I've never heard before. It would help knowing I have an additional interpreter."

Jack and Jonathan both laughed and Jonathan replied, "One of my old mates was from Sheffield like Jack is."

Jack grinned, "So this family has a thing for mates from Sheffield then. You have great taste if I may say so myself. Now, you look absolutely lovely Elle, no one tonight is going to be able to take their eyes off you."

Eleanor turned to look in the mirror in the lounge. She hadn't really been paying attention as she was getting ready, just going through the motions and trying to get ready as quickly as possible. But her hair, for once, was behaving and it was gathered loosely high on top of her head with a few pieces delicately framing her face. Her makeup gave her face a soft glow and her blue eyes popped against the blue of the dress, which fit her perfectly. The dress had 3/4 length sleeves, with a scoop neck and was fitted to the waist and then flared out down to her knees. It was bright cobalt at the bodice but the ombre color faded to a soft bluish-silvery-grey at the hem. She was normally self-conscious about her figure but in this dress, even she had to admit she looked good. With a blue and silver necklace and bracelet to match and a cobalt sequined clutch and grey suede heels, the complete outfit was unlike anything Eleanor had ever allowed herself to wear before. Michael always dressed so plainly and made subtle comments any time Eleanor indulged in a more creative or whimsical approach to her wardrobe. Looking at herself in the mirror she barely recognized herself, and while it scared her a bit, it thrilled her too.

She turned to look at Jack and Jonathan, who were still staring in admiration, and she blushed a little, "Thanks guys. And thank you Jack for helping me put this together."

Jack grinned, "As soon as we found that dress I knew it was perfect for you."

Clapping his hands, Jonathan announced, "Alright, time to get this party started."

Grinning cautiously Eleanor asked, "Where are we going?"

"That is a surprise my darling," Jonathan said with a smile. "Ok, everyone downstairs."

They all headed out of the flat and down to the street where Eleanor found a taxi waiting for them. She looked at Jonathan, who replied, "I ordered it while you were getting ready. I'm not expecting you to walk anywhere in those shoes," he finished with a pointed look down at her high heels. Eleanor was grateful, though the shoes were remarkably comfortable given their height, she knew she wouldn't be able to walk for too long in them.

They all piled into the taxi and Jonathan gave the name of a club that Eleanor had never heard of, though that was not surprising given that she was busy writing most nights.

After a drive they arrived somewhere in Knightsbridge, in front of a club Eleanor had never noticed before, even though she thought she must have walked by it a half a dozen times on her various trips to window shop at Harrods. There were men at the door wearing meticulously cut suits and just beyond them an impeccably dressed and astonishingly beautiful woman holding an iPad in a sleek leather case. Eleanor felt a little self-conscious looking at this woman and was grateful she'd indulged in the new outfit, nothing she already owned could have come close to competing with this gorgeous blonde.

Jonathan took Eleanor lightly by the arm and Jack flanked her on her other side and they approached the door. Eleanor noticed the long line of people wrapping to the right of the entrance but felt Jonathan leading her straight ahead. Glancing up at him she noticed that his posture was straight and his eyes locked on the hostess. He gave a slight nod to the two bouncers and they gave casual nods back at Jonathan. Sometimes she forgot how posh Jonathan and his family were, they were always so down to earth. Eleanor felt like she was in a movie. She'd never been to a club, let alone skipped to the front of the line and waltzed in like she owned the place. As they walked up to the hostess she looked up and her stiff demeanor dropped when she saw Jonathan.

Smiling warmly, "Mr. McNeil, what a pleasure to see you again. We have your table ready and several of your guests have already arrived."

"Thank you, Celeste," Jonathan replied, lightly kissing each of Celeste's cheeks, in a casual way.

Eleanor thought she noticed Celeste's attitude lighten even more as she seemed to blush slightly in response to Jonathan, and Eleanor wondered if she was just like every other woman who seemed to have a crush on her cousin or if there was something more there, considering Jonathan was smiling more warmly than Eleanor had noticed him do with any other woman.

Celeste directed her gaze at Eleanor, "You must be Jon's cousin, Eleanor. He's spoken very highly of you. I hope we've managed to put together a lovely evening for you here tonight, Jon and his mother have been very meticulous in their planning."

Celeste's shortening of Jonathan's name confirmed that there was something going on with them and Eleanor made a mental note to ask him about it later. For now, she smiled brightly at Celeste and replied, "Yes, I'm Eleanor, pleased to meet you Celeste, and thank you, I'm looking forward to tonight, even though I have no clue what's been planned!"

"My, what a charming accent!" Celeste responded sincerely, which made Eleanor laugh inwardly, she thought her American accent was boring, but so many here seemed to love it. Celeste gestured to someone behind her and another immaculately dressed woman walked up. "Please show Mr. McNeil and his guests to their table," Celeste instructed, and with that Eleanor felt Jonathan's hand at her elbow and Jack's at her lower back as she was moved forward into the middle of the club.

"Do you come here often," Eleanor said quietly to Jonathan, both curious about his choice of venue, and his relationship with Celeste.

"Well, mum redesigned the place a couple years back, so yeah, I do come here a bit. Just one more perk of being the son of the great Victoria McNeil," he said with a quiet laugh.

Looking around Eleanor tried to process her surroundings. The club was incredible! She could definitely see her aunt's aesthetic in here. Low lighting cast a soft glow over all the patrons. The sound of glassware tinkling and laughter mixed pleasantly and added to the overall atmosphere of fun and happy, glamorous people. The walls were a combination of dark, gleaming wood and mirrors and one side of the main room was dominated by a massive and impressive bar. The furniture consisted of large wood tables with matching chairs and clusters of plush arm chairs and sofas gathered around low tables for more intimate gatherings. Looking at all the people in the club Eleanor felt like she was on a movie set with all the extras straight from central casting. The men were all very good looking and impressively dressed in casual suits, while the women were all immaculate in beautiful dresses and high heels, hair and makeup done to perfection. Once again Eleanor was relieved she'd taken the extra time to dress up, she never imagined that Jonathan would take her somewhere like this.

They approached one of the clusters of arm chairs and sofas off to the side from the end of the bar. As they got closer Eleanor realized that all of Jonathan's LSE friends that she'd met the night school started were there along with some of the girls she'd become friends with in the program, clearly Jonathan and Jack had teamed up on the guest list and Eleanor was grateful. The group was big enough to feel festive but not full of people Eleanor didn't know, which she had been a little afraid of. When they saw Eleanor, Jack and Jonathan approaching a large cry of "Happy Birthday" sounded, ringing out over the sounds of the rest of the club and Eleanor felt herself blush as people at the nearby tables and bar looked their way.

Eleanor felt a glass of champagne be put in her hand and then heard Jonathan exclaim, "I am so happy you all could be here to help celebrate my dear cousin's birthday tonight. We've been lucky to have Eleanor here in London for a while now and I know I'm not the only one who's noticed how well London seems to suit her." Eleanor blushed again as the group nodded and exclaimed in agreement to Jonathan's compliment. He continued, looking at Eleanor,

"I am so happy to have you living here this year and getting to spend so much time with you. I love you like a sister and I can't wait to see what this year brings for you. I wish you the happiest of birthdays tonight and all the best wishes for the coming year, may it be as brilliant as you are. To Eleanor!" he finished, raising his glass.

Everyone else raised their glasses and exclaimed, "To Eleanor!"

As everyone sipped their champagne Eleanor felt tears prick her eyes. Jonathan looked down at her and quickly wrapped an arm around her, drawing her close. He said quietly so only she would hear, "You deserve all this and more. I want you to enjoy yourself, and so do our mums. Ok?"

Looking up at him she grinned and reached up to dab the tears that had formed in the corner of her eyes, "Ok," she agreed with a small laugh.

Jack came back over to Eleanor and stated loudly, "Don't you dare start crying missy, now is not the time to get all soppy and humble. Tonight we party!"

"Alright, alright, give the poor woman some room and a chance to drink her champagne," Mark exclaimed, reaching between Jonathan and Jack and taking Eleanor by the arm he guided her into the group and sat her in an open spot next to her friend Clara. Mark sat next to her and clinked his glass against hers, "Cheers darling, happy birthday."

Smiling, Eleanor replied, "Cheers, and thank you."

Over the next couple hours the group chatted excitedly and there was a lot of seat swapping as Eleanor made the rounds around the group, determined to talk with everyone. She spoke for a bit with Clara and her other girlfriends from school, Maggie and Alexandra, with Jack joining in while they were talking about school and then drifting over to talk to the guys while the girls started talking about Eleanor's outfit and shopping. The guys talked a bit about school and also asked Jack about his writing. Eventually Eleanor got caught up with Zaf, Malcolm, Henry, and Ioan and how they were doing at school.

She and Malcolm shared a nice moment when he caught her in between conversations, "School seems to be suiting you," he said with a small smile.

Eleanor smiled at the memory of their first meeting when he had confessed he'd almost dropped out of LSE after his first day. "Yes, I'm glad I went back. It's still tough and they work us hard, but it's definitely been worth it."

"I knew you'd be just fine," Malcolm said kindly.

They chatted for a bit longer and after a while the group settled down in a large circle and conversation flowed between them all, along with more champagne and mass amounts of food. Eleanor thought the food in this place was the best she'd ever had. Looking around at all of her friends Eleanor thought about the life she was building for herself in London. She never would have imagined this was actually possible. She felt like she was living in a dream, or a movie, particularly tonight in this incredible place. Her face hurt from smiling so much but she didn't care. The confidence she gained from her new outfit had her feeling like she might actually belong in a place like this.

Eleanor glanced up after laughing hard at something Mark had said and she noticed Celeste walking over to the group. Jonathan leaped up and said something to Celeste and then turned and gestured for Eleanor to come to him.

Getting up she exclaimed, "What have you done now?!" Looking past him and Celeste she saw a cake with sparklers being brought over to their table. Eleanor's eyes flew wide at the sight and with the sparklers it all looked so magical she couldn't help but clap her hands together and laugh like a little girl. She didn't realize it, but several men in the area, including Mark, were looking at her admiringly. In that moment, Mark especially noticed her, thinking to himself the she looked more beautiful than he had ever imagined a woman could be.

The group all wished her a happy birthday again and sang, with people at the surrounding tables joining in with the singing and cheering as she blew out the candles that had been lit after the sparklers had died. They all ate cake and chatted some more until the dance floor started to fill up. Before she knew it, Eleanor found herself dancing. First with Jonathan, then with Jack, then for a few songs with the girls. For once in her life Eleanor felt completely unselfconscious. She just threw her head back and laughed and enjoyed herself. The music shifted and a slower song came on and Eleanor found herself in Mark's strong arms. Maybe it was the giddiness of the night, maybe it was the champagne, probably it was both, but she allowed herself to dance with Mark for a few songs. Sometimes they talked, sometimes he just held her in his arms, guiding her expertly around the floor.

Jonathan's information that Mark was attracted to her bounced around in the back of her mind, but she didn't want to make herself nervous so she tried not to think about it. She just wanted to enjoy the fact that a cute guy was dancing with her.

"Penny for your thoughts," she heard him say suddenly.

Looking up at him, she laughed, "Nothing really, just thinking about how amazing tonight has been. I wasn't sure what my birthday was going to be like, with all my friends being back in the states. But I really do have friends here now, don't I?"

"Yes you do. And we care about you very much."

Between the effects of the champagne and the way Mark was looking at her, Eleanor started to feel a bit lightheaded.

Looking concerned, Mark asked, "Are you alright Elle?"

"Yes! Yes, I'm fine. Just a bit too much champagne. Excuse me for a moment Mark, I just need to visit the ladies room."

"Of course, I'll meet you back at the table."

Nodding she quickly cut across the dance floor towards the opposite side of the room where the toilets where. Unsurprisingly the ladies room was just as impressive as the main room. More plush sofas and vanities with lights and various lotions and perfumes and makeup samples for the patrons to help themselves. After a quick visit to one of the stalls Eleanor came back out to the lounge area of the ladies' room and crashed on one of the sofas. She was having a great time, but the lounge was so much quieter compared to out in the club and she enjoyed the momentary break in the festivities. Eleanor was an introvert through and through. She replayed the night's events so far in her head. She couldn't believe how incredible everything had been.

She also didn't know what to think about Mark. He obviously liked her. And she thought she liked him. But she was still gun shy after Michael. And there was something about Mark. She couldn't quite put her finger on it. They'd hung out together a few times, always in a group, or chatted for a few minutes in the flat when he'd come over to work with Jonathan. She always felt a bit off kilter with him. He was always so pulled together and seemed to always know what he was doing. Whereas she always felt like she was making stuff up as she went along. Maybe someone like Mark was what she needed. He certainly wasn't controlling or manipulating in the way Michael sometimes was. She leaned back and closed her eyes.

After a few minutes, she collected herself and headed back out to the party. She knew if she was gone too long she'd be missed.

She was still thinking about everything when she felt

someone bump into her. Between the champagne and the high heels, she quickly felt herself losing her balance but just as quickly felt two strong arms reach around to grab her and set her right again. She looked up suddenly, apology already on her lips, when she found herself staring once again into the eyes of Patrick Reynolds.

"I'm so terribly sorry!" he said at once, "I wasn't paying any attention to where I was going, I didn't see you!" Concern was etched all over his face, making him appear even more handsome. But the concern changed to recognition suddenly. "Wait. It's you! Oh my goodness, I'm so sorry! I can't believe I've collided with you twice now, you must think I'm terribly clumsy. Are you alright?"

Eleanor knew she needed to respond but she was still struck silent by being once again in the arms of her favorite movie star crush. *Is this really happening?!* she thought. Forcing herself to speak, she slowly placed her hands over his, which were still grasping her around the waist, and steadied herself. Looking up at him and feeling a bit mesmerized by his eyes she shook her head slightly and tried to speak, "Yes. Yes, I'm fine. You just caught me off guard. I'm sorry."

"Please don't apologize, I swear this was my fault," he said with a shy grin.

"If you say so," Eleanor said with a laugh.

"You ran off before I could properly apologize last time—"

"Yes, well I still maintain that I was at fault for that one, I was too busy staring at my map!" Eleanor interrupted.

"Sorry, I'm afraid I can't let you take the blame," he countered.

"Do you apologize for everything?" she asked.

Grinning sheepishly, "I have been told it's something I do. Sorry?"

Eleanor laughed, loudly. She couldn't believe the

craziness of the situation. Here she was standing in front of one of her favorite actors, chatting with him, and laughing with him. He smiled at her and she suddenly felt dizzy again under the power of it. On screen it was one thing, but when that smile is aimed directly at you in person, well, Eleanor understood why the women who show up at his premieres end up screaming and almost fainting.

Trying to focus herself, "Well, let's just call it a draw then, shall we? Thanks for catching me again though. It's been a long night and I've been enjoying perhaps a bit too much champagne."

"Champagne? Are you celebrating something?"

"Umm, yeah. My friends surprised me tonight with a birthday party —"

"It's your birthday?!" he exclaimed smiling even wider.

Struggling to maintain her composure, "Umm, uh huh. Yep."

"Happy birthday! That's fantastic!" Patrick replied enthusiastically.

His smile and enthusiasm were so sincere Eleanor felt her body tingle under his attention. She knew she needed to get back to her table before she made a complete fool of herself.

"Well, I should get back to my friends, and let you get back to yours," she said, feeling a bit foolish as she did, for some reason.

"Wait," Patrick said quickly, "at least tell me your name this time. I'm Patrick, Patrick Reynolds," he said, extending his hand to her.

Shaking it firmly, Eleanor replied, "I know...er, I mean, I'm Eleanor Gordon. Pleased to meet you Patrick."

"Very pleased to meet you, officially at last," he said sincerely. "I'll let you get back to your friends, I shouldn't keep the birthday girl held up chatting to a prat like me."

"It really was nice to bump into you again. And thank

you for the kind birthday wish."

"My pleasure. Truly. I hope you have a wonderful rest of your evening."

"Thank you." Smiling at him one last time, Eleanor walked past him and headed back across the room to her friends.

Jonathan rose when he saw her approaching, "Is everything alright?"

"Yes, I just saw someone I knew and stopped to chat for a bit."

"Someone you knew?" Mark asked curiously.

Eleanor paused, "Well...we've only met one other time, it's a long story. Sorry I took so long."

Jack looked at her puzzled expression and quickly said, "It's your party and you can talk to whoever you want. But we're glad you're back, we've been missing you."

Eleanor sat down between Jack and Mark and started chatting with them both, trying to put her encounter with Patrick in the back of her mind to replay later when she was home. A few moments later Celeste appeared with a server from the bar holding two more buckets of champagne.

"Did we order more champers?" Jonathan asked looking around at the group.

Before anyone could answer Celeste replied, "These are compliments of the gentleman at the bar, along with this," she finished, handing Eleanor a small card, folded over once. Eleanor unfolded it and read the short message:

My apologies again for being such a clumsy git. Happy birthday beautiful Eleanor.
xx
-Patrick R.

Eleanor felt herself blush reading the message and

quickly folded it back up and slipped it in her clutch before anyone else could read it.

"Who's it from Ellie?" Jonathan asked curiously.

Eleanor replied to Jonathan but looked directly at Celeste, "the friend I bumped into coming out of the ladies." She didn't want to make a big deal about having champagne delivered from one of Britain's most up and coming young actors. Celeste seemed to understand and gave a slight smile and nod. She left the ice buckets with the bottles and the group refilled their glasses and toasted Eleanor again. As she took a sip she glanced beyond their group to the bar and saw Patrick standing there in a group with his friends. He raised his glass in her direction and took a sip. She smiled in return.

The party continued for another couple hours and sometime around 2 o'clock in the morning they all stumbled out of the club laughing. Eleanor thought she'd seen Patrick wave in her direction as she was walking out but between Jack and Jonathan and Mark all bending over backwards to give her an arm to lean on, she was pretty distracted.

Eleanor said goodbye to all of her friends one at a time. Jack headed off with the girls from school as they all lived in the same area. It was down to just Eleanor, Jonathan, and Mark, when Jonathan said suddenly, "I forgot to talk to Celeste about something. Mark, can you get Eleanor home alright?"

"I can wait for you Jonathan," Eleanor said, feeling slightly alarmed with the thought of being alone with Mark. She was still somewhat uneasy about him "liking" her.

"No, you need to get home and go straight to bed. You're looking dead on your feet dear," Jonathan replied a little too quickly.

"I'll see she makes it home safely mate, no worries," Mark interrupted.

Eleanor felt herself being guided into a taxi before she could say anything else and suddenly was whisked back to Holborn. There was light traffic that late at night so the drive didn't take long. Mark got out first and paid and then offered his hand to help Eleanor get out of the taxi, which she accepted gratefully. Suddenly the lateness of the hour caught up with her and she suddenly felt so tired. While she had been careful with the champagne and wasn't drunk, she was still a bit tipsy. She realized suddenly that a bit too much alcohol, high heels, fatigue, and gravity were a potentially dangerous mix.

"Steady there," she heard Mark say with a laugh.

"I swear I was doing just fine in these shoes until about thirty minutes ago," Eleanor grumbled in return.

"Shall I carry you upstairs my lady?"

Appalled at the idea Eleanor gasped, "Absolutely not, thank you very much. I can manage on my own for another few minutes."

Mark continued laughing, "Very well then. Let's get you upstairs."

After a short and quiet ride in the lift they were soon at Eleanor's front door. She fished her key out of her clutch and opened the door. She turned to say goodnight to Mark and saw him looking down at her, a very serious expression on his face.

"Is everything alright Mark?" Eleanor asked with concern.

Shaking his head, as if to clear his mind, he smiled and said, "Yes, I was just thinking."

"Thinking about what?"

"Would you like to have dinner with me? I mean, not just as friends, not like we've done before, but, you know...as a date? What I mean is...what I'm trying to say, very clumsily I'm afraid, is...Eleanor, would you go on a date with me, to dinner? Wow, that was still rubbish, wasn't it?"

"No! That was sweet, and sincere. Thank you," Eleanor said with a smile. She felt a moment of hesitation. Did she really want to go out on a date with Mark? She liked him, but was she ready to date again? As quick as the questions came into her mind she squashed them even quicker and said suddenly, "I would love to go out to dinner with you. As a date. Thank you."

Mark beamed down at her, "That's great! Brilliant. How about Friday? Say, 7 o'clock?"

"Friday at 7 it is. And now if you'll excuse me I really must go to sleep, before I collapse," Eleanor said, pleadingly.

"Right, off to bed you go. Sweet dreams."

And before Eleanor could realize what was happening, Mark reached his hand up to tuck a strand of hair behind her ear and leaned in to kiss her. She was surprised but quickly found herself kissing him back. His hand moved from by her ear to the back of her head, his other hand wrapping gently around her back. He was a good kisser; his lips were smooth and gentle but there was no mistaking his interest.

Her eyes were still closed when he broke away, and said, "See you Friday then?"

Eyes fluttering open, Eleanor struggled to bring her mind into focus, "Yeah, um, yes. Friday. 7 o'clock. Um, do you want me to meet you somewhere?"

"No, I'll pick you up here. Alright, I'll let you go. Get some sleep." He gave her one last smile and then turned and walked back to the lift.

Eleanor stood there for a moment before stepping back and closing the door. What a night! She couldn't believe everything that happened this evening. The shopping, the surprise party, bumping into Patrick Reynolds. Again. And now Mark asking her out? And that kiss! She felt like she was living in one of the romance novels she loved to read. Smiling to herself as she walked into her room and kicked off her shoes Eleanor thought to herself, *this was the best night ever! And moving to London?* she thought as she collapsed on her bed, still wearing her dress, *definitely, absolutely, the best decision ever!* And with that she promptly fell asleep sprawled diagonally across her bed and slept better than she had in months.

Chapter 7

The next week Eleanor felt like she was floating through life, living on Cloud 9. School was going so well, her latest assignments had come back with top marks and Eleanor felt like she was finally getting into a rhythm. She spent hours in the afternoon in her favorite coffee shops writing and wandering around the One New Change shopping center behind St. Paul's Cathedral. She was looking forward to her date on Friday. Thursday found her taking advantage of the few days they had off from school before the next term began. She decided to pick up some new jewelry at Accessorize before treating herself to a cream tea at Bea's of Bloomsbury, which had quickly become a favorite after Jack had taken her there one day after class earlier in the term. While she enjoyed sipping her tea, Eleanor thought about everything that had been happening over the last few days and weeks. For once it felt like things were going her way and things were working out.

On Friday she headed straight home from school, arriving back at the flat around 5:45 in the evening. She frantically flew around her room trying to put together the perfect outfit, but nothing seemed right. She didn't know where Mark was taking her. She didn't think it was appropriate to dress up as formally as she'd been the week before for her party but she felt like jeans and a sweater weren't nice enough. Finally, with only a few minutes to spare she settled on a slim black pencil skirt with tights and knee high boots and a plain peacock blue sweater with a deep cowl neck and one of her favorite new blue and green statement necklaces from River Island. It was dressy but not too dressy and the neckline hinted at cleavage without actually showing any. Eleanor blushed at the thought, considering she would have never worn this sweater on a date with Michael, then immediately pushed all thoughts of Michael out of her head. She grabbed her black handbag, threw her scarf and coat over her arm before walking out into the foyer just as the bell rang letting her know Mark had arrived downstairs.

Pressing the button on the intercom, "Hello?"

"Hi, it's me," came Mark's voice from the front door below.

"Be right down."

Once she got to the ground floor and stepped outside the building Eleanor was hit with a blast of cool night air, it had become much cooler than it had been earlier in the day.

"Oooh, it's gotten chilly, hasn't it?" Eleanor said with a laugh. As she struggled to put her coat on, "I should have put this on upstairs," she said sheepishly.

"Here, let me help you," Mark said, taking Eleanor's coat and stepping around behind her. He held it out so she could slip her arms through the sleeves and then pulled it up over her shoulders. Eleanor reached up to pull her hair out from under the collar just as Mark stepped back in front of her and leaned down to kiss her lightly on the lips. "Good evening," he said with a smile.

Startled slightly and feeling thrown a bit off balance by the sudden display of affection Eleanor stammered back, "G-g-good evening."

Mark continued to stare at her for a second, as if

thinking, before reaching out to place his hands on either side of Eleanor's face and drawing her towards him, he leaned down and kissed her, gently at first, but soon growing in intensity. Eleanor felt thrown even further off balance and placed her hands on his chest to steady herself, which made Mark kiss her even more intensely, reaching one hand around to the back of her head and the other down around behind her waist. Eleanor felt like her head was spinning off into space and she struggled to keep up with Mark as his mouth explored hers.

Finally, Mark broke off and Eleanor found it difficult to catch her breath.

"I've been dreaming about doing that all week. I was going to wait until the end of the date but then you came out that door looking so ravishing. I'm afraid I've quite undone your lip color though," Mark said with a laugh.

Trying to focus her vision, Eleanor looked up at Mark and started laughing, noticing that he had indeed messed up her lipstick and was now, in fact, wearing some of it himself. Cocking her head to the side she quipped, "You know, it almost looks better on you." She laughed as Mark blushed sheepishly, and she quickly pulled a tissue out of her bag and wiped the lipstick from Mark's mouth and then wiped the remains off hers as well. She had brought the tube with her for touch ups but if this was how the date was starting she figured she'd better stick with her trusty Burt's Bees lip balm instead.

Mark reached out for her hand and tucked her arm through his as they walked off down the road towards Holborn Station, "Do you mind taking the Tube?" he asked.

"Not at all. I do it every day," she said with a smile.

"Yes, but this is a date. Not every woman appreciates taking public transit on a date."

"I wasn't expecting you to splurge on a cab. Where are we going," she asked, changing the subject.

"A friend of a friend owns a little Italian place in Kensington. How does that sound?"

Thinking about what had happened the last time she had been at an Italian restaurant on a date, Eleanor quickly pushed the thought out of her mind and tried to smile, "Sounds good."

Noticing her false brightness, "Are you sure? We don't have to, it's just I know you and Jonathan eat spag bol all the time, so I figured Italian was a safe guess."

Trying for a more sincere smile Eleanor insisted, "Yes, I love Italian. I'm sorry, it's just Jonathan and I eat at home. It's been ages since I've been to an Italian restaurant for a meal and to be honest, the last time wasn't the most spectacular experience. But that was back in Arizona, I'm sure it will be much better here," she finished in a hurry, hoping Mark would think it had been the food that had been the disappointment, and not her ex-boyfriend.

"Right, ok...," Mark said, clearly thinking about something, finally he said, "Ok, change of plans – "

" – oh no! We don't have to change the plans!" Eleanor interrupted.

"No, it's fine. I want you happy and comfortable and not worrying about a single thing. Tonight is meant to be fun. How do you feel about Chinese?"

"Umm, I'm really boring with my selection but I do like it, a lot."

"Ok, I know a really good spot, we can walk there if that's alright."

"I can walk," Eleanor said with a smile.

"Good, off we go then."

They headed towards Holborn Station but went past it and Mark led her towards Soho. Before long they were walking through Chinatown, but Mark kept leading her past one Chinese restaurant after another, until they'd almost reached the other side of Chinatown, when he suddenly led her down a small side street, away from the hustle and bustle of the main area of Chinatown where all the tourists were hanging out. Eleanor had finally managed to learn the larger roads in the area but she knew that she would have never found her way to this place, it was so tucked away. They finally walked up to a small, unassuming restaurant that was sandwiched between a dry cleaners and a newsagent in a small square with a couple office buildings around it. It was brightly lit from inside, with little Christmas tree lights twinkling around the windows.

They walked inside and were greeted by a kind looking older woman, who greeted Mark with a hug. They exchanged a few words of greeting in Mandarin, Eleanor recognized a couple words, thanks to having a friend during undergrad who was an exchange student from China, but she was impressed with how much Mark seemed to know. Finally, they switched to English.

"Mark, it has been too long," she said with a British accent, only slightly marked by her native language. Glancing at Eleanor, she smiled and asked, "Table for two?"

"Yes," agreed Mark. "Lois, this is my friend Eleanor. Elle, this is Lois, her family has owned and operated a restaurant in this space since the 1950s."

Eleanor's eyes grew wide and Lois said smiling, "Yes, I grew up in the flat upstairs. Please, take a seat wherever you like."

Mark led Eleanor through the tables, which at this time of night were mostly full, but Eleanor soon found that the restaurant was much deeper than it looked from the front. Mark led them back into an interior room that was much quieter and looked out over a small patio, lit up with more Christmas lights. The room was smaller than the main dining area but still a decent size and there were no other customers sitting in it.

"This room is usually used for private parties but Lois always lets me sit here or out on the patio when it's nice," Mark explained.

"How lovely," Eleanor replied, looking around.

They walked to a table by the window, looking out on the patio, and Mark came around behind Eleanor and held out her chair. Eleanor couldn't help but compare Mark's behavior to Michael's. Michael had never been one for holding open doors, pulling out chairs, and she couldn't remember the last time they had held hands or walked arm in arm. At the time she'd told herself she didn't need those little gestures, but experiencing it now with Mark, she found herself really enjoying and appreciating them.

The next couple hours seemed to fly by. Even though she had spent a lot of time with Mark and the rest of Jonathan's friends, they still had so much to talk about. The conversation ranged from their favorite TV shows (both couldn't decide between *Sherlock* and *Doctor Who*), favorite books (his sci-fi, hers chick lit), favorite bands and music (both admitted sheepishly to having Britany Spears on their iPods) and chatted about places they'd travelled to. The only pauses and silences were caused by stopping to eat the delicious food that had arrived. Somewhere around 10 o'clock, three hours after the date had started, Eleanor realized how long it had been and couldn't believe how easy going the date had been. She'd been a nervous wreck the first time she went out with Michael, and for the few horrid first dates she'd gone on during their first breakup. She knew it had to have been because unlike those dates, she already knew Mark. With Michael, it had just been a couple book club meetings and the others a very brief (and immediately regretted) foray into online dating.

Suddenly she heard Mark's voice break through her thoughts, "Where did you go just now Sugar?"

"Sugar? I don't think anyone's called me that before,"

Eleanor said with a laugh.

"Oh no, I'm sorry! That was probably a bit forward of me," Mark said in a rush, looking a bit embarrassed.

Realizing how he had taken her comment Eleanor said quickly, "No! It's fine, really. I don't mind. I'm just not used to it," smiling generously.

Smiling back at her, "Ok, as long as you're sure. I wouldn't want you to think I wasn't respecting you or anything. I think you're grand Elle, I really do. Oh, shoot, do you mind my calling you Elle? I know Jon calls you Ellie sometimes."

"Eleanor, Elle, Ellie, E...Sugar," she smiled and continued, "I'm good with any variation."

"Good," Mark said with a smile. "But back to my previous question. You disappeared for a moment, you weren't here having dinner with me. Where did your mind go?"

Cringing slightly, "I'm sorry, I do that sometimes. I wasn't thinking anything really, just that I am having a really lovely time this evening."

Grinning widely, "Good! I'm glad," Mark replied. "I've been wanting to ask you out since that first night we met in the pub. But Jon had mentioned to us before you arrived in London that you had just gotten out of a relationship and I didn't want to overstep."

Eleanor's smile slipped slightly at the mention of her failed relationship and Mark quickly said, "I'm sorry! I shouldn't have said anything. It's your business, and I'm sure you don't want to talk about it."

Cutting him off before he could make himself feel worse, "No, really, it's fine. It's a bit of a long and really boring, stupid story. I don't mind talking about it but I'm happier talking about being here with you."

"Fair enough. And I'm glad you're enjoying yourself tonight. You looked like you were having fun last week at your party but the other times I've seen you recently you've seemed a bit distracted. I hope things are going well for you here," Mark asked, voice tinged with concern.

"Oh yes, they are. Much better than when I started. I guess I'm just noticing how quickly the year is going, it will be the holidays before we know it."

"I know, I need to start my shopping, or my mum is going to be very cross with me come Christmas."

Eleanor laughed, "Well, you don't want that, do you?"

"No, I don't!" Mark replied laughing.

They laughed together for a moment and then Mark suddenly looked at Eleanor quizzically. "The thing is," he started cautiously, "I'm trying to figure out how any guy would let go of a woman like you? And how there weren't at least a dozen guys lined up waiting to step into his place when he did?"

"I don't know…," Eleanor started, faltering, trying to answer Mark's questions, "there just weren't, and he didn't want to be with me anymore. Pretty simple really."

"Are the men in your town just blind and stupid?"

"Yes," Eleanor answered a little too quickly, and perhaps a little too bitterly. "I mean, no. I'm sure there are some perfectly lovely men back home, I just never met them. I thought I had…but…well, it didn't work. And now it's done and I'm here in London and out with you," she said, attempting a smile.

"And I'm very glad for that," Mark said genuinely. Looking around Eleanor to peer past her towards the front of the restaurant, "Well, we don't have to go home just yet, but they do close around now, shall we get the bill?"

"Of course. Yes, I'm sorry," Eleanor started, apologetically, "I shouldn't keep you out all night anyway, I'm sure you have work to do."

"Not at all, I'm right where I want to be," Mark said with a grin. "It will be a bit chilly outside, but we could go for a bit of a walk, take the long, scenic route home?"

Smiling, Eleanor replied, "That would be nice."

Mark paid the bill for their meal, and wouldn't even hear it when Eleanor tried to contribute for her part of it.

"It's a date! What kind of wanker would I be if I expected you to pay for half the bill?! Do American blokes do that?"

Sheepishly, "Some do, I'm sure some British men expect to split the check as well. Not everyone is as generous as you."

With mock seriousness as they walked out of the restaurant, "I don't know what you're talking about. All British men are gentlemen and we all take care of a lady when we are fortunate enough to be in the presence of one. Split the check? Silly American men. They should learn a thing or two from one of us proper English gentlemen," he finished, puffing his chest out and lifting his chin pompously.

Poking him in the side as she slipped on her gloves, "Alright you, point made. I'm in the presence of a gracious and generous gentleman, I curtsy to your superior ways compared to American men," Eleanor replied with mock seriousness, slipping one foot behind the other and dropping into an exaggerated curtsy.

"Hey, not bad. You could be presented to the Queen with a curtsy like that," Mark said with a laugh.

Slapping the back of her hand against his arm gently, Eleanor shifted her handbag up onto her shoulder and laughed, "Oh yes, my date at court is next week, I've been practicing."

Taking her hand and slipping it through his arm again, Mark laughed and then smiled sincerely, "You would look ravishing at court."

"You say that like you've been," Eleanor said with a laugh.

"Well, I haven't been formally presented, they don't really do that anymore like they did in the old days, but I have met several members of the Royal Family. Both my parents work for them in different ways," Mark said, his voice getting a little more serious.

"What?" Eleanor said, startled at the news. "Are you serious? How did I not know that? Does Jonathan know?"

"Oh yeah, my closest friends do. Which is why I'm telling you now. I don't broadcast it," Mark said, looking at Eleanor cautiously.

"Well, I won't say anything, of course. But what do they do?"

"Dad works high up in the bank that keeps most of the family's personal finances. He's constantly getting invited to different events and parties and is on close terms with Charles, William, and Harry. Then Mum has always been a society darling, as Dad calls her. Growing up she was what you would have called a socialite, they still exist in the younger generations today but not like then. My grandmothers, in fact, were both part of the last generation of debutantes to be officially presented at court, one was presented to King George VI and the other a few years later after Queen Elizabeth became Queen. The official presentations ended in 1958 so mum missed out by a couple decades, but she's still very much part of that social crowd. She's involved in a number of charities that have attracted the attention of various royals, so if there's a ribbon cutting ceremony with the Queen or Camilla, Kate, or Meghan, even sometimes Beatrice, Eugenie, or Sophie, Mum is usually there in the background. I've lost count of how many charities she's on the board of or volunteers with. Especially once I went off to boarding school."

"Wow...that's impressive. I had no idea I was on a date with someone from such a connected background," Eleanor said with a grin.

"Well, at the risk of making you change your mind, I'm not the one who's 'connected', my parents are. I've been invited to a few of these things, but usually through my parents or when I was working at my father's bank between undergrad and going to LSE. I don't know any of these people personally, just been introduced here and there. And I think I was about 10 when I met the Queen, so it's not like I was hanging out with her just last week."

"Still, you've met the Queen. *The* Queen! I can't say that about myself," Eleanor said in awe and with a laugh.

They walked in companionable silence for a while, eventually arriving at the river. Lights glittered off the water and after they'd walked along the river for a while they could see Big Ben lit up in the distance. Eleanor still hadn't gotten used to seeing London's iconic landmarks every time she turned a corner. Every time she did it always gave her a thrill and she fought the urge to pinch herself. There was a cold wind blowing up the Thames. Despite her coat, Eleanor still felt the cold and shivered. Mark let go of her arm and placed his arm around her shoulders, pulling her close to him as they walked.

"Getting cold?" he said with concern.

Laughing, "Maybe a little, but I still enjoy it. It's still mid-90s back home right now. The cold is a novelty."

"Mid-90s? What's that in Celsius?" Mark asked curiously.

"Umm, low 30s? Something like that," Eleanor replied laughing.

"Bloody hell that's hot! How do you all stand it?" Mark replied incredulously.

"Air conditioning. We stay indoors a lot," Eleanor replied matter-of-factly.

"But still, this late in the year? And still that hot?"

"Some people get used to it. I only got less tolerant. So I'm enjoying being here," Eleanor said with a smile.

Mark stopped them and stepped in front to face her, "I'm enjoying you being here as well."

The look on his face was much more serious than the casual statement Eleanor had been making about the weather and London and it made her catch her breath. Before she could speak he placed his hands on both sides of her face and tilted it up, his lips meeting hers. Soft and inquiring at first, the kiss soon became heated and demanding as his mouth explored hers. She'd never been kissed like this. Eleanor felt a warmth spread throughout her entire body, in a way that the cold weather couldn't penetrate. With Michael it had always been very mechanical compared to this. Eleanor almost hated herself for comparing them but she couldn't help it. Michael had been her first kiss, so it was all she had to go by. With Mark, he seemed so enthusiastic and excited. It was a bit of a challenge for Eleanor to keep up.

Both the night of her party and tonight she felt out of her depth and swept away when Mark was kissing her. It made her both nervous and excited. Even when she and Michael had first started dating he'd never seemed this attracted to her. She'd always felt simply accepted as a part of his life, like she ticked a box on a list of his.

Eleanor tried to stay focused on the moment, Mark seemed in no hurry to stop kissing, but despite her warm coat and his arms wrapped tightly around her she couldn't help shaking from the persistent cold. Mark slowly pulled his lips away from hers and looked down at her with concern as Eleanor began to shake even more.

Rubbing his hands briskly up and down her arms, "You're freezing! You should have said something."

"I didn't really notice it until I started shaking," Eleanor said with a small grin. "You're very distracting."

Smiling broadly, "I'm terribly sorry to say that I'm not sorry in the slightest for distracting you from the cold. I quite enjoy kissing you."

"I enjoy kissing you as well," Eleanor replied shyly.

"Still, it's getting late and you're freezing, so we should probably get you home."

Eleanor was going to protest, but her chattering teeth told both her and Mark that it probably was time to get home.

"I guess I'm still getting used to the English cold after years of Arizona heat," Eleanor said laughing.

Mark laughed as well, then rushed to the side of the road and was able to wave down a cab. He gently helped Eleanor get in and then slid in beside her, reaching his arm across her shoulders and pulling her close for warmth.

Within minutes they had pulled up in front of Eleanor's flat and Mark walked her upstairs to the door to the flat.

"When can I see you again?" he asked, staring down at Eleanor intently.

Again, she felt something inside her twist under his focused attention, but pushed it aside. "I'm busy working on a project for school this weekend that's due on Tuesday, but I'm free after that's turned in."

"Tuesday evening for dinner then? Or Wednesday if you'd rather take the night off, but maybe we could celebrate it being finished," he said with a hopeful smile.

"Tuesday evening would be nice, but I already have plans with my classmates to celebrate that night," she replied with an apologetic smile. "We've all been stressing about it. But Wednesday would work," she finished, looking up at him hopefully.

"Wednesday it is. I'll plan something special and you can celebrate finishing your project twice."

"Deal," Eleanor said with a laugh.

Mark reached up and pulled her close again, leaning down to give her another kiss, this one just as insistent and mesmerizing as the others. When he stopped Eleanor felt as if she was swaying. They said goodbye and Eleanor somehow managed to get inside to her room. She shrugged out of her coat and quickly changed into her yoga pants and U of A hoody that she'd brought from home.

Looking at herself in the mirror she tried to see what Mark saw in her. She barely recognized herself anymore. Jonathan and Jack were right. She was a different person, in a lot of ways, than she was when she arrived. She was wearing her hair down more often, because it wasn't a million degrees outside. Her skin seemed to love the bit of humidity in the air and was clearer than it had been in years, and thanks to some new skincare products her girlfriends at school had recommended her skin was practically glowing most days. She hadn't lost weight, but she found she wasn't as self-conscious about it in London, seeing so many different body types around her, and with all the walking she did on a daily basis she just *felt* better in her body, even though her clothes all still fit the same. She was feeling better about herself physically and mentally, feeling so much more confident in her writing abilities and feeling like she was making friends and connections and building a life for herself in London. She no longer felt like the awkward tourist pretending to fit in.

But in so many ways she was still the shy and awkward girl who'd just "gone along" for years in order to maintain her relationship with Michael. With Mark things felt completely different, but almost to the other end of the spectrum. He was so interested and attracted to her, even Eleanor had to admit that. But did she feel the same way about him? They seemed to have a bit in common, conversation was always easy. He was happy to listen to her talk about school and her life back in Arizona. But part of Eleanor wondered if she was more attracted to the idea of him than anything else. It felt nice having someone pay so much attention to her. She liked being liked. But did she really like Mark as much as he seemed to like her? Was she ready to dive into another relationship with someone that she wasn't sure about? This whole year was supposed to be for Eleanor to focus on her writing and focus on herself. She was afraid to lose herself in another relationship and things with Mark felt like they were moving so fast.

Suddenly feeling very tired Eleanor quickly washed her face and brushed her teeth and then crawled under the duvet and fell asleep. She'd think about all of this later.

Chapter 8

The weekend went by in a blur of writing sessions in various coffee shops around London and at school, sometimes by herself, sometimes with Jack or other classmates. This project that had carried on from the first term was killing them all but Eleanor was happy for the distraction. Jack tried pressing her a few times for details about her date with Mark, so did Jonathan, but she managed to evade them each time. Tuesday finally arrived and Eleanor actually felt fairly confident about her work when she submitted it. She knew it wasn't perfect, nothing ever was, but it was one of the best pieces she'd written in a while. That night a group from school went out to the Knightrider pub near their building and ate way too much fish and chips and drank a lot of ale and cider. They were happy to be done with the project and excited about what the new term would bring and the new workshops they'd be attending. The Harrison didn't operate on a normal academic schedule, and Eleanor loved the workshop and project based format of it. It was the complete opposite about how her MA program had been set up.

The next night Eleanor got ready for another date with Mark. He hadn't told her where they were going but had said that she should wear a dress and that he was picking her up in a cab if she wanted to wear heels. On the one hand, she was impressed by his thoughtfulness to let her know about the dress code and that he was willing to get a cab for them, but on the other hand she kind of wished the date would be a little less formal. She'd been hoping for something more casual.

She pulled her hair up into an elegant twist in the back, securing it with a crystal encrusted clip she had found at Accessorize, which had quickly become one of her favorite shops, and applied her standard evening makeup look, slightly smokey eye, lots of mascara, a bit of blush and highlighter, natural lip. She dressed in her plain black shift dress from Hobbs, its streamlined darts accentuating her waist and its simple three-quarter sleeves able to provide just enough warmth wherever they ended up. She added a large statement necklace from Zara that framed the collar of the dress perfectly and then slipped on her usual stacking rings that she'd brought with her from home, each one a gift from her mom and aunt for various occasions, milestone birthdays, graduations, and the most recent one from her mom before she left for London.

She heard the intercom ring and Jonathan answer it as she grabbed her scarf, gloves, and coat and slipped into her most comfortable kitten heels. Cab or no, she wanted to be able to walk for at least a little while before her feet would start hurting. She said a quick goodbye to Jonathan and headed downstairs to meet Mark. As soon as she came through the door to the front steps he wrapped his arms around her and gave her a long, deep kiss. Eleanor felt immediately thrown off balance, while she loved the attention it was almost disconcerting how *much* attention he gave her. She thought to herself, a simple hug would have been just as nice and then immediately felt ungrateful for thinking that. Maybe this was just how a normal couple beginning to date interacted. She knew she had to stop

120

comparing everything Mark did to how Michael had behaved. Mark was a completely different man and she wanted to be able to just enjoy herself.

"Are you ready?" Mark said, breaking through her thoughts.

"Y-yes," Eleanor stammered slightly in reply. "I can't wait to see where we're going."

Grinning, "Well, you only have to wait a little bit longer. I pulled some strings and made some calls. Shall we?" he finished, indicating to the waiting taxi behind him.

Eleanor smiled back at him and they quickly slid into the cab and sped away. It took a little bit of time, winding through London traffic, but Eleanor could tell they were heading into the Knightsbridge area. They passed Harrods, aglow in its usual bright lights, and shortly after pulled up in front of a smaller but almost equally glowing and sparkling building. Eleanor registered that it was one of the luxurious boutique hotels in the area that had impeccable reviews for its in-house restaurant. From the outside the whole place looked magical with its sparkling lights around the exterior and the glow of candlelight illuminating each window. But as beautiful as it looked it also made Eleanor's heart jump to her throat. The whole place screamed expensive.

Mark reached out his hand to help Eleanor get out of the taxi and she suddenly became very self-conscious trying to do it as gracefully as possible, there were other people arriving and doormen at the entrance that she didn't want to look foolish in front of. She felt very much out of her comfort zone in this place. She suddenly thought back to the last time she'd been taken somewhere like this, not on a date, but by her father on one of the few times she visited him in Manhattan. It did not go well and the memory sent shivers up her spine.

As Mark led her up the steps she frantically tried to

remember the order of forks and spoons. It looked like the kind of place that would have multiple courses. She felt her heart racing slightly as they walked into the reception. She took a deep breath to try to calm herself as Mark helped her out of her coat and handed it, along with her gloves and scarf, to the waiting coat check attendant, followed by his own coat and scarf. Eleanor gripped her small clutch to keep from fidgeting with her hands. Mark looked so sure and confident as he guided her into the restaurant. It was beautiful, truly stunning. And Eleanor thought she saw Daniel Craig and Rachel Weisz at one of the corner tables. She couldn't have felt more out of her element than she did in that moment. Mark helped her into her seat and there was a flurry of activity as various servers poured wine and opened menus with a flourish. Eleanor tried not to make a face when she saw the prices. This was way too much. She should have made Mark tell her where they were going beforehand. She felt so ungrateful for not just going along and enjoying it. She knew other women would likely give anything to be out with a guy like Mark and in a restaurant like this. She felt her heart start to pound again.

Noticing the creeping signs of distress on Eleanor's face, Mark asked with concern, "Is everything alright Elle?"

Trying to cover, "Yes, it's lovely. Just a bit more than I was expecting." She smiled to try to hide her anxiety.

"Well, you deserve it. We're celebrating remember? I figured we'd celebrate in style."

"Côte Brasserie or Belgos would have been sufficient Mark. You didn't have to go to all this trouble."

"It's no trouble Elle, really. My parents know the owners. I can get a table here any time. And Côte or Belgos is not where I wanted to take you tonight. You deserve something more special than that. Now, what looks good? Tonight you'll have anything you want."

Eleanor knew he was trying to make her feel better but,

if anything, she just felt worse. This was too much for what was technically only their second date. She tried to calm her nerves and look at the menu. They soon ordered and Eleanor let herself get lost in the conversation, trying to make Mark do most of the talking. It was pretty easy, he was in the middle of a big project at school himself and Eleanor kept asking him questions, letting it distract her from her discomfort. Dinner went by in a blur, she tried not to drink too much champagne, she nearly gasped when it arrived thinking about the cost and she prayed that maybe it was a complimentary perk because of who Mark's family were. She tried to avoid ordering dessert but Mark insisted. Eleanor continued to try to keep up with the conversation and be pleasant company, but her back was starting to ache from sitting up straight — she wasn't about to slouch or lean back against her chair in this place — and her head was starting to hurt from the internal struggle to make sure she was saying and doing the right things. She knew she should just relax, and she'd hoped the champagne would help with that but mentally adding up the costs of the evening was just stressing her out again.

"Are you alright sugar?" Mark's voice broke through Eleanor's interior dialogue, one side stressing out, the other side trying to chill out and enjoy herself. She startled slightly at Mark's use of "sugar." Again, it just sounded odd to her ears. She wasn't sure how she felt about him being so familiar after only a couple dates. She'd gotten used to her friends using terms like darling or babe or luv, she figured they were just more common here in England but sugar felt extra familiar and personal. After the way they'd been kissing she supposed it was a natural progression, but it also seemed a bit forward considering she wasn't sure they were technically a couple. Eleanor felt so confused.

"Yes, I'm fine. Just a bit tired I guess. It's been a rough past few days since I last saw you," Eleanor said with a small sigh.

"Poor baby. I'm sorry, I hope you're having fun tonight, that's all I wanted," Mark replied. Eleanor could tell he was trying to be charming, but again she found herself cringing inwardly at his word choice. She really wasn't sure how she felt about him calling her "baby," it felt even more familiar, and not a little demeaning, than sugar. She felt like she'd missed a step in the relationship and was trying to catch up to where Mark was.

"Eleanor?" she heard him say, and she realized she'd missed what he'd said.

"Sorry, yes?" she replied apologetically.

"Do you want to get out of here? We don't have to stay if you don't want to. You've been quieter than usual tonight, was the choice of restaurant not to your liking?"

Mark looked so concerned, Eleanor didn't have the heart to tell him that she would have preferred somewhere else, so she lied, "No, the restaurant is lovely! This whole night has been incredible. I'm sorry I've been quiet, I really have just been interested in your project. We don't have to leave if you don't want to."

"We could go somewhere else? You could come back to my place...?" Mark asked suggested.

The hopeful tone of voice combined with the last suggestion sent up a red flag in the back of Eleanor's mind.

"Your place?" she repeated with confusion. "I'm not sure that's really a good idea, do you?"

Looking slightly thrown, for the first time since she'd met him, Mark slowly placed his hand on top of hers and replied, "I really fancy you Eleanor, a lot. I was thinking maybe you could come back to mine after this and we could have another drink? And chat some more perhaps and, you know, just see..." he trailed off, tracing a circle over the back of her hand with his thumb, giving her a look that shot straight through her and landed like a ton of bricks in her

124

brain. Mark may have been trying to be seductive, and for any other woman he probably would have succeeded. But for Eleanor it just flipped a switch in her brain.

"Just see what Mark? If I would sleep with you?" Eleanor asked bluntly, pulling her hand out of his and clasping both her hands in her lap. If her napkin had been paper instead of the finest linen she would have been shredding it to pieces.

Trying to maintain his seduction routine and this time not picking up her obvious discomfort, "Well, baby, if you want to. I think you are amazing Elle, I've thought so since the first night you came to the pub with Jonathan," he leaned towards her, trying to close the gap between them, "I love kissing you. I think we'd be wonderful together. Would you like that?"

A million thoughts collided in Eleanor's brain at the same time, part of her wanted to take up Mark on what he was offering, wondering what it would be like. Another part felt scared and just wanted to be home under her duvet. But instead she heard a voice that didn't even sound like hers. A voice that had been long hidden during her people pleasing childhood with a hard to please father and a long relationship with a man who preferred to hear her only when she was in agreement with him.

"No Mark. I would not like that. I like you too, but I'm not going home with you tonight," she replied plainly. "And if that's what all of this was about then you are very mistaken and I doubt you even know me at all. Did you really think I was the type of woman who would go home with you after a couple dates and a lavish meal at a fancy restaurant? We may have known each other for a while now but this is only our second date. Do I owe you something because you brought me here?" She spat out the last word like it was a dagger and she felt her blood starting to boil. How could she have been so stupid?! She felt like she'd walked herself right into this miserable situation. She wasn't ready for this. She had no business being out on a date with Mark.

Mark, to his credit, looked suitably shocked and horrified that his plan had gone so wrong. "I'm s-sorry," he stammered. "Of course not baby—"

"—Don't call me 'baby' please. It's a bit familiar don't you think?" Eleanor fired back, perhaps more forcefully than the situation required but she felt cornered, and fight or flight mode was kicking in.

"Eleanor, I'm sorry. I don't mean to make you feel uncomfortable and I didn't mean to pressure you or disrespect you," Mark insisted, trying to back pedal and regain some footing in the conversation.

"Oh, don't worry Mark," Eleanor said with a definite edge to her voice, "no one pressures me into anything. Look, you seemed to be a great guy and I liked you. I really enjoyed our last date and tonight had been lovely, until now. But no matter where you took me tonight I wasn't going back to your place with you. I'm sorry but I'm just not ready for that, with you or anyone else." Eleanor suddenly felt very tired, not just tired from the long day and long week but a fatigue that had been building since long before she got to London. She also felt sad. She'd been so hopeful for her time here but tonight she felt like she was just messing everything up. The progress she thought she'd made was just superficial. Placing her napkin on the table and picking up her clutch she started to rise from her seat. "I'm sorry for spoiling the evening Mark, it really was lovely, I'm sorry you wasted it on me. I'm going to leave now."

Jumping up and rushing to her side, Mark exclaimed, "Elle...Eleanor, I'm sorry, really. You didn't spoil anything, please don't think that. This is all my fault. I put what I wanted ahead of what you needed. Of course, I understand now, that you aren't ready. I just thought, we'd hit it off nicely and you were on the same path I was. I totally misread you. In my defense, well, you're gorgeous and easy to talk to…Please, don't let this spoil things between us. I can slow down, we don't have to rush. Please!"

Feeling defeated, she said sadly, "Mark, I don't know what I want. And it's unfair to keep you hanging while I figure it out. I value our friendship, I don't want to ruin that."

Placing his hand on her arm, and then removing it quickly for fear of offending her, Mark said in a rush, "You're not ruining anything, I am. I'm so sorry. Look, we can slow down. Take some steps backward. If you don't want to be in a relationship right now, I understand. But please don't ask me to stop seeing you entirely or to see you only as a friend. I couldn't bear that. Don't answer now, think about it. I'll take you home now."

"I can get home on my own, you don't have to take me," Eleanor insisted.

"I could never live with myself if I let you leave by yourself. And Jonathan would kill me."

"Jonathan is not my keeper. I can go home by myself if I want. And to be honest I could use some air and time to myself. Trust me, you're off the hook."

"Eleanor, please, let me take you home. You don't have to say another word, just let me get you home safely."

Not having any energy left to argue, Eleanor simply shrugged her shoulders and nodded. Without another word between them Mark quickly paid for the meal and they collected their coats and Eleanor silently accepted Mark's help getting her coat on. They walked out to a waiting taxi and Eleanor beat Mark to the door, opening it quickly for herself and swiftly sliding all the way across to the other side. She heard Mark sigh and get in behind her. They drove back across town, sitting in a heavy silence.

When the taxi pulled up in front of the flat Eleanor quickly got out but Mark was faster coming around from the other side, "Eleanor, wait, don't just run away." He quickly paid the driver and the cab sped off. "Eleanor, please, let me walk you upstairs."

Eleanor turned to look at him and said apologetically, "I'm sorry Mark, I really am. You planned this lovely evening and I messed everything up. I thought I was ready. New life, new me, and all that. But I'm not ready for this. You clearly want so much more than I'm able to give you right now. I don't think I've really changed that much, not as much as people seem to think at least. You should be with someone who is in the same place as you, not someone who's struggling to keep up." Eleanor felt tears prick her eyes and she knew she needed to get upstairs and fast. "Mark, you've done nothing wrong, this is all me. I'm sorry. I'm just not ready. Good night." Eleanor turned on her heel and quickly let herself in through the building door. Not wanting to wait for the lift she used what little energy she had left to fly up the stairs. All she wanted was to get into the flat and into her room. Arriving at the front door she turned her key in the lock and burst into the flat, colliding with Jonathan in the hallway.

"Back already?" he asked curiously. Then he took in the frantic look on Eleanor's face and the tears welling up in her eyes, threatening to spill any moment. "What did he do?! Ellie, are you ok? Are you hurt? What did Mark do?!"

"Oh come off it Jon, Mark didn't *do* anything, he was a perfect gentleman. Or at least he was after I told him I wasn't going to sleep with him tonight."

"He thought you were going to sleep with him?! I'm going to kill him," Jonathan thundered.

Eyes flashing in anger, Eleanor was suddenly feeling very angry again and was not too concerned in the moment about taking that anger out on Jonathan. "You will do nothing of the sort Jonathan McNeil! I can take care of my own business thank you very much. And I will not have you punishing Mark for misreading the situation. He had no way of knowing I wasn't ready. I'd certainly been kissing him enthusiastically enough the last couple times we've seen each other. He's not to blame for tonight, I am."

Backing away from the fierceness of Eleanor's angry outburst, Jonathan put his hands up in a placating manner. "Ok, ok, I won't kill him. But Ellie, are you sure you're alright? Whatever happened it *wasn't* your fault. I don't care how many times you'd kissed him or how enthusiastically you did so. Mark should have known better than to try to seduce you on your second date. I don't know what possessed him, he never moves this fast with women."

"I don't know Jon. He says he fancies me. And I believe him. I just don't know if I feel the same way. I like him a lot but I'm not sure I'm ready to get involved with someone else so soon. Or at least I'm not sure I want to get involved with him. I...," Eleanor broke off, not sure she should continue.

"Ellie, what is it?" Jonathan asked with concern. "Here, come sit down." He gently led her into the lounge, taking off her coat and scarf and wrapping a throw blanket around her shoulders.

Eleanor, feeling deflated, sank into the sofa as Jonathan walked back to the kitchen, coming back a moment later with two glasses and a bottle of whiskey. He poured a small glass for Eleanor and in response to the disgusted look she gave him, ordered, "You're freezing. This will warm you up. Drink it. And continue with what you were going to say before you decided to censor yourself."

Sipping at the drink, feeling it burn at the back of her throat, Eleanor started, "he's your friend Jonathan, it's not fair for me to put you in this position."

"Sod him. You're like a sister to me Ellie, and I told him

at the beginning that he better not hurt you. You come first and he knew that."

"I don't want this to ruin your friendship. He was nothing but kind and polite, and absolutely horrified with himself when I told him how I felt about the situation. I feel so bad for him Jonathan! He didn't do anything wrong other than move things along too quickly. He took me to a lovely restaurant. It's a shame he wasted it on me. I wanted to enjoy it but you know how I feel about extravagant places."

"Oh Ellie, I'm sorry. That was my fault. He told me where he was taking you. I didn't even think about that time in New York with your dad. Mark was just so excited he'd managed to get a table, and you'd seemed fine at the club the other week."

"We were in a large group at the club. And it wasn't a formal dinner setting, it was a club," she said with a small voice. After taking another sip of whiskey, "I like Mark. He seems like a great guy and I'm flattered he likes me. He's funny and kind and generous and gorgeous. Any woman with half a brain would be attracted to him. But while I enjoy hanging out with him I don't feel like we have that much common. I feel like he could just be a different version of Michael." Noticing Jonathan about to jump to Mark's defense, "I don't mean he's *like* Michael, just that I feel kind of similar to how I felt with Michael, just in a different way. I feel like I'm just going along with it and letting Mark determine where things go. It's partially my fault that things went so badly tonight, I could have insisted on knowing where we were going. I could have suggested something that wouldn't have felt so high pressure. I could have put the brakes on a bit. But I've just been going along and letting Mark think that I was ok with everything. And I'm not. I'm not ready to be in a relationship. At least not with Mark. I don't feel like myself when I'm with him. I

130

thought that was because I'm a 'new person' as everyone keeps telling me. But I'm still the old me, with all the same issues. Just new hair and a new wardrobe," she finished, smiling bitterly.

"Aww, Ellie. You're still getting over things. That's understandable. Mark's a big boy. You need to focus on yourself and do what you need to do to take care of you and to figure out what you want. And if that's Mark, then he'll have to be patient. And if it's not, he'll have to accept that."

"I wish I knew what that was..." Eleanor's voice trailed off in thought. "I'm just so tired. I can't think straight."

"For now, go to sleep. Tomorrow you'll think of something."

Eleanor went to her room, still wrapped in the throw blanket, kicked off her heels, and collapsed on her bed.

Chapter 9

The next day dawned brightly through her window, a beautiful sunny day in late fall. Eleanor groaned realizing she'd fallen asleep, still dressed and with all her makeup on. She crawled out of bed and stripped out of her clothes, and dragged herself into the shower. An hour later she was clean and feeling human again. Jonathan was back from a seminar.

"So, any ideas what you want to do?" he asked brightly.

Glumly twirling her teaspoon in her mug, "No, as a matter of fact, I do not."

"Hey," Jonathan replied laughing, "I didn't mean as far as life goals or solutions. But you need to do something. Get out of town or go lose yourself in a museum, you haven't done that in a while. Though I vote out of town. You should take a day trip or something."

Perking up at the idea, "A day trip? I hadn't thought of that. Leave London?"

"Sometimes we all need to get out of London for a day. You could go to Bath, you could stay the night at mum's. There's a lot of Jane Austen stuff there. Or Winchester, where she's buried? Ummm, Cardiff is cool, I know how much you like *Doctor Who*," Jonathan suggested helpfully.

"I don't think I'm in the mood for anything related to

Jane Austen or romance. And I'd rather wait to go to Bath when Aunt Vickie is home, she's still in New York. Cardiff would be fun, how far is that?" Eleanor asked, warming to the idea of going somewhere.

"About two hours I reckon, little more maybe?"

"Hmm, is there anything closer?"

"Sure, it's not the time of year for the beach, so maybe not Brighton. But Cambridge isn't far. Neither is Oxford."

"Oxford! How far is Oxford?"

"Only an hour, really close. You want to go to Oxford? I can give you some recommendations of things to do and places to see."

"Yes, that would be great," Eleanor said brightly, feeling better than she'd felt in days.

It was too late to go that day, so Eleanor puttered around the flat for a while and went for a walk while Jonathan went to the library to work. But that evening they sat down and Jonathan helped her purchase train tickets online and dug out an old map of Oxford and started circling places and marking things Eleanor should do.

* * * * *

The next morning Eleanor got up early and took the Central Line from Holborn to Oxford Circus and switched to the Bakerloo Line, getting off at Paddington Station. She collected her tickets from the machine and waited under the electronic departure signs until her train platform number flashed up. Clutching her latte from Caffè Nero and shrugging her bag filled with her iPad, notebook, map, and list of sights, she excitedly boarded her train. Soon she was being whisked away from London. The city gave way to suburbs and soon to open countryside. For the first time since she left Phoenix, Eleanor could look out for miles to the horizon and not see buildings.

As the train pulled into Oxford, Eleanor gave another look at her map. Getting from the station to the city center looked easy enough and Jonathan had described it to her as well. At first glance, taking in the large, modern business school across from the station and the standard off-license shops and dry cleaners across the road in the other direction, Oxford didn't seem that different from some of the outer areas of London. But as she walked across the bridge over the Thames, or the Isis as it was known out here, she could make out the top of Oxford Castle and the Mound.

Walking up the road she soon came to the center of town. Being that it was late fall, Jonathan told her there likely wouldn't be a whole lot of tourists and looking around Eleanor was relieved to see he was right. Most of the people walking by looked like locals, particularly students and university workers. All the students looked so smart, dressed casually, wearing jeans, tweed blazers, thick wool jumpers, lace up brogues, and nearly all of them were carrying a leather satchel of some kind or backpack, and many had a bicycle helmet clipped to the strap of their bag. Eleanor was pleased with her outfit for the day and felt she fit in well in her dark skinny jeans, tall brown boots, wool blazer with the fine navy and rust brown hounds tooth pattern, cream scarf wrapped several times around her neck, and her hair piled high on her head. The weather had called for clouds so she skipped her contacts and was wearing her glasses and though her bag wasn't a satchel, the distressed brown leather shoulder bag matched her boots.

She spent the next hour and a bit poking around the shops on Queen Street and Cornmarket, a lot of them the same high street shops she could find in London, but she did find some interesting little shops in the Covered Market and picked up a couple small trinkets and some new hand lotion from a shop that sold a bunch of amazing body and skin care. Leaving the Covered Market, she decided to look at the map. Even though it would be cold, Jonathan suggested visiting University Parks and walking around there for some peace and quiet. She decided to start there and wind her way back through town before getting dinner somewhere later in the evening. She headed straight out to the park, passing by some of Oxford's most impressive sights. On her right was the History of Science Museum, the Sheldonian Theatre, and the Bodleian Library. On the left, Blackwell's bookshop and the "New" Bodleian, the Weston Library, which still looked older than most buildings back in Phoenix. She walked around the corner and headed down Parks Road, passing Trinity and Wadham Colleges and the gothic looking Pitt Rivers Museum, then the impressive red-bricked Keble College.

She thought that Oxford had a very different energy to London. It had that quintessential "college town" feel. Like she had grown up with in Cambridge, Massachusetts and kind of like Tucson, Arizona when she was at U of A, though the scenery was very different here than in Tucson, she thought, laughing to herself as she gathered her scarf more tightly around her neck. She loved Oxford. She'd only been in town a few hours and already she knew she'd have to come back soon. Finally, she came up to the gates of the park and walked through, seeing the expansive playing fields stretched out before her. She took the path to the far right and walked along the far edge of the park.

It was quiet. And very peaceful. Every now and then a jogger would pass her or she'd pass someone sitting on one of the benches along the path or someone out walking their dog. She kept to the path, ignoring the ones that seemed to split off to the middle of the park until it eventually made her turn left or leave at another gate at this end. She could tell she was by a river and a check of the map told her she must have been at the opposite end of the park from where she'd started, where the River Cherwell bordered the south end. She saw the trail meet with another one up ahead, as she approached the main trail she heard a voice from just over her left shoulder.

"Eleanor?"

She turned suddenly towards the voice and found herself bouncing back off of whoever the voice belonged to. Stumbling backwards slightly she looked up into the eyes of Patrick Reynolds just as he reached his arms around her to keep her from falling.

Grinning, "We really need to stop meeting like this. If you want my arms around you all you have to do is ask," he said smoothly.

Pushing herself out of his embrace and tugging at the hem of her blazer to straighten herself out a bit, she replied tersely, "well maybe if you would quit startling me I'd be able to keep my balance and wouldn't need you to put your arms around me. Believe me, I don't make a habit of throwing myself into the arms of strange men."

"So I'm just lucky then?" Patrick replied, raising his right eyebrow in the way she'd seen him do a million times in his films.

Stammering in reply, "I-I-um...well..."

Patrick tried to stifle a laugh, as he looked at Eleanor, blushing and trying to come up with a response, he couldn't help but think she was absolutely adorable. Taking pity on her obvious discomfort, his expression shifting to the picture of contrition, "I'm sorry, really, I'm being rude, I just meant to tease. I really am sorry I keep barreling into you every time we meet. And I shouldn't be so cheeky, I don't mean to make you uncomfortable. I really am very happy to see you though."

His smile was so genuine and lit up his entire face, it nearly took Eleanor's breath away looking at him this close up. "Happy to see me? Why?" she asked, trying to figure out why on earth he'd want to see her again.

"You looked so dazzling at your party the other week. I haven't been able to get you out of my mind. Of course, you had so many good looking blokes hanging around you that night, I figured I didn't stand a chance."

"Blokes?" she repeated dumbly. "My cousin's friends? Yeah, they're a good group. Oh! And thank you, so much, for the champagne you sent over. That was very sweet of you. Incredibly sweet," she finished in a rush, hoping she sounded appreciative enough.

"Any time, I was happy to do it," he replied kindly. "So...none of those guys were with you in particular?"

"Well, no, not really. I mean, well...it's complicated," she finished, sighing with exasperation over her current situation with Mark. "To be honest, I'm trying not to think about it. But if you're asking if any of those men have any sort of 'claim' on me, no. They don't."

Noticing her defensive tone and the way her brow was knitting together, Patrick put his hands up and took a small step back, as if in retreat. "Hey, you don't need to give me any explanations. I was merely curious if you were single and I could risk asking you for a pint without having to duel at dawn with some guy back in London." He gave her a shy smile and Eleanor felt her heart stop for a second.

"No, dueling would not be necessary," she heard herself answer, a bit shocked to think that she was standing in University Parks...in Oxford...flirting...with Patrick Reynolds. THE Patrick Reynolds. He was standing there, less than a foot away from her. Her boots had a slight heel, but even still he towered above her and the way he was looking down at her right now...she shook her head slightly, trying to clear her mind, and took a substantial step backward to put some more space between them.

"I'm sorry," she said in a rush, "I didn't mean to run into

you like that again. You'd think I'd be better at watching where I'm going at this point."

"Really, it was my fault," he said sincerely, "I could tell you were lost in thought, I should have found a better way of approaching you. I was just very happy to see you again, I couldn't believe my luck, I was just thinking about you too."

"Thinking about me?" Eleanor kicked herself mentally, she really needed to stop repeating everything he said to her. *He's going to think I'm a parrot*, she thought, annoyed at herself.

"Yeah, as I've been walking around the park here I've just been thinking about the times we've run into each other and kicking myself for not taking advantage of each situation to ask you out for a drink. I was thinking about asking one of the hostesses at the club if they could get a message to you. So, I guess...now that I have you here and there's no one else to distract you...I'd love to have a drink with you and chat, get to know you a bit? I mean, we do seem to have a habit of running into each other, so maybe it's destiny?" He said with a slightly embarrassed laugh.

He looked so shy and unsure all of a sudden, the complete opposite of how he always seemed on film or in interviews. His normally confident and smooth voice now stammered and stopped, trying to find the right words, uncertainty mixed with hopefulness.

"A drink would be nice...although, it's not even quite noon yet. And I haven't eaten since breakfast, so...coffee might be more appropriate than alcohol," Eleanor replied with a shy smile of her own.

"Well, if you haven't eaten since breakfast, how about lunch? I know a good place not far. Have you been to Oxford before?"

"Not since I was little, this is my first time since moving to London in August. My cousin gave me a list of places to go and things to do, this was the first one I thought I'd check off. And lunch would be good, I am starting to feel a bit peckish, as you all would say," she said with a grin.

Smiling widely, "Well, we'll have to fix that. Permit me to walk with you around the remainder of the park and then I shall take you for lunch," he said with mock formality, like the 19th century heroes he'd played on screen, holding out the crook of his arm expectantly.

Laughing, and playing along, Eleanor slipped her arm through his and said, "I accept your kind offer sir, thank you."

Their arms relaxed into each other and they walked arm in arm along the Cherwell.

"So, what brought you to Oxford?" Patrick asked inquisitively.

Thinking for a moment, "I'm not sure. I mean, I've read some books set here and have heard about and seen the famous buildings like the Radcliffe Camera and St. Mary's and the Bodleian. Both my parents are academics, so I grew up around university towns. I came here once, when I was little. My dad was presenting at a conference here one summer and we took a family trip to London, coming out here for the weekend of the conference…"

Patrick noticed her voice trail off, and saw her face cloud over slightly. She was back in Oxford, so he didn't think it was a bad memory of her visit that she was thinking of, but something was clearly bothering her. Attempting to change the subject slightly, "So, what have you seen then so far today?"

Snapping out of her memories, "Umm, not a lot yet. I've walked by a few things on my way here but I was going to start here and then explore things in more detail on my way back."

"Brilliant! Let me be your tour guide!" Patrick exclaimed enthusiastically.

"You want to show me around? Don't you have anything better to do with your day?" Eleanor replied, a little more dismissively than she intended.

"I grew up here, I love showing people around my town. I don't have any other plans, I'm just in town visiting my parents and getting away from work for a few days. I'm in between projects at the moment," he responded with a sincere smile. "Please? I really would love to show you around, and it would give us time to chat and get to know each other a bit more."

"Alright, if you're sure it's not an imposition." She mentally kicked herself, was she kidding herself, this was THE Patrick Reynolds practically begging to spend time with HER! And she almost pushed him away!

"Not at all. It will be a delight."

By now they were going around the duck pond in the park and Eleanor couldn't quite believe the sudden turn the day had taken. It seemed so surreal to be here, walking arm in arm, with one of her favorite celebrities. Though she wasn't thinking of the celebrity bit, obviously not, since she almost turned down his request to show her around Oxford. He was so easy and natural to talk to. For the rest of the walk through the park she lost herself in their conversation. Telling him about her life in London and the work she was doing at school. Him answering her questions about his most recent projects and things he had coming up.

It turned out he had been working on a play in the West End back in August when they first bumped into each other. He'd been on his way to the theatre early for the performance that night. Eleanor had been aware of him doing the play, but tickets had sold out in June for the remainder of the run so when Eleanor arrived in August she'd put the play out of her mind. Now he was reading a bunch of different scripts and auditioning for different things. By the time they walked out of the park and back up the same road she'd taken to get there, he was telling her about growing up in Oxford and getting his undergraduate degree here. They bonded over their mutual studies in English as they walked up to the Kings Arms pub, kitty corner from the Bodleian Library.

"I used to come here after studying all afternoon in the library when I was at uni here," he explained, holding the door of the pink painted building on the corner of the road.

"I'm jealous. There were never any bars this close to the library at any of the schools where I attended," Eleanor said with a laugh.

Looking confused, Patrick asked "Where were they then?"

Laughing, "Campus wasn't broken up into distinct colleges like this, the whole university made up the campus, and alcohol isn't allowed on campus. So you had to walk off campus a bit to get to the bars. And even then, there weren't any cool places like this," Eleanor explained, looking around. "Not to mention, back home the legal drinking age is 21. It's 18 here in the UK, isn't it?

"Yes, it is. But still, no bars on campus. That's cruel and unusual for those that are of age" Patrick said dismissively, then laughed, "It's like they expected you all to learn or something." Eleanor laughed as well. Patrick walked them up to the side counter where you made food and non-alcoholic orders and turned to Eleanor, "What would you like Eleanor?" he asked politely with a wide smile.

"Umm, fish and chips?" she replied and the woman behind the till nodded. Eleanor scanned the list of tea and then added, "And a cup of PG Tips."

"Good choice," Patrick said with a smile, then made his order, "fish and chips for me too, and a cup of Earl Grey."

Eleanor started to pull her wallet out of her bag, but as soon as Patrick saw he exclaimed, "Don't you dare, this is my treat."

Still uncertain after her experience the other night with Mark, Eleanor kept reaching into her wallet and pulled out enough to cover her share and handed it to Patrick, saying firmly, "That's very kind of you but completely unnecessary. And I insist."

Something in her eyes told Patrick that she meant it, and he instinctively felt that if he didn't accept her money she might bolt for the door. He'd known some independent women before but there was more than independence in her eyes, there was also a tinge of fear. Smiling to try to put her at ease once more, he accepted the cash, determined to find some way to return it to her.

"Thank you," she said simply, but Patrick could hear the relief in her voice.

"Let's go sit," he replied. They grabbed their teas and Patrick took the board with their order number on it. He didn't know where her mind had gone just then but it didn't look like a very happy place, he was determined to get her smiling and laughing again. They walked around to the other side of the bar to a small room in the back. There was a fire going in the fire place and a selection of couches and arm chairs. Patrick turned to look at Eleanor for approval and asked, "is here good or would you rather a proper table?"

Immediately falling in love with the fireplace and the cozy atmosphere Eleanor replied enthusiastically, "this is perfect!"

She went straight for the small sofa across the room next to the fireplace. Patrick, not wanting to make her feel more uncomfortable than he worried he already had, chose to sit across the coffee table from her in the arm chair in front of the fireplace. As she sat down Patrick could see Eleanor visibly relax and get comfortable, the glow of the fireplace making her eyes sparkle even more.

"So tell me more about school back in the States?" he

asked kindly.

"What do you want to know? I just attended a couple of the state universities. Nothing special."

"Yes, but you went to graduate school, I'm jealous. I always thought I'd try it one day, but then got sidetracked," Patrick said, appearing wistful, if not even slightly regretful.

"Sidetracked? Oh yes, by RADA and then a successful acting career. I wish I could get sidetracked like that," Eleanor replied with a laugh, thinking it must have been wonderful to be accepted to the Royal Academy of Drama Arts.

Looking chastised, "Well, yes, I got very lucky after uni, getting into drama school. It was a great experience and one that worked out positively. But still, I envy that you were able to spend more time studying and learning."

"Well, it's never too late to go back to grad school," Eleanor said very matter-of-fact. "You're never too old to pursue higher learning. Or at least that's what my father always told me."

Noticing the flicker of a frown pass across Eleanor's features Patrick asked softly, "And is that what you want to do? Is that why you're here in England?"

Looking up at him across the top of her tea cup as she went for another sip, "Umm, in a way. I'm doing a special MFA program in creative writing. So technically I guess I am back in grad school, just *not* the type of program my father always hoped," she explained, her frown deepening as she thought about it.

"I'm sorry, sore subject?"

Seeing the concern in his eyes, "No, I'm sorry, it's not that big of a deal. I've learned to live with being a disappointment to him."

"Surely he doesn't see you as a disappointment."

"I honestly have no idea. We don't really speak

anymore. And I don't visit him. The last time I did...well, it ended badly. Honestly, he's a bigger disappointment to me than I could possibly be to him, not that he would see it that way." Noticing the deepening concern in Patrick's face, Eleanor quickly changed gears of the conversation, "Anyway, that's my sad little story. It's fine. My issues with my father are the last things I want to talk about right now."

Smiling slightly, eyes practically twinkling, Patrick said, "Alright, change of subject then. Favorite thing about England so far."

Eleanor smiled brightly back and they spent the next two hours sitting, happily chatting about London and Oxford and other places Patrick insisted Eleanor visit. Eleanor had a brief thought a couple times about how remarkable this day was becoming: running into Patrick again, having lunch with him, talking with him and feeling more like friends than actor and fan, it was all too surreal. After they'd talked extensively on the topic of London, they left the pub and Patrick led Eleanor on a walking tour of central Oxford and all of its iconic sights. He knew lots of facts about the city and all its iconic landmarks. They started with the Sheldonian Theatre and Bodleian Library and Patrick indulged Eleanor's need to stop in to the gift shop. She knew her mom would love something from there. Then they walked back through the courtyard and went out through the opposite archway than they'd arrived through and Eleanor suddenly saw the Radcliffe Camera building once they came through the other side.

It had always looked impressive in the pictures but seeing it looming above her it was even more impressive. Cylindrical with a large dome on top, it's golden stone facade with arched doors and windows along the lower level and columns around the upper level, Eleanor had always wondered what it would be like to go inside.

As if reading her thoughts Patrick said, "I wish I could

get you inside today. You'd love it in there."

Incredulously, "You've been inside?!" Eleanor exclaimed.

"Of course," Patrick replied with a laugh, "The Bodleian is the library for all Oxford students. I loved the upper reading room in the Radcliffe, that's where I did most of my studying."

"I can't believe that is your 'school library.' You all are so spoiled!"

"What was your library like then?"

"Well, at ASU, Hayden Library is nice enough, it certainly had everything I needed for my research. So did the main library at U of A. But both were built in the 1970s or sometime around then. They're nothing like this!"

Grinning at her excitement, "Well come on then. If you like it from down here, you'll love it from a little higher up."

"What do you mean? Higher up?"

"You afraid of heights?" He said raising an eyebrow.

"No, just curious what you're talking about," Eleanor replied laughing.

"You'll see," Patrick said cryptically.

He walked them around the building and soon another building behind the Radcliffe came into view. Eleanor found herself walking in to the University Church of St. Mary. Patrick left her to stare in wonder at the beauty of the church for a moment and when she looked over at him she noticed him handing over a few coins to the undergraduate age girls behind the souvenir counter, chatting with them politely. Both girls were looking at Patrick shyly and grinning nervously, when he was finished at the counter they both said, "bye Patrick!" and as he walked towards Eleanor they both started giggling and quietly shrieking.

"Friends of yours?" Eleanor asked casually.

"Sometimes it feels like I'm friends with all of Oxford. Between growing up here and meeting a lot of people throughout my childhood and uni time here. And now people recognizing me a little more from my work, people are always saying hello and goodbye but I've stopped being able to remember if I actually know them or not," he explained looking a bit embarrassed. Before she could ask him more questions, Patrick grabbed her by the hand and started leading her towards a doorway off to the side.

"Follow me," he said mischievously.

Follow him she did, and soon Eleanor found herself navigating upwards along one set of twisting and climbing stairs after another.

"Is the fame thing hard to deal with?" Eleanor asked, partly out of curiosity and partly to distract herself from all the stairs.

"Well, thankfully, I don't have to deal with it that much. Film premieres or outside the stage door after a performance can get a big wild. And if I happen to cross the path of paparazzi who're trying to get a shot of a bigger celebrity, they'll take my picture if they recognize me fast enough. But they don't hang out in front of my place. On my own, I'm not worth enough for the tabloids to stalk me. Thank goodness. I honestly get more response from people in Oxford, because I do know a lot of people here and over the years as my career has grown I've gotten more coverage in the local press back here."

"Local boy does good?" Eleanor teased lightly.

Laughing, "Exactly. I'm not the only person in the entertainment industry from Oxford, there are a few of us and Oxford is usually happy to claim us as their own. But still, the fame thing, as you put it, has never been that crazy or hard. I haven't had to change much in the way I go about my daily life. In London, I might occasionally get recognized and asked for an autograph or a selfie, which I'm happy to do, but here in Oxford it really does just feel like everybody knows me, and we're all old friends, even if

I can't remember all their names. Honestly, sometimes I worry about my career getting any bigger. I want to keep pushing myself with the projects I take on but I don't want my life to change too much from how it is now. My agent and manager keep pushing me towards projects they think will be a career breakthrough and make me an international household name. Neither of them was that thrilled with me doing the play back in the summer, but I'd been dying to work with that director since I started drama school."

It was interesting hearing Patrick talk about this side of his career and hearing his thoughts on the progression of his career and project opportunities.

"So you're not trying to get more projects in Hollywood?" Eleanor asked.

"Don't get me wrong, I'm not opposed to expanding my career options, but I'm not intentionally working towards being a bigger part of the American film scene. My main requirements for choosing a job is to do with the script and the production team. Is the script good? Do I respect the director and want to work with them? Will the project challenge my acting skills and help me grow? If the answer is yes to those questions then I seriously consider the job. So far all the projects that have met those requirements have been here in the UK. BBC film adaptations or West End plays or productions with the National Theatre or small British indie films. And I'm happy with that. But there are some possible scripts coming up for bigger projects and a couple of them are really exciting, even though I know they'd introduce me to a much bigger audience. Sometimes getting to do the really cool projects means accepting losing a little bit more of my anonymity when out in public."

As the stairways got narrower Patrick maneuvered Eleanor in front of him and whenever she felt herself get a little off balance from the steepness of the stairs she became well aware of Patrick's strong arms and chest behind her.

"Almost there," she heard him say, and as she looked upwards from the steps immediately in front of her she could see sky through an open door.

She stepped out into the walkway that seemed to go around the edge of the tower of the church and looked out over the chest high wall that protected them from falling off. Spread out before her was all of Oxford and the surrounding countryside. Stunned by how beautiful it was, she stopped in her tracks and just stared.

"You like the view?" Patrick asked, standing close behind her.

"Like?! Like doesn't even begin to cover it." Eleanor's words came out in almost a whisper, the view had truly taken her breath away. It was a mostly cloudy day, but in the distance she could see some breaks in the clouds and the rays of sun beaming down on the distant countryside. "This is an incredible view! I mean, Arizona has its share of sweeping landscapes but this is gorgeous. We don't have views like this back home. It's so…green! It's like a story book."

Looking down at her and smiling Patrick said, "I've never been to Arizona. Is it anything like California?"

Eleanor threw her head back and laughed, and Patrick thought in that moment that she was more beautiful than the view stretching out before them.

Laughing, "If you're comparing it to LA or Northern California, then no, Arizona is nothing like California. Even the California desert, the Mohave, is different from Arizona's Sonoran Desert. I suppose Phoenix is similar to LA in some ways. Large, very spread out, lots of highways and cars, good shopping and dining. We don't have movie stars though," she finished with a sly look towards Patrick and then blushed when he winked at her.

"Oh yes, all of us movie stars wandering around LA, can't walk more than a few feet without bumping into one of us," he said with exaggerated seriousness.

Wryly, "I can't seem to walk more than a few feet without bumping into you."

"Well, that's just because I'm a clumsy git who can't watch where I'm walking."

Eleanor laughed again and Patrick thought it would be worth it to make it his mission to make her laugh as much as possible just so he could hear that sound.

They stood up there for a while looking at the views from three sides of the building and taking some pictures. It felt like ages but Eleanor noticed it had only been thirty minutes. They slowly made their way back down the stairs and out of the church and Patrick led them back through the Bodleian courtyard and then past the Sheldonian Theatre. Eleanor was about to ask where he was taking her next when a sight in front of them made her stop in her tracks and then start to grin from ear to ear.

Leaning down and smiling, Patrick said, "I thought you might appreciate a stop at Blackwell's bookshop."

Nearly breathless with excitement, she looked up at him and said, unselfconsciously, "It's like you read my mind!" She quickly looked both ways and then darted across the street.

Patrick laughed and ran to catch up with her, amazed at how quickly she got to the door of the book store. As soon as he got inside he realized he'd already lost her as she had gotten swept up in the crowd of people milling around the front of the bookshop. When he finally found her upstairs with the secondhand and rare print books, her nose buried in a copy of *Persuasion*.

"Now, I would have pegged you for *Sense & Sensibility*," he said with a laugh.

Eleanor jumped, startled out of her mental trip back to Regency England. She looked at him and laughter in her eyes, "Why? Because my name is Eleanor?"

"Umm, yeah. It's a beautiful name by the way. And you said your parents were both into Literature, so I guess I assumed..."

Laughing gently, "Thank you, and I am partially named for Eleanor Dashwood, *Sense & Sensibility* is mom's favorite Austen novel. But my grandmother was also named Eleanor, so it was a natural choice for my parents. It's also why name is spelled differently from the Austen character. I'm E-l-e-a-n-o-r, not E-l-*i*-n-o-r."

"So is Grandma Eleanor your mum's mum or your dad's mum?"

"My mom's. My dad was adopted. He never knew who his parents were. He used to tell my mom, when they first started going out, that he was an 'enigma.' Like it was one of his appeals, being so mysterious. And she thought it was, for a while. But he likes to use it as an excuse not to let anyone get too close," Eleanor's face clouded over, as she looked down at the book in her hands, and she spoke so quietly Patrick almost missed it when she said, "If you're going to be a mystery to your wife and child, what's the freaking point."

Patrick was amazed at how unguarded Eleanor was, and the way she'd let snippets of her life slip out. Determined to get her smiling again, "So, *Persuasion* then? What's the draw? Kind of a sad story isn't it?"

Eyes brightening a bit, and a defensive look coming across her face, "Not in the end!" Finger jabbing at the cover, the thumb of her other hand still holding her place, Eleanor pronounced defiantly, "This book proves that it's never too late. Even when you think all hope is gone and you're out of second chances, you can still find love. After everything that Anne and Wentworth went through and all the ways they were pulled apart and all the misunderstandings and confusion, they still end up together!"

Hands up in surrender and backing up a step, Patrick laughed, "Ok! I take it back. Not a sad story at all. Rather, it's the perfect story of love and second chances. I stand corrected."

"Thank you," Eleanor replied smugly. "Plus, my middle name is Anne."

"Ahhhh, that makes more sense then too."

"And Rupert Penry-Jones is totally gorgeous," Eleanor said with a devious smile.

"Ok, now I get it. You just like it because of the actor that plays the main character! Admit it!"

Laughing genuinely, "I admit nothing! I loved the book long before I saw the BBC production of it. I just really love the movie too. And the earlier version with Amanda Root and Ciaran Hinds."

"Ok, I'll try to believe that."

"You can believe anything you like, it won't change the facts. I read this book ten times by the age of 18."

"Wow! Ok, I believe it, you're a genuine fan of the book and not because of who plays Wentworth." Glancing down at the book in her hand, "So are you going to get it? Don't you already have a copy?"

Bashfully, "I have several actually. I kind of collect them."

Raising an eyebrow, "Really?"

Feeling slightly embarrassed under his scrutiny, "I'm sure it sounds silly, but I tend to pick up a copy any time I travel. I have it in English, German, French, Italian, and Spanish. My oldest copy was printed in the 1920s. And I'll get this copy because even though it's not a terribly rare edition from the 1980s, it has this inscription on the inside cover," she opened the cover and placed her finger below a block of writing that read:

To our darling Anne,
Enjoy your first term studying at Oxford.
We're so proud of you!
Love always, mum and dad
xoxo

"It's probably silly, but it mentions Oxford, I'm buying it in an Oxford bookshop, and Blackwell's at that, and the previous owner was named Anne, like Anne Elliot," Eleanor stated simply.

"And like you," Patrick said, looking down at her with a sincere smile.

"And like me, or like my middle name at least," she said, smiling back.

"Are you ready to continue our tour? Or do you want to keep looking here."

"No, I'm good, we can go."

They paid for the book and left the shop. They walked along the road a ways before coming to a main intersection and then headed to the right. Patrick was doing his best as a tour guide, pointing out different buildings and colleges and explaining the history and story of things they passed. Before long they crossed the street and kept walking along the other side. Soon Eleanor saw another sign that made her stop and squeal with joy.

"The Eagle and Child! Oh can we stop there for a bit? Just one drink?"

Looking down at her with amusement, "So you've heard of the place?"

"The pub where J. R. R. Tolkien and C. S. Lewis and the Inklings met to discuss writing and philosophy and such? Umm, yeah." She replied, rolling her eyes. "I've heard of it. So can we stop?"

Laughing, and putting his arm lightly across the back of

her shoulders, steering her in towards the door, "Yes, this was our next stop. At least I don't have to try to remember all the facts about this place now, since you already know about it. We can just have a drink and enjoy sitting among the history."

They went inside and Patrick settled Eleanor in a quiet corner before going for their drinks at the bar along with a side of chips to snack on, this time flatly refusing to let Eleanor pay. She watched him walk up to the bar and place their order, chatting casually with the bartenders behind the bar. This was different from the giggling girls at the church, she could tell he actually knew these people, a girl and two guys working the bar, the four of them chatting and laughing, catching up quickly.

He came back with their pints, beer for him, cider for her. "Here you go, a pint of Aspall cider m'lady" he said teasingly.

Laughing, "Thank you kind sir. Friends of yours?" She asked nodding towards the staff at the bar.

Patrick smiled, "Yeah, this is one of my favorite pubs, even if it is really busy with tourists half the year. I can usually sit in a corner with my face buried in a book. I've gotten to know a bunch of the staff here, they're good people. A couple of them are artists, one is a writer, there's a couple who are trying to break into acting. It's nice to talk to other creative people who care about the art of their craft, you know?"

Eleanor nodded. "I know what you mean for sure, that's how it's been with the friends I've made at the Harrison. Especially my friend Jack. But Clara, Maggie, and Alexandra have been amazing too. I'm used to being the only writer and creative person in my friend group. Grace and Carly back home are great, and they'll listen to me talk about writing, but it's not the same. It's nice to have people to talk to about the intricacies of writing, of plot and character development. People who understand how and why you might be struggling with something, not just because they're readers, but because they're writers and creators themselves."

"Wow, I'm not used to being around someone who can articulate that feeling, but you're so right. The business is hard, I mean, it's easier in the UK where a lot of actors go to drama school and actually study the history and craft of acting, but even here we still have the occasional person who just had the right look and was in the right casting room at the right time. They're less fun to work with. It's challenging, but not in a fun way." Patrick frowned in frustration. Eleanor could tell he was thinking of some specific experiences.

"Yeah, I can imagine. There's some people at the Harrison who really don't care about what they're writing. Like, none of us care about someone's genre preference, if romance or horror or whatever is your thing, cool. And our professors are very accepting of that, it's not like other creative writing programs I've heard about or researched in the past. But some students just don't even try! They just think they can get something published and become the next hit author. I think that's why Jack, Clara, Maggie, and Alex and I gravitated towards each other. We're some of the few in the workshops actually workshopping our work and the only ones interested in forming a writing group outside of classes. I don't think I'd be doing half as well without all of them."

"It helps when you find your fellow creatives to bounce ideas off of," Patrick said with a smile.

Smiling back, "It really does," Eleanor agreed.

The chips, actually what would be considered thick French Fries in the U.S., arrived a few moments later, piping hot and so delicious. They settled once more into easy conversation. This time about random things like books they'd read recently or places outside of the UK they'd each visited. They also occasionally lapsed into easy, companionable silences.

Eventually, Patrick broke the silence that had fallen, "You're very easy to talk to Eleanor. I don't often meet people that I can spend a whole day talking to like this. You'll have to pardon me if this sounds a bit mental, but...well, it feels like we've been friends for ages."

Feeling a bit taken aback by what he was saying, and the sincerity in his voice and expression, Eleanor, smiled shyly. "I know what you mean. I've had a great time today. I didn't know what to expect from Oxford, but spending this day with you has far exceeded any possible expectations."

"I hope this isn't too forward, but, can I see you back in London? We could get a drink, or just do coffee? Whatever you'd like."

He looked so hesitant and vulnerable, like he was afraid she'd say no. Eleanor still couldn't believe she'd run into him again and now he wanted see her again? On purpose?

With a calmness she didn't feel inside, she heard herself saying, "That would be nice. Coffee sometime would be great."

They sat for a bit longer smiling at each other, neither quite sure what to say next. Eleanor looked around at the pictures on the wall and thought about Tolkien and Lewis and their friends sitting in this very pub discussing their work and ideas. This made her start to think about her father again and her smile dropped a bit.

"What are you thinking? You're frowning all of a sudden," Patrick said with concern.

"Sorry, I didn't realize," Eleanor replied, trying to smile again.

"You don't have to apologize, I just hate seeing you unhappy."

"Trust me, I'm very happy. Today has been incredible.

Thanks to you."

Eleanor heard her phone alert that she had a text. "Sorry, but I should probably check this text." She said as she dug her cell out of her jacket pocket, a quick glance showed her it was getting towards evening, and that Jonathan had texted to see how she was doing.

"Everything ok?" Patrick asked.

"Yes, it's just my cousin, wondering how I'm doing. When I left this morning I wasn't sure how long I would stay here today."

"Is your ticket just an open one?"

"Yeah, I can just get on any train I want, whenever I'm ready."

"Well, I hate to say goodbye to you today, but whenever you need to leave just say so. I'm staying here tonight at my parent's place, but I can take you back to the station and make sure you get on a train."

"That's so sweet, you really don't have to do that," Eleanor said, protesting slightly.

"I insist. Do you want to get dinner first?" Patrick asked, looking adorably hopeful.

Eleanor wasn't sure how she managed to refuse, but she did. "That's a nice idea, but I'm not super hungry after the fish and chips earlier and the extra chips just now. I might just grab a sandwich from the M&S I saw at the station and eat on the train."

Recovering quickly from his disappointment, "Right, well shall we go then?" he asked, noting their empty glasses. "We can get a cab or walk."

"I'm not in a huge rush, walking would be nice," Eleanor said brightly.

Smiling, "Brilliant! Let's walk then."

As they walked back towards the city center they passed an older couple who smiled and said hello to Patrick, who waved back in a friendly way. In response to Eleanor's inquisitive look, Patrick explained, "Friends of my parents." Eleanor smiled in response. Another several yards down the sidewalk they passed a younger couple who smiled brightly at Patrick and said hello, this time when Eleanor looked at him Patrick said, "No clue who they are, I think they're local, maybe I met them in a pub one night, but definitely don't know them" he said sheepishly. "Like I told you, coming back to Oxford it's like everyone knows me and I'm the prat who keeps forgetting everyone's names."

Eleanor just laughed in response then said, "I suppose if you're going to be famous and get recognized constantly this isn't all that bad."

"No, it's not. I'm definitely lucky."

Patrick turned them down a quieter road that passed in front of the Ashmolean Museum.

"It's not really that much of a short cut, but it gets us away from all the busy-ness of the center of town," he explained.

Eleanor couldn't help but notice that he kept glancing over at her and seemed a bit nervous. Or at least, he didn't seem like his usual self-assured, confidence that he always had in the characters he played, interviews, and red carpet appearances. She also noticed that even as they crossed the street, he always moved himself to be closest to the curb and had a way of gently guiding her without actually touching her. She thought about how all day, she'd just felt so at ease with him.

Eventually they reached the train station and Patrick went into the M&S with Eleanor and watched as she picked out a sandwich, some crisps, and an elderflower juice. He also managed to keep her from seeing him smile when she swiped a pack of Percy Pigs from the rack by the till and added them to her purchase at the last minute.

Purchases stowed in her bag, they walked back out into

the main area of the station and Eleanor checked the board showing all the train times. There was a train back to London Paddington in about twenty minutes.

"I'll stay and keep you company," Patrick said.

"Oh no! You really don't have to, I'll be fine," Eleanor protested.

Glancing over her shoulder as if looking for something, "No really, I insist. I don't want to leave you until I know you're getting on a train, there's a spot to sit over there." He led them over to an empty bank of seats and they sat. Eleanor noticed Patrick checking the time on his watch.

"I'll make sure I don't keep you and make you miss your train," he said with a mischievous grin.

Laughing a bit, Eleanor could only smile in reply. She noticed a few people taking notice of Patrick, but no one approached them. Some smiled and waved at Patrick and he smiled and waved back. She was starting to be able spot the difference between when it was some stranger recognizing him as "Patrick Reynolds the Actor" and when it was a local who knew him personally. Patrick's smile was always genuine, but there was an extra depth to it when directed at someone he knew personally.

They sat in silence for a bit, before Patrick spoke again, "Thank you for spending the day with me Eleanor. I'd thought it was going to be just another quiet day here when I went for my walk in the park. Running into you was the best thing that could have happened today."

A bit taken aback by his sincerity, Eleanor stammered slightly, "You're welcome...And thank you. For being such a great tour guide, and for spending the day with me. It was a lot of fun."

"Good, I'm glad you enjoyed it," Patrick said, smiling brightly.

They continued making general small talk for another fifteen minutes, Patrick asking Eleanor what her plans for the week were. And then about five minutes before her train was due he walked her to the barriers.

"The train will come to Platform 1 which is this one right in front of us through the doors, so you're already pretty much where you need to be," Patrick told her.

"Great," Eleanor replied, not quite sure what to say or how to say goodbye. He'd said he wanted to see her again but she figured once she was gone he'd forget all about her.

Almost as if reading her mind, "So, how can I reach you?"

"Umm, let me give you my mobile number, that's probably the easiest."

"Great!" Patrick took out his phone, the latest model of the iPhone that Eleanor had been lusting after, and opened up a new contact before handing the phone to Eleanor to put in her number. Fingers fumbling a bit she entered it in and triple checked she'd done it correctly.

As she handed it back he leaned over and gave her a quick peck on the cheek, "Better get going, I promised I wouldn't let you miss your train," he said with a smile.

Slightly dazed, she turned and put her ticket through the barrier and walked through the doors to the platform. Moments later she heard her phone ping again. She slipped it from her pocket and looked at the screen. It was from an unknown number and read:

Testing...testing ;)

She turned and looked back through the doors and saw Patrick waving his phone at her and smiling. She threw her head back and laughed at how silly his grin looked. In that moment he was no longer Patrick Reynolds, he was just Patrick, a really cool guy she was starting to get to know. She had definitely seen a different side of him today than she figured most people got to see.

Her train pulled up and turned to wave goodbye one last time and then boarded the train and found a seat by the window. Once she was settled, she tapped a response into:

Afraid I'd given you the wrong number? ;)

A few seconds later:

The thought had occurred to me. Glad (and honored) you gave me the real one.

She smiled and then replied:

Of course I gave you the real one. Use it whenever you like.

She saw the three dots indicating he was typing and a few moments later:

I plan to, though be careful what you give me permission for. I might start texting you every day. I'll be busy the next couple days but once I'm settled back in London with some free time I'll be in touch. You promised to meet me for coffee, I'm going to hold you to that. Enjoy your train ride back. :)

She typed a thank you and then plugged in her headphones and turned on her music before putting her phone back in her pocket. She really couldn't believe the crazy turn this day had taken. Or how easy it had felt to be around Patrick. She replayed their conversations and she was surprised at herself with some of the things she revealed but he made it so easy to talk and he seemed truly interested in her. She didn't know when she'd hear from him again, and she couldn't help but hope it was soon.

Chapter 10

The next day Eleanor spoke with her mom over FaceTime. She needed advice, about Mark and Patrick and everything that was going on. They talked for a while, and Cassie understood Eleanor's discomfort with Mark and his extravagance, but didn't quite share Eleanor's cautious excitement about Patrick. Cassie was afraid that Eleanor was getting swept up by the glamour of seeing not just a movie star, but her movie star crush. Reality was often different than the dream. Eleanor assured her mom that they were not "seeing" each other, they were just friends. But she couldn't help but feel like she was telling a slight white lie with that. Did she want to be more than just friends? Was she really attracted to him or just the characters he'd played? She was scared, that was for certain. After the time wasted with Michael and then the false start with Mark, she didn't want to get swept away by Patrick's charm and gorgeous smile. After assuring her mom that she was not going to get into anything serious with anyone they ended the call.

Still feeling like she needed some advice she managed to get her friends Grace and Carly on FaceTime. They, of course, were very supportive about Eleanor's decision concerning Mark but totally freaked out when she told them about her day in Oxford with Patrick Reynolds. They'd gotten excited back in August when Eleanor told them about her encounter with him in Covent Garden and then again when she told them about seeing him at her birthday party, but this was a whole different level of excitement.

"Date him!!!! Marry him!!!!" Grace exclaimed, practically vibrating with excitement.

"I don't know that I would go that far Grace," replied Carly, the more practical of the two. "But I honestly think you should give him a chance. You need to get back out into the dating scene Elle. Michael was an asshole. And Mark sounds nice but a bit showy, and I know how you feel about guys like that. Patrick certainly lives a glamorous life but he seems much more down to earth and relatable than Mark, from what you're saying, based on what you all did and talked about in Oxford."

"Yeah, I don't know," Eleanor replied quietly. "I mean, sending over the bottle of champagne at my party was a pretty flash move, but he did it quietly, just a private note to me, not a big gesture making everyone know it was him sending it. And in Oxford he just seemed so different from what I'd expected. He was so easy to talk to. I honestly started to forget that he was an actor."

Grumbling, Grace replied, "I don't know how you got so lucky."

Laughing a bit, and feeling better about things, "I'm sorry, I will try to be more grateful. It's just all so overwhelming," Eleanor said.

"I'm sure it is sweetheart," Carly said. "You've only just finally adjusted to living over there and I know there's still stuff you're dealing with as far as Michael goes. You don't get over a relationship like that overnight."

"Yeah," Eleanor agreed. "Mostly I just don't want to make a similar mistake. If I start seeing someone again I want to know that he's the right guy. I know there are no guarantees but looking back there were clearly red flags with Michael, I just want to make sure I'm not missing any red flags. Mark was pushing things too far, too fast and it freaked me out. Patrick seems willing to get to know me a bit. But who knows, it was just one day. He'll probably forget all about me."

"Stop that," Carly said sternly. "After those cute texts he sent you from the train station I doubt he's going to just forget about you. And it wasn't just one day. He sent you champagne for your birthday. And he probably would have asked you to coffee that first time you bumped into him if you hadn't run off. I think he likes you. I think you should be careful, but I definitely think he likes you. We'll just have to see how smart he is."

"Thank you 'Ms. Voice of Reason,'" Grace said dramatically. To Eleanor she said, "Look, Carly is right about everything. You need to see how things go but don't shut yourself down to any possibilities. If he's smart, Patrick will treat you right and he'll be patient. Besides, bumping into someone three times is kind of, you know Karma, or fate, of destiny, or angel, or *something* that means it's meant to be!"

"Thanks Grace," Eleanor said with a laugh.

"No prob," Grace replied smugly, then with narrowed eyes, "And when you two get married you have to invite all his hot British actor friends to the wedding and introduce me to them all. No reason Carly and I can't benefit from you getting with Patrick Reynolds."

Carly and Eleanor both laughed. Grace was definitely the more boy crazy and celebrity obsessed one between the three of them.

Suddenly there was a knock on the door.

"Come in," Eleanor called.

Jonathan poked his head around the open door, "You

got a minute? Oh, sorry, didn't realize you were on FaceTime," he said with a hushed voice when he saw Eleanor's computer screen.

"We're just about done, the girls have to go soon. Be right out?"

"Sure thing," Jonathan said.

Eleanor wrapped things up with the girls and promised to give them regular updates. She walked out to the lounge and joined Jonathan on the sofa. She noticed he'd made two cups of tea and picked up hers from the coffee table.

After taking a sip, "So, what's up? Miss me yesterday?"

"Yes, desperately," Jonathan replied sarcastically.

Laughing, "I thought so. Ok, seriously, what's going on. Since when to you do 'tea and chat'?"

Jonathan looked uncomfortable and Eleanor's heart sunk, thinking something was seriously wrong. Finally he said, cautiously, "Mark keeps texting and calling me. He's really worried about you and feels terrible."

Now it was Eleanor's turn to look uncomfortable, "I'm sorry...," she stammered, not really knowing what else to say.

"No, you have nothing to be sorry about Ellie. I told him I would talk to you but made no promises. I still think he's an idiot for trying what he did, and I've told him so. He agrees. And he's the one who's sorry, as he should be."

"Maybe, but I still feel bad, like I led him on. Our first date was nice and the conversation was good. We've known each other for a while now so it's easy to talk to him. But...," she trailed off frowning.

"But what Ellie?"

"It started the night he took me home from the birthday party. He walked me upstairs and kissed me goodnight. Like full on, proper kissing. And I kissed him back! I mean, it took me by surprise and I was thrown a bit off guard but I still enjoyed it. Then there was more kissing on the first dinner date, but that's when I began to feel, I don't know, rushed? Like too fast. And, I don't know, there were just other little ways that seemed overly familiar, like calling me 'sugar.' I don't know, by the second date and the extravagance of it then asking me to come to his place, like I owed him. It just felt like things had accelerated faster than I could deal with. I know we've known each other socially for a few months now, but hanging out at the pub with the group isn't the same as dating for months. It felt like he was way ahead of me. He clearly wants so much more than I do right now. I thought I was open to dating again, but it was too much or maybe just too much too soon, but either way, I just can't. And I feel horrible Jonathan, he's your friend, and I thought he was my friend too. But now there's no way that's going to work out."

"I know, I told him he was screwing everything up," Jonathan said bluntly.

"He clearly has no interest in being just friends. He pretty much said as much. He'd rather 'wait' until I'm ready. But that's not fair to either of us, but especially to him."

"Sod what's fair to him. You have to do what's best for you and he can just deal with it. I don't like the way he pushed. You were right to be put off."

"I know, but I still don't want him waiting around, hoping I change my mind. But I really don't want to make things awkward with you. You and Mark are friends."

"Look, Mark and I will be fine. It's you I'm concerned about. You seemed different after you got back from Oxford yesterday. Did something happen? You've been holed up in your room all day, I know you were talking to your mom, and then were those your girlfriends back home?"

"Yeah. And yes, something did kind of happen in Oxford. I ran into Patrick Reynolds again and we kind of spent the day together."

"Wait, the actor guy you bumped into in Covent Garden when you first got here?"

"Yeah," Eleanor admitted sheepishly. "He's also the one who sent over the champagne at my party. He was the person I bumped into coming out of the ladies' room."

"Wow," Jonathan said, seeming a bit shocked. "So, are you interested in him?"

Cringing and leaning her head back against the sofa, "I have no idea what I'm interested in or what I want. He was very friendly and showed me around. We had great conversations, he was so easy to talk to. With Mark it was a lot of superficial things, favorite TV shows and music and such, I don't feel like I really opened up to him, but with Patrick...I don't know, I just found myself telling him things about me. It just felt easy and natural. But it also wasn't a date. It just felt like hanging out with a new friend. There was no pressure."

"I hate thinking that Mark was pressuring you," Jonathan said sadly.

"He didn't know he was," Eleanor said in a rush. "Any other woman would have probably been thrilled. There was no way he could have known that I wasn't ready. And I hate comparing Mark to Patrick, because it's not fair."

"Yeah, Patrick is a movie star," Jonathan said laughing.

"That's not what I mean," Eleanor said frowning slightly. "I just mean, with Mark the interest was clearly there. He wanted more, and for a moment I thought I did too, then it just ran away from me. But with Patrick I've been clearer that I'm not rushing into anything. And I'll continue to be clear about that. But we really just spent the day together as friends, I think he's interested in me, maybe? But I'm not sure. He said he wanted to meet me for coffee sometime, if he actually remembers that and texts me I'll make sure he knows it's just a friendly coffee and not a coffee *date*. But yeah, I kind of like him. At least, I like hanging out with him, as friends. Beyond that, it's like I told Mark. I'm just not ready."

Jonathan placed his hand over Eleanor's, "Well, like I keep saying, you need to do what feels right for you. If you want to be done with Mark, then fine. If you hit it off better with this Patrick bloke, then good. But be careful, actors and movie stars seem a bit unpredictable. Plus there's the possibility of paparazzi tabloids, don't they like to make things up? "

"Yeah, I thought of that, but he's really not an A list celebrity, yet anyway. I honestly have no idea what to think about Patrick. But as far as Mark is concerned, I just don't see that going anywhere. It was too much, too soon, and I don't know how to come back from that. It feels so awkward now, the thought of seeing him in a social setting. I know he wants more and I really don't."

"That's fine. You don't have to do anything you won't want to. And if you don't want to hang out with Mark and the guys anymore, you don't have to. You and I can start doing stuff on our own or with your friends."

"I don't want to mess up your social group Jonathan," Eleanor said worriedly.

"You won't," Jonathan reassured her. "I'm just saying we'll make adjustments. Not that you seem to need me that much anymore, you've got all your school friends and now a movie star to hang out with," he finished with mock hurt.

Giving him a light shove, "Oh knock it off. You know I'll always have time for you. Doing stuff on our own and having you join my friends and I could be nice." Taking another sip of her tea and glancing at him over the top of her mug she added slyly, "Am I going to meet Celeste again sometime?"

Pretending he didn't understand, "Celeste? From the club? I...I don't know what you mean."

"Oh come off it Jonathan, you totally have a thing for

her, and she seemed to like you. Just because my own love life is a complete disaster doesn't mean I'm an idiot. Are you seeing her?"

"I don't know," he said, a look of confusion on his face.

"You don't know? What the hell does that mean? Has she turned you down?"

"I haven't asked her out," he replied, realizing as he said it how lame it was.

"Wooooooooooow," came Eleanor's drawn out reply. "You know, a girl can't say yes if you don't ask her out on a date."

"I'm an idiot," he said putting his head in his hands.

"Yes you are."

"Thanks," he said with a frown.

Smiling brightly, "You're very welcome. Seriously Jon, just ask her out, something simple, lunch or coffee."

"What's the hesitation for? I know it's not because she's a hostess, not upper class enough, or some such nonsense. We've talked about not being snobbish about social standing.

"Naw, it's not that. She's actually from an upper class family. Believe it or not."

"Oh wait, so now we are snobbish the other way?" She poked him in the ribs.

"No, no, it's well, I guess, I've got a little of the same feelings you do." He paused, "not sure she'd be interested in me?"

"What! You jerk, you couldn't tell? She practically glows whenever you looked at her!"

"Really?" He asked doubtfully

"Yes, really! And so did you, so ask her out!"

"Yeah, ok, I might do that."

"You better."

They smiled at each other and chatted for a bit longer about school and their moms before they went to their separate rooms to work on homework. Before going to sleep that night Eleanor replayed some of the events of the last several days, from her party, to her dates with Mark, to spending the day with Patrick. It all felt so overwhelming, and even with her head against the pillow she felt as if her head was swimming.

* * * * *

Eleanor spent the next couple days working on school stuff and generally trying to distract herself. She hadn't heard a word from Mark, and was relieved. But she also hadn't heard anything from Patrick, and she didn't quite know what she thought of that. She tried to tell herself, that it had just been a nice day in Oxford and that was that. He was a celebrity after all and must have been just spending down time with someone who kept bumping into him, she laughed to her herself, or rather tried to.

After class one day she decided to skip her usual writing session and go for a walk. She couldn't focus on writing so she thought a walk through a new neighborhood might clear her head. Dropping her school stuff at the flat she switched to her smaller cross body bag and headed to the Tube. After several stops she arrived at Hyde Park Corner and with a quick check of her map, she headed away from the park and towards Belgravia. Her Aunt Vickie had told her about a great French bakery somewhere on Elizabeth Street and Eleanor was determined to find it.

The more she got away from the bustle of Hyde Park Corner and into the more residential area the clouds above started to look a bit ominous. The map didn't look like the bakery was that far from the Tube but Eleanor began to think she might have to make this a quicker trip than she'd anticipated. As she walked through Belgrave Square and marveled at all the incredible iconic white townhouses that had been turned into embassies, the clouds got darker still, and by the time she walked along Eaton Square the first rain drops started to fall. At first it was just a drizzle, and Eleanor's umbrella was able to protect her, but once she turned on to Elizabeth Street it was starting to come down a bit more. She was relieved to see the sign for Poilâne Bakery and ducked inside just as the rain started to chuck down.

Eleanor took a deep breath to calm down and process her surroundings. The smell of fresh bread quickly overwhelmed her senses. Looking around the bread was all neatly laid out on display on the shelves and there were little cookies bundled up in plastic bags in front of the window. It was all so incredible! She said a quiet prayer of thanks to her aunt for recommending the place.

"Hello, may I help you?"

Eleanor heard a woman with a soft French accent say from behind her. Eleanor turned around towards the counter and saw a pretty young woman, with blond hair twisted up into a bun. She was wearing an apron with a dusting of flour on it.

"Umm, yeah, I mean, I'm kind of just looking...," Eleanor hated how American she sounded, she took a deep breath to calm herself down, "My aunt recommended this place, she said you have the best bread in all of London."

The woman smiled, "You must thank your aunt for us, we are always pleased to hear such lovely compliments from our patrons. What is your aunt's name?"

Figuring there was no way this woman could know who her aunt was, Eleanor casually replied, "Victoria McNeil."

The woman's eyes sparkled as she smiled brightly, "Ahhh, yes! Dearest Vickie. Tell her it has been too long and she must come to see us soon."

Laughing inwardly, Eleanor thought to herself, *of course they know Aunt Vickie, she's probably best friends with the owner.*

"I am Isabelle, your aunt usually comes here every week."

"That's what she told me. She's working on a project in New York at the moment, so she said I should come visit for her sometime. Today was the first day I had a chance," Eleanor explained smiling at Isabelle.

"Well, we are very happy to see you visit us today. Is there anything in particular you would like Miss…?"

"Oh, well, I just thought I'd pop in and see what you had, I'm certainly open to suggestions. And I'm Eleanor."

"Well, Eleanor, allow me to show you what we have to tempt you," Isabelle replied with a smile. "With that rain outside, you can't be in a hurry to leave us."

Eleanor smiled in response and spent the next hour being told all about the different breads they make and was able to sample a few, including trying one of the cookies she saw in the window. Crispy and slightly sweet, they were called *punitions, French style buttery shortbread cookies.* Eleanor couldn't help but buy some to have with her tea and coffee. When they'd finished, and all the breads and cookies were wrapped in plastic and placed in a carrier bag, it was still pouring out, but Eleanor thought she could make a dash back to the Tube.

Saying a cheerful goodbye and promising to be back soon, Eleanor clutched the bag to her chest and kept her umbrella low. She made it to Eaton Square when the rain started coming down even harder and she could feel it start to seep through her clothing. She immediately started feeling cold. Between the rain and the late October cold, the temperature felt wintery to Eleanor. Her coat was waterproof but she could feel the rain dripping down inside of her boots and drenching her tights and skirt. She kept looking around but there weren't any taxis in sight, nor any bus stops. She came up to a large tree that was hanging low over the sidewalk and noticed it was dry underneath so she stopped for a second to catch her breath. She was so cold. The paper carrier bag was starting to get soggy, but thankfully the bread inside was safe.

Just as Eleanor was trying to brace herself to start walking again, a car drove past and then quickly stopped and reversed and stopped right in front of her at the curb. Eleanor was about to start walking again, thinking it must be some creep inside, when she heard a familiar voice call out.

"Eleanor?"

Peering, through a rain and into the back window of the car, Eleanor couldn't help but exclaim, "Patrick?!"

Looking at the state she was in, Patrick quickly threw the car door open and slid to the other side, saying, "Get in."

A moment of hesitation, trying to process what was happening, Eleanor rushed to the curb and dove into the car, landing in a wet soggy mess on the seat.

"Oh my goodness, I'm going to ruin the leather!"

"Don't worry about it. Are you ok?" Patrick looked at her, concern etched all over his face.

"I'm f-fine. J-just cold and w-wet," Eleanor said through chattering teeth. The cold felt like it was going through to her bones now.

"I can't believe I found you like this, I just sent you a text."

"You d-did?" Eleanor said, still not sure what was going on.

"Yes, my schedule is finally clearing up and I wanted to see about that coffee you promised to have with me. But we'll talk about that later. Right now we need to get you somewhere warm and dry. Where do you live, the driver was taking me home but we can take you to your place first."

"Oh, I, umm, thank you. I live in Holborn, Red Lion Square."

Patrick knitted his brow, "Well, we can take you there for sure, but my place is actually just not far from here. At the risk of sounding forward, it might be better if you came to mine. You can dry off and warm up, and then I'll call the car back to take you home."

Eleanor wanted to protest, and just go home, but she felt like she was about to literally freeze, so before she could think about it any further she heard herself say, "That would be great, thank you."

The car drove a several streets over and down the road a bit, traveling from Belgravia into Knightsbridge, before turning into Ennismore Mews. Eleanor had wandered around here admiring the homes one day while exploring around Harrods and the surrounding area. She was fascinated by the mews houses, these former carriage houses, stables, and servants' quarters behind the enormous white fronted townhouses had been redeveloped over the years into charming homes tucked back from the main streets and squares of London.

"It's lucky I passed you, I was just being driven back from a meeting, I don't have a car myself so I'm glad I happen to have one at my disposal today."

Trying to concentrate on something other than how cold she was, Eleanor could only murmur, "Mmm hmm," in response.

Patrick glanced down at her, she was soaking wet and visibly shaking from the cold. They pulled up in front of his place and the driver got out with a large umbrella and Patrick rushed around to help Eleanor out of the car, she felt like her joints were frozen in place, she never knew cold could hurt so much.

As soon as she walked through the door the warmth of Patrick's place hit her frigid face. She could hardly take in her surroundings, all she wanted was more of that warmth. She felt Patrick take her shopping bag and her handbag, and then helped her out of her coat. Though her top was still dry, rain had dripped down from her neck at the same time her skirt was wet from driving rain. Eleanor felt herself being led up the stairs to the right of the door and down a short hall upstairs and finally into a bathroom. Eleanor stood there not sure what she was supposed to do, Patrick moved around her quickly and with purpose, turning on the shower and pulling out some towels. He left the bathroom and came back with a large terry cloth bathrobe.

"Ok, the fastest way to warm you up is a hot shower. Stay in as long as you want, I'll get some tea going, that will warm you up some more. Change into the dressing gown and bring your wet clothes downstairs, we'll put them in the dryer. You can stay here as long as you want and once you're feeling up for it I'll call a car to take you home," looking at her for some response, all Eleanor could do was nod her head. Patrick quietly slipped out of the room and shut the door behind him, leaving Eleanor in privacy. The shower was already starting to steam up the small room.

Chapter 11

It took some effort to get the soaking skirt off. The collar of her shirt was sopping wet, so she really was more wet than dry after all. In short order, she stepped into the shower.

Patrick's shower.

She tried really hard not to think about that. She wasn't sure exactly how long she stayed in there but she was feeling warm again by the time she got out. She wrapped herself in the fluffy towels Patrick had left. She towel dried her hair and then twisted it back up into the bobby pins that been holding it up before. She changed into the bath robe, or dressing gown, as Patrick had called it, and then gathered up her wet clothes and her boots.

She hesitantly edged her way back down the hall to the stairs. The doors to the other rooms were open, so she couldn't help noticing the other rooms. The one past the bathroom looked like a walk-in closet, and the door across from the bathroom was clearly Patrick's. It was tidy, but she spotted the sweater he'd been wearing in Oxford thrown over a chair and on the table beside it was a book, flipped upside down, open to a page. As she went back to the stairs she had come up earlier, she noticed two more bedrooms and another bathroom, as well as a staircase leading up to another floor. Downstairs she could hear Patrick in the kitchen. It was definitely a roomy flat for one person, she thought, maybe he had a roommate?

She came back down the stairs into the lounge, holding her wet clothes slightly in front of her so they wouldn't get the dressing gown wet. Patrick had put out tea and a range of snacks and had lit a fire. He was standing in front of it when Eleanor came down the stairs. At the sight of her he rushed over and grabbed the wet bundle from her.

"Anything in here that can't go in the dryer?"

"No, it's all good to go in, thank you. That's great that you have an actual dryer. We do too, but some of my fellow classmates seem to think that's quite a luxury."

"Yes, I got spoilt whilst in L.A." he grinned. "Right, you sit, help yourself to the tea. Just relax, I promise you're safe here and welcome to stay as long as you want."

Eleanor crashed on the sofa, instinctively pulling the throw blanket from the back and drawing it around her. She suddenly felt so tired.

Patrick came back in and saw her curled up in the corner of the sofa. He poured her a cup of tea and then one for himself. "I put your boots by the radiator, unzipped. That should help dry out and warm up the insides of them without damaging the leather."

"Thank you, really Patrick, for everything. This is very kind of you," Eleanor said sincerely.

"Think nothing of it. Least I could do. I could hardly leave you there."

"No, but you could have just taken me home, or dropped me at the nearest Tube station. You didn't have to invite me into your home like this, so thank you."

"You're very welcome Eleanor. I'm happy to see you, though I wish it had been under drier circumstances. But, I guess I wouldn't have you sitting on my sofa right now if that had been the case."

Laughing slightly, "No, I suppose not." Eleanor smiled at Patrick over the top of her tea cup.

"Umm, your purchases look fine, but the carrier bag is drenched. I'll give you a new one when I take you home."

"Thank you. That would have been a wasted trip if the bread had gotten soggy," she said with a smile.

"It's my favorite bakery actually," Patrick said, smiling back at Eleanor. "Though it's a bit of a trek from Holborn."

Noticing his questioning gaze, Eleanor couldn't help but sigh slightly. "I couldn't focus on writing so I thought exploring a new neighborhood would be good, my aunt recommended the place. I thought it might rain on me but I wasn't expecting a downpour of biblical proportions."

Patrick laughed, and Eleanor's heart jumped. The sound of his laughter was incredible, even better hearing it in person.

"You think I'm exaggerating but I've been here for a few months now. This isn't English rain, this is Arizona summer monsoon thunderstorm rain!" Eleanor exclaimed defensively. And as if to prove her point, there was a sudden flash of light in the growing darkness outside followed a second later by a loud clap of thunder. Patrick jumped at the sound.

Peering out from under a fan of dark lashes, over the top of her tea cup, Eleanor raised an eyebrow at Patrick and smiled smugly, "See? I told you. This is not English rain. Are you scared of thunder?"

"No!" Patrick replied, a little too quickly.

"You sure about that? It's a perfectly natural thing to be afraid of, lots of people are."

"Ok, thunderstorms are not my favorite thing. Fortunately, as you point out, we rarely get them here in London, especially this time of year. But my family used to spend summers at an estate in Scotland—"

"An estate in Scotland?!" Eleanor interrupted.

"It's not as grand as it sounds, I promise. It belongs to my father's side of the family, he and his two brothers and one sister. Anyway, we all share it, my family, my aunt and her family and my uncles and their families. When the weather is nice it's great fun, but as a kid when it would storm it could be downright terrifying."

"Sounds like something out of a Bronte novel," Eleanor said wistfully.

"Minus a crazy wife in a tower," Patrick said winking at her.

"I would hope so. I mean, that's sooo 19th century," Eleanor replied sarcastically, earning another laugh from Patrick. "So tell me more about it."

Eleanor spent the next hour listening to stories of Patrick's family's estate, a rambling property on the border of the Scottish Highlands. An 18th century stone property, with some 19th century additions, including a large conservatory in the back that led out to manicured formal gardens of the English style and surrounded by fields of heather and sheep. She listened, enthralled by his stories of running around the hedge maze or riding horses through the hills around the estate, swimming in the several lakes around the house, picnics that lasted until sundown, and late nights playing with his cousins in any of the many rooms of the estate. Or if the weather was good enough, having sleepovers in the hayloft of the large barn.

"It sounds incredible!" Eleanor said, sighing a bit. Suddenly her stomach growled, sounding embarrassingly loud in the quiet little house.

"Hungry?" Patrick asked laughing.

"I might be a bit hungry," Eleanor replied meekly. "Maybe I should think about getting home…" she said, an invisible question mark hanging in the air.

"Nonsense," Patrick stated dramatically, "Stay for dinner, I insist. How does bangers and mash sound? I do a pretty good gravy with ale."

"Sounds amazing. Though you've made me so comfortable already, you might end up stuck with me," Eleanor said with a laugh.

"I wouldn't mind that one bit," Patrick said with a smile, but there was a seriousness in his voice. For a moment they both were frozen, the mood suddenly feeling much heavier than it had been.

Sensing the sudden changed mood in the room, Patrick spoke quickly, "Come on, you can cozy up in the kitchen and keep me company while I cook," and bounded into the kitchen.

Eleanor followed, taking in the sight of the amazing kitchen. It had clearly been redone recently, judging by the beam in the middle of the room she guessed it had been two separate rooms. Where the dividing wall used to be there was a large island made out of an antique butcher's block with wood shelving and storage underneath. When entering the kitchen, to the right against the wall were more counters and cabinets as well as the stove and oven and other appliances. She guessed the fridge and dishwasher were concealed behind the cabinetry. To the front of the island, in the middle of the second half of the room was a sitting area of a few cozy chairs and small coffee table and in the far side by the window was an inviting dining area tucked into the corner with benches covered with cushions running against the wall and the window in the corner and arm chairs along the other two sides of the large table. It really was a dream kitchen. She immediately went to the arm chairs by the island.

"This is really nice." She said.

Noticing her looking around at all the design elements of the kitchen, Patrick explained, "I've lived here for a couple years, the kitchen was the first thing I redid. I tend to spend a lot of time in here, either cooking or eating and reading. Before the kitchen was small and cut off here at the back of the room," he explained, indicating with a wave of his hand the space behind the island. "And the rest of the space was set up as a formal dining room. I love having people over but I don't do formal entertaining, so I wanted a larger space to cook while still having an open and comfortable space for people to sit and chat and for all of us to sit and eat. That play I worked on back in the summer was a relatively small cast and crew, about 15 people total. I loved having everyone over for dinner and drinks."

"It's incredible!" Eleanor exclaimed. "It's like a dream house. I've walked around this area before, I love all these mews streets, the houses are like out of a fairytale, each one so different. But I've never seen the inside of one before. I wasn't expecting it to be so spacious inside."

"Well you have to remember that back in the day the whole downstairs would have needed to fit at least one carriage, if not two or more, plus stables for at least four horses or so, then upstairs would have been more storage plus servants' quarters. The fronts of the mews houses can be very deceptive. I've seen some that are only a few meters wide in the front, but then you go inside and they seem to go back for miles. It also depends on if the renovator broke them into smaller flats to make more money. I've been in several mews houses when I was house hunting, probably about fifteen in several different streets, as well as some that were next door to each other, and none of them were the same."

"That must have made it hard to choose," Eleanor replied.

"It was. But then my estate agent showed me this one and I knew it was it. I could see the potential with this room, as well as the rooms upstairs, and I fell in love with the room on the top floor with access to the roof terrace. Not every mews house has outdoor space and that was something I really wanted."

"It's great that you were able to invest in such an incredible property."

"I'm *very* lucky," Patrick replied with emphasis on the word very.

"Well, you've also worked *very* hard," Eleanor responded with equal emphasis.

"Yes, I have," Patrick said laughing. "But still, I scrimped and saved every penny, living in a flat with four other actors when I moved to London at the start of my career and staying there for far longer than others thought I should. My agent wanted me to move into a flat on my own and stop living like a student or starving actor. But it was in Zone 5 and I was paying peanuts for rent since I had the smallest room. When I started getting bigger paychecks from my early projects I knew if I could save ninety percent of them I could eventually buy something like this. I saw it as my security plan. If the whole acting career went bottoms up I could sell this at a profit and have enough money to float me for a long time while I went back to grad school or something and figured out what to do next."

"That's amazing, though, surely you don't see it as a security plan anymore? The way your career is going, this home is more likely your retirement plan than a backup plan," Eleanor said with a laugh.

"You never know, audiences change, new actors come along. I suppose it's a little easier on me than it is on my female actor friends, which is unfair, but I'm still at the mercy of hoping that casting directors think I'm worth casting. It could all end at any time."

Taking a sip from her tea, Eleanor said quietly, mostly to herself but Patrick heard, "Doubt it." Then looking at Patrick as he smiled at her while making himself busy getting pots and pans together, she suddenly felt guilty.

"I should help you," she stated suddenly.

"Nope, you stay right there."

"I'm feeling much warmer, I really should help after everything you've done."

"No, I insist, you're my guest, please make yourself comfortable, I have dinner under control. Rest for now, and maybe I'll let you help me wash the dishes later," he finished with a wink.

Smiling and shaking her head, Eleanor nestled herself deeply into the cushions and watched as Patrick busied himself around the small kitchen.

"So, if your acting career goes bottoms up, what would you do instead? Surely you wouldn't give up on acting completely?" Eleanor asked curiously.

"No, not completely. I've thought about it a lot. You might think it's doubtful but I've had a few friends over the years who looked like their career was taking off and then the next year they were back to not getting any work at all. It happens. I might be past the risky stage, but it's still something a good actor has to think about. I thought I'd go back to school, study theatre history a bit more, I also thought about studying theatre management and business. Whether my acting career continues on its current trajectory or not, I've always thought I'd like to own my own theatre one day. Keep acting but also do some directing and producing," he admitted, looking a bit sheepish and shy at this confession.

"That sounds incredible!" Eleanor exclaimed. "I bet you'd be brilliant at that."

Patrick grinned. "Thanks, I haven't told many people about that plan." He smiled shyly at Eleanor again, and then went back to chopping vegetables. Changing the subject, he continued, "So, I've told you about my childhood adventures and vacations. What about your childhood, any places your family would escape to?" Patrick asked.

Eleanor smiled, "When I was little, we always went somewhere different each summer, typically wherever my dad needed to go for a conference or to do research during summer vacation from his teaching responsibilities. A lot of that time I would spend with my mom, wandering around and sightseeing while dad was presenting or in a library. Paris, Berlin, Prague, Barcelona, New York, Chicago…London. The list went on. Sometimes two or three places in one summer, and we'd always rent an apartment. Then summer would end and we'd go back to Cambridge." Noticing Patrick's raised eyebrow, "Massachusetts, Dad was working at Harvard at the time."

"He's not anymore?"

"No, he's at Columbia now. In New York. It was a big to do at the time I remember. This was shortly after my parents had divorced. Mom and I were in Arizona by then. I was only 16 when he left Harvard. Dad was offered a position of Chair of some fancy program in the English department at Columbia and within less than a month he'd moved to Manhattan."

"You look like this wasn't a good thing."

"Mom was so upset, I didn't find out until later, much later, but mom had had an offer from a small but good school in Manhattan, a private college. But dad wouldn't let her take it because of his job at Harvard. Anyway, it's done now, and mom and I were in Arizona, so it didn't really matter."

"That's pretty far from your dad, did you visit regularly?"

"All the major school breaks, a week in the fall around Thanksgiving, one week of Christmas break, usually for New Year's, a week for spring break, and then a month in the summer," Eleanor rattled off, as if reading from a court decree. Bitterness tinged her voice.

Hesitantly, "Spending your breaks in somewhere like

Manhattan must have been fun though?" Patrick asked as he began the preparations for the meal he was making.

"Well, some of them were still when dad was in Cambridge, and that was fun, because I still had friends there. Manhattan was ok I guess, I could go to the library or wander around Central Park, or in the winter when it was freezing I could get lost in Macy's."

"But what about spending time with your dad?" Patrick asked.

"Oh. Well, he was often busy, grading papers, writing journal articles or his books, preparing conference papers, meeting with his teaching assistants..." Eleanor's voice trailed off, and a strange expression that Patrick couldn't quite read came over her face.

Trying to change the subject, "And how did you and your mom end up in Arizona? That's a bit far from Cambridge."

Eleanor gave Patrick a smile that didn't quite reach her eyes, "Nearly opposite sides of the country. Phoenix was like another planet compared to Cambridge. Cambridge is more like England, bigger than Oxford but definitely not a huge city like London. Mom was a bit...adrift when she and dad got divorced. I was thirteen, I still don't know all the details. I was too young at the time, and once I was older, I didn't want to stir up all the old pain with my mom. I know she wasn't happy, even at thirteen I could tell their marriage wasn't like the marriages of some of my friends. But Jonathan's parents had gotten divorced a couple years prior, so had the parents of a girl I knew at school, so it wasn't a strange concept. I think my mom had been trying to keep the family together for me. I overheard them arguing one night and my dad said something about not being able to wait another five years to end things. I think mom had been trying to get him to wait until I was eighteen and going to college. I definitely got the feeling at the time of the divorce, from what snippets of conversations and arguments I could eavesdrop on that the divorce was definitely my dad's decision in the end, he couldn't wait to end the marriage.

"The divorce was awful, truly horrific. I can't imagine what it had been like for my mom, because I know I was being shielded from the vast majority of the horror show. My dad was paying child support but no alimony, despite the fact that mom's career had never really taken off. She and dad had met in grad school. They were both pursuing a PhD in English Literature, dad was 19th century British Lit and mom was Modern American. I gather it was terribly romantic at the time. They graduated at the same time, both with honors, dad was offered a place at Harvard, which was a huge deal. So mom followed. She tried getting jobs but nothing ever worked out for her at Harvard and eventually she took a very unprestigious job at a small public college outside of Cambridge. It feels terribly unfair when I think about it now, but mom was in love and dad was full of what turned out to be false promises," Eleanor said bitterly.

"When they got divorced mom only had the one college position and only a handful of conference presentations and research projects, and only a few publications. Once she'd had me she'd become more of a part time academic. She thought she was doing it for her husband and family. But suddenly she was divorced, with a teenager, and a job that couldn't support us on our own, even with child support from dad, in a town like Cambridge. To be honest, my dad was a major asshole about it all. He insisted on splitting everything 50/50. I had been going to a really good private school but the fees were astronomical. Mom couldn't afford even a fifth of the cost on her own, let alone half. My riding lessons, piano lessons, extra French and math tutoring, dad would only cover half. Child support only covered the rent on the small apartment mom rented for us, mom had to cover all other expenses. My new school was nowhere near as good as my old one and all the extra tutoring and after school activities and lessons stopped, it was a mess.

"While they were married he was happy to pay for everything, it kept up the appearance of what a happy Harvard family should look like. I think he knew that by not helping to support me more than what the court mandated, which his bastard of a divorce attorney made sure was as low as possible, mom would be forced to leave Cambridge. I later heard through some of my friends that he lied and told their parents that my mom wanted to leave and had deliberately taken me away from him. Heaven forbid his colleagues realize what a jerk he was.

"Anyway, mom and I couldn't afford to stay in the Cambridge area but mom didn't have a job anywhere else. There was talk about moving to England, to live with my aunt, mom's sister, and my cousin, but dad went to the court and mom was forbidden from taking me out of the country, even though it's the about the same flight time from Cambridge to London as it is from Cambridge to Phoenix. He was just trying to make life difficult.

"Thankfully, mom's lawyer managed to keep the court from preventing mom and I from leaving the state. I don't think dad realized that nothing would stop my aunt from helping us. Thank god for my Aunt Victoria. She swept in like a hurricane of love and support and whisked me and mom, away to Arizona. Aunt Vickie had a house in Paradise Valley that she used in the winters to escape the English cold and as a show home for her southwest and west coast clients. It was like a fairy godmother had appeared and saved us. We went from living in this tiny one bedroom apartment outside of Cambridge to staying in my aunt's 5,000 square foot, Tuscan style mansion with a four car garage, movie room, and giant pool in the back yard. We'd always visited Aunt Vickie and Jonathan in England or New York, I'd never seen the Arizona house before. My aunt had always been successful, even before her marriage, and then with my uncle's support she built her career even more. During my parent's marriage, our families never felt that different from each other, but after the divorce the reality of my aunt's wealth was hard to ignore. But through it all, she was nothing but love and support for my mom and I, her generosity was absolute, there was no arguing with it. She was determined to help mom and I, no matter what and no matter how long we needed help. I know my mom felt guilty occasionally but Aunt Vickie, and even my uncle were so adamant about helping us. They were horrified how my dad was treating my mom and me. Their divorce hadn't been a walk in the park but it was nothing compared to what my dad did in court. Through all of their help, we were never made to feel like we were the poor relations or anything like out of a Jane Austen novel or something.

"We had a place to stay, for as long as we needed, mom was able to take her time finding a job, eventually she got lucky and was hired as Chair of the English department at a local community college, and Aunt Vickie helped her get into some consulting work on the side, over the years mom not only recovered from the initial financial damage of the divorce but now she's doing better than ever with her career. We bought a house in north Phoenix, I finished high school, went to college, visited dad when I had to, he didn't insist on alternating holidays once we moved but he did insist on the longer breaks from school, like spring break or winter break, and one month in the summer. Though I don't know why he insisted on the visits. Eventually I stopped. I was in college, legally I could do what I wanted, he never paid attention to me when I visited, and then the last time I went to Manhattan…well, it wasn't good. I haven't visited, or seen him since."

A heavy silence hung in the air as Patrick finished cooking and quietly brought the plates with their dinner over to the table and sat down. He couldn't take his eyes off Eleanor as she finished her story and as he watched a tear slip down her cheek he wanted nothing more than to take her into his arms and comfort her.

Looking up at him, and seeing the look of grave concern on his face, Eleanor blushed. "I don't know why I just told you all of that," she cried, trying to laugh while reaching up to wipe the tears that were now flowing more freely.

"Maybe you needed to. Have you shared that story with many people?"

"No! God, no. Not even my ex-boyfriend knew all of that."

"Really?" Patrick asked, sounding surprised. "How long were you together?"

"Oh no, I've spilled my guts enough this evening, you're not getting any more personal information out of me tonight," Eleanor said defiantly, trying to laugh it off as a joke.

"Fair enough," Patrick replied. "I hope you know you can tell me anything, I won't judge and I won't share your stories. Sometimes it helps talking to people," he said gently.

Feeling deflated and even more exhausted, "I know. Thank you for listening. And I do talk about it. But only really to Jonathan. We both know how it feels to have divorced parents, though his dad is actually a really decent man, unlike mine," she said bitterly.

"Well, I'm always happy to listen. Or provide a distraction. Whatever you need."

Smiling at him, "Please distract me, I'm tired of talking about myself and my miserable past. And these bangers and mash smell delicious. No more of my sad life."

"Alright then," Patrick replied with a gentle smile.

As they ate dinner Patrick kept Eleanor entertained with stories from the set of his last film and the antics of his crazy costars. Eleanor felt herself relax and Patrick was relieved to see her smile return and her eyes brighten. After a while, Patrick asked her about teaching and Eleanor shared some of her crazier stories from the classroom and the silly things her students would do.

"I still couldn't believe it!" she exclaimed. "When I called him out on watching football on the computer classrooms, his response was to close the blinds of the window behind him so the screen wouldn't reflect off the window! Little jerk."

"Wow, kids these days," Patrick responded dumbfounded.

"Oh, these aren't kids. These are 18 and 19-year-old adults. Shame their parents don't bother to treat them that way. I swear, they're over-managed throughout high school and then they get to my college classroom and don't know how to behave like the adults they legally are. It's so obnoxious," Eleanor said with disdain. "But most of them are decent enough, so I've kept doing it. Honestly, I do love it, and I love my students, even when they're totally ridiculous. But the salary wasn't enough to live on, and when my ex and I broke up, it seemed like a good time to try something new."

"So, who is this ex? And how did he let you get away?" Patrick asked with genuine curiosity. Noticing Eleanor's smile drop, he quickly said, "Never mind, you don't have to answer that, I forgot I was supposed to distract you, not pester you with personal questions."

"No, it's alright," Eleanor said quietly. "Michael's not my favorite subject these days. I still don't understand how foolish I was, I wasted so much time, years of my life, that in the end meant nothing."

"It must have meant something to you, that's not

nothing," Patrick said gently. "And if that wasn't enough for him, then he's the fool."

"Thank you. He wasn't a horrible person. But he just never cared for me as much as I cared for him. We broke up for a bit and then he asked for another chance. But honestly, I think he liked the idea of a relationship more than he actually cared about me. We met at our favorite Italian place for dinner, and I thought he might propose, instead he broke up with me. This time I knew it was for real."

"And what about that guy you mentioned, Mark?"

"We're just friends," Eleanor said, a bit quickly. Sighing, "He wants more, and I'm flattered, he's a great guy and a good friend of my cousin. But I just can't get involved with someone right now. I can't," she finished, sounding almost defiant.

"Why not?" Patrick asked gently. He knew he was treading on fragile ground with Eleanor, he didn't want her to clam up again, but he couldn't help himself.

Raising her eyes to meet his, Eleanor could see that there was no dark motive in Patrick's question, just honest curiosity, so she took a deep breath and replied, slowly, "I feel like I lost myself with Michael. I wasn't myself, I was 'Michael's girlfriend.' I only had a couple friends of my own, most of the people we hung out with regularly were his friends. He never liked the topic of me going back to school or looking for a serious job, because he liked how much time I had to spend with him when he was free. Looking back I can see now how much of my life revolved around him. And at the time I felt justified. Every now and then we would talk about marriage and starting a family. It was always hypothetical but it still felt real, like it was part of the long-term plan. So I thought I was waiting for a reason. Then it was over, and I'd invested years of my life in a guy and a plan that was never going to happen. His life was just fine, he had all he needed, but I was the one who was still working two part-time jobs and living with my mother. It's almost like...I guess...I almost repeated what happened to my mom.

"Coming to London, starting this MFA program, it allowed me to take my life back, to figure out who *I* am. Without a guy, without being the sad girl with no real job who lives with her mom. I mean, I'm far from rich but I'm lucky my mom can help me and that my aunt continues to be exceedingly generous and is allowing me to live in the Holborn flat with my cousin. Who knows what will happen at the end of the year. But with Mark it was getting too serious, too fast. He doesn't know me. He can't, because I barely know me anymore. I just feel like I need to figure myself out before I can get involved with someone else. I need to trust myself again."

"What do you mean, 'trust' yourself?"

"I chose to stay with Michael all those years. I chose to get back together with him after he broke up with me the first time. I chose to stay with him after we got back together even though it became increasingly clear that nothing had really changed, and probably wasn't going to. I held on to dreams and fantasies of a life that would never be. That's on me. I can't blame Michael for everything, because the red flags were there, I just didn't want to see them. I need to figure out who I am and what I want for me before I can get involved with someone else. Mark doesn't seem to understand that. He'd rather wait around for me to be ready, but I don't want that. I just want to be friends. I don't want any complications," she said firmly.

"I think what you're doing is incredibly brave, and smart. And Mark, or any man, who would try to rush you into something you're not ready for is an idiot. I won't lie to you Eleanor, I fancy you. A lot. But listening to you this evening, you're right. You need to figure out who you are and what you want. Any man who would rush you through that doesn't deserve you. I hope we can be friends, because I really do enjoy spending time with you, and I promise, you'll get no pressure from me. Though, I must admit, if you decide one day that you might be able to fancy me as well, I'd be delighted," he finished with a smile.

Smiling back at him, "You really are wonderful Mr. Reynolds, do you know that?"

Laughing at her mock formality, and echoing it, "For you Miss Gordon, I will always endeavor to deserve that compliment."

They smiled at each other, and sat in the quiet kitchen for a bit, just enjoying each other's company. Eventually they cleaned up the dishes from dinner, Patrick washed while Eleanor dried, and then Eleanor changed back into her, now dry, clothes. Patrick called a taxi and took her home.

As the taxi pulled up in front of Eleanor's flat, Patrick turned to her.

"Would you have dinner with me again? This time, planned and proper, in a restaurant. Just as friends, I promise."

Eleanor smiled and quickly agreed, "Dinner would be nice. Just let me know when."

"Ok, I'll check my schedule and call you tomorrow."

"Sounds good."

"Let me walk you up," Patrick said, moving to get out of the cab.

"Oh no, don't worry about it. But thank you. I'll talk to you tomorrow," Eleanor said firmly.

Noting the defiant independence in her voice, Patrick relented. He quickly leaned over in the cab and gave Eleanor a quick peck on the cheek, and then reached across her to open the door, "Talk to you tomorrow then," he said with a smile.

Grinning at him and shaking her head slightly, Eleanor

192

slipped out of the cab and walked quickly up the stairs to the front door of the building, letting herself in. Patrick watched her enter the building before allowing the cabbie to pull away.

Chapter 12

Eleanor was still smiling to herself, as she let herself into the flat, and thinking about what a crazy day it had been and how amazing Patrick was turning out to be. Once inside she immediately heard voices in the lounge. As she walked in her smile faltered slightly when she saw Mark sitting on the sofa with Jonathan. She immediately plastered her smile back on as the men turned to look up at her in the doorway.

"You're home! I was worried about you when the storm started, where have you been?" Jonathan asked with concern.

Dropping her bakery purchases on the table and shrugging off her coat, "I went to that bakery in Belgravia your mom mentioned. I got caught up in the storm and...um," Eleanor suddenly didn't want to tell them, or Mark at least, that she'd spent all afternoon in Patrick's flat, wearing Patrick's bathrobe. "I managed to duck into a coffee shop and got lost in my writing," she fibbed, knowing she'd tell Jonathan the truth eventually.

"It's nice to see you Eleanor," Mark said quietly.

"Nice to see you as well Mark," Eleanor said with a brightness she didn't quite feel. "You two having a nice time?"

"Actually," Jonathan said cautiously, "Mark arrived an hour ago to talk to you."

"If that's alright?" Mark asked, sounding equally cautious.

Looking between the two men, Jonathan looking unsure and Mark looking hopeful, "Sure," Eleanor agreed. "That's fine."

Jonathan looked at her as if to double check she really was ok with it and she nodded slightly at him. He got up and walked past her, giving her hand a slight squeeze as he went.

Eleanor moved to take Jonathan's place on the sofa, careful to keep a distance from Mark. She heard Mark sigh slightly, as if he'd noticed and disapproved of the distance between them.

Taking a deep breath, Mark dove in to what seemed to Eleanor to be a previously rehearsed speech.

"I'm so sorry about what happened, I never meant to make you feel rushed or uncomfortable. I certainly never intended you to feel pressured in anyway. I thought we were on the same page, clearly we weren't. I really enjoy hanging out with you Eleanor, I don't want to lose that. And I don't want you to feel like you can't come out with Jonathan when he meets up with all of us from school. I'd hate to feel like you're avoiding us or that there's an awkwardness between us. I'll do anything to make it better. To make it right," Mark finished, his voice full of contriteness and sincerity.

Now it was Eleanor's turn to take a deep breath, she began to speak slowly, "Mark, I had a great time on our first day, and I've always enjoyed hanging out with you and the guys, you were some of my first friends here. It wasn't entirely your fault that our last date went so wrong. But it just proved that you really don't know me, if you did, you'd have known that restaurant was one of the worst places you could have taken me. A private dinner, in such an extravagant place was just too much, especially for what was essentially only a second date. Maybe other women would have been thrilled with such a date, but it just made me uncomfortable. If you knew me better you'd have known that. But that's partly my fault. I'm still figuring out who I am since my last relationship ended. I'm just not ready to open myself up to another relationship like that. I need to figure out who I am now, and what I want."

Mark suddenly looked hopeful, "I understand that now. And I can wait. I'll give you time if that's what you need," he interjected.

"No," Eleanor cut him off, taking control of the conversation back. There was a firmness in her voice, "I don't want you to *wait*. I don't want to sit here and give you false hope that it might work out for us down the road, because that would be dishonest. The fact of the matter is I'm not ready for a relationship. I don't know when I will be ready for one. Right now I need to focus on my life and school and my writing and my friendships. After years of trailing around supporting my ex, I need to be a bit selfish and take care of myself. And I need you to understand and accept that."

Mark frowned, "I won't say I'm not disappointed, but I do understand. I hope we can still be friends?"

Eleanor smiled gently, at least he had come to terms with being friends, unlike his previous declaration. "I would like that."

Mark smiled back and Eleanor hoped this could be the end of some of the awkwardness that had existed between them since their disastrous date.

"If you'll excuse me though, it's been a long day and I'm exhausted," Eleanor said apologetically.

"Of course, I understand. I'm just glad we got to talk. I'll leave you alone now. But hopefully I'll see you at the pub with Jonathan soon."

"I'll try to find time to join you all, I promise."

She walked Mark to the door and they said goodbye. Eleanor knew she wouldn't feel up to seeing him for a little while, but maybe in a week or so she would accompany Jon to the pub like she used to.

* * * * *

The next day passed in a fog. Eleanor went through her classes, distracted the whole time. She couldn't help but think about Mark, and Patrick. And because of thinking about them, she couldn't help thinking about Michael and wondering what he was doing right then. She knew it was morning in Arizona, he'd probably be up making his coffee and getting ready for work, everything laid out the night before as always. She realized she had tears forming, quickly blinked, and tried to focus on what the professor was saying at the front of the classroom. Jack gave her a quizzical look, as if asking what was wrong, and she forced a smile and mouthed, "allergies" and rolled her eyes. He seemed to believe her.

By the end of the day she was exhausted. She and Jack spent some time writing in their favorite Starbucks in Paternoster Square, and then Eleanor went for a wander down by the river. She walked across the Millennium Bridge and then west along the South Bank. She sat on a bench outside the National Theatre. It was a cold day but the sun was out, though it was nearly to the horizon, and she watched it flicker through the branches of the tree above her, empty of all its leaves. There weren't many people out, just some tourists rushing by. Eventually the cold got to her and she had to get moving again to warm up.

She walked up the stairs to street level of Waterloo Bridge, she loved this bridge. From here she could see east to the City and down to the Tower Bridge, to the west she could see the London Eye and Big Ben. As she walked, she could hear Big Ben chime the hour, it was four o'clock. In another few days, British Summer Time would end and it would be pitch black by now. She laughed at the thought, living in Arizona for so long she had forgotten what it was like to have to change the clocks and "fall back" an hour. Arizona was just about the only state that didn't follow Daylight Savings Time. She crossed back to the north side of the Thames and then made her way back towards Holborn and the flat, stopping for a takeaway latte from Caffè Nero on Kingsway. Just as she was standing at the corner in front of the Sainsbury's and across from Holborn Station, her phone rang and she saw Patrick's name on her screen.

"Hello Eleanor, have I caught you at a good time?" Patrick's warm voice came from the other end of the line.

Smiling in spite of herself, "Yes, I was just walking home."

"Good. I'm glad to hear it. I wasn't sure what time you got out of school, but I'd hoped I'd be able to catch you."

"Oh, class got out ages ago. I've just been writing and then wandering down along the river. Until I started to freeze," she said laughing.

She heard Patrick laugh on the other end of the call, "Please don't go and catch a cold, it's bloody freezing out there today! I'm just calling to ask if you want to meet up sometime? Coffee, lunch, dinner, whatever you want." As if sensing her hesitation, he quickly added, "Just as friends, I promise."

"I know," she said laughing slightly, "I was just trying to think about my schedule. I'm really only free in the evenings until the weekend."

"Well, I know it's late notice but I have some unexpected free time and I'm near Holborn. Otherwise I'm probably not free until the weekend, the rest of my evenings are already booked with meetings."

"I guess I can do dinner tonight, I'm pretty tired though, can we meet somewhere between your place and mine?? I'm not sure I have the energy to trek across town."

"You're in luck. I actually just had a meeting in Bloomsbury. Whereabouts in Holborn are you?"

"Red Lion Square, where are you?"

"I'm at Russell Square. I know it's early, and I'm not entirely sure what's around here but I'm sure there's something."

"If you don't mind meeting me near my flat, there's a place around the corner called The Bountiful Cow, if you're up for a burger or steak?"

"A burger sounds great, I'll see you there soon?"

"Should be less than five minutes," she said quickly, stepping into the crosswalk as the green man lit up on the walk sign. Saying goodbye, she pressed, "end call" on her phone and slipped it back in her pocket. She couldn't help it, but she was actually feeling excited.

* * * * *

Picking up her pace, she made it to the restaurant in just under five minutes. Somehow Patrick had beat her there and was already seated in a corner booth in the back.

"I promise I didn't ask for a romantic booth, just something tucked away from view of the entrance," Patrick said, getting up to give Eleanor a quick hug and peck on both cheeks.

Laughing, "I understand. Just as well, I'm a bit disheveled today, not sure I'd want too much attention looking like this."

"You look lovely, a bit rosy cheeked and windblown, but still lovely, as usual."

Blushing, "Thank you, that's sweet of you to say."

They quickly ordered their dinner and fell into an easy conversation. Patrick told her he'd been in Bloomsbury to meet with his agent and manager and the projects they shared with him and she filled him in on her day at school and how distracted she'd felt. He was so easy to talk to she found herself telling him about Mark's visit and thinking about Michael. Patrick just nodded with understanding and encouragement.

"You've been through a lot lately Eleanor. A lot of changes for sure, some good, others not so good. You've every right to be confused. But you'll figure it all out eventually. And London is the perfect place to figure out what you want."

"I hope so."

"So was it just the MFA program that brought you to London or was there another reason?"

"Well, the program seemed like the perfect solution. My mom has been pushing me to figure out what I want to do with my life. She knew how much I love writing, I spent all my free time sitting in coffee shops back home writing on my laptop, iPad or scribbling ideas in a notebook. I never go anywhere without something to write on," she said with a laugh.

Patrick raised his eyebrow and then glanced at her bag beside her.

Laughing at the look on his face, Eleanor reached into her bag and pulled out both her assortment of three notebooks and her iPad, clipped into its keyboard case.

"Three journals! What on earth do you need three separate notebooks for?"

"Well, this one," she said defensively, indicating the bright green notebook with 'Don't Wait' embossed on the cover, "is for my general tasks, notes, to do's, lists et cetera. Then this one," holding up the floral notebook she'd found at Ted Baker on one of her first shopping days in London, "is for random notes and observations since I've arrived in London. It's not really a diary, I'm rubbish at keeping a daily journal, but it's where I put all my personal thoughts and ideas. Finally, this one," holding up a slim notebook with a map of London on the cover, "is where I keep all my continuity notes for the book I'm working on."

"Continuity notes? And what book? I've never really asked you about what you write."

"It's just a novel, I don't know, it's hard to explain. I'm struggling with it right now. But the notebook is where I write down all the facts about the characters, timeline of when things happen, it's just how I keep things straight. When I'm writing, it's hard to keep going back up in the document to see what I've already written about characters, locations, plot twists, and such. By keeping it all in a notebook I can keep myself more organized as I write," she said with a shrug of her shoulders.

"Have you ever thought about writing screenplays?" Patrick asked curiously.

"I've thought about it," Eleanor replied hesitantly. "Not seriously, but I am a very visual writer. I tend to see everything as I write it and hear the dialogue between my characters. Although, as a writer I can also get into the head of the character, which I suppose is part of what you do as an actor," she said smiling.

Patrick nodded, smiling back.

"I guess I always figured getting a novel published was nearly impossible enough, but living in Phoenix it just seemed completely outrageous to think that I could get a screenplay seen by the right people and have it actually get produced. But maybe, if I'm lucky, I can get a novel published and get it adapted to the screen. That's the pipe dream anyway," she said with a laugh.

"Hey, not quite so impossible you know," Patrick said

seriously.

"Oh? And how do you figure that?" she asked inquisitively.

"You seem to be forgetting that you are now friends with an almost major, international movie star," he proclaimed with fake self-importance.

Eleanor couldn't help but laugh at the silly look of pretend arrogance on Patrick's face. And Patrick broke into laughter as well.

His face turning a bit more serious, he said, "But for real, as your friend, I am happy to help you meet agents or get your work seen by the right people. Is there any character in that novel that I could play?" he said winking at Eleanor.

Laughing lightly, "Maybe. Seriously, though, that's sweet of you to offer. The program offers a lot of assistance with finding agents and getting our work seen. I wouldn't want to take advantage of our friendship. But I'll keep it in mind."

"It wouldn't be taking advantage. In this industry...films, TV shows, books, music...you have to make connections. I'm a connection for you now. So if I can help at some point, I hope you'll let me."

"I promise I'll keep that in mind. But I kind of need to have a finished product first."

"Better get writing then," he said smiling.

They got quiet again as they looked at the dessert menu. Eleanor couldn't help but notice, as she had in Oxford, how easy it was to not only talk to Patrick but also to sit in silence with him. They weren't uncomfortable silences, far from it. She felt something shift slightly in the back of her brain, she couldn't help but wonder what it would be like if this *was* a date with Patrick. She definitely liked him and it felt easy and natural to be with him. However, as quickly as the thought occurred to her she dismissed it. She knew she wasn't ready, or strong, enough to think about dating again, especially not with someone like Patrick Reynolds. But she had to admit it felt nice being out with him, she felt safe, and comfortable, and she wasn't constantly second guessing herself or waiting for the other shoe to drop as it felt with Michael, and even with Mark in their couple of dates. With Patrick, she felt like she could just be herself. *Well, isn't that the point of being friends with someone?* she thought, frustrated with herself for trying to complicate things.

Once they finished their drinks and desserts Patrick offered to walk her home. She was freezing in the cold, and Patrick kept close to her side, as if to try to warm her up without actually putting an arm around her. She had to fight away her brain's wish that he would.

The pub was literally around the corner so they made it to the front of Eleanor's building in less than a minute. Patrick didn't say anything and she didn't question it when he followed her through the front door downstairs and up the stairs to her floor. He walked her to the door of her flat and as she turned to say goodbye she saw a flicker of something in his eyes. She knew, though she couldn't explain how, that in that moment he wanted to kiss her, and in that moment she wanted him to or thought she did. In that moment of her hesitation, he took a quick breath and was giving her the same casual, friendly smile he always had when she saw him.

"I had a great time tonight, thanks for joining me for dinner," he said easily.

"Thanks for calling, it would have been ready-to-eat spag bol from Waitrose and Graham Norton on the TV if you hadn't called when you did," she replied, half jokingly.

"What an exciting and decadent life you lead Miss Gordon," Patrick replied with a laugh.

"Don't you know it. You think you're the one with the fabulous life Mr. Almost Major International Movie Star, but my life is way more fabulous." She said with a laugh.

"You'll get no arguments from me there. Maybe you'll let me join you some night. I love Graham Norton," he said, and Eleanor noticed there was a seriousness in his expression.

"You're more than welcome, any time. All my friends are welcome over for dinner and the BBC. Though, it wouldn't be a ready-to-eat meal from the shop, I'd make spag bol from scratch," she said with a smile.

"Well, if that's the case, how about this weekend?"

"I think that should work, call me?"

"Deal," he said, smiling. "I'll double check my schedule and call you in the next day or so. I'm pretty swamped the next couple days with meetings, but we'll sort it out and confirm something soon, I promise."

"Great," she replied. "And...thanks. Not just for dinner, but, well, for everything. For helping me out yesterday in the rain, for listening, for being a friend."

"You never have to thank me for being kind or being a friend to you Eleanor. I promise you can trust me. You've been honest about not being ready for a relationship and I understand and respect that. So if a friendship is what you can handle right now, then I'll be here, as your friend. But when you decide you know who you are now and what you want, I'll be there fighting for my chance."

Before she could respond, he leaned down and brushed a strand of hair from her face and kissed her lightly on her cheek, then he quickly turned on his heel and walked away and down the stairs. She walked in to the flat in a daze and walked to the window in her room, she watched as he walked out the building door downstairs and back out to the square. As she watched him go, she found herself hoping, desperately, that he was telling the truth, and that he would still be there waiting for her when she was ready.

Chapter 13

The next morning Eleanor woke up late, her sleep had been interrupted by thoughts of Patrick, and Mark, and Michael. And what a confusing mess everything had become. She dashed around the flat, frantically getting ready. She pulled on her skinny jeans, a thick ivory sweater, and her tall brown boots. Thankfully her bag was still packed from the night before since she'd taken everything to the restaurant with her, so she threw on her coat, grabbed the bag, and raced out of the flat. Her phone dinged and as she was rushing down the road she whipped it out of her coat pocket and glanced at the screen. It was from Jack.

Have time to stop at Caffè Nero. Want owt? Xx

Eleanor was still getting used to Jack's Yorkshire slang, especially over text, but she got the gist of the offer and appreciated him asking if she wanted anything. Breathing a sigh of relief, she quickly tapped her reply on the screen.

You're an angel! A latte and a pain au chocolate. Running late. Xx

Running up Ludgate Hill she was out of breath by the

time she turned towards the river and down to the school, but fortunately made up the time she'd lost. She slid into her seat in the classroom just as the professor turned to start class. Jack winked at her and slid her latte and pastry over to her side of the table they always shared. Somehow, she made it through the class and the rest of the day, even though she could hardly think straight. Even Jack noticed she was a bit off as they settled into their usual spot at Starbucks after class.

"Alreyt luv?" he asked with concern.

"Yeah, just distracted. I overslept. It's been pretty crazy lately."

"Don't I know it. All these writing workshops are doing my head in. It's like my work will never be good enough," he said mournfully.

"At least you know what you're writing, I'm still stuck, I can't seem to get things to work," Eleanor replied bitterly.

"You'll get it sorted eventually. Is everything else ok? Is it just writing that has you distracted or is there something else going on?"

Before she could answer, her phone dinged with a text message. She glanced at the screen and saw it was from Patrick. She quickly opened up the message to read it.

So sorry, I won't be able to meet up this weekend after all. Possible new roles, have to fly to New York and LA for a while. I'll keep in touch when I can, text me anytime if you need to talk, vent, whatever. Talk soon. x :)

Eleanor couldn't help but smile at the sight of both the kiss and the smiley face at the end of his text, but she was disappointed that he was leaving and didn't seem to know when he'd be back.

"Who's the boy?" Jack said, interrupting her thoughts, smile on his face.

"What? Oh, it's nothing. Just a friend."

"No, that's not how this works. *I'm* your friend. One of your *best* friends. Now spill, who's texting you and making you smile like that? Because I'm bloody well sure that it's not that mardy wanker Mark."

Realizing that he was right, Jack was one of, if not the best, friend she had here in London, Jonathan aside. She felt guilty for not having mentioned Patrick before.

"Be nice, Mark isn't all that bad. It was just a misunderstanding."

"Oh no dearie, I saw that train wreck coming at your birthday party. He was far too possessive of you all night," he said, a dark expression covering his face.

"Well, speaking of my birthday, that's actually a good place to start filling you in. There's so much to tell you. I hope you'll forgive me for not saying something sooner," she replied apologetically.

"Spill," Jack ordered.

She told him about Patrick sending over the champagne. About bumping into him on one of her first days, running into him again at the party, then spending the day with him in Oxford. Getting caught in the rain and rescued and spending the afternoon and evening at Patrick's flat. And then finally catching him up on having dinner with him last night and his text saying he was going to the States.

"Eh by gum! I can't believe you've been keeping all this to yourself," Jack said incredulously.

"I'm sooooooo sorry! Please forgive me, I swear I wasn't keeping it from you deliberately. I really have just been so distracted and out of my head. Between Mark and Patrick and still thinking about Michael, I just don't know what's going on anymore. And it's having an impact on my writing."

"You should be writing about your life. You're living in a freaking soap opera!"

"More like a three-ring circus," Eleanor said frowning.

"I'd give anything to have Patrick Reynolds trying to get close to me, you jammy dodger!" wiggling his eyebrows in mock suggestiveness.

Laughing, "Oh Jack, I wish I was ready to get close, no not yet, but yes, he's seems so wonderful. Oh gosh, that's all part of what's been going through my head! We're just friends right now. I told him that's all I can handle. He's being amazingly understanding about it all."

"Yes, but he *does* fancy you. He said so, twice, based on what you've just told me. I think you've got a winner there, Ellie luv. A guy like him could have any woman he wanted, right now, but he's willing to take the long road to get to you. Sounds like a keeper to me."

"Maybe, I just still feel so confused. Every time I think about getting into a relationship again I think about Michael. Or my parents. I don't have a good track record, nor do I come from a healthy background when it comes to relationships."

"Who did you date before Michael?"

Biting her lip, "well, I went on dates, but I didn't really date anyone seriously before Michael. My parents got divorced and mom and I moved just as I was getting to that age. I went to two different high schools when we moved to Arizona. I was terribly shy and didn't really fit in. Then in college I was still shy and too scared to put myself out there. Finally I gave up and went on an online social meet up website. I attended a few different groups and then I met Michael."

"So Michael was your first relationship?" Jack asked gently.

Tears starting to well up, "Michael was my first *everything*. He told me I was his and I truly believed him. I don't know how I was so wrong."

Jack's eyes flew wide, "Oh luv. You poor thing." He

reached across the table to take Eleanor's hand and gave it a squeeze. "No wonder the breakup has been so difficult. Also not surprising you're struggling so much now with Mark and Patrick."

Wiping the tears away, "Mark wants too much. I'm not ready to get that swept away by someone with lovely promises. At least, I learned that from Michael. Patrick seems more patient, but I worry that he still wants more than I can give, that he's just keeping it to himself."

"Darling, you've been upfront and clear with both of them. You're not ready for a relationship. You just want to be friends. If they can't understand and respect that, then on their heads be it."

Eleanor couldn't help but laugh at Jack's dramatic proclamation, but she knew he was right. And Patrick going out of the country for a while certainly allowed for a bit of distance and breathing room.

"You're right," she admitted finally.

"Of course I am," Jack said smugly.

They chatted for a bit longer and then said goodbye. Jack headed off towards Islington where his flat was and Eleanor walked down to the river and wandered around for a bit, thinking about everything.

* * * * *

When she got home, Jonathan was waiting for her in the kitchen. She said hi as she passed by on her way to her room to drop off her stuff. Changing into her yoga pants and her hoodie, she joined Jonathan in the lounge and saw that he'd prepared a cup of tea for her.

"What's up cousin?" she asked casually.

"I was going to ask you the same thing. We really haven't had a chance to talk lately, especially since Mark came over. You never told me where you really were that day but I have a feeling you weren't escaping the rain in a coffee shop. You've been distracted for a while now. What's going on?" he asked, concern on his face.

Eleanor sighed, and for the second time that day found herself talking about everything that had been going on and the time she'd been spending with Patrick. Jonathan listened patiently and other than raising his eyebrows a couple times, he didn't really give away how he was feeling about the situation. When she finished, he looked at her and finally spoke.

"What did you really come to London for?"

It was a simple question with such a complicated answer.

Haltingly, Eleanor attempted to answer, "I came to write. I came for school and to do something with my life. But I also wanted to make new friends and start over fresh, somewhere without memories of Michael. I don't want to be alone for the rest of my life Jon. But it wasn't right with Mark. And I don't know if it will be right with Patrick, but he's at least willing to be friends and not pressure me for anything more."

"Mark says he's willing to be friends," Jon said gently.

"And I hope he means that!" Eleanor exclaimed. "I like Mark, I really do. He's a great guy, and a girl would be lucky to be with him. But I'm not the girl for him. I'm not capable of being spontaneous and just go with the flow and take a risk and hope it works out. I need to go slow, I need to get to know someone first. Mark rushed it, and I can't quite get over that."

"Fair enough. You've been hurt so much already. I don't want to see you get hurt more, by Mark or by Patrick. I also don't want to see you get distracted by either of them. Friendships and relationships are important. And you won't be alone for the rest of your life Ellie. It's ok to focus on your writing and your school, at least for the rest of this year. When the program is done, what are you going to do?" Jon asked, clearly trying to get Eleanor to think past her confusion over Mark and Patrick.

"I know, I know. I've been so focused on surviving school, and yes, getting distracted by guys, this year is just going by so fast. I need to start looking for jobs and ways to stay. Aunt Vickie said I could keep living here for a little while after graduation," she said, looking pointedly at Jonathan.

"You are more than welcome to stay here for as long as UK immigration will allow you my dear. But you're definitely going to need a job, and one that will sponsor a visa. Which is not an easy thing to find. It's nearly the holidays, you're done with school in August. That gives you about eight months after New Years to find something."

"I need to talk to the career services office. They have some different options, as well as fellowships and grants I can apply for. I just haven't gotten around to it. But I will. I *can't* go back to Arizona after this year. I can't go back to my old life. You're right, for the rest of the school year at least, I need to focus on school and writing and finding a job. Everything else can wait," she finished, her voice stronger and more determined.

"Now hold on, you're still allowed to have some fun. And keep pursuing your friendships, even your friendships with Mark and Patrick. You need balance. I've just been noticing you lately and it seems like you've been so distracted and not focused on maintaining that balance."

"You're right. I'll work on it. I promise," she said with a smile.

Jonathan excused himself to work on homework before bed. Eleanor stayed on the sofa sipping her tea and thinking about everything that had been going on and everything that she knew she needed to start paying more attention to.

Finally, she got up and cleaned her mug and then got ready for bed. She lay awake for a while, thinking about her writing project and the problems she'd been having with it, and after a while she fell into a fitful sleep.

* * * * *

The following day was Friday and Eleanor needed a break from her routine. She knew Jack would miss writing with her, but she needed the time alone. That afternoon, after wandering around the Victoria & Albert museum, she walked over to Hyde Park. As she walked through the park she remembered being there with her parents on one of their trips to London. It was a sunny, summer day, she remembered she was about nine years old. She thought often of that day. Her dad had taken the afternoon off from his conference and it was one of the rare times Eleanor remembered being out as a family. It was one of the few 'perfect' memories she had of her childhood. Her dad was smiling and laughing and she could tell her mom was genuinely happy. As she walked by the Peter Pan statue, she remembered her dad chasing her around the statue, as she bubbled with laughter. Her mom catching her in her arms and her dad pulling them both into a giant hug. Walking along the Serpentine, cold and half frozen now, she remembered feeding the ducks and geese and swans, and her dad making up silly stories and names for them all as the sun sparkled on the water. They got ice cream from one of the stands and ate it sitting in the grass as the sun filtered down through the trees. It was a perfect, idyllic day that had brought her comfort.

In the years that followed, leading up to her parent's divorce, the atmosphere in the house, on the summer trips, between her parents, had all started to get tense. They tried to cover it with false brightness and unity in front of

Eleanor. Which was why that summer day in London, in Hyde Park, always stood out in her mind. It was the last time they spent together as a family that she *knew* with absolute certainty, that they had all been happy as a family. Despite the bitterness, anger, hurt feelings, yelling, slamming doors, and eventually the divorce and the estrangement from her father, on *that* day, they were happy.

As she continued walking through the park, she noticed a family further ahead of her on the path. A mother and father, with a little girl who looked around eight or nine years old. The little girl was running circles around her parents, soon her dad started chasing her around her mother. The girl shrieked with laughter as her mom reached out and caught her and both her parents started smothering her with hugs. Eleanor's heart dropped into her stomach at the sight. It was so similar to her family that summer day, so long ago. Though it had been so many years since that day, the old wounds came rushing back. The name calling, the hurt feelings, the shouting and yelling, her mom crying and trying to tell her that everything would be ok. The way her dad left one night and she didn't see him again for two weeks after she and her mom had moved into their temporary apartment near her mom's college.

Tears started to fall, at first just a few, but soon streams of tears down Eleanor's face. She was crying so hard she could no longer see the family ahead of her and her pace had slowed so much that they were soon well ahead of her. Eventually Eleanor had to stop and sit on a bench. All the pain she thought she'd dealt with she now realized she had just pushed it deep down. She now understood where her writer's block was coming from. She'd been trying to write the story of a happy family. Like hers had been on that summer's day when she was nine. But that's not her story to tell. That wasn't really her family and that memory wasn't as perfect as she remembered it.

They may have been happy in that moment, a moment that she had been using as a safety blanket to cover what had come next in her family life. Her father was still deeply flawed and the plain truth was, he never loved them enough. Not really. If he did the divorce wouldn't have been so nasty, he wouldn't have treated her and her mother so poorly. He wouldn't have cut Eleanor out and used her when he needed to maintain the appearance of doting father to his colleagues. *If he truly loved me*, Eleanor thought angrily, *that horrible night in Manhattan would never have happened*. But she and her mom had only been pawns. They served a purpose for a time and then when they were no longer of use, her dad discarded her mom and kept Eleanor on the side, as if he could just call up Central Casting and order "one dutiful daughter" for the annual faculty and family luncheon.

It made Eleanor sick to think about it now, but her professors were always telling them to "write what they know." Eleanor realized now that she didn't know about happy families and happy endings. She knew about pain and loss, heartbreak and destruction. She knew how to move on and start over, and she was learning how to reinvent herself. She understood that people aren't perfect and you can't make them be. Her father is who he is. She couldn't change him or their past. All she could do was move forward with her future, just as she did half a lifetime ago when she was thirteen. She learned she couldn't trust her father, but she could trust her mom. And Aunt Vickie and Jonathan and Uncle Edward. And eventually she learned she could trust Grace and Carly, just as she's started trusting Jack, and Patrick. But by not dealing with her past, she opened herself up to Michael, who she now realized, never deserved her in the first place. He treated her just like her father did. And Mark may or may not have been the same story if she'd continued with him.

Suddenly she knew her whole project needed to change, the characters needed to be completely reworked. There would be no magic happy ending like the movies she loved to watch when she was upset. Because that wasn't real life. Her protagonist needed to figure things out on her own and make her own happy ending, just as Eleanor was trying to do. Eleanor wiped the tears from her eyes furiously, and with a new determination raced out of the park. She got the Tube at Hyde Park Corner and headed to one of her favorite coffee shops back by the flat, scribbling notes in her notebook the whole way. She sat in Caffè Nero until it closed, taking one last large latte back to the flat with her, where she continued writing in her room until well past 2 o'clock in the morning when her eyes, tired from staring at the screen for so long, finally fluttered shut.

Despite the late hour she fell asleep, she was back up at 7 o'clock the next morning, and at the Caffè Nero on Kingsway by 8 o'clock. She spent all of Saturday writing, taking breaks to walk around and moving from one coffee shop to the other. Sunday was the same thing, up before Jonathan was awake and out in coffee shops or the occasional pub for a meal, writing until late, coming home and writing in her room, barely aware of Jonathan in the flat outside her door. But it was working, her book was finally working! She had so much to write, her fingers couldn't type fast enough. She had to give up on writing on her iPad, her little Bluetooth keyboard couldn't keep up with her. So every day she packed up her laptop and found new places to write.

That week at school she could barely pay attention in class, all she wanted to do was go write. Jack kept glancing at her, fidgeting and bouncing in her seat, tapping her pen against the desk until she caught him glaring at her and she suddenly stopped moving, clasping her hands together tightly in her lap.

After her last class of the day she found Jack waiting right outside the classroom.

"What is going on with you?!" he asked worriedly.

Eleanor grinned, "I'm writing. It finally clicked, I know what I'm writing now! Are we going to write now? Which coffee shop do you want to go to?" she asked, practically hopping from one foot to the other waiting for Jack's reply.

Picking up on the energy radiating off of Eleanor, Jack raised an eyebrow and said, "Do you even need more coffee? You look like you could power all of London with the energy coming off you right now."

"Shut up, are you joining me or not? Because I need to get back to writing, if I can keep going at the rate I'm going, I might be able to catch up to where I need to be by the spring term mentor meetings and career workshops."

"Ok, crazy lady, let's go. But since I'm pretty sure you're going to ignore me as soon as we get settled at the coffee shop I'm choosing the location, and I pick the Caffè Nero at the OXO Tower. So you have from here to there to fill me in on what's happened since last week."

Eleanor frowned, because she knew even at a quick pace it would still take at least ten minutes to get there, and there were coffee shops much closer, but she reluctantly agreed and pulled on Jack's arm to get them moving. As they walked across the Millennium Bridge, Eleanor filled him in on her walk through Hyde Park, she didn't share all of the details about her family memories, but enough to make Jack speechless with shock.

"No offense, Elle darling, but your dad is a proper arsehole of the highest order."

"You'll get no argument from me on that," Eleanor said quickly.

They soon arrived at Caffè Nero and got their coffees and cakes and settled in. Jack couldn't help but stop and watch Eleanor for a couple minutes, her fingers flying across her keyboard, a series of different expressions flickering across her face, her lips moving slightly as she wrote streams of dialogue between characters. As he worked on his own project, slowly but steadily, he would notice how every now and then Eleanor would pause and take a sip of her latte or bite of her cappuccino cake and look off into the distance before something would spark in her eyes and her fingers would start flying again, as if there was some great energy inside her, desperately trying to get out.

* * * * *

The rest of the week passed in the same way. Halloween came and went, she knew Jonathan went out to a party but she stuck to her routine. Class during the morning and early afternoon, then writing with Jack, though they barely spoke once they got to whichever coffee shop they were writing in for the afternoon. They'd sit there for hours, until Jack would force Eleanor to stop for dinner. But even then, they would talk about their projects and help each other out with places they were getting stuck. She'd stay up late writing and reworking her novel. There was so much work to do but she felt so much more confident about it now. There were days where she'd look back and count how many pages she'd done that day and find it was only four or five, but she knew instinctively they were good pages so she didn't let herself feel discouraged.

After New Year's there would be a series of meetings and conversations with their assigned mentors and she was finally feeling like she had some solid material to show for her work so far this year. She just hoped it would be enough to get a fellowship or grant, or to help her get a job at one of the publishing companies the school had connections to. The weekend went by in a blur of coffee and writing and the following week had gone the same as the previous week. October turned into November and Eleanor had about four weeks left to the term before the winter holiday break.

She was vaguely aware that Jonathan was concerned about her. She'd catch him hovering by the front door when she got home and he was constantly offering to bring her tea at night while she was working. There had been texts from Patrick too. To some she replied quickly, others she meant to reply to later and then forgot. He flew to LA after his meetings in New York and was about to start a series of meetings for a couple new roles in some high profile projects. He sounded excited and Eleanor was excited for him. She'd believed him when he said he'd keep in touch, but she was surprised to receive at least one text a day, if not two, from him. By the end of the second week, even Patrick was starting to sound worried about Eleanor.

You ok? You've been really quiet the past couple weeks. :/ x

Feeling guilty, Eleanor quickly tapped a reply and then turned back to her writing.

Yeah, everything's great. Just finally writing. A lot of work to catch up on! Promise all is well. Can't wait to see you when you're back in London :) x

She felt awkward adding the kiss at the end, but he'd included one so it felt awkward not including it in her reply. She groaned inwardly thinking about how bad she was with men. Even as friends, she got flustered where Patrick was concerned. Some part of Eleanor thought it was because she wanted to be more than friends with Patrick, but another part told herself to be sensible and that she was just getting confused by her long time crush on him as an actor.

That Friday night she returned home, ready to start writing again after eating the sandwich she picked up at Pret but she was stopped at the door by Jonathan.

"This has gone on long enough. I'm glad you've got through your writer's block but you need a break Ellie, you can't keep writing all day and night, you'll burn out. I'm going to the pub, you're coming with me, and I won't hear any arguments. Now go put your laptop and notebooks away, freshen up if you want, and we leave in five minutes."

Before she could respond he turned and went to his room, shutting the door behind him, but through the closed door she heard him call out, "The clock is ticking Ellie! Four minutes and forty-five seconds!"

Sighing, she gave in. She knew that when Jonathan got determined about something like this there was no stopping him or arguing. She put her food from Pret in the fridge to eat later, then went into her room and put down her bag. She transferred the essentials into a smaller cross body bag and changed from the dress and tights she'd been wearing into skinny jeans and a sweater, putting her tall black boots back on. With a minute to spare she was back out in the hall just as Jonathan was coming out of his room.

Looking at her, "Good, you're ready. Let's go."

Chapter 14

They walked down the road to their usual pub. As they approached, Jonathan suddenly looked a bit nervous.

"Umm, Mark will probably be here. I wasn't thinking about that. Will you be ok? I just wanted to get you away from your computer for a while, but I don't want to put you in an awkward situation. You and I could go out somewhere on our own instead if you want."

"No, it's fine Jon, really. I was going to see him again eventually. And we talked, he's willing to be friends, I am too. May as well get the initial awkwardness over with."

They went in and soon found Zaf and Malcolm, who told them that Ioan was out for the night, but Henry would be there soon. Which made Eleanor happy, she liked Henry and his stories of growing up in Nigeria. They both liked to talk about the shock of arriving in a new country, with a different culture, and coming from much warmer climates. Before they could take their seats, Eleanor heard a voice behind her.

"Hey Jon. Hi Eleanor," Mark said quietly.

The whole table seemed to hold their breath, and she could feel Jon's hand on her back. Not wanting to make things more awkward then they already felt, she turned and smiled brightly at Mark.

"Hi Mark, it's good to see you again."

Mark grinned at Eleanor, "Good to see you too."

Turning to Jonathan, she said, "I'll have my usual please. You're paying, since you dragged me away from my writing tonight."

Jonathan just laughed and as he walked off Mark put the three drinks he'd brought back for himself, Zaf and Malcolm. Eleanor grabbed a seat at the end of the table, next to Malcolm, and Mark sat down across from her.

Before things could get uncomfortable again, Malcolm turned to Eleanor and made her fill them in on school and all the writing she'd been doing, saying, "Jonathan says you've been very busy, I think he's been worried."

Eleanor just laughed. "Jonathan worries too much. But there's only a month left to term at the Harrison and I only just started to solve the problem with my project, so I'm frantically trying to get caught up. Like he's never spent all day and night working on a project before," she said stubbornly.

"Aye, very true," Malcolm said laughing. "Trust me, we all feel your pain."

Just then she heard a loud voice cut across the pub, "Gorgeous Elle! How are you?!"

Eleanor looked up to see Henry rush across the pub and she jumped up to give him a hug. "Henry! I'm good, how are you?"

"I'm good, I'm good. Exhausted, but I'm sure you feel the same way, right? Jonathan says you're burning the candle at both ends and writing day and night. You must sleep Elle," he said, looking worried.

"Oh stop being so dramatic, I'm sleeping, I promise," she said laughing.

She heard Jonathan laugh behind her, "Yeah, you sleep for like six hours and then you're back up again. You need *more* sleep Ellie."

"He's right, Elle, you need to sleep. It's very important." Henry gave her a very worried look.

"Oh fine. I won't set my alarm tonight, I'll sleep in as late as I can tomorrow. Happy?" she said with mock anger.

"Yes," said all the men at the table at once.

"Oh god, it's like I have five brothers now instead of one," Eleanor said mournfully.

Henry pulled up a chair next to hers and wrapped his arm around her shoulders, "Elle, if you were my sister I'd have hidden your laptop and notebooks by now and forced you to relax. You deserve at least one day off each week. Even God rested on the seventh day, and He was creating the world. Your book will survive your absence for one day."

"Oh now you're really being dramatic Henry, stop it," she said laughing. "And you lot," she said, her gaze sweeping the faces around the table, "are hardly in a position to give me any lectures. Jonathan, you've been working nearly as hard as I am. Every time I come home you're hard at work at your own computer. When you're not hovering outside my door with a cup of tea, that is. And I know the rest of you are working just as hard with the end of term coming up. This is crunch time for all of us."

"Yes, Ellie," Jonathan agreed. "But we've all still taken at least a couple nights off each week. You didn't even come out for Halloween with us. And you're American!"

"What does that have to do with anything?" she asked laughing. "I don't celebrate Halloween back in the States. I haven't dressed up and done anything for Halloween since I was eighteen my senior year of high school."

"Still, you need to give yourself a break every now and then."

"Ugh, fine," she said petulantly. "I'm taking a break now and I'll have a nice lazy lie in tomorrow morning, satisfied?"

"Yes," the whole table responded again. And then they all laughed.

They all chatted about school and work for a while, and Eleanor felt comfortable sitting between Malcolm and Henry, Henry's arm was still draped casually across the back of her chair. After a couple hours, Zaf and Malcolm had to leave but the rest of them were willing to stay for one more drink. Henry and Jonathan went to the bar to get the drinks, leaving Mark and Eleanor alone at the table.

"I'm glad to get you alone for a minute. I've been wanting to talk to you since we spoke a few weeks ago," he said hesitantly.

"Oh? What's up?" Eleanor replied, trying to sound casual.

"I've missed hanging out with you. I was wondering if we could get coffee sometime. Maybe tomorrow, while you're taking a break from your work?"

He looked so hopeful, Eleanor couldn't bear to turn him down, even though she really wasn't sure. It was one thing hanging out with him in a group like this, with the others around as a buffer, but just the two of them alone? Even in a busy coffee shop, she just wasn't sure.

"Yeah, that would be nice," she heard herself saying. "I can't afford to take the whole day off tomorrow, no matter what you all think. But I could meet for coffee before I start writing. Would one o'clock work?"

"Sure, brilliant," Mark said with a giant smile. "Just say where and I'll be there."

"How about the Caffè Nero across the street from here?"

They agreed, and Jonathan and Henry arrived back at the table with the last round of drinks. An hour later they all left and headed home. Eleanor suddenly felt very tired, and the idea of sleeping in the next morning sounded like the best idea ever. Though she would never admit that to Jonathan she thought, smiling to herself. She was a little nervous about meeting Mark tomorrow, but she figured that would take care of itself. No sense worrying about it now.

* * * * *

The next day, Eleanor woke up to the sun streaming through her window. She knew based on how bright it was when she removed her sleep eye mask, that she had definitely slept in. She reached for her phone and saw that it was past noon. She hadn't slept that late since she arrived in London with jet lag. She also realized with a start that she had less than an hour to get ready and get to Caffè Nero to meet Mark and then go write.

"Bugger," she cursed, leaping out of bed. She dashed around her room getting ready. Another quick glance at her phone told her that it was only going to be in the mid-30s Fahrenheit, nearly 0 Celsius, as a high for the weather that day, almost freezing. Sunny days in London tended to be colder than cloudy ones since the clouds kept the city insulated. She put on the same skinny jeans from the night before and her boots again, then pulled on a long sleeve t-shirt and one of her thickest jumpers, a gorgeous sapphire blue chunky cable knit she'd found at Jigsaw. It had cost her a pretty penny but once again she was grateful for her part time job as a writing tutor. It wasn't a ton of money, and if she had to pay her share of the rent she'd never make it. She and Jonathan were very lucky that Aunt Vickie spoiled them both so much. But what she earned kept her clothed and caffeinated and she was grateful.

Grabbing the bag from last night, she dumped out the contents and organized them back into her trusty navy Longchamp tote bag. It had been a gift from her aunt several years ago. No one in Arizona carried the simple Le Pliage nylon tote, the women in Phoenix all seemed to favor

Coach or Gucci or Michael Kors. But since arriving in London Eleanor had been amused to see every fourth or fifth woman carrying the bag, in a range of colors. She never realized how European she'd been all these years.

She laughed at the memory as she double checked that her laptop and notebooks were still in the bag. She grabbed a hairband from her bedside table and scraped her hair up into a messy topknot and then went to the mirror on her dresser and grabbed a tube of Rimmel mascara, quickly putting a few coats on her lashes and then dabbing some cream blusher on each cheek. This was *not* a date, so she wasn't going to waste time doing her hair and makeup. *Just a quick coffee with Mark and then you need to get back to writing,* she thought, wondering just how long a 'quick' coffee should be. Was an hour long enough? Too long? She didn't want Mark to feel like she was ditching him. But she really did need to write. *Oh well, I'll just play it by ear and see what happens. But definitely no longer than an hour.*

She threw on her wool coat, scarf, and gloves, and dashed out of the flat. She saw Mark walking up from the opposite direction just as she was racing up to the coffee shop.

"Afraid you were going to be late?" he asked with a smile?

"Well I took everyone's advice and slept in. I only woke up about forty-five minutes ago. I didn't think I'd sleep that long!" she said laughing incredulously.

"Clearly you needed it," Mark replied kindly. "I'm glad. You could have texted me you know, I could have met you later."

"No, this is good. I need to get back to writing this afternoon anyway. But I definitely need some coffee first. And it's kind of freezing out here, so maybe we could go inside?" she said with a smile, hopping from one foot to the other trying to keep warm.

Mark laughed and ushered her inside. For a Saturday afternoon the coffee shop was fairly quiet. The tourists had long ago stopped flooding the coffee shops of London. The city seemed to be in a lull between the busy summer season and the holidays. There were still plenty of tourists around, but definitely much less than there had been when she first arrived. They ordered their coffees, paying separately at Eleanor's insistence.

"But I invited you out today! It's bad manners to make you pay," Mark protested.

Still, he gave in and she felt better about paying for herself. They got a table near the window and soon fell into an easy conversation. He told her stories of what he'd been up to lately and gave her the gossip about Jonathan and Celeste. All the guys were on Jon's case as well to just ask her out. Eleanor found herself enjoying Mark's company more than ever and was glad she'd agreed to continue their friendship. After spending so much time writing it was nice to be talking to someone and feeling social. She didn't realize how much she'd missed it.

Feeling like no time at all had passed, Eleanor caught a glimpse of the time on her watch, "Oh! It's after three! I'm so sorry Mark, this has been lovely but I really do need to write this afternoon," she cried apologetically.

"Don't worry about it. I shouldn't have kept you so long," he said reassuringly.

"I really have had a wonderful time. Thank you for inviting me, this has been really nice."

They got up and Mark helped Eleanor back into her coat. "So where do you go from here?"

"Oh, I'll just wander and think about my writing for a bit, once I'm done thinking I just stop at the nearest coffee shop and start writing," she said with a laugh.

They got outside the door and were hit with a blast of cold air. Eleanor laughed as she started shaking. Mark turned to her and gave her a big hug, rubbing her shoulders and back briskly to warm her up. Suddenly he stopped and was looking at Eleanor, before she could move he was kissing her, passionately. She was too stunned to do anything at first, but after a couple seconds, as Mark took her inaction for permission and started to kiss her more intensely, she flung her hands up between them and pushed him firmly away from her, taking a couple steps backward at the same time. Her heart was pounding in her ears and for a moment she was back in a different time and place. She felt fight or flight kick in, and like one night several years ago, fight took over and a rage began to build up inside her.

Furiously, "What the bloody hell do you think you're doing Mark?!"

"Oh come on Eleanor! You felt that, you know you did!" Mark replied pleadingly.

"What I felt was your tongue down my throat you creep! Something you most definitely did *not* have permission to do. I thought you understood, I don't want to be with you Mark, I just want to be friends! I thought I could trust you, god, how stupid can I be?!" she asked, more to herself than to Mark.

"You're not stupid Eleanor, you're smart and beautiful and amazing, why is it so hard to understand why I want you?"

"You don't want me, you don't even know me! Not really. And you certainly don't respect me, so why would I want *you*?! You know what Mark, you can take your ideas of friendship and go fling them in the Thames. And then you can leave me the hell alone. I'm so done with you." Eleanor felt a rage she hadn't felt in a very long time. Not since her trip to Manhattan and the events that led up to her falling out with her father. Before she could say anything else, or worse, slap Mark across the face, she turned on her heel and stalked off down Queen Street towards Covent Garden, she could sense Mark start to follow her and she whipped around to face him.

"In case I wasn't clear enough before, let me put this in language your one track mind might be able to process. Back off Mark. If you keep following me I will flag down the next cop I see and report you for stalking and harassment. Respect me, just this once, and I'll *consider* not telling Jonathan about what you've done today and we'll just politely ignore each other from now on. Keep following me and I'll tell him what you've pulled. I think we both know what his reaction will be."

Without waiting for a response Eleanor turned away from him and kept walking into Covent Garden. Thankfully this time he didn't follow. She walked straight through Covent Garden and towards Leicester Square, the anger was still too strong and she still felt filled with adrenaline. She knew there was no way she was going to get any writing done today, so she kept walking, eventually making it to Oxford Street. Since it was now nearly four o'clock, it was starting to get dark, and much colder. She bundled her coat and scarf around herself more tightly. She soon spotted a Waterstones bookstore across from Selfridges and veered left, sailing through the doors without thinking. A bookstore was the perfect place to calm herself down. Inside the store it was significantly quieter compared to outside. She wandered up to the second floor, instinctively seeking out the Jane Austen shelf, hoping for comfort from familiar characters and words. She walked up and down the aisles, scanning the book spines, knowing she was getting closer. She could feel the tension start to dissipate and her shoulders began to feel more relaxed. As she reached the end of the aisle, and was about to turn down the next one when she looked up and spotted Patrick a few rows away, a few books in his hand. She suddenly remembered she hadn't responded to the text he sent a couple days ago, she didn't even know he was back in London. She was unsure if she should say hello, she felt guilty for neglecting his texts but she desperately needed a friend right now.

As if sensing he was being watched, Patrick glanced up and saw Eleanor frozen in place. His eyes lit up at the sight of her and Eleanor's heart leapt.

"You're, umm, back in London," she stammered, for lack of anything better to say as he approached.

"And you, Miss Gordon, have been ignoring me," Patrick replied with a serious expression.

"No! I haven't! I mean, not really, or at least not intentionally, I'm so sorry Patrick, I am. I've been a crap friend and you've been so nice to text me even though I know you've been so busy and traveling and I'm sorry I didn't respond to your last text I've just been so busy writing and it's finally working but that's still not an excuse to ignore you and be so horrible," Eleanor blurted out, not taking a breath as she tried to apologize, a look of horror on her face at the thought that Patrick had thought she was deliberately ignoring him. Just when she thought this day couldn't get any worse.

Suddenly Patrick started to laugh, holding his hands up, "Slow down Eleanor, I'm only teasing you! I know you've been busy writing. I just got back last night, I was going to text you today but then got stuck in a meeting this morning. I'm glad to bump into you like this, it saves me the trouble of texting you this evening to ask you to coffee tomorrow." Noticing that Eleanor still looked distraught, "Hey, Eleanor, really, it's ok, I didn't really think you were ignoring me. Wait, has something happened? Are you ok?" Concern spread across his face, "You look like you're about to faint. What's wrong?"

"Oh nothing, I'm fine, it's just been a bad afternoon.

Well, it wasn't all bad. It started out fine, but then it took a sharp turn into total crap and I'm still so angry I could punch something—"

"Whoa, hold on. What's made you so angry?" Patrick asked worriedly, seeing her seething with anger, it was radiating off her in waves. "Wait, let's not talk in the middle of the book store, I need to pay for these books, then we'll go find a quiet place to sit and you can tell me everything from the beginning."

Eleanor could only nod in agreement and she followed Patrick downstairs to the till where he paid for his books. They walked out and Patrick flagged down a cab and ushered her inside. She didn't even hear where he told the cab to go, she just put her head in her hands and rubbed her temples a little, trying to relieve the headache that as building. A few minutes later they pulled up outside a small, unassuming restaurant on a quiet street somewhere in Mayfair Eleanor thought. She took Patrick's hand when he offered to help her out of the cab and she followed him inside. He said hello to the man who met them at the door.

"Hey Charles, got a table for two?" Patrick said with a smile, shaking hands with Charles, a kind looking man in his mid-40s.

"For you I always have a table Patrick. But as we don't open for dinner for another couple hours you have your pick of the place," Charles said with a wink.

"This is my friend Eleanor. Eleanor, this is Charles, a friend of my family's and owner of this fine establishment."

"Pleased to meet you," Eleanor said automatically, even in her current state she knew there was no excuse for bad manners.

"A pleasure m'dear," Charles replied. Looking between Patrick and Eleanor, "What can I get the two of you, I can have the chef whip something up."

"Oh no," Patrick replied, "We don't want to cause a hold

up with your dinner preparations. If we could just trouble you for a pot of coffee and any pastries left over from this morning?"

"I'll bring it out myself, just give me a few minutes. Sit wherever you like." Charles hurried back towards the kitchen and Patrick lead Eleanor to a booth in the back corner.

"I hope this place is ok, I knew they'd be between services today and it would be quiet. Charles often lets me come in for coffee in the middle of the afternoon like this when it's quiet."

"It's fine," Eleanor said distractedly. Looking around, "It's nice."

"We can stay for dinner later, if you want, or I can take you home after we've had coffee and warmed up. And after you've filled me in on what's happened, if you feel like talking about it."

Charles soon brought over a couple giant croissants and a pot of coffee with cream and sugar. Haltingly at first, Eleanor started telling Patrick about what had happened since the night they had dinner. About coming home to find Mark at the flat with Jonathan and them agreeing to start over as friends. The time she spent in a haze of writing and feeling better than she had in weeks. Seeing Mark at the pub last night and agreeing to meet him today. As if sensing where her story was going, a dark expression came over Patrick's face. When she got to the end of the story and told him how she'd threatened to tell Jonathan about Mark's behavior today Patrick interrupted.

"As well you should! I can't believe that bastard! How dare he force himself on you like that."

Quietly, "I wouldn't say he forced himself, I mean, I didn't want him to kiss me but at least that's all he tried." Although as she said it, she knew she lying to herself. Past experience had taught her better.

"Eleanor, you just said it. You didn't want him to kiss you. But he did. By definition, he forced himself on you. Just because he didn't drag you down an alleyway and do something worse doesn't make his behavior any less reprehensible. And your cousin has a right to know!"

"They're friends Patrick," Eleanor cried out quietly. "They've been friends for a long time, even before LSE, they went to Eton together. And then Cambridge for their undergrad studies."

"Your cousin went to Eton? When?"

"I can't remember."

"Sorry, not important. I was just wondering if I knew him, or this Mark fellow. I went to Eton."

"Oh, well, if you were there at the same time, I'm sorry to say my cousin doesn't remember you," Eleanor said with a small laugh. "He only vaguely knew who you were when I mentioned you were in that football movie."

Patrick laughed, "Fair enough."

Eleanor gave a small smile at the memory of that conversation. It felt like a lifetime ago.

"But seriously," Patrick said, "You need to tell Jonathan. He deserves to know. And you definitely shouldn't be around Mark anymore."

"Oh, believe me, I will be avoiding him like the plague," Eleanor said bitterly.

"I'm sorry this happened Eleanor," Patrick said sincerely. "You don't deserve this."

"Thanks. And thanks for bringing me here and for listening."

"That's what friends are for."

"Well, thanks for being my friend. I really needed this. I'm glad I ran into you this afternoon."

Patrick smiled gently, "I admit, I was a little worried when I saw you. I knew you weren't ignoring my texts but I still worried that I was making you feel pressured. Truth be told, I don't have very many friends myself. A few good mates from Eton and Oxford and from drama school, but for the most part it's a small group, and only a couple of them live in London. It's rare that I connect with new people enough to develop a friendship. I've enjoyed my time with you and getting to know you, so I wouldn't want to do anything to make you feel uncomfortable." Again Eleanor noticed a rare moment of vulnerability in his expression.

"Oh Patrick," Eleanor sighed, suddenly feeling really bad for not texting him back, "you haven't made me feel uncomfortable, far from it. You've been a good friend, and I loved hearing from you while you were gone. I swear, the only reason I didn't respond all the time was because I was so busy writing. I have so much catching up to do but I think I'm actually going to make it."

Looking down at the plates covered in croissant crumbs and checking his watch, "It's nearly time for them to start serving dinner. Why don't we order something and you can tell me about your writing?" Patrick suggested with a smile.

Charles brought over menus and once the kitchen had reopened they ordered dinner. Eleanor told Patrick about her walk in the park and her idea for the book. Just as she'd done with Jack, she didn't tell Patrick all of the personal inspiration that went into her idea, but kept to the story of the characters and how she was finally getting to understand her protagonist.

Patrick watched and listened, enthralled, as Eleanor filled him in. Her entire face lit up as she talked about writing, she was so excited. He thought that he could sit here for hours listening to her talk about her work and after seeing her so upset earlier it was a relief to see her look so happy now.

As they ate their dinner Eleanor asked him about his trip to the States. He gave her the full story of the meetings he'd attended in New York and LA. There were two major productions that wanted him in the starring roles. The one he'd met for in New York would start right after New Year's but would shoot in the London area. It was a small film, a personal story about love and relationships he said, it would be just him and three other actors and he was really excited about the chance to do serious character development with the character he would play. The second film, that they had flown him to LA for, was a huge action film, sort of *James Bond* meets *Mission: Impossible* and *Bourne Identity*. He'd play the mysterious MI-6 agent, that could possibly be a double agent for the Russian FSB. There were several other major movie stars signed up already to play various CIA and MI-6 agents, none of them knowing who might be double crossing the others. It would be the highest profile role Patrick had played, and though his part was not the largest, it was one of the most dynamic he thought. It was scheduled to start filming in LA in March and would then shoot on location around the world from April through July.

He was clearly very excited and Eleanor knew both roles would be a huge deal for him. He'd had very prominent roles in the UK and was already fairly well known, with a small but ardent fan base. He was all over Tumblr and though he didn't post often, his Instagram had almost a million followers. And Eleanor would never admit to how many hours she'd spent watching clips, torrents, and fanvids of him on YouTube. But despite his status as one of Britain's most crush-worthy actors, next to the likes of Tom Hiddleston or Benedict Cumberbatch or Tom Hardy, he still wasn't super well known in the States. The small film was bound for Sundance and was predicted to be an indie hit but the big spy film would put him in a major summer blockbuster, opening the following year, starring Brad Pitt, Michael Fassbender, Idris Elba, Kate Winslet, Jessica Chastain, and others yet to be announced. It was going to be a near-guaranteed hit and would make Patrick a household name on both sides of the Atlantic.

"Or at least that's what my agent and the producers tell me," Patrick said with a laugh. "I'm doubtful."

"Oh stop being so modest. This is a huge opportunity for you! You must be over the moon," Eleanor replied enthusiastically.

"To be honest I'm scared out of my mind," Patrick said, his voice lowering.

"You're going to be brilliant, as always, in both roles. You have accepted them, right?"

Patrick nodded. "I took a couple days to think about each one before signing the contracts, but yes, I'm officially committed to both. Terrifying as that feels."

"Each one is just another role. Just like you've done a bunch of times already. Different characters but the process is the same. You're going to be great. I just can't wait for them to come out, I want to see each one already!" Eleanor said laughing.

"You know, to be honest, I want to see the spy film so bad!" Patrick admitted, smiling like an excited five year old. "It's exactly the kind of movie I grew up watching. Playing a spy in an action film like this is a dream come true. It's the kind of project that got me into wanting to do films in the first place, as opposed to focusing only on stage work."

"See? It was meant to be," Eleanor stated with finality.

As Patrick smiled at her, she thought about how nice it was talking to him and how much better she felt. She needed the day to end like this. It was amazing how much better she always felt with Patrick. He always put her at ease and she didn't feel awkward talking to him, even about her writing, something she usually struggled talking to people about. And after hearing all his good news, she was so happy for him she could burst.

Once they were done eating, they paid their bill, Patrick

not even blinking an eye when Eleanor fished out her wallet to pay her half. They got a taxi and Patrick took her home, walking her up to the door again.

"Sleep well Eleanor, I'm glad I got to spend time with you tonight, it was a welcome change of plans."

"Thanks, I enjoyed it too," Eleanor said. "I'd invite you in, but after today's emotional rollercoaster, I'm shattered."

"No, don't worry about it, I need to get home, I have an early meeting. But I'm still hoping to come over for spag bol and Graham Norton soon."

Eleanor laughed, "Definitely, we'll plan it soon."

Patrick held out his arms and when she nodded her that she was open to a hug, he pulled Eleanor into a giant hug, that warmed her whole body. She hugged him back until he let her go and with final smile, turned and walked away. It felt lovely not to have to worry about a hug turning into something else.

Slightly dazed, Eleanor let herself into the flat. Jonathan wasn't in, she decided she'd tell him about Mark later. She made herself some tea and a bath, and soaked away all the remaining stress of the day, though she really did feel much better thanks to Patrick. Eventually she crawled into bed and fell into a deep, dreamless sleep.

Chapter 15

The following week, Eleanor kept up her steady routine of classes, working in the writing center, and writing with Jack, but listening to Jonathan's advice, she started spending the evenings at home reading or watching movies on her laptop. On Thursday she went about her usual routine, and it wasn't until she got out of school later in the afternoon and was walking past St. Paul's Cathedral that she realized what day it was. There was a sign outside advertising their special Thanksgiving Day service for Americans in London. Eleanor's heart dropped realizing it was Thanksgiving back home. She hadn't talked to her mom in a few days and Cassie hadn't mentioned it. The service was already done at the Cathedral so she'd missed that too.

It had never been her favorite holiday, Christmas was her favorite. But since moving to Arizona she and her mom had made their own traditions that included a small turkey and all the traditional side dishes. In the morning, they would set the table, laying down a piece of butcher paper on the table, and throughout the day, while they cooked, they would each add different things they were thankful for that year. Then after dinner they'd type up the list and hang it on the fridge. This would be followed by a weekend of decorating the house for Christmas and watching their favorite Christmas films. Eleanor sank down onto the front steps of the Cathedral and tears started falling. She suddenly felt terribly homesick and lonely. She missed her mom.

Suddenly her phone started to ring and she fished it out of her coat pocket. It was Jonathan, answering quickly, she was suddenly worried, Jonathan rarely called her, he usually stuck to text.

"Hi cousin, how are you?" she heard him ask, he sounded very casual and upbeat.

"Umm, I'm fine?" she said, though her voice went up in the end adding a question mark to her response and there was a slight catch in her voice as she tried to stop crying.

"Uh oh, you are not 'fine', I can hear it in your voice. What's wrong? Where are you?" he said, sounding worried.

"I'm sitting in front of St. Paul's. Oh, Jonathan, it's Thanksgiving and I completely forgot. And I already missed the service at the Cathedral which I told myself months ago that I needed to look up the time and put an alert in my phone because I wanted to go. And I should have planned something to distract myself this evening because all I can think about is how much I miss mom and our usual plans," she cried out in a rush, tears starting to fall again, this time harder than before. The exhaustion of her schedule and the emotional drama she'd been dealing with had gotten to be too much and she was finally at a breaking point. She felt a sudden urge to just go home and bury herself in her duvet.

"Come home Ellie, we'll figure something out to distract you. Ok?"

"Ok," she replied in a small voice. She hung up before she had to say anything else. She was crying too hard to talk. She got up and started walking back down Ludgate Hill towards home, hugging her arms around herself, as much as to keep warm as to try to comfort herself. By the time she got to the flat she was fighting tears again and felt so tired. She turned the key in the door but it was flung open by Jonathan, who had a big smile on his face, which immediately fell when he saw Eleanor's tear-stained face and red eyes.

Pulling her into his arms and shutting the door behind her, "Oh Ellie, it's ok. You need to stop crying now, because I have the best surprise for you," he said, looking suddenly very mischievous.

Frowning, "What do you mean? And what smells so good?" Then she noticed the door to the living room was closed, which they never did, and she swore she heard something get knocked over followed by a giggle. She looked at Jonathan, who put an arm around her shoulder and led her to the lounge, opening the door to reveal Jack, Clara, Maggie, and Alexandra from school, Celeste, and by the window Patrick, all smiling at Eleanor and shouting "Happy Thanksgiving!" She looked at the rest of the room, the dining table had been extended to fit more than the usual four people and was now taking up half of the lounge. The table was beautifully decorated with flowers and mini pumpkins and gourds. Eleanor also noticed a long piece of butcher paper covered the whole length and she could see that people had already started writing on it.

Realizing the thought and planning that had gone into the preparations, and the fact that Jonathan must have contacted her mom, made Eleanor start to cry all over again. She turned and buried her face in Jonathan's chest as fresh tears spilled over.

"Oh poppet," she heard Jonathan say as she felt his arms wrap tightly around her. "Did you really think I was going to let Thanksgiving pass without doing something for you? I know you miss Aunt Cassie, we're going to FaceTime her and Grace and Carly later, it's all planned. But in the meantime, your mom gave me all the details and recipes."

A thought occurred to Eleanor after hearing that last part and she lifted her head off Jonathan's chest and wailed, "but you can't cook anything besides spag bol!" Everyone, including Jonathan, burst into laughter. Eleanor hadn't meant to be funny, she meant it. Jon was a rubbish cook who was limited to scrambled eggs, beans on toast, and spaghetti Bolognese, technically he also made a curry but Eleanor found it inedible.

But Celeste suddenly spoke up. "Jon can't cook, but a friend of mine is a chef. He's prepared everything and left it all in the oven and refrigerator with instructions for heating and serving. I promise he followed your mum's instructions to the letter."

"Right," Jonathan said firmly, "enough crying, it's like you're American or something. Really, I wonder how we're related sometimes," he said jokingly. "Let's eat!"

Everyone got their food and took a seat. They kept scribbling new thoughts on the butcher paper throughout the meal. Which was delicious. Celeste's friend was indeed an amazing chef, it tasted just like her mother's cooking, which while simple, still had quality of a different kind to what you usually found in fancy restaurants. They passed the bottles of Prosecco around the table and refilled the glasses frequently. Looking around the table, with Jonathan to her left and Patrick to her right, and Jack giving her sly winks and glances towards Patrick throughout the meal, Eleanor was so filled with joy and gratitude for her friends and her life here.

As dinner was cleared away and two large pumpkin pies were brought out, they began to go around the table and share the things that had been written down before and during the meal, sharing what they all were thankful for. Friends old and new, family, getting over writer's block, surviving LSE, and new opportunities were all mentioned.

When it got to Eleanor, she found herself suddenly feeling very shy and quiet. She thought she noticed Patrick shift almost imperceptibly closer to her, without actually touching her.

Looking up and around at all the faces around her, she said softly, "Last year, I would have never imagined that this is where I would be this year. It's like I've been transplanted into someone else's life. Last year I thought I was happy. I thought I had so much to be grateful for. And I did have some things. But I learned that others weren't as lasting as I'd thought or hoped, and there were plenty of disappointments. But those were followed by a second chance. A chance to start over and do things the way I wanted to. That chance led me here, to London, and to all of you. Jonathan, you've always been like a brother to me, which I've always been profoundly grateful for. And to have this time to spend with you and have a life with you here in London, has been an absolute gift. I don't know what I would have done without you and Aunt Vickie, not just since I've been here, but always. You've always been my big brother, my hero.

"And all of you, have been so kind and welcoming and generous with your friendships. Jack, Clara, Maggie, Alex...I wouldn't be surviving school without you all. Celeste, you made my birthday party one I would never forget, Jonathan told me how involved you were in the planning and I'm glad to have the chance to thank you properly. And Patrick, when I bumped into you, literally, in Covent Garden that day, I never thought that all these months later we'd be friends and you'd be sharing this day with me. And I'm so happy to have your friendship and for all the good things that are coming your way. I'm so happy to have all of you," she finished, her voice cracking as she started to cry again.

Before Jonathan could comfort her, Patrick reached an

arm around her and pulled her close, Jack and Jonathan both exchanging a glance as they saw Eleanor curl into him for a moment. Quickly Eleanor pulled away and dried her eyes.

"Let's eat pie," she commanded. And they all started serving up the pumpkin deliciousness. While eating the pie, Jonathan brought in his laptop and got Eleanor's mom, and her friends Grace and Carly on FaceTime. Eleanor was surprised to see them all at her mom's house, and they told her that since Grace and Carly knew Cassie was going to be alone on Thanksgiving they'd both given up on flying home to their own families and were spending the holiday and the weekend with Cassie. Eleanor nearly started crying again thinking of how generous that was of her friends.

After pie, Jonathan surprised Eleanor again by putting *White Christmas* in the DVD player and the group rearranged the coffee table and pillows and blankets to create a more comfortable space to watch the film. Eleanor was shocked when Jack admitted he'd never seen the film. Before long Eleanor was entranced by the film. She always loved the music, the dialogue, and oh the costumes! What she would give to go back in time to experience the golden era of Hollywood. To have seen films like this in giant movie palaces rather than on a small TV.

Finally, around eleven o'clock, everyone started saying goodbye. Everyone but Patrick and Celeste had class the next morning, but Celeste had work at the restaurant and Patrick had an early morning meeting. Jack and the girls headed out together, since they lived in the same area. Patrick offered to share a taxi with Celeste, since they were both headed across town. As Eleanor fell asleep that night, she couldn't help but think about how truly blessed and lucky she was to have such wonderful friends.

* * * * *

242

Christmas break soon arrived at school and Eleanor would have a full month off. However, as much as she wanted to spend that time writing, the lure of Christmas in London was too strong to resist and her routine was temporarily altered. She'd spend a few hours each day writing, but the rest of the time was spent shopping for Christmas gifts, enjoying festivals and markets like Winter Wonderland in Hyde Park, and attending Christmas parties. She was spending increasing amounts of time at Patrick's flat, baking cookies or wrapping presents, or writing while Patrick read his script and worked on preparing for his next film. Things felt very easy and comfortable with him, never awkward or difficult. One night Eleanor and Patrick had been out at the cinema at the Brunswick Centre, watching a screening of *It's A Wonderful Life*, When they got out of the film it was so quiet and still with a light snow that had started to fall while they were inside and had dusted everything in sight with a thin layer of white.

Eleanor had been so excited by the snow, it seemed so magical! And Patrick couldn't take his eyes off her face and her brilliant smile. He walked her back to the flat, through the quiet and the snow, and without really thinking about it, she'd slipped her arm through his. He just made her feel so safe. In the back of her mind she knew that he was interested in her, but he was always so focused on being her friend and never put his own wants and needs ahead of hers. Whenever Eleanor would think about this she'd feel a little confused and guilty, like she was holding him back.

On the one hand, she knew she wasn't ready for anything more than being just friends. Especially with someone who's life was as crazy as Patrick's was. On the other hand, he was always so patient and kind, and allowed things to progress naturally between them which was making her start to feel things that she wasn't sure she was ready to feel. She also increasingly felt as if she was afraid of losing him. It all just felt so complicated, sometimes she worried she was making it more complicated than it needed to be but then she just cycled back around to the beginning of her cycle of worry where Patrick was concerned. So she didn't say anything and just focused on enjoying the holidays and the time she got to spend with Patrick. Patrick also came over to Eleanor's flat a couple times, and as much as he teased, he thoroughly enjoyed Eleanor's homemade spaghetti Bolognese and watching Graham Norton with Jon and Eleanor, who was also happy to see Celeste joining them more often.

On the 20th of December, Eleanor's mom arrived and she was there to meet Cassie at Heathrow. Though it had only been four months it felt like forty and mother and daughter embraced tightly and with loud shrieks of laughter in the middle of the Terminal 3 arrivals hall. This time, instead of taking the Tube back to the flat as she had done with Jonathan, Eleanor ushered her mom down to the Heathrow Express train and within twenty minutes they had met Jonathan at Paddington Station, who was waiting with Eleanor's bags. The three of them were soon on a train to Bath Spa Station and were met there by Aunt Vickie. Cassie and Vickie hugged for a solid minute, neither sister wanting to let the other go, it had been nearly a year since the last time they'd seen each other when Aunt Vickie had gone out to Arizona for New Years.

After everyone had exchanged hugs and hellos, they piled into Aunt Vickie's Range Rover and drove to her sprawling country house, about twenty minutes outside of Bath. There were plans to drive back to town the following day to visit the shops and see some of the sights. Despite being a huge Jane Austen fan, and a general nerd about England and its history, Eleanor still hadn't made it to Bath.

Aunt Vickie had been doing a lot of traveling that fall and Jonathan hadn't wanted Eleanor to without him as he wanted to be her tour guide since he knew the city so well. So she was excited to spend the Christmas holiday in this amazing town and with the people she loved most in the world. Time with her mom and aunt was just what she needed, Eleanor was convinced of that.

Over the next few days there were long walks in the country around the house, shopping and sightseeing trips into Bath, including the Jane Austen Centre, the Royal Crescent, and the Fashion Museum, all of which Jonathan willingly obliged the women and enjoyed as well. Evenings were spent cozied up by the fire in the den, drinking tea and hot chocolate, telling stories and catching up, and watching classic Christmas films. Eleanor felt more relaxed and happy than she'd been in months. It felt so good to be together with her mom, and as much as she loved living with Jonathan, it was nice being in a house with two other women.

Eleanor and her mom made sure to spend plenty of time together on their own, giving Jonathan and his mom some time together as well. For Cassie, getting this time with her daughter was priceless, definitely well worth the cost of the ticket to come visit. After having Eleanor under the same roof for so long, it was hard living without her. Even when Eleanor had gone away to college, she was never farther than Tucson and they would take turns doing the hour and a half drive between Tucson and Phoenix for visits. Having her daughter across an ocean, after having her entirely to herself for more than ten years since the divorce was almost more than Cassie could bear. The two were already planning another trip in the spring, Eleanor wouldn't be done with school until the end of July, and even then, she might not come back to Arizona. Cassie knew she wouldn't last another several months separation.

Eleanor filled Cassie in on all the little details that had been glossed over in their weekly Skype calls. She also finally told her mom about her awkward coffee "date" with Mark. Cassie shared Patrick's sentiment that Eleanor should tell Jonathan.

"You have to tell him Ellie. Mark may be his friend but you're his family. I'm not saying he can't be friends with the guy, but he should know how his so-called 'friends' treat you," Cassie said emphatically.

Looking down at her tea mug, Eleanor wrapped the blanket more tightly around her shoulders. Despite sitting next to the fireplace, in the large plush chairs that furnished the den, thinking about the incident outside the coffee shop still gave Eleanor the chills.

"I know, I just haven't known how to bring it up. They've been friends for years mom. I don't want to ruin that."

"Honey, Mark is the one who's ruined it. If Jonathan chooses not to be friends with him, that's Mark's fault for not respecting you, not yours. And Jonathan deserves to have the chance to make that choice for himself."

"Fine, I'll tell him. But after Christmas, not right now."

"You should do it before you both head back to London sweetheart. Don't keep putting it off."

"Ok," Eleanor said, her voice small. She knew her mom was right. She hated when her mom was right.

"Now, what's going on between you and that movie star?" Cassie asked, winking at her daughter.

Blushing, "Mom!" Eleanor exclaimed. "Nothing! We're just friends."

"So?" Cassie retorted. She'd noticed what Jonathan and Vickie had noticed as well, that every time the conversation turned to Patrick, Eleanor's whole face lit up. She'd told them about the time she'd spent with him preparing for the holidays and his coming over to the Holborn flat a few times and to spend the evening with Eleanor, Jonathan, and Celeste.

"Really, we're just friends! If you want to interrogate someone about their relationship you should try Jonathan. He keeps trying to say that he doesn't want to 'rush' things with Celeste, but glaciers move faster than he does."

"Oh don't worry, Victoria and I plan on talking to him about Celeste. Vickie says she's a darling girl. Now stop deflecting and tell me about Patrick," Cassie said firmly.

"There's nothing to tell mom, we're just friends," Eleanor repeated emphatically.

"Me thinks thou dost protest too much my dear," Cassie said dramatically.

Eleanor rolled her eyes and groaned, "Mooooom," dragging the word out into several syllables, sounding like an annoyed teenager.

"What? You are friends, ok, I get that. And? You know the best relationships start as friendships. I'm glad you're taking things slow, but you clearly like this guy. I know you said you wanted to spend time figuring out what you want, and I completely agree. But you're not a nun. I want you to move on with someone new at some point and despite my initial misgivings because of his career, he seems like a decent man and perhaps not the stereotype I imagined."

"Well, I'm not sure I'm ready to 'move on'. And when I am, I'm not sure if it will be with Patrick. I'm grateful for his friendship. And no, he's nothing like the stereotypical actor. But I don't want to mess up our friendship by leading him on to think that I might be ready for more with him."

"Darling, he sounds like a very special man. He's certainly very handsome. I won't say I'm not still a little nervous about his career, but if he treats you well that's all I care about. Just make sure that you're not holding yourself back out of fear."

"Fine," Eleanor said quietly.

Cassie knew that Eleanor was finished on the subject and knew better than to continue pushing her. She'd made her point, she just hoped that Eleanor had listened.

* * * * *

Christmas day arrived and Eleanor woke early, the room seemed much brighter than it had the previous morning and for a moment Eleanor thought she'd slept in. But a check of her phone showed that it was only eight o'clock, the sun was just barely up. Thinking that the clouds from the previous day must have cleared, she was about to get out of bed to look out the window, when she heard the sound of footsteps running loudly down the hall outside her room.

The door was suddenly thrown open and Jonathan burst through exclaiming with all the excitement of a five-year-old, "IT SNOWED!!!!!!!!"

Grinning widely, Eleanor threw back the heavy duvet and ran to the window. Looking out she was blinded by the thick, fresh layer of white, sparkling below her as the first bit of sunlight bounced off of it.

Smiling at Eleanor, Jonathan said cheerfully, "Happy Christmas cousin."

Reaching her arm around his waist, she gave him a light hug, "Happy Christmas cousin."

Jonathan gave her a big hug and then turned to the door to leave, "Hurry up! There's presents to open and food to eat. And in that order." And in the blink of an eye he was gone.

Eleanor laughed and then turned to look out the window again at the real life winter wonderland the spread out below her. Snow as far as the eye could see, covering every inch of the farmland that surrounded Aunt Vickie's house. It was like something out of an old-fashioned post card. Even the trees around the property were covered with inches of snow on each branch. It was a good thing it was Christmas Day and their only plans included staying at the house to celebrate. There was no way they were getting down the driveway today!

"It's perfect," Eleanor said to herself, smiling.

She heard Jonathan shouting gleefully downstairs and knew she'd only have another few minutes before he'd come back upstairs and drag her down to the tree. The two families had spent more than a few Christmases together, especially in the years after both Cassie and Victoria had been divorced, neither sister being able to bear the thought of spending Christmas alone. So Eleanor knew that Jonathan had the patience of a small child on Christmas morning, there was no sleeping in or lounging over breakfast before opening presents. She quickly threw on a thick, chunky cable knit cardigan, that came down to her knees, over her plaid flannel men's style pajama set that she'd picked up a week before at Marks & Spencer. She slipped on her warm, fuzzy slippers from Primark and tossed her hair up into a quick top knot. A couple swipes of mascara on her lashes and she rushed out of her room and downstairs.

The snow outside wasn't the only surprise that morning. When she came into the living room and saw the tree, she gasped. She should have known her aunt and her mom would go overboard, but it was still beyond her expectations. The night before, the tree already had a more than sufficient number of gifts underneath it. But now, the brightly wrapped presents spilled out in all directions from under the brightly lit and decorated tree. Her mother must have had Aunt Vickie do some of her shopping for her, there was no way even a fraction of these gifts had come from her mom's suitcase. Jonathan sat in the middle of the pile, grinning from ear to ear.

"I think our mums might have outdone themselves this year," he said excitedly.

"Umm, you think? This is insane! What on earth could be in all of those boxes!"

"Let's get those two crazy mums of ours in here and we can start opening them and find out!"

"Calm yourself, at least for a few more minutes. I need coffee. And knowing our moms, that's probably where they are. Now come and make yourself useful."

Eleanor turned and headed off to the kitchen. Sure enough, Vickie and Cassie where there gathering snacks and coffee.

"Both of you," Eleanor said bossily, "into the living room. Go make yourselves comfortable. Jonathan and I will finish getting the tray together. After seeing what you've been up to I have a feeling Santa's elves need a break this morning."

Not needing further encouragement, the women smiled and left for the living room, while Eleanor and a grumbling Jonathan bustled around the kitchen. Soon they headed back into the living room, Jonathan carrying a heavy tray with a big pot of coffee, cream, sugar, and mugs for them all, while Eleanor brought in a tray with cookies and thickly iced cinnamon rolls, a Christmas morning tradition.

Over the next couple hours, they enjoyed their coffee and treats, and opened all the gifts. For all his excitement, Jonathan was very good at pacing the gift opening process. He'd always liked to make it last as long as possible, so even with just the four of them, it never took less than two hours. They went one at a time and often took things out of their store packaging to inspect more closely before moving on to the next gift. He was thrilled with the new iPad his mom gave him, and insisted on turning it on and taking a couple pictures of them all with the iPad's camera. When their moms opened his joint gift to the two of them, a day at one of London's premier spas, he spent a full ten minutes telling them all about the various treatments that they could choose from. Eleanor had been so excited for that particular gift. Both their moms worked so hard, and while both of them had long since gotten their lives to a position where they could afford such a luxury, neither was good at taking the time for themselves to book an appointment.

Eleanor's mom and aunt and cousin had outdone themselves indeed with their gifts to her. She was now well stocked with jumpers, scarves, a new coat (from Ted Baker at that, the bright cobalt blue one she'd been eyeing all autumn), a gorgeous new pair of black flat heeled boots, and a gorgeous black dress from Reiss that she knew would be perfect for New Year's Eve. She'd also received a new iPad, complete with a Bluetooth keyboard that doubled as a cover, a notebook and pen with a touch screen stylus at the end, and an assortment of home accessories and jewelry. Her family really had gone overboard and it was a Christmas she'd never forget.

Once all the presents had been opened, and the carnage of all the wrapping had been cleaned up, they all curled up on chairs around the tree and chatted while eating more snacks and drinking more coffee. Later in the afternoon, Eleanor and Jonathan put on their jeans and wellies and heavy coats, and headed out into the snow. Vickie and Cassie took pictures from inside the warm house of the two acting like kids as they threw snowballs and built a snowman. After about an hour, Eleanor complained of being cold and they headed back in.

By the time she crawled into bed that night she was exhausted but deliriously happy. It had been a perfect day. Getting away from London for a while and spending Christmas with just the family was a gift in and of itself and she was glad to have a few more days at Aunt Vickie's house before returning to London on the 30th. Just as she was falling asleep she heard her phone alert her to a new text message. When she opened the message, she couldn't help but smile, Patrick had sent a picture of himself with a huge smile on his face and covered in Christmas wrapping and bows, with a caption that read:

My nieces and nephews decided I needed to be "decorated". Hope your day was full of Christmas magic. Happy Christmas Elle xx

Eleanor quickly tapped out her reply:

Christmas was perfect. Can't wait to see you and catch up. Happy Christmas Patrick xx

She put her phone down and quickly fell fast asleep.

* * * * *

The next morning when she went downstairs to the kitchen, she found Jonathan alone sitting in the breakfast nook.

"Mum and Aunt Cassie went out for a walk, they said they'd probably be an hour or so. But considering mum was planning to walk by the Peterson's house and say hi, they could be closer to three or four hours."

"Sounds like fun," Eleanor said with a smile.

"Not that I don't love all of you women, but I for one am happy for some quiet in this house for a few hours," Jonathan said mischievously.

"Oh, knock it off. You're loving spending the time with them as much as I am," Eleanor reprimanded, laughing.

"You're right. Of course. Come over here, I've made plenty of food and tea for both of us. I assumed you'd be awake about now. It's been awhile since we've had a proper chat, we both were so busy in the lead up to Christmas."

Knowing she still needed to talk to Jonathan about Mark, Eleanor hesitated for a second.

As if reading her mind, "Is there something I need to know about Mark?"

Eleanor's eyes widened, "How did you know? Err...I mean, um, what makes you say that?"

"The look on your face just now, for one. For another, he's been acting weird since the two of you met for coffee. I assumed something happened, but you haven't said anything." Jonathan looked hurt and confused. "You know there's nothing you can't tell me, right? Even about my friends. No one is more important to me than my family."

Sitting down next to Jonathan, Eleanor suddenly felt exhausted, even though she'd only been awake for less than an hour. "Jon, Mark is like your family, you've known each other since school. He's practically your brother, you've told me as much, several times."

Taking her hand, "Yes. But I told him when he first wanted to ask you out, that if he did anything to hurt you, I wouldn't accept that. I don't know what happened, but I want to know. Mark is one of my oldest friends, but that also means that I know better than anyone how he can be. He's been through a lot over the years. He's been hurt, by more than a few people. Unfortunately, he uses that as an excuse for a number of bad behaviors. He's not perfect, no one is. I've always felt he's a basically decent person, and I saw him acting towards you in a different way than I've seen him act towards other women. But I knew you weren't really ready for something serious and needed to take things slow. That's not something Mark is very good at. Ever since your coffee date, or non-date, whatever you want to call it, he's been acting very weird around me, like he's expecting me to rip into him. I know he's done something Ellie. You have to tell me."

Eleanor took a deep breath and started telling Jonathan the whole story. How it started out fine and she thought they would be able to be just friends, and finishing with Mark kissing her and their fight outside the coffee shop. Eleanor could tell that Jonathan was struggling not to blow up in anger. He was clenching her hand a bit tightly, and his face was turning slightly red.

"It's ok Jon, it really is. Like you said, he's mostly a decent guy, we just got our signals crossed. He was trying to be romantic or whatever and it just backfired. I probably made a bigger deal out of it than I should, I just got spooked. And I was tired of feeling like I wasn't being heard or understood. It just made me feel like I used to feel with Michael sometimes. And how I felt with my father. Like my opinion wasn't important and I just needed to be brought around to a different way of thinking about things. This is my problem with Mark, it doesn't have to be yours. I really don't want this to mess things up with you two."

"Well, I'm definitely going to have a talk with him about it. It's not fair, to you or to me, how he's treated you. God, Elle, after everything you went through in New York—"

Eleanor interrupted, "that's a completely separate case. Everything with Mark was nothing like New York. And Mark doesn't know about New York."

"He doesn't need to know about your past trauma to treat you right! Still Elle, I feel awful. If I'd known Mark would go that far I would have never encouraged him."

"I know Jon. Look, I don't want this to ruin your friendship with him. Personally, I can't hang out with him anymore. It would be too awkward, for all of us. The best thing is for him to just forget me and move on. But he hasn't done anything unforgivable Jon, there's no reason the two of you can't still be friends."

"Maybe, but he still owes both of us an apology," Jonathan replied frowning.

"I don't want an apology, I really just want to forget it ever happened. I just want to move on."

"Fine, but he owes an apology to me then, for treating you so poorly and taking advantage of my friendship to insinuate himself into your life."

"Look, talk to him if you want. Make him apologize if you feel you need that from him. But don't blow this up into something bigger than it is. It's not like he took me to bed or got me pregnant or something. So don't go getting all Victorian Era and demanding pistols at sunrise or some such nonsense."

Jonathan laughed slightly, "I think dueling was illegal by the Victorian Era. But fine. I'm still going to talk to him though. It's not right how he treated you. And I'm pretty sure he knows that, or he wouldn't be walking on eggshells around me."

"You do what you feel you need to do. Just keep things in perspective, ok? Now, are you going to eat the last piece of bacon, or can I?" Eleanor asked with a smile.

Laughing, "Go for it. I'll make some more."

After more bacon had been produced, along with more tea and toast and eggs, they continued sitting at the table, with the snow sparkling in the sunlight outside, talking about Christmas and their plans for the last few days in Bath. Later, their moms returned and the four of them played board games and watched movies the rest of the afternoon and evening.

The rest of the trip passed quickly, and soon they all headed back to London. Aunt Vickie and Cassie were going to spend time together in London before Cassie flew back to Phoenix on the 3rd, after New Year's. Though Eleanor was reluctant to get back to London, she was grateful that her mom wasn't leaving just yet and that she also still had another week and a half before school started again.

Chapter 16

New Year's Eve arrived the day after they got back to London from Bath. Jon and Eleanor spent the morning having brunch with their moms at the hotel near their flat. Since the flat wasn't big enough to accommodate two guests, their moms had decided to treat themselves to a stay at a boutique hotel just a couple blocks from the flat so Cassie and Eleanor could still spend plenty of time together. After brunch Eleanor and Jon returned to the flat to get ready for the party they were going to that night. Their moms were going to spend a quiet evening together at the hotel but Jon had gotten Eleanor and her school friends on the guest list for the big New Year's Eve bash at the club where her birthday party had been held.

Eleanor took her time getting ready. Her long brown hair was curled to perfection and pulled loosely up and away from her face. The crystal hair pins sparkled in the light. Her makeup was flawless, her skin glowed and her blue eyes popped thanks to the dark blue and black eye shadow she had meticulously applied, along with a set of lush false lashes. She knew Jack would be proud of her handy work. As it got close to time to leave she changed into her dress.

It was the black dress from Reiss that she'd received for

Christmas from her mom and Aunt Vickie. It was stunning and quite daring compared to Eleanor's usual style. In front, the neckline was a modest round neck, cut just below the collar bone. It had 3/4 length sleeves and was fitted down to just below the waist and then flared out into a full skirt that was knee length in front and nearly floor length in the back. It was made out of a luxurious satin so the skirt had some weight and volume as it floated around her legs.

The back of the dress was the real focus of the dress. It closed at the top but opened into a large cutout that went more than halfway down Eleanor's back. Dangling from the clasp were three strands of crystals that fell down her back to the bottom of the cutout. She could feel the strands sway across her back as she moved. She added a large cocktail ring to her right hand and a pair of stud earrings to complete the look. She grabbed her clutch and slipped into the same pair of shoes from her birthday party and Jonathan helped her into her new cobalt coat to keep her warm. Giggling like teenagers they dashed down to their waiting cab and were then whisked across town to the club.

As they approached Eleanor began to feel a bit nervous, as she always did before large social events, but she knew that this would be like her birthday party. Jonathan had reserved a space in the club just for their group. They got to their table and saw that most of the group was already there. Eleanor quickly spotted Mark among the group and she veered off to the other side where she saw Jack and the girls from school. She was determined to have a good time but she kept noticing Mark staring at her. She and the girls were sitting on the sofa, with Jack on a chair opposite and they all filled each other in on how everyone's Christmas went and what gifts they'd given and received. Everyone wanted to know how Eleanor's mom was enjoying the visit and Jack kept insisting he be able to meet her.

Eleanor soon fell into easy conversation with her friends

and was able to pay less attention to Mark. The atmosphere in the club was exciting as midnight drew closer. However, half way through the evening Eleanor noticed that Mark was getting increasingly drunk. Jonathan was doing a good job of running interference but it was starting to grate on Eleanor's nerves feeling like she couldn't hang out with the whole group, even though Malcom, Ioan, Zaf, and Henry had all come over to chat with her at least twice that evening.

Finally, with less than an hour until midnight, Mark came over to Eleanor in a moment where he was able to catch her alone.

"I hear you had a good Christmas," he said, with a definite edge to his voice.

Not looking at him, "Yes, we had a lovely Christmas, thank you."

"I don't know why you had to tell Jonathan. I thought you said you wouldn't."

Turning slowly and deliberately to look Mark in the eye, "I said I would *consider* not telling him. After thinking about it I realized he had the right to know. I also explained that to him that I didn't want it to affect your friendship with each other but that I did not want anything to do with you. If you'll excuse me I'm going to go join my friends."

As she got up to leave Mark grabbed her by the wrist and pulled her back down onto the couch. Leaning in close to her, she could smell the alcohol on his breath.

Angry and slurring, "Why did you have to be so difficult?! Was I not *good* enough for you?! You were lucky I wanted you."

Eleanor felt panic rising and frantically looked around but in that moment, couldn't see anyone else from their group as they were all on the dance floor and Mark's grasp on her wrist was getting tighter. Everything around Eleanor slowed down, she could hear her heart pounding in her ears. Before she knew what she was doing, she had wrenched her wrist out of his grasp, feeling a sharp pain shoot up her arm. Pushing hard on his chest she managed to launch herself off the couch while simultaneously forcing him deeper into it. A second later Jonathan and Jack were at her side, the rest of the guys right behind them. Jonathan looked horrified and beyond angry.

"Are you ok Ellie?" He asked, shooting daggers at Mark over Eleanor's shoulder.

"I'm fine, really. But I'm leaving," Eleanor said firmly, trying to catch her breath and slow her heart rate back down. She held her wrist to try to rub out the painful twist.

"No, Mark will leave," Jonathan said angrily.

"Damn straight," Jack said in agreement, he also looked angrier than she'd ever seen him.

"I don't give a damn if Mark stays or goes, but I'm leaving. I have a headache, I just want to go somewhere quiet."

"Fine, we'll go back to the flat," Jonathan said, but she could see the reluctance on his face. She knew he was looking forward to ringing in the New Year with Celeste.

"Don't be ridiculous. You all stay here, everyone's having a good time. I'll be fine. I'll text you when I get back to the flat. But you stay here, if you don't give Celeste a proper kiss at midnight I won't speak to you for a month," she said with as much conviction as she could muster.

Before anyone could argue with her she headed towards the exit. She quickly grabbed her coat from the coat check and headed out of the club, texting Patrick as she did. She quickly tapped out the low points of the evening and that she was going home to ring in the new year by herself. As she got to the bottom of the steps and saw a taxi waiting she quickened her pace and waved at the cabbie, when she heard her phone alert her to a new text message. It was from Patrick:

Come over. I'm home.

*****

About a short drive later, and just minutes to spare before midnight, the taxi pulled up in front of Patrick's home. As she finished paying the driver and got out of the car the front door opened and Patrick was standing in the light. Within seconds he had taken her coat, settled her on the couch by the fireplace wrapped in a warm blanket, and got her a glass of champagne.

"All you have to do now is relax Elle. You shouldn't spend New Year's Eve alone if you don't want to."

As usual, she automatically felt at ease in Patrick's presence. He had the TV on the BBC and they were counting down to the fireworks. At midnight, Big Ben struck twelve times as fireworks started to explode. For the next fourteen minutes, she sat mesmerized by the fireworks over the Thames. When it was done she noticed she had finished her champagne.

"Would you like another?" Patrick asked.

"I should probably switch to something else," she replied with a small laugh.

"Tea?"

"That would be great," she said with a smile.

Patrick soon returned with two mugs of tea and some shortbread biscuits and sat at the other end of the couch from Eleanor. "Do you want to talk about it?" He asked hesitantly.

"Not particularly," Eleanor said glumly, and paused before continuing, "But only because it feels like all I do is complain to you about Mark. It's not fair to you."

"Elle, we talk about so many other things than just Mark. Besides, that's what friends do, they listen to each other. What happened?"

Eleanor then filled him in on everything that had happened over Christmas and that she had told Jonathan about everything. Patrick nodded approvingly and Eleanor continued to catch him up on the evening's developments. When she got to the part where Mark grabbed her by the wrist she saw Patrick's eyes dart down to her hands, which were wrapped under the blanket.

"Really, Patrick, it's fine, it was nothing." But even as she said that she could feel her wrist still throbbing and remembered the sharp pain she had felt when she yanked it out of Mark's grasp.

"Let me see Elle," Patrick said firmly.

When Eleanor gingerly brought her hand out from under the blanket she and Patrick both gasped at the sight of her wrist, now turning pale shades of blue and purple. It was faint, but still a noticeable bruise. Looking up at Patrick she saw his expression had gone very tight. He quickly got up from the couch and went back to the kitchen. She heard him rummaging around for a bit and then silence before the faint sound of Patrick taking a deep breath. When he came back he had a bag of ice wrapped in a towel. Eleanor winced as he placed the ice on her wrist, but within seconds the ice had started to numb the pain.

"Does Jonathan know where you are Eleanor?"

"Yes, I texted him during the taxi ride over."

"Ok, I think you should text him and tell him you're staying over. I'll take you home at any time if you want, but you may as well stay here. We can keep an eye on that wrist and just relax tomorrow."

"Don't you have any plans? I feel like I'm imposing on you enough as it is."

"No. There were some parties I was invited to tonight but I didn't feel like going. I'm working on preparing for my next two films and I have nothing planned for tomorrow, other than practicing lines."

"But I don't have anything to stay the night…"

"I have some clothes you can sleep in and some skincare stuff from a swag bag at a party I went to a couple months ago, there was some women's stuff in the mix that I thought I'd keep the next time I had a guest. Looks like that's you," he said with a smile.

Feeling very weary, "Alright, if you're sure it's ok," she agreed after a slight pause.

"Of course I'm sure," he replied and then left to get the guest room set up.

Eleanor texted Jonathan to let him know she was staying over and not to worry. By the time she went upstairs to the guest room, Patrick had set out some basic toiletries and the same t-shirt and sweat pants she had worn that first day she came over. She smiled at the memory of that day and at the friendship that had developed since then.

Soon she was changed and cleaned up and ready for bed. Climbing into the soft and luxurious guest bed, she sank into the pillows and duvet and fell into a deep, dreamless sleep.

* * * * *

The next morning, she woke up, late, judging by the amount of light coming into the room through the window. She slipped on the large pair of wool socks Patrick had laid out the night before, to use as slippers, and slipped into the bathroom to wash her face again and brush her teeth. By the time she was finished she could smell something amazing baking in the kitchen. As she walked into the kitchen she was overwhelmed by the smells of fresh coffee, fresh baked scones, scrambled eggs, bacon, sausages, and an assortment of other breakfast goodies.

"What have you done?!" She exclaimed.

"It's New Year's Day, we have to do breakfast right," Patrick replied with a sly grin.

Sitting down in the window seat side of the table, she tucked her feet up under her and pulled one of the throw blankets that Patrick kept around the flat over her shoulders and placed a napkin in her lap.

"Well, you won't hear any complaints from me, but I hope you haven't done all of this just for me."

Placing a plate of eggs, bacon, sausage, and sourdough toast in front of her, Patrick said, "No, this is entirely for me, I'm just glad to have someone to share it with." He got his own plate and came back to sit in the corner across from Eleanor. "This is kind of a family tradition. My parents always made a huge breakfast on New Year's Day, with scones and other treats and we'd have a late large breakfast, or brunch essentially, and then snack on the rest throughout the day. It's been years since I've spent this day with them at home, but I usually have friends over to cook for. This was going to be the first year I'd be by myself. So I'm glad you came by last night and stayed over. It's like it was fate," he finished with a wink.

Eleanor listened to him share this bit of his past and couldn't help smiling at how happy he looked. As she reached for butter for her toast the sleeve of the sweater she put on that morning slipped back and she saw Patrick notice the darkening color of the bruise on her wrist, but to her relief he didn't say anything. She knew she'd have to deal with Mark eventually, but she didn't want to waste time thinking about him or talking about it today. She just wanted to enjoy the first day of a new year.

Patrick seemed to sense her desire to change the subject, so as he began buttering his toast, he asked, "So, what about you and your family? Any special holiday traditions?"

"Well…" Eleanor began slowly, "As a kid there weren't many, my dad always said he, *'didn't go in for all that nonsense'* whatever that meant. But my mom tried. She still signs some of my Christmas gifts 'from Santa' every year." Eleanor laughed warmly at the thought.

Patrick grinned in response, "So does my mum."

Eleanor continued, "Since the divorce my mom got much more into creating routines and traditions for the two of us. You saw the one at Thanksgiving, writing what we're grateful for on the paper on the dining table." Patrick nodded and Eleanor went on. "But for Christmas...well...we're both Christmas fanatics. Sometimes I think my mom is the long-lost daughter of Santa Claus. She always goes crazy with the house. I think she'd always wanted to do that, but my dad never let her when I was little. Plus, half the years of my childhood we weren't even home for Christmas, we were off in some other city for my dad's research. Winter break was valuable time for him to work on projects in between terms.

"But when it was just mom and I, the tree was always up Thanksgiving night, as soon as dinner had been cleared away, and the rest of that weekend was spent decorating the rest of the house, inside and out. We'd go raid our favorite stores for new stuff to add to our collection of Christmas decorations." Eleanor smiled at the memory, and continued, "But there were also traditions like going Christmas shopping together, watching Christmas movies almost every night between Thanksgiving and Christmas Eve, reading *A Christmas Carol* every Christmas Eve night, and every year we did something with my cousin and my Aunt Vickie. Either they came to visit us or we went to visit them in Bath."

"How long has your aunt lived in Bath?" Patrick asked as he took a sip of his coffee.

"Oh gosh, it's been years. Since I was about 17? Not long after the divorce. Mom and Aunt Vickie are originally from Kansas, Overland Park, just outside Kansas City. Mom went to university at Yale, which is where she met my dad. Aunt Vickie went to uni in Edinburgh, and then got her first job in London, where she met my uncle. They moved to Cambridge, which is where Jonathan grew up. My uncle works for the university there, some fancy administrative position, I forget the details. Aunt Vickie is also divorced, a few years before my parents, she moved back to London for a bit, and then half settled herself in Bath. She travels a lot. Having divorced parents was something Jonathan and I bonded over. I mean, we were already close, but that made us even closer. But Aunt Vickie was in a very different situation. Her ex isn't a complete jerk, like my father, so he continued to support and take care of Jonathan, paying his school fees for Eton and such. And Aunt Vickie had a career of her own, still does. She's a successful interior designer, more successful every year. She has clients around the world and has designed her own collection of furniture and accessories for various interiors companies. It's one of the reasons she has properties all over, she uses them as portfolio showcases. So, we stayed in her place in Paradise Valley when we first moved to Arizona, but she's also got a townhouse in London, a loft in New York City, and her personal home, the cottage in Bath. But over the last ten years she's also bought and sold at least five places that I can think of. I remember one in Canada and one in France. She also rents out her various properties to film projects, editorial shoots, and events, whatever and earns extra income that way as well. She's a smart lady. And also incredibly generous. She owns the Holborn flat Jonathan and I live in. She's always supported Jon as long as he's in school. And she wanted to help my mom make this all happen for me. I don't know what I'd do without her and Jon.

"So yeah, they always spent time with us for the holidays, whether here or in Arizona. And if we couldn't afford the flight one year, Aunt Vickie would just pay. She's always been like a fairy godmother to me. She and my mom were a good team, getting me through the divorce and high school and college. Between her and my cousin I always had someone to talk to if I didn't want to make my mom worry or make her feel worse about things after the divorce."

"It's great having support in different places," Patrick said kindly, thinking not for the first time, that for someone who'd been through so much, Eleanor seemed remarkably adjusted.

"I'm very lucky," Eleanor agreed, "And privileged. A lot of people don't have that kind of support. When the divorce was really bad in the beginning, my aunt kind of swooped in to take care of us while my mom sorted out what we would do. As soon as my aunt realized my dad was going to make things difficult she stepped in to help. I remember spending a couple weekends in New York with Jonathan and Uncle Edward, while Aunt Vickie was home with mom helping her make plans. I think they spared me from the worst of it. There's still a lot of details from that time I don't know about. Things they protected me from. I haven't seen my uncle recently, I know Jonathan sees him every month or so, he goes to Cambridge to visit him. But he still sends me a birthday gift every year and something for Christmas, this year it was a stunning matching monogrammed notebook and fountain pen, and I'll probably go out to Cambridge with Jonathan soon. I certainly feel closer to my uncle than I do my own father," Eleanor concluded with a furrowed brow, staring darkly into her coffee mug.

Patrick, looking around at the remnants of brunch, offered, "Change of subject?"

Looking up and smiling at him, Eleanor replied gratefully and laughing gently, "Yes please. You make it so easy to talk to you that I end up saying way more than is probably appropriate."

"Well, I'm always happy to listen, that's what friends are for. But it's New Year's Day and I don't want you feeling gloomy and sad."

Smiling, "So what should we do then?" Eleanor asked brightly.

"Well…," Patrick started, "Could I tempt you, or rather *beg* you, to help me practice lines for my next project? We start in a week and I really want to get the first several scenes we're shooting memorized before we start."

"Ooooh!" Eleanor squealed girlishly, "That sounds like fun! Of course I'll help you. Just tell me what to do."

"Well, for you it will be very simple, and you don't have to move. Just sit there with the script and let me know what I'm getting wrong." Patrick jumped up from the table and ran to get his script from the kitchen counter. Eleanor had thought she'd heard him talking to himself when she first walked in to the kitchen that morning, now she realized he'd been rehearsing.

Eleanor poured herself some more coffee and snuggled down into her seat and reached out for the script. They spent the next few hours with Patrick pacing the kitchen, rehearsing his lines as Eleanor watched, mesmerized by how completely transported he seemed. Seeing him act in person like this was a real treat and Eleanor was transfixed.

Later in the day they relaxed in the lounge, Patrick sprawled out on the sofa, Eleanor cozied up in what had become her favorite armchair by the fireplace, watching films and drinking mulled cider and picking at leftover food in the fridge. All in all, Eleanor thought, the perfect New Year's Day.

Around seven o'clock, thoroughly stuffed with good food and relaxed from good company, Patrick called a car and took Eleanor home. Ever the gentleman, he left the car waiting in front of Eleanor's flat and walked her up the steps to the door of the building

"I'm glad you came over," Patrick said, "It really was the best New Years I've had in years."

"Me too," Eleanor replied.

"Get inside before you freeze," Patrick teased.

Eleanor laughed, "I'll see you soon?"

"Yep, I'll call you when I confirm the shooting schedule for next week."

Patrick leaned down and kissed her lightly on the cheek and Eleanor felt her heart flutter a bit. She said goodnight and turned to let herself in to the building and walked up to the flat.

As she entered the flat and closed the door behind her, she heard Jonathan watching TV in the lounge. She started walking to her room and stopped when she heard Jonathan call out, "Eleanor, is that you?"

She walked to the lounge and leaned against the door and said teasingly, "Who else would have a key? Did you give one to Celeste?"

Jonathan muted the TV and turned to her with worry on his face.

Before he could speak, Eleanor held up a hand and pleaded, "Please, I will tell you everything tomorrow, but it's been such a great day and I don't want to spoil it by talking about last night. I just want to go to sleep right now."

Jonathan relented and leaned back against the sofa, "As long as you're ok. You were really upset last night."

"I'm fine. We'll talk about it tomorrow, ok?"

"Ok. Goodnight Elle."

"Goodnight Jon."

Eleanor walked to her room and took off her New Year's Eve dress that she had changed back into for the drive home from Patrick's place. She kicked off her heels, fell into bed, and was soon fast asleep, with a dreamy smile on her face.

Chapter 17

The next day Eleanor woke up feeling like she'd been asleep for a month. She couldn't remember the last time she'd slept that deeply, but it felt great. She walked into the lounge and saw Jonathan sitting at the dining table. As soon as she walked in, he shuffled with what looked like a couple magazines, as if he was hiding something from her.

Laughing Eleanor asked, "What are you doing? Trying to hide something?"

Jonathan's face was tight and hard to read.

"Oh my god Jonathan, what's going on? You're kind of freaking me out."

Jonathan sighed, paused, then said, "I guess it was going to happen eventually. I worried about this when you started your friendship with him."

Eleanor sat down at the table across from him, feeling very confused. After another moment, Jonathan slid the magazines he had been looking at across the table to her.

"I went out to get some milk, we had run out. I was just walking past the off license and saw this on the newsstand."

Eleanor looked down and realized it was a one of the trashy tabloids she always spotted when she was out running errands. Looking closer at the front page story, she took in the headline, "Patrick Reynolds' New Flame?" And then she saw the photo, or rather, two photos, one of her and Patrick leaving his home, with his arm around her shoulder, and another of him saying goodbye at her flat, taken just as he had kissed her goodnight. Only, from the angle taken from the street, it looked like significantly more than an innocent kiss on the cheek. Eleanor flipped to the third page to read the full story, and was horrified to see that the reporter had clearly been looking into them for more than a day or so. They knew where she was studying and had a quote from a "classmate," but based on what was said about her she doubted this so-called classmate was someone she really knew. It was all fairly positive and generic, just that she was an American studying in London who had "caught the eye" of London's rising star. There was a clearer picture that they'd clearly taken from her Instagram, as well as pictures of her school and of Patrick's mews house. It was a long enough story considering the reporter didn't seem to actually know much of anything.

"So much for not getting into any complicated relationships," she heard Jonathan say.

"Oh Jon, this is not what it looks like," Eleanor said with a sigh.

"No judgement cousin, you know I like Patrick. I'm honestly surprised this hasn't happened sooner, by what you've said, it's not like you all have been hiding away, you've seen each other out in public. But I don't like that it seems like they were waiting for you to leave his place and then followed you back here."

"I know, that's pretty creepy. But I'm sure it will blow over. Patrick starts filming his new movie next week. We're not going to be able to see each other very often, and school will be starting the new term next week as well. We'll just lay low and this will pass. I'm sure some football player or reality TV star is going to do something much crazier and will take the attention."

Jonathan didn't look convinced. "Are you sure you're ok though? You still haven't told me what exactly happened."

"Ugh," Eleanor groaned, "Do we really have to talk about it?"

"Well, no, not if you don't want to. I'm not going to make you talk about Mark if you don't want to. But he said some weird things after you left, and I was really worried."

Eleanor looked up, worriedly, "What did Mark say?"

Furrowing his brows, "Just that he was sorry, and he didn't mean to hurt you? That it was an accident? You looked ok when you left, angry and upset but physically ok, so I assumed he meant he didn't mean to make you upset, but he looked really freaked out Eleanor, like he expected me to punch him. Eventually he left, about ten minutes after you did. What happened before you left?"

"Oh Jon, it was…well it wasn't nothing, but it wasn't serious and I don't think he intended to hurt me." Seeing Jonathan's face change from worried to anger, she rushed to continue, "He just grabbed my wrist to stop me from walking away, he was holding it a little too tightly and I panicked and when I yanked it out of his grasp it got twisted a bit. It's fine though, I put ice on it at Patrick's and you can barely see the bruise anymore."

"You were bruised?!" Jonathan gasped. "Let me see Elle, please."

Reluctantly Eleanor put her hand on the table. The bruise was already fading and was only a very yellowish green now. But it was still noticeable.

"I don't want to make this a big thing Jon. It's over. I don't want to see Mark anymore. I don't think we're good for each other. He just can't let it go and seeing me just makes it worse. He's not a bad guy and I don't mind if you keep hanging out with him. But I'm done discussing him or trying to give him a chance to be my friend. Even if I wasn't friends with Patrick, I really have no interest in Mark. He honestly reminds me too much of my father. Charming on the surface, but very thoughtless and careless of others when you get down deeper. Maybe he's different with all of you guys, but I don't think he ever really cared about me at all. I can't make the same mistakes my mom did."

Jonathan watched as a tear slipped down Eleanor's cheek.

"And it's different with Patrick?" He asked gently.

"Oh Jon," Eleanor said, sighing softly. "It's the complete opposite. Patrick truly is a friend. I mean, I know he's interested in more, but he's also very respectful. And just for the record, I slept in the guest room the other night, and despite what the angle of that picture looks like, he only kissed me on the cheek, for like, half a second, when he dropped me off last night. We're friends. Full stop. Maybe, *eventually*, it will turn into something more, but for now we're *just* friends. Which is just what I need, and I think he's enjoying the friendship too. Like, there's no pressure from him. He seems genuinely happy just hanging out. I've never been with a guy like him. And I'm not talking about the celebrity stuff."

"All I care about is that you're happy Ellie. Really. And I do like Patrick, he's a good bloke, in more ways than one from what I've seen. I'm not going to tell you what to do. You're a grown woman and you've never needed me to make decisions for you, so please believe me when I say I'm not trying to be the big brother, protector figure here. I just want you to be ok. And for the record, I think Mark has burned his bridges with both of us. I don't care if he didn't *intentionally* bruise you. He should have never grabbed you in the first place."

Eleanor tried to interject but Jonathan held up his hand to stop her, "No. Mark has a bad habit of acting impulsively. He's not a bad guy, I agree. But he's never been rejected, that I'm aware of, and he's always had a sense of entitlement, like the same rules don't apply to him and that all he has to do is say he's sorry and didn't mean to cause harm or offense. Well that's pathetic. Because I've gotten upset with girlfriends in the past, but whenever one turned to walk away from me I *never* tried to physically stop them from going."

Sighing, "I know Jon. I know. There's no excuse for him. Look, I really just want to move on from Mark, and from this," Eleanor said, gesturing at the tabloids. "I'm going to go for a walk, maybe down to St. Paul's or something. I just need to get some air and clear my head."

"Ok, do you want me to come with you," Jonathan asked kindly.

Smiling at him, "No, I'm ok. But I can pick us up some takeaway for dinner on my way back if you like? Cozy night in, just us cousins?"

"Sounds perfect," Jonathan agreed.

Eleanor went to her room and changed into some jeans and a sweater, and pulled on her favorite black over knee boots. As she was walking out into the entryway and pulling on her wool coat, there was a knock, or rather, more of a pounding, on the front door. Eleanor stopped at the sound.

Jonathan came out of the kitchen and looked at her, both of them frozen.

"Did you buzz anyone up?" He asked puzzled.

"No, did you?" Eleanor replied. They never had unannounced visitors, they always had to buzz guests up from downstairs.

There was another knock at the door, and Eleanor heard what sounded like Patrick's voice talking to someone outside, but he sounded angry or frustrated.

"That sounds like Patrick," Eleanor said to Jonathan.

Jonathan opened the door, and sure enough, there was

Patrick, looking very angry and speaking heatedly to Mark.

Looking between the two of them, Jonathan demanded, "How did you get in the building?"

Before Mark could say anything, Patrick said, "I saw him hanging around the door as I was walking up. Before I could get to him someone came out of the building and he slipped in, I managed to get to the door before it shut. I'm sorry we didn't call up first."

"Oh sure, aren't you just the knight in shining armor. Eleanor and Jonathan are *my* friends—"

Jonathan interrupted, "—*your* friends? You sure about that mate? After the way you've been acting lately and the way you've treated Eleanor? She was a good friend to you. Because *I* told her she could trust you. You're walking a thin line with both of us Mark."

"Oh, she's been a good friend huh. Leading me on, telling me she's not open to a relationship, meanwhile she's sleeping around with this guy, she needs to just make a damn choice about what she wants!"

Patrick and Jonathan both stiffened where they each stood, at the same time they both started, "She—"

Loud enough to be heard over the rising voices of the men, Eleanor silenced them all, "—*She* can speak for herself, so would all of you shut your mouths." Seeing the three of them ready to rip into each other had Eleanor seething with rage.

To Patrick and Jonathan, "I appreciate that you both want to stand up for me, but just stop. I can deal with this myself." To Mark, "You've got some bloody cheek coming over here uninvited. Maybe you were too drunk New Year's Eve to fully understand, so let me make myself clear now that you appear to be sober. We're done. Over. I don't want anything to do with you. I have no problem with you salvaging your friendship with Jon, if you can, but you and I will never have any kind of relationship going forward.

You have shown more than once that you are incapable of listening to me or respecting my decisions. My relationship with Patrick is completely separate from my relationship with you and is none of your damn business and you have no right to judge me for those photos or for whatever twisted assumptions you have about my friendship with Patrick. And as for making a *choice* about what I want, I would think someone as smart as you would have figured it out by now. If you want me to choose between you or Patrick, I'm going to choose Patrick, since he's never once made me feel uncomfortable or pressured in any way and since he's always respected my desire to be friends and nothing else."

"Oh sure, those pictures look soooo friendly," Mark snarled.

Rolling her eyes, "Oh grow up Mark. This is just getting annoying now. You're not four years old and I'm not some toy that's been taken away from you. I don't owe you any explanation and quite frankly I don't give a damn what you think about me. I'm not ashamed about any aspect of my relationship with Patrick or about those photos. So if we're done here? I have plans."

Patrick put his hands in his coat pocket sheepishly, "Eleanor I'm sorry, I only came over here to talk about the photos in person and make sure you were ok."

"It's ok Patrick."

Mark looked like he was going to say something, but Jonathan spoke before he could, "Mark, you and I need to talk. Go into the lounge and wait for me." Mark looked like he was going to argue but Jonathan stared him down, after a few seconds, Mark sighed and walked into the lounge. Jonathan looked at both Patrick and Eleanor and then followed Mark into the lounge and shut the door, leaving Eleanor and Patrick alone in the entryway.

"Are you ok?" Patrick asked gently.

"I'm tired. I'm just…tired. I don't need this drama with Mark."

"Umm, about the photos, I'm sorry Elle, I've never had paparazzi hiding outside my flat, I wasn't expecting them to be there."

Patrick looked so sorry and worried, Eleanor couldn't help but feel bad.

"It's not your fault. I'm not even that upset about it. It was kind of you to come over to see me."

"You're not mad?" Patrick asked, relief starting to show on his face.

"Of course I'm not mad. Look, as long as you and I are on the same page about our friendship, that's all I care about."

Patrick took a step towards Eleanor and put his hand gently on her arm. "My friendship with you is one of the most important relationships in my life right now."

"Thank you Patrick, really. That means a lot to me."

"So, you have plans? I don't want to keep you."

"I just wanted to go for a walk and maybe do some writing."

"Do you want some company?" Patrick asked hopefully.

"Honestly I think I just need some time to myself. Is that ok?"

"Of course it is. Can I walk you downstairs?"

"I'd like that," Eleanor said with a smile.

She grabbed her bag with her notebook and iPad and together she and Patrick walked downstairs and turned towards the square. They walked and made companionable small talk about the weather until they made it out to the main road near Holborn Station. There they said goodbye and Eleanor headed in the direction of Oxford Street.

* * * * *

Eleanor walked for a while, the road she was on eventually turned into Oxford Street and she began passing by all the big department stores. The Christmas lights were still hanging over the road and the Christmas displays were still in the windows of the shops. Seeing all the festive displays made Eleanor feel a little calmer. The last several days had been such a roller coaster. Christmas had been fantastic, then New Year's Eve started great, turned sour, then was rescued by going to Patrick's. New Year's Day at his place was fantastic and she'd woken up this morning feeling really good. Then there were the pictures in the tabloid and the confrontation with Mark and the lingering unsettled feeling in the back of her mind about Patrick.

Before she knew it she reached Marble Arch and found herself walking into Hyde Park. She could see Winter Wonderland was still going on but she turned to continue away from the fair and the busy crowds. She could hear the screams of laughter coming from the rides, and though it was still daytime, the clouds and the shortened daylight of winter made two o'clock feel much later than it was. As the noise of the fair faded behind her, she continued walking into Hyde Park and towards Kensington Gardens.

Eventually she came to a bench that overlooked a large field and the intersection of a few park paths. She sat down and began watching other park visitors as they walked along the path or played in the little bit of snow that dusted the field. As she sat there she found herself replaying all the events of the last few months since her arrival in August. Meeting Patrick, starting school, getting to know all of Jon's friends—including Mark—and making her own friends at school, getting to know Patrick and becoming friends with him, all the problems with Mark, Christmas, New Year's Eve and then New Year's Day, and now the tabloid photos. She couldn't help laughing out loud at the ridiculousness of it all. She thought back to what her life had been like this time last year.

Jon and Aunt Vickie had come to visit Eleanor and Cassie in Phoenix. She and her mom had taken them to see Zoo Lights at the Phoenix Zoo and the luminaria walk at the Botanical Gardens. She and Jon had gone for long hikes on Christmas Day and New Year's Day. Michael had joined them all for dinner at the house a couple times, but even then, it felt like he was only there out of a sense of obligation, not that he actually wanted to spend time with her family. Of course, at the time she had dismissed those thoughts and put on a happy face for Jon. She remembered how envious she was when she and Cassie dropped Jon and Vickie off at the airport for their flight back to London, how desperately she had wished she were flying back with them. The fact that she could have so easily left her life — and Michael — behind in that moment should have been a sign of things to come. If she had known that only a few months later he'd break up with her, she probably would have spent her savings on a ticket right there and then and gone back with Jon and Vickie.

She continued thinking about the past year. All the boring and monotonous days teaching in a department that didn't care about her, countless shifts in her old job at the bookstore, all those days spent writing and day dreaming in the coffee shop after class wishing for something exciting and different to happen to her.

She started laughing, loudly and almost hysterically. Her life in the last twelve months had been like one of her favorite chick lit novels or romantic comedies. "Girl with boring life gets broken up with by boring boyfriend. Girl decides to move halfway across the world and chase her dreams. Because why not? Upon arriving in London, girl meets movie star crush AND catches the eye of a charming but perhaps inappropriate friend of her cousin's." It was all too ridiculous. She'd craved something exciting and different, well...she had gotten that, and then some. Be careful what you wish for, that's what they always said right?

Eleanor was so grateful, the more she thought about it. She really had been given such an incredible gift being able to come live and study in London, making so many amazing friends. Everything that had happened with Mark had been unfortunate but still a learning experience. Between Mark and Michael, she was learning exactly what she didn't want in a relationship. And Patrick had been slowly showing her many of the things she did think she would want, when she eventually felt she was ready for a relationship again. Her laughter quieted as she thought about Patrick. As she looked out over the field she spotted a young couple walking hand in hand and leaning into one another. Even from a distance she could tell how close and intimate their relationship was.

She sat there, for how long she didn't quite know. It only felt like it had been twenty minutes or so since she'd sat down, but the sky was getting noticeably dark, night was definitely descending. She looked at her watch and sure enough, it was now nearing 4 o'clock. Even if it wasn't cloudy, it would be dark as the sun was most surely setting by now. She stood up, and felt how stiff the cold had made her legs sitting on that bench for so long. She began walking briskly down the path, not quite sure which direction she needed to go. Eventually she saw Winter Wonderland in the distance and headed in the direction of Marble Arch Station. She checked her phone as she neared the station and saw a text from Jonathan:

When will u be back??? I know we said takeaway but feel like getting out of flat. Carluccio's at Brunswick? Let me know when.

Before heading into the Underground, Eleanor quickly tapped her reply on her phone:

Catching Tube at Marble Arch. Meet you in 15? Get us a table if u get there first.

She stowed her phone back in her pocket and fished her Oyster card out of her handbag. She headed down to the Tube and let herself get lost in the evening crowd of post-Christmas shoppers.

* * * * *

When she came back up above ground from the Tube at Russell Square Station, and caught sight of the Christmas lights at the Brunswick Centre, she thought about how much she was going to miss all the festive lights and displays once they started taking them down in a few days. She walked across the street and as she walked up to Carluccio's she saw Jonathan standing at the host's stand just inside the entrance. She walked in and joined him.

"Hi, you made it," he said with a smile.

"Yep, doesn't look like you've been waiting long."

"Nope, perfect timing."

They followed the host back to their booth and settled in, shedding their coats and relaxing into their seats. It was pretty quiet in the restaurant, as it was now only just before 5 o'clock, far too early for the dinner rush. Eleanor suddenly felt very tired. The server came over and they quickly ordered their meals.

Jonathan noticed the look on her face, "It's been a long day hasn't it?"

Eleanor laughed, "Well it was fine until I woke up." Jonathan laughed as well. Eleanor continued, "Ok, seriously, it really wasn't that bad, but definitely interesting. I might have slept an extra hour if I'd known I was going to wake up to my picture in the tabloids and have both Mark and Patrick pitch up unannounced on my doorstep."

Jonathan laughed in response, then asked, "Was everything ok with Patrick?"

"Yeah, he was just concerned about my reaction to the photos and wanted to make sure I was ok and not mad or something."

"Are you mad?" Jonathan asked gently.

"Noooo," Eleanor responded slowly. "Not mad. A bit…disconcerted maybe. Patrick seemed upset at the thought that they clearly were waiting outside his home and that they obviously followed us back to the flat. And I won't lie, the pictures definitely look more scandalous than they are. Leaving his place New Year's morning in what clearly looks like my New Year's Eve party outfit. And from the street at our place, that angle at that particular second, an innocent kiss on the cheek looks like much more. I'm sure I'll hear about it at school."

"Are you worried about that?"

"Not really. I mean, I was, at first. But after talking to Patrick, I realized his friendship is really important to me. And being friends with him means I'm probably going to have my picture in the tabloids from time to time and things speculated about us. It's not ideal, but I think his friendship is worth it. And you know, I really can't complain, I feel like I brought this on myself."

"How do you mean?"

"After I said goodbye to Patrick, I walked to Hyde Park and wandered around there for a while just thinking about everything that's happened since last New Year's when you and Aunt Vickie were visiting us. It's been such a crazy year. Last winter and spring when I was in Arizona I kept wishing that something exciting would happen, that my life would get more interesting and I'd have a new opportunity for something. I think I've gotten what I wished for. I shouldn't get upset if it's been a little more *dramatic* than I anticipated. I'm just sorry that your friendship with Mark has gotten mixed up with all of this. I should have never pursued something with him."

"It's not your fault. I encouraged you. And I warned Mark. I told him I wouldn't defend him if he hurt you. That if he did anything and it came down to choosing sides I'd always choose you. I just never thought he'd be such an arse. I thought the worst that could happen was that you wouldn't be interested or that you'd date for a bit and then break up with him. I'm sorry for ever encouraging you to give him a chance in the first place."

"You couldn't have known. I don't blame you. What happened with you two after Patrick and I left?" Eleanor asked gently. She had been worried that their talk hadn't gone well after she'd left them at the flat.

A sad look spread across Jonathan's face and he sighed. "He's angry. He thinks you led him on. I told him he's wrong of course, and that you'd been right when you told him that what you did and who you saw was none of his business. You never made him any promises and were free to see whoever you wanted. I also told him that I felt that Patrick had nothing to do with your relationship with Mark, that Patrick hadn't come between the two of you."

"You're right, they were two separate relationships. From the very beginning."

"I know. Unfortunately Mark doesn't want to believe that. He thinks he's the wronged one. I gave him several chances to see how he's gone too far. He should have backed off and left you alone ages ago. I'm so sorry Elle. I've never seen this side of him. I would have never encouraged you if I'd known he'd be like this."

"You're not responsible for him. But I'm sorry that you've had such a falling out."

"I'm not, I told him you were my top priority. The fact that he can't even acknowledge that he's done anything wrong or apologize for his actions is just unacceptable. What's worse is he's tried to get the guys on his side. I've been getting texts from Zaf, Malcolm, Henry, and Ioan all day."

"Oh Jonathan —," Eleanor burst out.

Jonathan put up his hand to silence her, "It's ok, they all agree with you and me. They think Mark has been a real jerk in this whole thing. Malcolm and Ioan both called him a 'bloody wanker', their words, not mine, Zaf called him something in French that I won't repeat, and Henry called him something in Nigerian, I'm not sure I want to try to translate it. I've told them they don't have to choose sides, but they've all told me that Mark is basically making them choose. They all refuse to listen to him say a bad word about you, but he just won't let it drop. It's not going to be fun for him once term starts again. He's cutting all of us out because of his foolish pride and ego."

"I know I shouldn't, but I still feel responsible."

"You're right, you shouldn't. It's not your fault. You were open and honest with him from the beginning. He's messed things up with both of us. I told him that until he's ready to at least recognize responsibility for his part of all this, we really have nothing to say."

"What a mess," Eleanor said, shaking her head.

"So, forget about Mark. What are you going to do about Patrick?"

"Nothing," Eleanor laughed. "I mean, we're friends, we'll continue being friends, and then, who knows? School starts on Monday, Mom flies home on Wednesday, Patrick starts filming his next project the week after. He and I will both be so busy, even if I was interested in something more than friendship this would be the worst time to test that out. And the future is so uncertain. By the time summer arrives, I might not even be able to stay in London once my program is done."

"Well I wouldn't let any of that stop you cousin, life is short. Didn't you say this first film is being shot in and around London? And you could very well end up staying here, we both know you're trying to. You have no real intention of going back to Arizona. Why delay your future? Why not start living it now?"

"You make it sound so easy," Eleanor said sarcastically.

"It is," Jonathan replied with a smug look on his face.

"Oh? Well then how's it going with Celeste?" Eleanor snapped back just as smugly.

Jonathan's face looked even more smug, if that was possible Eleanor thought, "Quite well actually, we have a date set up for Monday. The club is closed on Monday's so it's her day off. We're going to Winter Wonderland, it will be the last night and neither of us have been this year."

Jonathan looked so happy talking about Celeste, Eleanor couldn't help but feel happy for him. But she also felt that twinge of envy, like she felt for that couple walking in the the park earlier. Why did it feel so easy for everyone but her?

As if reading her thoughts, "Ellie," Jonathan said gently, "It really can be that easy if you just let yourself go. Patrick is a good guy. In all the times I've met him, I've never gotten a bad feeling off of him. And you completely change when you're with him, in all the best ways. You're calmer and happier, much more relaxed. It reminds me of when you were younger, before your parent's divorce, before New York, and then everything with Michael. You were so naturally happy then. It's like Patrick brings out the side of you that doesn't worry about every little thing."

"You think I worry too much?" Eleanor laughed, trying

to make light of the conversation. But Jonathan wouldn't let her.

"Yes," he replied seriously. "You worry about everything. School, your writing, your friendships, your parents, Michael, Mark...I could go on. You constantly worry and second guess all of your decisions. You are so much smarter and braver than you know. You don't have to be afraid. You've had some bad luck with men in the past, I get that. Mark, Michael, and we all know what a tosser your dad is. But you also have had some good luck with men. Me, Jack, the guys — they all love you, you know, and so does my dad, he asks about you all the time. There have been so many men who haven't betrayed your trust or disappointed you. I think Patrick is one of those good guys."

Eleanor thought carefully about what Jonathan was saying. Deep down she knew he was right. It was fear that was holding her back. But she wasn't sure how to go forward.

Speaking gently, "Elle, listen. If you're still working through feelings for Michael and the breakup and still need more time to process all of that, then that's totally understandable. You were together for a long time and it was your first serious relationship, and it's only been eight months, which seems like a long time but compared to how long you dated it's understandable if you're still dealing with it all. And if that's the case, starting a new romantic relationship isn't the best idea. *But...*if you're completely over Michael and past that relationship and you're holding yourself back from starting something new with Patrick, or anyone else really, out of fear that's not good. Be brave Elle. Trust yourself to make the right decision."

At that point their food arrived. They started eating quietly before Jonathan said, "Look, you don't have to say anything right now. But think about what we've just been talking about. You don't have to make any decisions right away but you should think about whatever is holding you back and try to resolve that. And not for Patrick's sake, but for yours."

Eleanor just nodded, and wiped away a small tear. Jonathan reached across the table and squeezed her hand. He then switched the subject to talking about something lighthearted, Eleanor couldn't even really remember what later, but it made her feel better and she was able to enjoy the rest of dinner.

They eventually walked home together. Eleanor talked on the phone with her mom, who was still at the hotel in with Aunt Vickie. She quickly mentioned the tabloid pictures so her mom wouldn't worry about her. She and Aunt Vickie hadn't seen them yet, so she was glad she had mentioned it. Her mom was concerned but reassured. They made plans to go to a service at St. Paul's the next day, Sunday, and then to meet for tea at Bea's in One New Change after school on Monday. By the time she got in bed she was looking forward to spending time with her mom. She knew her mom wouldn't let her off easy, just as Jonathan hadn't. But they were the two people she trusted the most. She fell asleep feeling numb and more confused than ever, but she just couldn't stop thinking about Patrick.

Chapter 18

Sunday with her mom had been nice. They attended the morning service at St. Paul's and then spent the rest of the day wandering around the City and along the Thames. They talked about everything and Cassie gave Eleanor a lot of good advice, even if it was hard to hear. She'd exchanged a couple texts with Patrick, each asking how the other was doing. Eleanor did have to admit, it was nice to have someone—who wasn't a family member—interested in how her day was going. She also had some texts from Jack, who was back in London after spending New Year's Day and the rest of the weekend with his family in Sheffield. She was excited to see him at school the next day. He'd found out about the tabloids, but typical Jack, he found it all a riot and said he hoped Eleanor would remember him when she was famous. Eleanor had just rolled her eyes at that text.

Monday arrived and it was time to go back to school. The time off for the holidays had been good, just what she needed. Despite the drama she had made good progress on her book and was more or less on track with where she should be. It was going to be a busy spring term.

As she walked up the steps of the school, she saw some girls she knew and waved. But when they waved back they also laughed and whispered to themselves. Eleanor had a weird feeling about it. That weird feeling was confirmed when she saw Jack in the lobby, he was grinning like the Cheshire Cat and held up a tabloid. She saw another ridiculous headline about "Patrick's New Love." She held out her hand for the rag, and began flipping through the pages as they walked to the lift. She scanned the story, which was thankfully short. They still didn't know much more about her beyond her name and where she studied. But there were pictures of her and Patrick walking near her flat from after they had left Jon with Mark, and more pictures of her walking down Oxford Street. Those ones made her uneasy, she didn't like thinking that she had been watched and photographed while she was on her own.

The rest of the day passed uneventfully. Patrick had texted her, worried about the new pictures. She told him it was fine, she wasn't terribly worried and that she was sure it would pass, especially once he started filming. She met her mom for afternoon tea at Bea's. It was so close to the Harrison and had become one of her favorite places and she was excited to share it with her mom. They enjoyed tea and then did some shopping there at One New Change. They were starting to take down the decorations, the holidays were officially over. Now London was just cold and dreary, but it didn't bother Eleanor, after years of living in the desert, she thought it would be awhile before she tired of the London weather.

She went with her mom to Heathrow on Wednesday after her classes. It was hard to say goodbye to her mom, it had been so nice having her close during the last couple weeks. To not have to deal with a seven-hour time difference or poor connection FaceTime calls. As she took the Tube back to the flat from the airport she couldn't stop herself from crying and immediately missing her mom. Jonathan was waiting when she walked into the flat and he quickly wrapped her in a giant hug. They spent the rest of the afternoon on the sofa watching movies on Netflix and eating popcorn and leftover Christmas chocolate. It was just what she needed.

Eleanor spent the rest of the week writing and meeting with her professors. They all agreed that she was making good progress and that her work had improved since the beginning of the program when she had been struggling. She also spoke with a couple of the recruiters in the career services office and there was talk of arranging interviews with companies the school was connected to and the possibilities of her getting a job somewhere after she completed the program. Her previous teaching experience was an advantage she was told, as well as the part time tutoring work she was doing. She tried not to get her hopes up, but the thought of staying in London, or even moving elsewhere in the UK after graduation was everything she wanted. Jonathan had been right, she couldn't bear the thought of going back to Arizona after everything she'd experienced in London.

On Friday Patrick called, he asked if he could come over. He would start filming on Monday and he wanted to spend some time together before then. Eleanor was excited to see him, but also nervous. Something in his voice on the phone sounded different. Hesitant. Uncertain. Eleanor couldn't help but feel the same.

* * * * *

Patrick arrived right on time, carrying takeaway from Rock & Sole Plaice, the fish and chips place in Covent Garden they both loved. They ate in the lounge, sitting across from each other at the dining table, drinking cider from bottles. They filled each other in on what they had both been up to that week, Eleanor telling him about her meetings and discussions with her professors, and the possibility of a job after graduation.

"You know if you want a job I can connect you with tons of different people, all you have to do is tell me what you're looking for."

"Be careful what you offer," Eleanor laughed. "I just might take you up on it."

Patrick laughed back. "I hope you do. London suits you. You shouldn't have to leave if you don't want to."

"You know, as much as I love London, I wouldn't be opposed to living elsewhere in the UK."

"Really?" Patrick asked, slightly incredulous. "I thought you lived for London."

Eleanor caught the joking tone, "Ha ha. I love it, but I don't live for it. I think as long as I was close enough I could take the train in for the day I'd be happy."

Patrick raised an eyebrow.

Eleanor laughed and then relented, "Ok, I do live for it. I've loved every day I've been here. Good weather, bad weather, busy with tourists or quiet, transit strikes that make you want to pull your hair out, I love it all. But I have to be realistic. Aunt Vickie is only paying for this flat while Jon and I are in school. Once we graduate we have to start contributing. She'd never charge us a realistic rent considering what she's spent on the place. She owns it outright, so there's no mortgage. Depending on the job I *might* be able to cover my half of the amount she quoted Jon, but it would be really tight. And Jonathan might stay in London after graduation but that will depend on where he gets a job. There's no way I could afford a place of my own this central."

"Do you want a place of your own?"

"Kind of," Eleanor said slowly. "I mean, I love Jon. And I love this flat and the location. But I also loved how quiet and peaceful Oxford felt. Not that I can afford Oxford either," she added with a laugh. "There are so many places around England, not to mention Wales or Scotland. If the right job pops up but just happens to be in another city, then I'll have to consider that. It might be fun to start a new adventure somewhere outside of London but still close. That way I could have my own life but still be near to Jon and Aunt Vickie. And you. I guess it will all depend on where I find a job."

Patrick appreciated being included in the list of people Eleanor wanted to stay close to, and he smiled as he picked up a chip off his plate. "Well, I think you'll have some say in where you end up. If you want a job in London, I know at least three different people that could make that happen. And probably at a salary that you could afford a nice little flat on your own. Maybe not in Zone 1 like this one," he said laughing. "But definitely still fairly central."

"I'd be happy with Zone 6 if it meant having my own place at a reasonable budget."

"Darling, you wouldn't be happy with your transport bills if you lived in Zone 6. Not unless you worked from home ninety percent of the time."

"Not going to lie Patrick, working from home sounds like my idea of heaven. I've never been built for the 9-5 office job. That's why I got into teaching."

"Well, think about what you'd like to do. Teach? Publishing? Writing? Let me know and I'll ask around and make some calls."

"I'll think about it. My professors and advisors were asking the same thing. It feels weird to think I could have options. I'm used to taking what I can get." *In more ways than one*, Eleanor thought silently as she thought about years wasted with Michael and how flattered she was initially by Mark. She really wasn't in the habit of thinking about what *she* wanted.

Patrick sensed Eleanor's mind had wandered somewhere other than jobs and he wondered what she was thinking. She was so expressive when she was deep in thought, one day he hoped she'd let him in on where her mind wandered.

"I hope the new pictures this week weren't too disconcerting," he asked cautiously.

"What?" Eleanor snapped out of her private thoughts and tried to rejoin the conversation. "Oh. No, they weren't too bad. I mean, I'm not thrilled they followed me down to Oxford Street after I said goodbye to you. It's weird thinking someone was following me and I didn't even know it. But I guess it is what it is. I thought I was aware of my surroundings but I guess I'll have to start paying more attention."

"I still feel bad about it. And about the confrontation with Mark. I hope there haven't been any more issues with him after he and I pitched up on your doorstep. Thank goodness the tabloids didn't get that on camera."

Eleanor grimaced at the thought. "I know. That would have been less than ideal. No, there haven't been more problems with Mark. He's basically cut himself off from all of us. Not just me and Jon, but the rest of their friends at school. They wouldn't take his side over mine or Jon's and he's not happy. I feel bad, but Mark can't just let things go. I've honestly been trying not to think about it this week. I've just been spending time with mom before she flew home and then focusing on school."

"I hope you had fun with your mum before she left."

"We did," Eleanor smiled.

"I'm glad you seem so ok about the photos and the articles, I really have been worrying about that."

"Oh Patrick, there's no need to worry. I assumed being friends with a what did you call yourself? An almost famous international Movie Star would eventually get some notice. It's not fun, but it's not the end of the world."

"But would it make you..." Patrick trailed off.

Eleanor could tell he really was worried about something. "Patrick? What is it?"

"I'm sorry Eleanor, I wasn't sure if I should bring this up but I've been thinking about it all week. I value your friendship more than anything. And I've always meant it when I said that if that's all this ever was between us I would respect that and would be grateful to have your friendship…"

"But?" Eleanor asked hesitantly.

"But…I am interested in more than friendship. I always have been, and I hope you know that."

Eleanor nodded silently, looking down and pushed a chip nervously around her plate.

"Seeing the tabloid stories, it just makes me worried you might never want to be more than friends. That you wouldn't be open to pursuing something eventually with me if it would mean having to deal with that on a regular basis. As my friend you can stay out of the spotlight more or less, if you were my girlfriend…well that would be different. I wouldn't want to hide that. I'd want to live our lives normally and go out in public. I'd want to go to work events at whatever job you got and I'd want you to come to my work stuff."

"Parties and premiers, you mean?" Eleanor asked, suddenly feeling anxious.

"Yeah, they're not always my favorite thing but it is part of the job. Ideally I'd want to be with someone who would keep me company at that sort of thing."

"I guess I haven't really thought that far ahead Patrick. I'm not sure I'm the right fit for all the glitz and glamour of the filmmaking industry."

"Elle, you're so intelligent and funny, you'd fit right in."

"I don't know Patrick. I just like how it is now. I like hanging out with you at home over fish and chips. This side of your life I feel very comfortable with. I understand it. I relate to it. But all your work and the business side of the industry…it's so overwhelming. I really don't like big social events, especially formal ones. And the thought of having tabloids caring about every little detail of what I do and where I go and what I wear just because I'm dating a celebrity…it just feels so odd."

"Even if I'm the celebrity," Patrick said, with a slight edge in his voice.

Eleanor sighed, "Don't twist my words, I think you know me well enough by now to know I didn't mean it like that. If I didn't care about you I wouldn't even bother to be friends with you." She was struck by how much she meant it when she said she cared about Patrick, even as more than just a friend. She was finding herself thinking about if they started pursuing their relationship more seriously and she wasn't balking at the thought as much as she'd expected she would.

"So you care about me?" Patrick prodded.

"Of course I do! Haven't I made at least that much clear already? You're one of the best friends and most important relationships I've developed since moving here. I'm grateful for you as well Patrick, believe me, that sentiment goes both ways, you're not alone in feeling that."

"But?" Patrick demanded, staring at her across the dining table.

"But is this really the best time to bring up this subject? You start filming in a few days. I'm up to my eyeballs in school work trying to get my manuscript sorted out and apply for jobs. We're hardly going to be able to see each other over the next few months. You want to talk about taking our relationship to the next level *now*?" Eleanor's voice became more agitated as she spoke and she could feel the fear creeping in. "Maybe it's best if we just focus on our own work for a bit. You go almost straight into your next film after this one. That's over six months of hardly seeing

294

each other. Hardly ideal for starting a serious romantic relationship. Maybe friendship is best right now."

"I think you're scared and making excuses" Patrick said plainly.

Eleanor knew instinctively he was right, and hated how he always seemed to be able to read her feelings. It was just like Jon or her mom or Aunt Vickie but they'd known Eleanor her whole life, Patrick had only know her for five months, if even that. A tear started to slip down her cheek. Eleanor suddenly felt very tired.

"Oh Ellie, I didn't mean to make you cry. Damn it. I'm sorry." Patrick got up and knelt beside her chair, reaching up to wipe the tear away.

"It's not your fault. I'm just so tired Patrick. It's been a long week and saying goodbye to mom was harder than I thought it would be."

"Elle, I don't think it's the long week that's making you feel so tired. You have been running from making decisions about what you want since I've met you. Your writing, a job after graduation, a relationship with me, or with anyone else...you've been doing everything you can to avoid making a choice about what you really want. You've got to be exhausted!"

With that it was like a dam broke inside Eleanor. Suddenly there was another tear, and then another, and then another. They just kept falling and Eleanor began to shake and her breathing became ragged. Patrick leaned in close to comfort her and while part of her wanted him close, the other part felt claustrophobic. It felt like the room was closing in on her. She couldn't breathe. Though she dealt with them rarely these days, she remembered all too clearly what a panic attack felt like when one struck.

She pushed Patrick gently away from her. She didn't want to offend him but she needed space. She stood up, trying to catch her breath and walked to the end of the lounge and up to the big bay window. Patrick followed her. She opened the window and let the cold fresh air in, trying to take a deep breath and let it fill her lungs. She knew Patrick was behind her but sensed he was keeping a slight distance. She leaned her head against the window frame and sat down on the windowsill. The cold air felt good against her face and filled her lungs. Slowly she was able to control her breathing a bit more but the tears continued to stream down her face.

"Patrick…" she started, in between small sobs.

"No Elle, I'm not leaving you right now. I'll go in the hall if that will help but I'm not leaving you alone in the flat like this.

"I don't…want you to s…s…see me…like th…this," Eleanor struggled to say the words.

"Too late," Patrick said, crossing his arms, frown etched on his face. He shifted from one foot to the other, all he wanted was to go to her but he could tell she needed space.

Eleanor just closed her eyes and leaned harder against the window. The tears continued for what felt like hours, but Eleanor supposed it was only five minutes or so. She eventually let Patrick guide her to the sofa where she curled into a ball, arms wrapped tightly around one of the throw pillows. Patrick put one of the throw blankets over her and rubbed her back through the fabric, moving his hand in a circle around her back, just like her mom had always done when a panic attack would hit.

Eventually the tears stopped and Eleanor managed to open her eyes. She immediately noticed how worried Patrick was.

"Does this happen often," he asked quietly.

"No, not anymore thankfully. They used to happen a lot when I was a teen, after the divorce and…everything." Eleanor had been about to say more than she would have been happy about, so she stopped. Patrick had such a habit of making her feel so at ease, like she could tell him all her secrets. But some things were too hard to think about, even after a long time had passed. "I can't believe you witnessed that. Only my mom has ever seen me like that. And Jonathan, once."

"I'm glad I was here. But I'm sorry if anything I said triggered it." Patrick paused, then continued, "Eleanor, I don't ever want to pressure you into making a decision about us. If you genuinely need more time, that's ok. We can continue our friendship and see how things develop after my next two films. But I think your hesitation is about something completely different from the tabloid photos and your worries about my so-called celebrity lifestyle. I saw you stick up for yourself with Mark, that took guts. You have been through so much in the past with your parent's divorce, with Michael, then moving half way across the world. Eleanor, you're incredible! You're excelling at school, you sound so much more certain and clear about your writing. And yet when it comes to personal relationships, specifically romantic relationships, you're like a deer in the headlights. I can tell you're scared but I also know you're not scared of *me*. So what are you scared of Elle? What are you afraid is going to happen if you let yourself fall for me?"

"I don't know," Eleanor answered in a small voice. She immediately squeezed her eyes shut and buried her face in the pillow.

Patrick sighed. "Elle, I think we both know. This is about the one subject you've never fully explained."

Eleanor looked up at him, not knowing where he was going with this, and yet deep down she knew exactly what he was going to say next.

"This is about your dad."

Eleanor felt the panic starting to rise again. She sat up on the sofa and clutched the blanket around her.

"You've brought him up several times but you've never said why you don't speak to him anymore. You've hinted that something happened on your last visit but you've never said what."

"Patrick, this has nothing to do with my dad. I'm not some cliche little girl with daddy issues."

"I beg to differ. Maybe you're not the cliche, but something happened. Something that broke off your relationship with him and that has impacted your relationship with every other man that's come into your life since."

"I don't want to talk about this Patrick. It's not relevant. He doesn't factor into the decisions I make about my life anymore," Eleanor said, trying to sound defiant, but knowing she wasn't succeeding.

"I think he does Eleanor," Patrick replied gently.

They stared at each other from opposite ends of the sofa for what felt like a minute. Eleanor hoped he'd give up on the subject but he refused to drop his gaze. He just sat there waiting for her to speak. Eleanor was the first to break the stare. She looked down at her hands, twisted around the edge of the blanket. *Maybe it was time*, she thought, time to tell him. She was so tired of keeping it locked inside. Tired of letting the past hold her back from making decisions about the future.

Eleanor looked up and opened her mouth to speak. But before she could, there was a knock at the door. Eleanor looked past Patrick towards the sound of the knocking. Patrick turned towards the door as well, then looked back at Eleanor.

"Are you expecting someone? I didn't hear the door buzz," he said curiously.

"I'm not expecting anyone. Maybe it's a neighbor?" Eleanor said confused.

"As long as it's not Mark again," Patrick said bitterly.

Eleanor gave a sour laugh. There was another knock at the door, this time more insistent.

"Well, whoever it is, they're not going away," she said grumpily as she got up from the sofa.

Patrick quickly followed her, "Elle, let me get it, you should rest."

But Eleanor was already to the door. As she opened it, Patrick was right behind her, watching over her shoulder as she opened the door.

There was a man standing outside, bending over to set a suitcase down on the ground. Eleanor's brain was trying to process who it was and what was going on. She felt Patrick put a hand on her shoulder and heard him ask, "Can we help you?"

The man stood up and looked at Eleanor and in that moment, she thought she might sink to the floor.

Eleanor gasped, "Michael?"

Chapter 19

"You have got to be kidding me," Eleanor blurted out. She was completely shocked. Of all the people she would have thought might show up at her doorstep one night, she had never once imagined this scenario.

"Hi Ellie Bean. Miss me?" Michael said with a goofy smile and a laugh.

Eleanor just stared back at him blankly. The use of one of his rare affectionate nicknames for her didn't even register through her shock. She did however notice that Patrick's hand on her shoulder felt significantly heavier than it had a few moments ago.

"Can I come in sweetie? It's pretty freezing outside and I'm chilled to the bone." Michael stamped his feet on the ground, like he was trying to get his blood circulating.

Eleanor's body defaulted to politeness out of instinct. He was cold, she should let him in. Then she'd decide what to do.

Michael picked up his bag and walked in. He gave her a quick kiss on the lips then set the bag down in the entryway and immediately strolled into the lounge, leaving Eleanor and Patrick in the entryway, staring at each other in dumbfounded silence. Michael came back into the hallway from the lounge, having removed his coat and shoes and looking far too comfortable in her flat than Eleanor liked.

The three of them just stared at each other. Eleanor felt like she was in some kind of farce but without the benefit of having a script. Patrick wasn't touching her anymore, but she could feel his presence. She could also feel the anger radiating off him. He was clearly less thrilled than she was to see Michael.

"What are you doing here?" She finally asked.

"We need to talk hun."

Ellie Bean, *sweetie*, *hun*. In less than five minutes he'd been more affectionate than he'd been in a typical week while they were dating. Eleanor's brain felt like it was melting as she tried to process what was happening.

"Without *him*," Michael finished, glaring at Patrick. "I've seen the tabloids, I know who you are and why you are trying to steal my Ellie Bean."

"I'm not leaving you alone with him Elle. I'm not," Patrick said defiantly.

"You're not needed here pal," Michael said, sounding so arrogant it made Eleanor cringe.

"Michael, stop. Go into the living room. Patrick was invited here and you weren't. I'll be there in a minute and I'll deal with you there."

"Eleanor!" Patrick protested.

Michael just smirked and turned back to go into the lounge and sit on the sofa, whistling a ridiculously cheery tune as he did.

Eleanor put her head in her hands. She could feel Patrick staring at her.

"I'm sorry. Really Patrick. I had no idea he was coming, I don't know what this is about. But I do know that he won't leave until he says whatever he needs to say."

"I'm not leaving you Elle. I refuse to leave you alone with him." Patrick was furious. Not at her, Eleanor could tell that much. But he was definitely angry about Michael being there.

"Please Patrick. Michael is harmless. But if you stay it's only going to make him dig his heels in further," Eleanor whispered, she didn't want Michael to hear her conversation with Patrick.

Patrick looked at her, hard, thinking. She held his gaze. The panic she'd felt earlier had gone, in its place was a steely resistance. "Trust me Patrick. I can handle him. You can go. I'll call you later."

After another few moments Patrick finally closed his eyes and sighed. "Fine," he said reluctantly.

He got his coat from the closet and leaned down to give Eleanor a kiss on the cheek, lingering slightly with the side of his face rested against her head. Eleanor squeezed his arm through the fabric of his coat. He turned without a word and left the flat.

Eleanor turned to walk into the lounge, but before she did she picked up her phone on the hall table. She quickly opened up her texts and found the thread for Jonathan. She may not have wanted Patrick to witness whatever was going to happen next, but she wasn't not going to deal with Michael alone.

Come home now.
Need you.

She tapped out quickly as two separate texts. Almost immediately she got a reply.

What's wrong? U ok?

She sent her response, then put the phone in her back pocket and walked into the lounge.

Michael is here. Need reinforcements.

302

* * * * *

Michael was sprawled on the sofa, as if he owned the place. Eleanor couldn't remember if he'd always seemed so arrogant and entitled or if this was a new thing. *He's probably always been this way,* she thought. *I just probably never noticed it as anything bad.*

Michael patted the space on the sofa next to him.

Eleanor deliberately sat on the armchair in the opposite corner of the small room. Determined to put as much distance between them as possible.

"How did you even find me? I never gave you this address."

"I was at Dylan and Jill's, Jill had a Christmas card from you in the kitchen. She'd kept the envelope and your address was on it."

He acted like he was Sherlock. Eleanor rolled her eyes. "What do you want?" She asked pointedly.

"Aren't you happy to see me?" Michael asked, frowning slightly.

"No. You had made up your mind the last time we saw each other. We're done. You broke my heart, well…at the time. But then I moved here and I moved on."

"What, to that stupid actor guy?"

"You don't even know who he is, do you?" Eleanor said, laughing bitterly.

"I know he's an actor, I saw your picture in a tabloid at Safeway. I couldn't believe it! My Ellie! In London kissing some actor."

"Some actor," Eleanor scoffed. "Shows how much you ever paid attention to anything I was interested in. You used to tease me about the films I watched. You've seen his face a thousand times, on my TV screen, but you never cared about what I cared about."

"Eleanor, he doesn't matter. Maybe I don't know every film you loved but I care about you. I *miss* you!"

"So you flew all the way to London to tell me that? What do you want?"

"I want you back," Michael stated. So definitely and matter-of-factly.

Eleanor just stared back at him, blinking uncomprehendingly. Then from out of nowhere she just started laughing. Slightly hysterically. Michael's face fell.

"Eleanor, it's rude to laugh," he scolded.

Eleanor's laughing subsided to giggles as she tried to calm herself down. "I'm sorry, I'm sorry. Oh Michael, you seriously have just wasted a lot of time and money. You will never get me back. Ever. I am so done and over our relationship. You did me a huge favor when you broke up with me last spring. Huge. And I'm grateful. But we are so beyond over Michael. You didn't want me anymore. And you don't get to turn up, unannounced at my flat, thinking you can make some grand gesture and I'll melt."

"Eleanor, you can't give up on everything we had. We're good together."

"No. We weren't good. You might have been happy enough. But I was happy only because I didn't know better." Softening her tone, "I'm sorry Michael, I really am. But you made the decision for us months ago. I accepted it and moved on and I'm happier now. So much happier. And I think you'd be happier with someone else. I'm not the same person I was with you."

"I refuse to accept this Eleanor. I was your *first*, you're really going to throw that away?"

Eleanor felt her face burn hot. "You threw *me* away Michael, so don't you dare put this on me. You gave me up *twice*. I was foolish enough to go back to you the first time, but that's it. I'm not falling for it again. You did this Michael, *you* bear the responsibility for ending our relationship. I don't owe you anything. You've gotten all you're going to get from me."

"You think that fancy actor man is going to want you? When he's used to being around supermodels and hot actresses? Like you could ever make him happy. Or satisfy him," he sneered.

Eleanor stood up quickly, "That's it. You're done. I'm not listening to anymore of this crap. You know nothing about my relationship with him. You saw me in those pictures and you got jealous. Just like you always do. You can't stand the thought of anyone else having something you want. And that's all I ever was to you, a thing. For you to put down or cast aside and then pick back up whenever you want. The fact is, Patrick has nothing to do with my decision. I wouldn't take you back now even if I was single. I. Don't. Want. *You*. Full stop. End of story. Now get out."

Michael's face dropped as he listened to Eleanor's furious statement. Like he finally was realizing she meant it and he'd failed.

"This isn't like you, Ellie, you must be feeling sick or confused."

"Get out Michael. Now. You weren't welcome here in the first place and my patience is wearing painfully thin."

"But, where will I go? I don't have anywhere to stay."

"That's not my problem. You're in Central London, Michael, five minutes from the West End. You're literally surrounded by hotels. Find one and check in. But get out of my flat."

"Eleanor, please…," Michael began to plead.

"She said leave," Jonathan's voice cut in, as he casually leaned against the door frame to the lounge.

Eleanor was very grateful to see him. Knowing Michael, he wouldn't listen to Eleanor alone.

Michael looked between Jonathan and Eleanor, as if hoping she would change her mind.

"Who are you, another boyfriend? Wow, you really have been busy, Ellie."

"We've met in case you don't remember. I'm her cousin and if you don't leave her alone you'll have more trouble than you know." Jon smiled threateningly.

Michael's smug smile slipped a bit, but she could see he wasn't going to give up easily. The fact that he didn't remember Jonathan from the time he'd visited really did show he was always disengaged from really caring about her.

"Leave Michael. There's a hotel around every corner, no matter the direction you go out the square, you'll be very comfortable at any of them," Eleanor said finally, crossing her arms.

Michael sighed and stood up. "Eleanor, you're going to regret this. When you change your mind it will be too late."

"Whatever," Eleanor said, shrugging casually.

"Time to go mate," Jonathan said.

Michael walked out of the lounge and picked up his bag and walked out the front door, Jonathan went with him. Eleanor stood alone in the lounge for a few minutes. Eventually Jonathan came back in.

"I walked him downstairs and watched him leave the building and walk around the corner."

"Maybe we should have given him directions."

"Please Elle, you know as much as I do that knowing Michael he was lying about having nowhere to go. He's got some nice hotel room booked. If you'd said yes, he would have swept you away there as a romantic gesture, if you said no, he'd have a place to crash."

Eleanor paused for a moment then put her hands to her face, "Oh my god, you're right. That's exactly what he would have done," Eleanor said with a bitter laugh, dropping her hands to her side.

"Are you ok?" Jonathan asked gently, Eleanor seemed

deceptively calm, still standing in the middle of the lounge.

She opened her mouth to speak. Then closed it. Then tried again. But before she could, the tears started falling again. This time it was different. There was no racing heartbeat, no tightening in her chest or feeling like she couldn't breathe. Just streams of tears falling steadily. Jonathan came to her side and led her to the sofa to sit as she continued crying silently. She'd reach up to wipe the tears away but they kept coming, almost from nowhere. Eleanor struggled to figure out how she was feeling and where this emotion was coming from. She hadn't been happy to see Michael and she was thrilled to see him leave, so why was she crying? Then it hit her.

She was finally and truly done with him. And on her terms.

Back in the spring, the breakup was all down to Michael. He'd made that decision for the both of them and she'd been blindsided. She never got to have her say. It wasn't that she'd wanted revenge but she'd always hated feeling like she'd just been thrown away, without any care or thought to how it would hurt her. But that had changed. She'd finally found her voice with Michael. It had felt good too. All those years she'd just gone along with whatever he wanted. Breakup? Ok. Get back together? Sure! Breakup again? Ok. But no more. He'd made decisions and now he got to live with the consequences, she was done getting sucked back in. And the best part was it hadn't even crossed her mind to go back. Even if she didn't have Patrick...then she remembered something she'd said to Michael just a few moments ago.

"The fact is, Patrick has nothing to do with my decision. I wouldn't take you back now even if I was single."

Even if I was single," she thought again. Had she meant that? Did she really see herself as not single? If she was really just friends with Patrick as she'd tried to tell herself so many times, why would she say that to Michael?

"Eleanor? Are you alright," Jonathan asked, concern plastered across his face. "I'm going to get you some water, I'll be right back." He got up and went to the kitchen. Eleanor vaguely heard him getting a glass from the cabinet and water from the tap.

She also started thinking back to Patrick's attempts to talk about her dad before Michael showed up, and the panic attack that felt like it was going to engulf her. Having the confrontation with Michael had left Eleanor feeling like she was finally released from all the pain and bad memories. She really did feel like she was finally and completely over him, he was part of her past now. Maybe telling Patrick about her dad could have the same result? Maybe she could finally let go of those painful memories as well?

Jonathan came back with the water, "Here Elle, just have a couple sips. You look like you've been put through the wringer."

"I have to go," Eleanor said abruptly, standing straight up.

"What? Now?! Elle, it's getting late. Where on earth could you need to rush off to now?"

"I have to find Patrick, he was here when Michael arrived and I asked him to leave. God, what an idiot! I shouldn't have done that! He was so mad, he didn't want to leave me with him." Eleanor rushed to her room to get her handbag and then grabbed her coat off the hook near the door.

"Elle, just call him, I don't like you going out there when you're in such a state."

Eleanor wiped her eyes, the tears finally gone, and smoothed her hair. She took a deep breath as she buttoned up her coat and slipped her bag over her head, cross body style. "I'm fine Jon. Better than I've been in ages. I have to go." And without another word she flew out the door and downstairs, leaving Jonathan standing, open mouthed in the doorway.

* * * * *

Even though it was Friday it was past the holiday madness, so Eleanor thought a taxi might be the fastest way to get to Patrick's. Even though mentally she was feeling clearer than she had in months, the physical toll of the shock of Michael and the panic attack before that left her feeling like navigating the Tube might not be the wisest thing. She ran down the steps of her building and dashed across Red Lion Square, heading towards Holborn Station. She figured she'd find a cab quick nearer the station and the main road. Sure enough she saw a few and threw her hand up to flag one down, something she'd never done very confidently before but this time it worked. She jumped in the cab and gave the driver Patrick's address.

There was still a little bit of traffic, but the drive gave her time to think about everything that had happened that day, particularly her conversation with Patrick. She'd known from the beginning he wanted more. He'd been flirty and sweet all the way back to that first day they bumped into each other. But under the flirtation, even then there was such a genuineness that Eleanor had rarely found in men she met. Then at her birthday, the way he'd casually but privately sent over the champagne, extending a kind gesture without making a big scene about it. He was always doing nice things for her without having to make sure that everyone around them knew he was doing it.

The day he spent with her in Oxford. Letting her pay when she insisted at the pub, sharing jokes with her, acting as the tour guide, the way he truly listened to her and seemed genuinely interested in her life and her thoughts, and the way he shared things about his life. And since then, all the million little ways he'd shown her true friendship and caring. She knew he fancied her, that he wanted to take their relationship further, but looking back at the past several months, she could see that wherever their relationship went in the future, it was already grounded in something so solid and precious. There was a real foundation, much more so than anything she'd had with Michael, or might have had with Mark. More so than even her relationship with her father, who she felt never really loved her or cared about her happiness.

She knew Patrick was different from any other man in her life, but was she brave enough to move forward? Did she trust herself to believe that he was different? The closer she got to Patrick's home the more nervous she became. Everything from past experience told her to turn around and go home. But everything from her time and experience with Patrick told her to keep going.

The cab arrived in front of Patrick's and she paid the cabbie and got out. The cab pulled away and Eleanor just stood there at his front door for at least a solid minute. Fighting her usual impulse to run away from a scary situation, she finally knocked on the door.

No answer.

She knocked again and waited. Still no answer.

Eleanor stood there, not knowing what to do. She hadn't thought about him not being home. She just assumed that he'd go home after he left her flat. He should have been here by now, so where was he? Eleanor leaned her forehead against his front door, suddenly feeling like she might pass out. The anxiety, the adrenaline, all the crying, she was beyond exhausted, she felt like she might shatter into a million pieces. And now she felt the tears starting to fall again. In that moment, all she wanted was Patrick. And he wasn't there.

She turned and leaned her back against the door and

slowly slid down until she was sat on his doorstep, legs outstretched in front of her. Her head leaned back against the door as she closed her eyes and let the tears just fall. She was too tired to try to fight them. She felt so cold. And so pathetic. What was she even doing here? Should she text him? Ask where he is? What if he was mad at her for asking him to leave? What if he went out to some bar or club? Should she just go home? He'd never know she was here, she could just leave? *Patrick would want you to text him*, she thought. She knew she was right. Patrick wasn't the type of person, or friend, to be mad at her right now or to go out drinking or something crazy to distract himself. He'd be mad at Michael and the situation, but not at Eleanor, that wasn't his style.

"Eleanor?!"

She heard Patrick's voice cut through her thoughts.

"How long have you been here?! Oh my god, are you ok? You're freezing." He crouched down beside her and pulled her close into a hug, rubbing her arms and back as if trying to warm her. "Why didn't you call me? Jonathan texted a few minutes ago asking if you'd made it to my place safely."

"I wanted to talk. To apologize...about earlier," Eleanor stammered uncertainly. She looked at Patrick and then looked down to where he'd set something on the ground beside them. Grocery bags. Eleanor sighed at herself and laughed slightly as she leaned against Patrick. *He went to the shop you ninny. Of course he didn't go off to some club.*

"We need to get you inside and warmed up, I can't believe you're just sitting out here on the ground Ellie, you're going to catch your death!"

He reached up and unlocked his door and stood up. Eleanor did in fact feel a bit frozen, not just from the cold but from the exhaustion of the multiple emotional episodes of the evening. Patrick bent down and in one swift movement, lifted Eleanor up off the ground and carried her into his house, setting her on the sofa. He stepped back outside to get his groceries and ran to set them in the kitchen. Eleanor tried to unbutton her coat but her fingers were frozen stiff. She heard Patrick doing something in the kitchen, and a few moments later she heard the kettle starting to boil.

Patrick came back to the lounge and helped Eleanor get out of her coat and boots and then helped her move to the armchair nearest the fireplace. He wrapped her in throw blankets and started building a fire. She heard the kettle squeal and he went back to the kitchen. He came back with a mug of tea and a hot water bottle, the latter of which she clutched to her chest and then cradled the tea in both hands. He went back to the kitchen and returned with a tea of his own, and a bottle of whiskey. He poured a shot into his glass, and then before she could protest, poured another shot into hers.

"Medicinal. No arguments," he said with mock sternness.

Eleanor took a small sip, the whiskey wasn't so bad, since it was diluted by the tea, which Patrick had made very milky and very sugary. The combination started warming her from the inside. He sat down in the chair opposite hers, watching her very carefully. She took another sip and then leaned her head against the side of the high-backed chair and closed her eyes. She'd always loved this chair. It was one of her favorite places in his home. By the fire, with views out the front window and through to the kitchen, as well as of his well-stocked bookshelves in the lounge. The first day she'd been to his place she'd thought to herself that everything was exactly as she'd have done it if she'd lived here and designed it herself. It felt like home.

"What happened after I left Elle?" She heard Patrick ask. She opened her eyes and saw him looking at her. His face was a mixture of concern and something else. Fear? She wasn't sure.

Eleanor sighed. "Well, long story short. Michael wanted us to get back together." She saw Patrick's face tighten. She looked at him pointedly and continued, "I told him hell no and to get out of my flat." Relief flooded Patrick's face. "Seriously Patrick, I swear, he wasn't there for longer than five minutes or so, ten tops. And Jonathan arrived near the end of it. He helped me get Michael to realize I meant it and that he had to leave."

"I wish you'd let me stay." He said it so simply and Eleanor knew he meant it.

"I know. And I wish you could have stayed. Believe me, I would have much rather let you or Jonathan just deal with Michael for me. But I had to do it myself. Does that make sense? I had to handle it. Once and for all."

"I can understand that," Patrick replied gently, looking down into his tea.

"You're always so good at taking care of me, just like you're doing now. But this was something I had to take care of myself or it would never be truly over. I didn't even hesitate Patrick. I don't quite know what came over me. But when he said he wanted me back I started laughing. Like, full on laughing. To his face. He told me I was rude, and maybe it was, but I couldn't help it. It was all so absurd. I felt like I was in some kind of farce. As soon as you walked out I wanted to go with you. But I knew I had to take care of Michael and just put the past to rest. After Michael left I started crying again, but it was so different. It was like I was crying out of relief. It was over, he was gone, I never have to feel bad about him again. I was released Patrick."

Patrick was silent for a moment, just looking at his tea, like he was trying to make a decision. Eleanor waited.

Finally he said, "So, you're released from Michael, and earlier you sounded resigned and past things with Mark."

"I am. They're both in the past. Firmly in the past."

"What about your dad?" He asked directly.

Eleanor paused, then said slowly, "That's why I'm here. I want to put that in the past too. So I can move on. With you."

Patrick's eyes grew wide, his mouth opened slightly out of surprise. "Do...do you mean that?"

"Patrick, I'll be honest, I'm scared out of my mind. Moving forward terrifies me, it always has, that's why I've wasted so much time stuck in the past. But I want more. Our friendship has been the biggest gift, but I've been unfairly holding us both back. I'm scared, but I don't want to let that fear guide me. I want to be brave...with you."

Patrick's eyes shined a little brighter in the firelight, and he reached up to wipe at them roughly with his sleeve. He collected himself and then looked at her solemnly, "Eleanor, I can't promise you that I'll never hurt you or that we'll end up being together forever. But I can promise you that I will never intentionally hurt you the way you've been hurt before. I'm not Michael or Mark...or your dad. I know what's happened with Michael and Mark, if you're finally ready to tell me about your dad I'm here to listen."

"Ok. Just...be patient. I've only ever told this story once. To mom. I know mom told Jonathan and Aunt Vickie, Jon tried to ask me about it, but I couldn't bear to get into it again, it was too painful. I thought I could just forget it, but you're right, it's been haunting me ever since and it's time to tell you. Because I trust you.

"Take your time, there's no rush," Patrick leaned back in his chair with his tea and just looked at Eleanor, a soft, neutral expression on his face.

Eleanor took a deep breath and began.

314

Chapter 20

"After the divorce, I would go spend a month in Manhattan with my dad. He never insisted on the whole 'alternating holidays and two weeks in the summer,' I think I told you that already, so the arrangement had been just one month in the summer. They were never terribly exciting, I was a teenager and I was mad at my dad for the divorce and for how sad mom was. But it was Manhattan, so it was hardly a punishment. When I was still 16, 17, he'd take me to some Broadway shows and there were always nice dinners out. But mom had always been the one that made us feel like a family. When it was just dad and me, I always felt like I was on a field trip with a professor. For those first few years after the divorce I gave him the benefit of the doubt and just tried to have fun and behave. He would still spend most of the day at work or in his home office doing research. It was hardly a vacation. After I turned 18 it never occurred to me to stop going to see him. He was my dad and if he still wanted me to visit I would. When I was 19 though, well, that was the summer it changed. That was the last summer I would see him.

"The summer had been good at the start. Manhattan is humid and hot but not nearly has hot as Phoenix. I had been looking forward to getting away from the desert for a bit. I had finished my first year at university for my undergrad. I felt like an adult," Eleanor laughed bitterly, then continued. "I had my own room at my dad's apartment. It was more like a hotel so it felt really luxurious. Dad gave me cash for every day I was there. Looking back, I should have been furious about that. When mom was taking care of me, in those first few years after the divorce, we had to be very careful with money, but as long as I was in my dad's care there was an envelope with $200 cash every day, just for me to spend on whatever, like a daily allowance. Some days I'd only spend $10 on some street food and save the rest for another day, then there'd be days where I'd take all that saved cash and go shopping for new clothes for the fall. Over the course of a month he'd give me several thousand dollars in cash. If he wanted to take me out to dinner somewhere nice he'd leave an additional $500 with the usual $200 so I could go buy a new dress. Now I can see how weird and problematic all this money was. But I was 19 Patrick. And living off of student loans and my mother's generosity living at home as an undergrad. I was 19, a legal adult, but I still felt 15 and wanting my dad's attention and love.

"Anyway, I'd spend most of the days wandering around. Dad was always working, so I'd hang out at the Met or the Public Library, I'd write in coffee shops or wander around Central Park. Some nights, usually once or twice a week I'd meet my dad for dinner somewhere extravagant. He never went anywhere casual, so that's why I would buy a new dress. Once I thought I'd wear trousers, but he made me change.

"Other nights I'd come back to the apartment and he'd be entertaining his colleagues. After the first week of being there I noticed one of them, one of the younger ones, watching me. I always tried to ignore my dad and his friends and just go to my room, but I had to walk past them to get there, so I always had to stop and say hello. But this one guy just made me so uneasy, the way he was looking at me. He was probably in his early 30s, a new associate professor in my dad's department, some kind of rising star in his field. Not that I cared. He'd always make a point of saying hello when I walked in. And each time he would ask me something about my day, something personal. I was always so shy and nervous; my dad's crowd was a whole different scene than I was used to back home. And being a 19-year-old girl in a room full of older men, it just made me uncomfortable. Even in my dad's home with him sitting right there.

"So, eventually, by the middle of the second week, I pretended to be talking on my phone when I got home, I just waved at the men in a friendly way and practically sprinted to my room. The next day my dad stopped me. He told me I was being rude and he expected me to talk to his friends if they are over when I come home. He told me he wouldn't be disrespected in such a way and with everything he was doing for me that summer the least I could do was have polite conversation with his friends. I knew he was referring to the money. He was paying for my respect and my time. That was the implication. I tried telling him that the younger guy, Brian was his name, made me uncomfortable. My dad just dismissed me and said I was being ridiculous.

"After that I tried coming home at different times, if I came home late they were often still there, but had usually been drinking a bit of brandy by then. If I came home early I could usually avoid them, but then I'd be stuck in my room the rest of the night. They'd stay over until 1 a.m. sometimes. It was at the beginning of the third week that it all started to unravel. Dad made a big deal about me going with him to some fancy charity gala he was connected to through work. Dad was always more than just a traditional academic. He liked the intellectual elitism of academia but he also craved social power, connections, and wealth. So there were always side projects and book deals that helped him afford his lifestyle, and then charity stuff that connected him with the New York elite. He loved all of it. I did not want to go, it sounded too formal and I knew everyone there would be older than me. But he insisted. Said if I didn't go I could just pack my bags and go home to mom. So like a fool, I agreed. He gave me the name of a stylist to go see the next day, one of the personal shoppers at Neiman Marcus. I would need a new dress and he wanted a 'professional,' his words not mine, to pick it out. All the dresses she showed me were gorgeous but very revealing and grown up. I was a 19-year-old from Arizona, not a Hollywood actress. We finally settled on one that was a little more covered up at the top, but it had a long slit in the skirt. It really was gorgeous though, and I felt like a princess in it. God help me, I was so naive.

"The night of the dinner, dad and I arrived and he made us mingle in the lobby for a bit before going to our table for the dinner. Patrick, it was awful. All these older guys with their dates, all of whom were either older but clearly trying to fight it or practically my age looking bored out of their minds but laughing mechanically whenever the guy said something. Looking back, I know most of them were only with those guys because of their money. And the men were all complimenting my dad on his 'hot date', lots of winking and slapping him on the back. They knew I was his daughter, he'd introduced me! I was so disgusted by the way they were joking about me. It was mortifying.

"We finally got our seats at the table and I immediately wished we hadn't. It was a formal table setting. Millions of glasses and cutlery, I had no clue what order I was supposed to use everything. Then, to make matters worse, Brian was seated next to me and my dad was across the table. I had to make conversation with him all night. He kept complimenting me, saying how beautiful the dress was and how pretty I was. But it was all so inappropriate. Like, it wasn't just 'that dress is beautiful' instead he added how perfectly it hugged my figure. Or that my lipstick made my mouth look so kissable. If he had been my age and not my dad's colleague I might have been flattered. But by this point I'd Googled him and he was 35, sixteen years older than me! What kind of 35-year-old goes after a 19-year-old?! It's disgusting. He thought it was 'cute', that's what he said, 'cute', that I didn't know which fork or glass to use, so he made a big show out of helping me out, like it was our little secret, and he wouldn't tell anyone. I was just trying to get through the dinner. But the wine was flowing and later champagne. Brian kept brushing his arm against mine, or would reach over and squeeze my hand in the middle of telling a joke. He'd brush his thigh against my leg. It just kept getting worse.

"After dinner, when dessert and more champagne was served, he started trying to place his hand on my leg, reaching through the slit in my dress to my bare leg beneath. Or he'd reach for my hand and try to place it on his thigh. Each time I'd push his hand off me or snatch my hand out of his grasp. He wouldn't even react. All of this crap happening under the table so no one could see, he'd be doing this in the middle of talking to my father or someone else at the table. He'd make a move and I'd resist, then he'd try again. I was on the defensive all night long, he just wouldn't stop. The couple times there was a break in the conversation I would try to lean over and tell him to stop and either he'd act like he didn't know what I was talking about or someone else at the table would make a joke about Brian and I sharing secrets. My father ignored the whole thing. It had to have been clear from the look on my face, that I didn't like what was happening.

"I just wanted to go back to the apartment so desperately. I had made up my mind that I was going to pack my things and get an earlier flight home. I wasn't even going to tell my dad because after all this I was afraid he'd stop me. Clearly, he knew about Brian and was helping him. I was convinced he'd orchestrated the whole thing. I was frustrated and angry and scared. At one point, before they cleared all the table servings away, I slipped one of the dessert forks under the table and just held it at an angle. Sure enough, a few minutes later Brian reached for my leg again and hit the fork instead. I was just staring straight ahead, acting like nothing had happened. I don't think it made him bleed, but he was rubbing his hand for a few minutes after that. He didn't reach under the table again.

"Finally, after five hours of this constant assault under the dinner table, we went home. Our table walked out as a group and Brian stayed very close to me. He kept trying to put his arm around me and I would wiggle out of it. Finally, as he said goodnight to my dad and I, he shook my dad's hand and they shared a joke about something, I wasn't even paying attention. Then my dad got in the car first and before I could get in after him Brian wrapped his arms around me in a hug and he whispered in my ear that he would see me soon, that he liked a girl with 'fight' in her.

"Patrick, I swear, in that moment it felt like a threat. I've never been so terrified. I refused to talk to my dad the whole drive home, I just told him I was tired. He kept trying to talk about Brian, how he was such a nice guy from a very prominent family, that it was time I had a real, adult relationship. Patrick, he was honestly trying to set us up! Like I was some Victorian Era daughter needing her father to make a good match. I knew then if I stayed the rest of my trip my dad was only going to continue trying to set me up. It was past midnight. As soon as I got home I got my computer and looked up flights. There was a morning flight, the day after next, that the airline would let me switch my ticket for, I just had to get through one more day and night. I thought I could do that.

"The next morning, I slept in and then went out and spent one more day at Central Park and visiting a couple of my favorite places. I got back to the apartment early, in order to miss my dad and his friends if they came over. I spent the rest of the afternoon and evening packing for my flight the next morning. I didn't even tell my mom I was coming back early, I was too afraid she'd call my dad and chew him out. I just wanted to get home and explain everything later. I thought it was all working out. I had picked up dinner from a deli, just a sandwich and some chips, and I ate in my room. My dad had come home but for a while didn't know I was in there. But when I hadn't come in at my usual time he texted to see where I was. I texted back that I was feeling sick and I was lying down in my room, that I was about to go to sleep.

"About an hour later there was a soft knock at my door, which I ignored. My lights were out, but I was reading my Kindle under the blanket. I was too afraid to go to sleep while I knew they all were still out there. I had locked the door but I heard the person jiggling the lock. I thought it was my dad coming to check on me so I just turned off my Kindle and pretended to be asleep. A few seconds later I heard a soft click at the door and then someone opened it. It wasn't a sturdy lock, it was just one of those standard bedroom locks, there was a little key that could open them all that my dad kept on the top of the door frame of his room. So again, I assumed it was my dad.

"Oh god. Eleanor. It was Brian," Patrick said horrified.

Eleanor just nodded and took a deep breath before continuing.

"I felt someone sit on the bed beside me. I foolishly thought my dad had come to check on me since I said I was sick. I was about to open my eyes to talk to him when I felt someone kissing me, hard. One hand slipped under my head to keep me from wiggling away and the other reached under my blankets trying to pull up my t-shirt. I immediately freaked out. I started fighting. I clawed at him. I realized then it was Brian. He just laughed quietly as he clamped his hand down around my mouth. In the distance, I could hear my dad and his friends talking and laughing. Brian smelled like brandy and cigars. I nearly passed out from fright. I knew in that moment what Brian was going do if I didn't stop him, with my dad sitting in the other room.

"I've never fought anyone so hard in my life. My whole body just snapped, like it had a life of its own. All my limbs were flailing and thrashing. At one point, he hit me in the head, the pain was literally stunning. I just froze. Then I felt him reach for the waist of my pajama bottoms and I just flipped. I didn't even think, I just reached beside me to the night stand and grabbed the lamp and arched it over the bed bringing it down on his head. That stunned him enough to let me race to the bathroom. I managed to grab my phone on my way and I locked myself in the bathroom and called 911.

"He followed me, but didn't yell. He just tried breaking down the door, thank god it was sturdy, I was praying so hard that the door would hold. I told the operator what was happening and that there were other people in the apartment but I didn't trust them. That when the police got there they shouldn't listen to anything said by whoever opened the door. I insisted that the police had to come into the apartment, into my room, and get me themselves. I was so afraid my dad would just try to explain everything away, just to avoid scandal. It's the only thing he ever really cared about.

"I just felt myself spilling out everything that had

happened that night, the gala, the sexual advances, Brian sneaking in to my room, I told that operator everything, and she was incredible, she just kept telling me it was going to be ok. She could hear Brian whispering furiously through the door and tugging on the door handle. He heard everything I was telling her and he was furious. He kept saying things like 'no one would ever believe me' and I knew it was true. The operator believed me, and I prayed the police would. But if it ever got out in public, I would just be the poor deranged daughter who my father should have been allowed to raise after the divorce. I already knew that's what people thought, he had them convinced he was some kind of prize father! All he ever cared about was appearances.

"Finally, the police arrived. The operator told me they were at the door. A few moments later I heard them come in the bedroom, followed by my father yelling at them, and then I heard them hauling Brian out and reading him his rights. After that the room got quiet but there were two officers outside the bathroom door, trying to get me to open it. The operator was telling me it was ok, that I was safe, but I was so scared Patrick, I was absolutely frozen. But they couldn't break the door down because I was leaning against it trying to barricade myself inside. After about five minutes there was a third officer who came in, a female, and she started talking to me. They eventually got me to open the door and come out. The paramedics had arrived, I panicked when I saw them, thinking I had seriously hurt Brian and afraid he was going to have me arrested. I was so disoriented and not thinking straight, eventually I realized they were there for me. The two paramedics and the female officer sat with me in the corner of the bedroom, looking over my injuries and asking me some questions while the other two started investigating the scene and taking pictures. But I knew it was pointless, ultimately it was going to be my word against his. I had bruises and cuts, but Brian had people like my dad who would help him sweep it away.

"The paramedics cleaned me up, they wanted to take me to the hospital to do a rape kit, but I told them I hadn't been raped, he hadn't gotten that far. They said they could still collect DNA evidence proving that Brian had assaulted me, but when I pressed the police on if it would ever actually make it to trial, they wouldn't commit to an answer. So I knew it probably wasn't likely. No rape had occurred, witnesses the evening before had seen me sitting next to him all night. I know I wasn't my normal self, but I knew none of them thought anything about how Brian was behaving. It would be a classic case of 'he said, she said'. The police were honestly amazing, they really did all they could. A couple detectives from the sex crime unit showed up, they talked to me. They kept me separate from my dad the whole night. I told them I was supposed to be flying out that morning, at that point in only about seven hours. Once they had finished up with everything at the apartment, they let me get dressed and then the detectives escorted me, and all my luggage, to the local precinct, took my formal statement, processed everything, and then, a couple hours before my flight, a social worker or liaison person, I can't remember their exact title, took me to the airport and made sure I made it safely through security. I was so afraid my dad was going to find out about the flight and would be there to stop me."

"Wait," Patrick interrupted, "did they not detain your father?"

"No," Eleanor said, shaking her head. "And by that point Brian was released as well. I know my father came to the precinct but they kept him in a separate room, they told him they needed to get his statement before they could do anything else. While he was doing that they had me whisked away to the airport."

Eleanor sighed, "I flew home, the flight attendants on the plane had been amazing, I was supposed to fly economy but when the police social worker woman helped me check in and check my bags she had a word with them and got me an upgrade. I barely remember any of the flight. Someone found me at the gate before boarding and took me on board early during pre-board, and then they kept bringing me water and blankets throughout the flight, just checking on me you know, making sure I was comfortable. I just zoned out. I had called my mom from the airport telling her about my flight and what time I was landing. I didn't explain, I just begged her to pick me up, which of course she did. I'll never forget the look on her face when she saw me with the bruises on my face. Despite the heat I was wearing a long sleeve shirt so people wouldn't see the bruises on my arms. Mom wanted to take me to the doctor but I told her no. At that point, all I wanted was to go home.

"I slept for days. I'd wake up, try to eat, have some water, go to the bathroom, then go back to sleep. I'd wake up screaming from nightmares. Then repeat the whole thing. Mom could only take a few days of that before she called my doctor and made a same day appointment. She took me in and they referred me to a psychiatrist. But I refused to talk about it. They gave me some Xanax to help with the anxiety, but it didn't do much except make me sleepy. Mom was ready to take me to another psychiatrist or psychologist and I broke down. I told her I couldn't talk about it, over and over again. I just wanted to move on. My dad had been calling her, wanting to talk to me, but he didn't know what I had said so he wasn't saying anything. The NYPD was calling too, in that first week home, updating me. When mom realized the police were involved she broke down and begged me to tell her what happened, however bad it was she had to know. So I told her. And then said I never wanted to talk about it again. The New York prosecutor's office called and said that as much as they regretted it they weren't going forward with the case, there wasn't enough evidence and witness statements complicated things. My dad and his friends backed up their version, which is exactly what I knew was going to happen. For some reason even a charge of assault wasn't pursued. But it was nice of them to call me.

"I don't know Patrick. I'm sure it sounds awful, and maybe I should have pushed them to do more, but I just accepted it. Brian is still free, teaching at some other university, I know he left New York. And I haven't talked to or seen my father since we got home from the gala."

"You didn't see him at all before or after the attack?" Patrick asked incredulously.

"No, that day he had left before I woke up, and then I was hiding in my room when he got home, then after the attack the police kept us separated. They could see how afraid I was of him. And after I'd told them about everything, the little things leading up to the gala, his behavior at the gala, then how he behaves when his friends are over and why I was hiding in my room, they promised they'd get all the statements and reports processed quickly and then make sure I left the state without seeing him. I left New York and haven't been back since. I don't think I'll ever be able to go back. Too many bad memories.

"My dad tried to talk to me, after I got back to Arizona. He'd leave voicemails on my phone. Eventually he sent me an email, explaining that he didn't know Brian was going to do what he did, that he thought Brian just wanted to talk to me that night. That he thought Brian was a good guy and that I was lucky he was interested in me. In his twisted way, I think he honestly thought it was a good match. I think he saw something of himself in Brian, the young, hot shot academic. When I'd Googled Brian, I saw he'd come from a wealthy family, very well connected. That's what my dad was really attracted to. Get me in with Brian and his family so my dad could continue his social climbing. He only ever cared about himself. My mom and I were just part of the decorations of his life for a while. He only kept me around after the divorce because I might still be useful. I just remember feeling so crushed, like it was the final cut that severed the tie. He really wasn't my dad. If he was, he would have protected me from Brian, not offered me up to a predator. He would have flown out to Arizona and begged my forgiveness, but that was beneath him apparently. I was done.

"Once I knew there wasn't going to be a trial I just tried to forget. School started a month later and by then all my bruises had healed so no one knew. I just focused on school and drew a line under the whole thing. It was in the past. Or so I thought. I dated a few guys in college, but they all fizzled out, none were very serious. Partly because we just weren't interested in each other enough but also partly because I was afraid of letting anyone too close. Fast forward several years to when I eventually met Michael, I had convinced myself that the past was the past. And Michael was nothing like my father on the surface. He had none of the charm or sophistication, he thought he did but he didn't. He was just plain, simple, boring, but generally kind. And I felt safe with that. I never told him about what had happened in New York or with my dad. Just that we didn't talk anymore. Michael was never really that interested in my life so he didn't press or ask questions. When we made love for the first time, my first time ever, he was kind and gentle, and I felt safe, so it didn't trigger anything. That was when I thought maybe I was truly over it.

"But hindsight is 20/20 and looking back I can see ways that Michael was similar to my dad, particularly in his complete lack of interest in me as a person. I was mostly a prop for him. Just like I'd been for my dad. And looking at how things played out with Mark and how it's brought all of this back to the surface, it's definitely not as dead and buried as I'd hoped."

"Eleanor, you never stopped long enough to process it. You never spoke about it with anyone who could help you. You can't just think something like that is going to stay hidden away in a little box."

"I know," Eleanor said quietly. "Every now and then I'd see someone who reminded me of Brian and I'd panic. Then it would pass. But you're right. I think after telling you, I might be able to talk about it with someone. A therapist or something. But now that you've heard, I hope you don't hate me."

"Hate you!? Eleanor, don't be daft, why on earth would I hate you after hearing all that?!" Patrick was dumbfounded.

"I've been keeping you at arm's length because I don't know how to trust people. Because my dad betrayed me and basically helped one of his colleagues to physically assault and attempt to sexually assault me. Please believe me when I say that it's not that I've ever thought that you would do to me what they did. I just don't know how to let my guard down, especially when I'm still getting to know people. But you and I have become such good friends, and I know in my heart that I can trust you to be more than friends. That's just easier said than done for me."

Patrick stood up from his chair and came to kneel on the floor in front of Eleanor. He placed one hand on her knee and the other on her hand resting on the arm of the chair.

"Eleanor Anne Gordon, I could never hate you. Never. And I can't even be angry at you for keeping your guard up all this time. You've been remarkably open towards me and our friendship despite everything that's happened to you.

I'm not going anywhere, I promise. I will wait as long as it takes and we can take things as slow as needed. Nothing in our relationship has to change until you're comfortable."

Eleanor was so overcome with emotion and exhaustion. All she could do was nod and smile through her tears that had started falling for the millionth time. They stayed like that, Eleanor crying, Patrick kneeling in front of her, for several minutes until Eleanor composed herself. She eventually looked at the clock and realized it was nearly ten o'clock, it had taken her almost two hours to slowly tell her story.

"You look exhausted," Patrick said gently. "Please stay the night, don't go home."

Eleanor just nodded, and then, looking down at her hands, knotted in the blankets, she slowly asked, "Can I stay with you?"

Patrick didn't quite understand her at first, and then realized what she was asking and how significant it was. He nodded and replied, "I can't think of anywhere else I'd rather you be."

He helped her get up, and let her lead him upstairs to his bedroom. He helped her get changed into an old t-shirt and sweat pants of his, never taking his eyes from hers. Then she climbed into his bed and he got changed into his t-shirt and flannel trousers and slid into bed next to her. She rolled over to snuggle in close to him as he wrapped his arm around her and with his other hand reached over to turn out the light. He pulled the blanket up tightly around them and within seconds Eleanor was fast asleep. He was so amazed with how strong and resilient she could be and felt so grateful that she trusted him so much. In that moment, he knew he'd cut off his own limbs before ever causing her harm or emotional distress and he hoped that he would always be the man that she deserved.

Chapter 21

The next morning when Eleanor woke she was momentarily disoriented. She'd slept so deeply after the exhaustion of the day before and it took her a second to remember she'd gone to sleep in Patrick's bed. She was buried under the luxurious duvet and extra cozy blankets and when she burrowed her way out and looked to the other side of the bed she realized Patrick wasn't there. Light was streaming through the window, an instant sign that it was a rare sunny January day. Before she could fully sit up, she heard Patrick coming into the bedroom.

"Wakey, wakey sleepyhead," he said cheerily. He was carrying a large tray filled with things that smelled incredible. Eleanor quickly sat herself upright and pushed her hair out of her face, leaning against the headboard. As Patrick set the tray on the bed she saw croissants, scrambled eggs, bacon, fresh berries and cream, orange juice, plus a large French press and two coffee cups. It was a breakfast feast.

Patrick began pouring the coffee, "You were still out like a light when I woke up that I thought I'd take the risk of leaving you here asleep to run out and pick up some fresh croissants. They came out of the oven at the baker's only a couple hours ago," he said with a smile.

"You are an angel!" Eleanor exclaimed as she reached for the coffee cup Patrick held out and also plucked a piece of bacon from the plate on the tray.

"Only the best for you," Patrick replied. He quickly jumped back in bed under the covers and slid next to Eleanor and put his arm around her shoulders. She nestled in close to him as he pulled the tray closer and they began to tuck in to the feast.

They ate quietly for a few minutes, just enjoying being close. Eventually Eleanor said, to herself as much as to Patrick, "I'm glad I came over last night."

Patrick fought the urge to hug her even more tightly to him, feeling like he was already pushing his luck by having her so close all night and now this morning, so he simply said, "I'm glad too."

Eleanor sensed a slight change in his energy, "Are you ok?" She asked looking up at him.

Patrick just smiled, then said, "Yeah, I'm better than I've been in months. To be honest I feel a bit like I'm dreaming. Having you here, wearing my old t-shirt and trackie bums, eating breakfast in my bed, after getting to hold you all night long? Elle, this has been everything I've dreamed about almost since the day I first bumped into you in Covent Garden back in August."

"You've thought about me, like this," she asked incredulously, gesturing to her clothing and the breakfast in bed, "since August?"

"Yep," Patrick said definitively, taking a big bite out of a piece of toast.

"You need better dreams," Eleanor replied jokingly.

"Nope, I just need you."

He said it so sincerely it melted Eleanor's heart. August was really only five months ago. Five months and a week, give or take, since she'd bumped into him on her first day walking around London. Not that long really. And yet it felt like a lifetime. She'd been through so much, and Patrick had been there for nearly the whole time. A kind and supportive friend. Never pushing or pressuring or making her feel bad for not knowing what she wanted this whole time. He knew what he wanted. Her. But he waited, with the patience of a saint, for her to figure out what she wanted. Which was him. It had probably always been him, she had just been too scared to say so.

In that moment, she wanted nothing more than to kiss him, but she'd never been the type to make the first move. She'd never been brave enough. And even now, after everything she'd shared with him and knowing that she could trust him, she still didn't think she had the courage to close that small space between them and kiss him. She wished he would just kiss her, and as she looked into his eyes she thought she saw something that indicated he wanted to kiss her, then it passed and he was pouring more coffee for them out of the French press.

Eleanor quietly sighed, so faint Patrick thought he'd imagined it, and then leaned back against the headboard and sipped her coffee.

They relaxed in bed for over an hour, lingering over breakfast and just cuddling against each other. It was strangely intimate considering all they had done was literally just sleep in the same bed, Eleanor thought. They hadn't actually *done* anything. She blushed slightly at the thought of them eventually doing something more than just sleep next to each other. She knew eventually they would need to talk about that, Michael had been trying to get a reaction out of her last night, and while she would never have given him the satisfaction of seeing her react, he definitely struck a nerve when he mentioned that she wouldn't be able to satisfy someone like Patrick in bed. Sex with Michael had been good as far as she knew, but she'd always felt a bit insecure, like maybe she wasn't very good at it. He was always very kind about it, but it was still a sensitive subject and his comment last night made her question a lot about her experience, or lack thereof.

"Where did you go just now?" She heard Patrick's voice break into her thoughts.

"Hmm?" She replied absently.

"You just got this worried look on your face and kind of went off with the fairies there for a minute. You alright?" Patrick looked at her with concern in his eyes.

Eleanor just smiled, then said, "I'm fine. Better than fine. It's nothing. Well...ok, it's not nothing. And we will talk about it, eventually. But not right now. I'm too happy right now. And after last night I don't think I can handle any tough, emotional conversations."

"Ok," Patrick agreed. "So, what do you want to do? Stay here or go out? It's a lovely day, but you look pretty comfortable," he said with a grin.

"I am very comfortable," Eleanor replied laughing. "But it would be good to get some fresh air."

"We can walk to Hyde Park from here. Let's head over there, we can get some hot chocolate on the way."

"Sounds perfect."

Eleanor went into the bathroom and freshened herself up, then changed back into the clothes she'd worn over to Patrick's the night before. She met Patrick in the living room and he helped her into her coat. They started walking in the general direction of the park, heading down one mews street after another before turning on to some of the main roads and walking past the beautiful townhouses that lined the street. Traffic got a little busier the closer they got to Hyde Park but once they crossed into the park and started walking down the paths, it got quiet again. They passed a little stand near the Serpentine that was selling hot chocolate and other sweet treats and they each got a drink. Patrick was making small talk, mostly about the weather or nerves about starting the new film. Eleanor assured him filming would go smoothly and that he'd be great. She was amazed that her simple belief in him could make him look so relieved.

"You really are nervous about tomorrow, aren't you?" Eleanor asked.

"I always get nervous before starting a new project, but this is different. It's such a small cast and every role is crucial, and not just in the way of the old line of 'there's no such thing as a small part, only small actors.' Like, if any of us don't pull our weight it will bring the whole film down."

"When have you *ever* not pulled your own weight in your work?" Eleanor asked pointedly.

"There's a first time for everything Elle."

Patrick sounded so worried it broke Eleanor's heart a little. "Look, I know a thing or two about imposter syndrome, it's a classic struggle in grad school and an inherent part of being a writer, or any creative person for that matter. They wouldn't have cast you if they didn't think you were the right person for the job. No one gets cast in a major film out of pity Patrick. They chose you for a reason. You just need to get out of your own head and stop talking yourself into a confidence crisis."

"You sound so sure of yourself," Patrick laughed lightly.

"Well, I can give advice, but I can't take it," Eleanor laughed. "That's basically what Jonathan's friends told me the night I first met them at the pub back in August after a terrifying first day at the Harrison. I know what it feels like to think you can't do something Patrick, or that you're not good enough. It sucks, I feel for you, I really do. But you know what? If I'm being honest, in all the years that I've come up against something I thought I couldn't do, I always ended up doing it and succeeding. My worst fears never came true. I survived my parents' divorce, that last visit to New York, I got through uni and then grad school, I moved half way around the world to study in London," Eleanor paused, "I went through so much shit with my dad and felt so worthless, especially after everything with Brian. And for years I thought I'd never be able to talk to anyone about it or meet someone who could make me feel safe and comfortable enough to be my true self. And then I met you."

"Do you really mean that Elle? That you feel safe and comfortable to be yourself with me? Because that's all I've ever wanted," Patrick was looking at her so intently as he reached to take her free hand in his.

They stood there frozen in the middle of the path clutching their hot chocolates and holding hands, not a single person around, just the sound of wind in the trees and ducks and geese on the lake and the sounds of the city in the distance. Eleanor thought about how, since that day in Oxford, she always found herself telling Patrick things she barely talked about with anyone else. How she always felt so at ease when she was with him. How she never felt like she had to pretend to be something she wasn't. She didn't have to be smarter, or funnier, or prettier, or cooler, he cared about her just as she was.

Once again, she found herself dying to kiss him, and again that little voice of fear held her back. She could see in his eyes he wanted to kiss her too and she was desperate for him to just lean down and do it. But thinking back on their relationship she thought how he always followed her lead, he always waited for her to show that she was comfortable. In that moment, she realized that's what he was doing now. It's what he had been doing earlier in bed as they ate breakfast. She'd been bold last night, asking to sleep in his bed, and it had been fine, he didn't reject her. And he wouldn't reject her now.

Before she could talk herself out of it again, Eleanor let go of Patrick's hand and reached up to touch his face, she leaned in and stood up on her tip toes, and Patrick leaned down until his lips were less than an inch from hers, she paused, thinking he was going to start kissing her, but he just stayed frozen, waiting for her to make her choice. Without giving it another thought, she closed the gap and pressed her lips to his, winding her hand around the back of his head.

The kiss was slow and gentle at first, but once Eleanor had made that first move, Patrick was very quick to follow her lead. The kiss deepened, Eleanor felt her whole body melt into his. Still holding her hot chocolate, she put her other arm around his waist, and Patrick wound both his arms around her.

They stayed like that, kissing and ignoring the rest of the world, for at least a minute. It felt like a blissful eternity to Eleanor. Time stopped in that kiss. She loved kissing Patrick, it felt so easy and so natural. She felt like an equal participant, not like she was trying to keep up. He reacted to every move she made. Which made it hard for her to not think about what it would be like to make love with him. She'd have blushed at the thought if she wasn't already feeling flush from all the kissing. She felt giddy and all of a sudden, she had to fight the urge to giggle. She wasn't very successful.

"Do you find kissing me amusing Miss Gordon?" Patrick asked with mock offense and formality.

"No...of course not," Eleanor protested through her giggles.

"What's so funny then?" Patrick asked, grinning.

"I think I'm just overwhelmed, today has been so amazing and I've wanted to kiss you since this morning, but I was too scared to do it, and then I finally did and..." Eleanor trailed off not knowing how to finish her thought.

Patrick hugged her tighter and said, "I'm really glad you finally did. I've been wanting to kiss you for months, but I was waiting for you to make the first move."

"Yeah, I finally realized that's what you were doing," Eleanor laughed. "Thank you, for waiting until I was ready. For, well, you know, everything."

"Eleanor, that is one thing that I can very easily promise you, I will never make you do something before you're ready. And you can talk to me about anything."

Eleanor had a feeling he was referring to something specific as well as to their relationship in general.

"I know that, and I'm grateful. It's nice to know that I can talk to you, that you understand," she replied, smiling shyly at him. She hugged him tightly and nestled her head into his shoulder.

"You're freezing. And our hot chocolates have gone cold. We should get moving again."

"Or you could kiss me again? That seemed to make me feel warm," Eleanor smiled girlishly at him.

"Don't tempt me darling. Let's get you back to the house and warmed up, then I'll kiss you some more."

"Deal."

They huddled together as they retraced their steps to leave the park, Patrick's arm wrapped tightly around her shoulders.

Epilogue

It had been a glorious summer, and Eleanor couldn't believe that it had been nearly a year since she'd arrived in London. It was a beautiful July day, and Eleanor was enjoying a leisurely Saturday afternoon picnic with Patrick in Hyde Park. January and February had gone by in a blur of writing and working at school and Patrick spending most of each week filming in London. Then in March he flew to LA to start his big spy film. He was finally home from filming in LA and on location around the world. It had been hard being without him for the four-and-a-half-month shoot, and he'd been so busy during most of it that they'd struggled to fit in regular FaceTime calls. But he'd texted her every chance he could and sent her letters and postcards from every city the film production had visited.

She loved receiving those letters and cards and would read and reread them over and over again. She kept them in a drawer beside the bed. When he first started sending the letters and postcards from the States he'd started signing them:

"With all my love, from across the pond xx PR"

He kept up the sign off in the letters even after the production left the States for other locations. But over the months "across the pond" had taken on added significance. All of this, school, her writing, her friendships, her relationship with Patrick, had all been possible because she'd taken a risk and allowed herself a brave start "across the pond" in London.

They hadn't officially moved in together but she'd taken to spending a lot of time at his mews house while he was gone, both to house sit and to have some quiet space to herself while she worked on finishing her manuscript for her MFA final capstone project. Now Patrick was back and she was still spending half the week at his place. The last two months of the program had switched to twice a week mentoring sessions and the rest of the time was open for writing, on the days she was at school for mentoring she'd spend those afternoons writing in coffee shops with Jack, Clara, Maggie, and Alex. But any night she didn't have to be up and in the City the next morning she spent at Patrick's. He was taking a bit of a break before taking on a new project and spent his time making Eleanor cups of coffee as she wrote and read scripts for potential new projects.

At Patrick's insistence, and Jon's and her mom's encouragement, Eleanor had been seeing a therapist once a week since late January. She thought it would be difficult, digging everything up and laying it all out to dissect it. But her therapist was amazing. Her therapist was only a few years older than Eleanor and she felt so comfortable with her, like she was being fully understood. She found that things that used to trigger her, triggered her less often and she was better at coping with things if she started to feel overwhelmed or panicked. She'd worried about not being able to be "fixed" but with her therapist's help, and with the way Patrick loved her so unconditionally, she was finally realizing that she'd never been broken in the first place.

Eleanor's student visa would be good for another three months after she graduated, but she had three good job offers with companies in London, each of them willing to sponsor a work visa, all she had to do was choose which one she wanted to work at. She also had two agents interested in signing her and start pitching her manuscript. She had to pinch herself when she thought about how perfectly things were working out. She'd be able to have a job, stay in London, possibly get a place of her own, or maybe move in with Patrick. They hadn't decided anything and Eleanor wasn't in a rush. It just felt like everything was falling into place.

She glanced over at Patrick, who was laying back on the picnic blanket, reading Eleanor's copy of *Persuasion* that she'd picked up in Oxford. Eleanor smiled to herself at the memory.

"What do you feel like doing tonight?" She asked him quietly.

Patrick placed the book down on his chest, thumb holding his place. He looked pensive for a moment, "I don't know. Dinner together at mine? Or is Jonathan missing you? Maybe we could go out with him and Celeste?"

Eleanor smiled, thinking about the growing relationship between her cousin and the gorgeous Celeste. "They've actually gone to Cambridge to spend the weekend with Jon's dad. Jon invited me along but I saw Uncle Edward a few weeks ago, just before you got back, and this is only the second time Jon's taking Celeste out there, so I thought it'd be better for just the two of them to go." She laid down next to Patrick and nestled her head on his chest. "So I'm quite afraid you're stuck with just me this weekend," she finished with a smile.

"Well aren't I just the luckiest man in the world," Patrick said dramatically with a big smile as he lifted his head to kiss Eleanor.

"Dinner at yours sounds good, if this sun holds out, we could eat out on the roof terrace," Eleanor said.

"Sounds perfect. I can cook or we can pick something up on our way back?" Patrick suggested with a questioning tone.

Eleanor smiled childishly, "Could we pick up takeaway from Pizza Express? I'm kind of craving pizza and their dough balls."

Grinning back, "With the garlic butter?"

"Especially with the garlic butter, duh," Eleanor said rolling her eyes and laughing.

Patrick laughed back and checked his watch. "Well, it's about five o'clock, we've been sitting out here for a few hours already. You ok to hang out here for a bit longer while I put in an order on my phone, then we can pick it up on our way back?

"Sounds like a solid plan," Eleanor replied smiling.

Patrick opened up his phone and placed their order online as Eleanor stretched out on the blanket. She was looking forward to the rest of the evening and spending more time with Patrick. They were still taking it slow, but enjoying every moment they had together and learning more about each other.

Eleanor's mom was planning another trip to visit at the end of the month for Eleanor's graduation. She'd been in the spring but still hadn't met Patrick as he'd been on location. So this next visit would be important. And Eleanor and Patrick were already planning a summer trip up to Scotland to spend time at his family's place up there, she'd already been to meet his parents in Oxford, and then they were tentatively planning a trip to visit Cassie in Arizona around Thanksgiving time in the autumn. Patrick had suggested sooner but as soon as she told him what August's usual temperatures were in Phoenix he quickly agreed that it would be better for Cassie to visit them in the summer and for them to visit her in the autumn.

Patrick finished ordering dinner and then laid down beside Eleanor, his head next to hers, reaching for her hand and then placing it on his chest. They stayed like that, for a little while longer, lost in their own little world, so many plans and hopes for the future, oblivious to the other couples and families with kids running around the park around them, as the summer sun shone above them, slowly working its way above large puffy white clouds, towards the western horizon, as London hummed with activity and the afternoon worked its way towards evening and everything felt just as it should.

The End

Acknowledgements

There are so many people to acknowledge and thank when comes to this book. I almost don't know where to start. So, I'll start with my parents. Dad, your career in the U.S. Army gave me a childhood full of travel and amazing memories and your knowledge of history and geography made me a huge history and travel nerd. Mom, you were always a million things at once when I was growing up. You taught me that I could be anything I wanted to be. You and Dad taught me a love of reading from a young age and watching you write your own stories taught me that writing wasn't something only certain people could do. Growing up with a writer in the family made me feel a little less daunted about writing my own books. Mom and Dad, you both taught me to believe in myself and in the power of following my dreams. You taught me that nothing was impossible. I love you so much.

Alicia, my parents gave me my first trip to London, but you gave me the London that I fell in love with. You gave me my first proper trip to London as an adult and it forever changed my live. This book wouldn't exist if you hadn't given me that first trip and shown me a side of London that only a local would know. Your generosity in opening your home to me over the next several years allowed me to visit more and get to know the city even better. You introduced me to places I might never have found. I am forever grateful. I'm also completely indebted for the wealth of knowledge, insider info, and background details on the expat life in London you provided to make Eleanor's experience more authentic. This book is so much richer and more detailed because of your feedback. Thanks a million!

Tamzin, I don't think I would have decided to go

forward with publishing this book without your encouragement. You were excited about it from the first time I told you about the story and you immediately wanted to know more. You read the first draft in one day and have had endless enthusiasm and encouragement ever since. Through all my moments of worry and self-doubt you've been there to support me and have believed in me when I struggled to believe in myself. Our friendship has been special from the first day we finally met in person, and in London of all places! You understand me and Eleanor so perfectly, I couldn't have gotten through the editing process without you. You helped me with a title and an ending when I was struggling with both and I know you've been holding my hand throughout this entire process through our endless WhatsApp messages, FaceTime calls, and pushing the limits of Marco Polo. And last but not least, thank you for helping me with Jack's Northern accent, just when I thought I couldn't love that character any more, you helped me add a bit more personality to him! I'm glad Eleanor has a friend like Jack, and I'm so grateful to have a friend like you!

Lisa, thank you so much. Not only for being an amazing sister but for also being such a brilliant artist. You took my idea for a cover and brought it to life even better than I imagined. The little details, that only I will fully appreciate, make me so happy every time I look at the cover. I'm so glad you got to be a part of this book and I'm honored to have your illustration on the cover.

To my test readers...Elizabeth, Shannon, Jess, Hannah, and Nicole. You took your valuable time to read part or all of an early draft of this book and give me feedback. Your feedback helped so much, both in terms of fixing the things that weren't quite working or making me feel better and validated about the parts that were working great. Writing can be a very isolating process and it's easy to get caught up in my own head and second guess everything. Your feedback helped me realize that I was doing a lot better than I realized and made me even more excited to finally be able to share it with others. Thank you so much for all your help and encouragement!

Finally, to my online community on YouTube, Instagram, Twitter, and my blog. For more than three years now, you all have been so unbelievably supportive and encouraging of all my endeavors. You've helped me in more ways than you could possibly know and I am profoundly grateful for each and every one of you. You've followed every step of the journey in publishing this book and have been excited to read it from the first time I mentioned it. You've encouraged me and reassured me every step of the way and I couldn't have done this without you. For someone who is never short of words in my vlogs and can't stop talking, I somehow don't have enough words to express my gratitude for you all and "thank you" just isn't enough, but it will have to do. So, thank you, a million times, thank you.

Join the fun!

Thank you for reading *A Brave Start!* Stay tuned for further adventures with Eleanor, Patrick and all their friends in future installments in the *Across the Pond* series!

Connect with me on social media and let me know what you think of the book! And follow along to stay updated on behind the scenes of writing, where I get my inspiration, deleted scenes and short stories, and updates on new work!

And if you want to be a real rock star, please leave a review of *A Brave Start* on Amazon.

Instagram: @jesuisjustemoi
Twitter: @SeversonSimotti
Facebook Group: Across the Pond Book
YouTube: JeSuisJusteMoi
Website: www.andreajseverson.com

About the Author

Andrea J. Severson lives in Scottsdale, Arizona. She has a PhD in English with a focus in fashion rhetoric and is a writing instructor at Arizona State University. Living abroad while her father served in the U.S. Army, she grew up loving European countries and experiencing other cultures. A family vacation to the United Kingdom when she was 9 made a strong impression and she dreamed of returning as an adult. A fateful first trip in late 2010 created a love affair with the country, and London in particular. She has visited and lived in London and Oxford numerous times. Now she loves to write about her favorite locations and dreams of adventures to come.

Printed in Great Britain
by Amazon